To Mom

Madness Heart Press
2006 Idlewilde Run Dr.
Austin, Texas 78744

This is a work of fiction. Names, characters, places, and incidents either are the product of the author's imagination or are used fictitiously. Any resemblance to actual persons, living or dead, events, or locales is entirely coincidental.

Copyright © 2011 Wrath James White
Cover by Simone Tammetta

All rights reserved. No part of this book may be reproduced or used in any manner without written permission of the copyright owner except for the use of quotations in a book review. For more information, address: john@madnessheart.press

Second Edition
isbn:
www.madnessheart.press

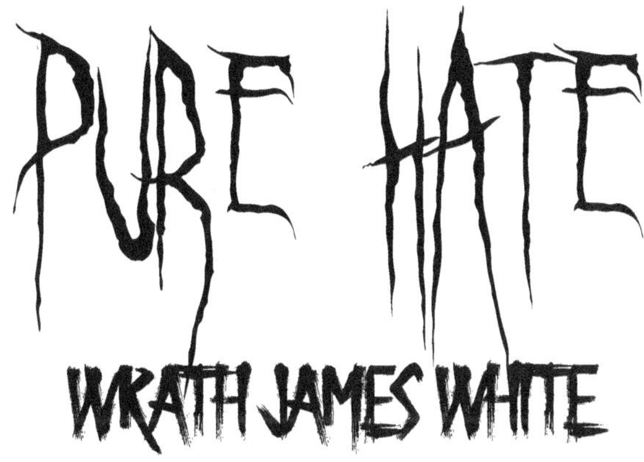


A Madness Heart Press Publication

# PROLOGUE

Something wasn't right. Malcolm rang the doorbell again. No answer. He could see furtive movements in the upstairs window, shadowy silhouettes darting around behind the curtains in Natasha's room. She was home. She was not alone. And she was not answering the door. A ricochet began in Malcolm's brain, a jumble of jealous, angry thoughts like a ballistic projectile bouncing around his skull, gaining momentum, tearing his mind apart.

*She's cheating on me. She's cheating one me! That lying whoring bitch is cheating on ME!*

The thoughts bounced around his mind at increasing velocity. Malcolm hated it when this happened, this loss of control. Even if he had to kill someone tonight, he wanted his head clear when he did it. If he lost his head, he'd be sloppy and get caught. He'd never killed anyone before, and if tonight was the night when he crossed that line, he needed to be calm and rational. But he didn't know how to do that. He didn't know how he could possibly stay calm with his girlfriend up there dirtying the sheets with some other stud.

"I knew this bitch would betray me," he whispered, shaking his head and breathing heavily, his pulse speeding up, muscles tensing.

All his friends had told him not to date outside his race.

*Stay with your own, Malcolm. You ain't got no business messin' around with those white bitches. They ain't nothin' but a bunch of triflin' whores, and you ain't shit to them but a cheap thrill.*

He'd ignored them all because Natasha was different. She loved him. She had told him so.

*That lying bitch! That lying bitch! THAT LYING FUCKING BITCH!*

Malcolm began grinding his teeth as he struggled to control his rage. He knew that if he allowed these thoughts out of his head, gave voice to them, let them take over him, he would smash through the door and kill everyone inside. He knew enough about himself to know that mercy was not part of his makeup. Holding the thoughts inside made his entire body shake. The veins in his neck and forehead bulged. His teeth gnashed. His eyes dodged back and forth in their sockets as his mind worked overtime, trying to steady itself. His hands clenched into fists so tight the skin on his knuckles threatened to rip. A scream, a roar, was trapped in his gut, and it churned there, indigestible.

A giggle came from somewhere in the house and then … Malcolm charged. The compressed wood particleboard that comprised the front door became wood particles again as Malcolm's entire body slammed into it—through it. The peephole flew across the room and shattered the mirror over the mantelpiece. Malcolm stood in the living room, wood chips scattered at his feet.

The house was dark and silent except for a lone light coming from Natasha's bedroom and the heavy, panting breath of a very large and angry teenager. Malcolm was halfway up the stairs when he heard her window open and footsteps on the roof. Whoever was in Natasha's room was trying to escape.

*That fuckin' coward!*

Malcolm ran back down the stairs and out into the yard. When he looked up at the figures silhouetted by the moon and crawling out of Natasha's window, his hand tightened around his ten-dollar swap-meet switchblade with the leopard on the handle. He could already imagine their blood staining the blade. He reached up and grabbed the man from where he dangled off the gutter and pulled him down to slam down on the lawn. Then Malcom stopped. He looked up at Natasha, frozen on the roof, and then down at his best friend, Reed, struggling to sit up in the wet grass like a dying cockroach trying to right itself on a waxed floor.

"What the fuck is going on!"

Malcolm was confused but still angry, still murderously angry. He could hear the voices of his friends in his head, the ones who had tried to warn him.

*You can't trust none of them muthafuckas. That White boy you kick it with spends more time with your girl than you do. Fuck do you think they doin' when you ain't around?*

But Malcolm had ignored all the warnings.

"Nothing, man. We were just hanging out. Just talking." Reed stayed on his back, obviously figuring it was safer down there than up where his six-foot-five-inch homicidal best friend raged.

"In her fucking bedroom!"

The ricochet had begun again, rebounding off his skull with increasing force. Malcolm could feel his mind rattling itself apart. His eyes searched Reed's, almost hoping the kid could provide some rational answer, something that would calm the maelstrom in Malcolm's head.

"Malcolm, we weren't doing anything! Don't hurt him!" Natasha screamed as she scrambled down from the roof.

"You don't answer the door? You sneak out the fuckin' window?"

The flaming projectile whizzed through his mind, and his entire body shook.

*My best friend and my girlfriend.*

It wouldn't stop. It flew faster and faster through his brain.

*My best friend and my girlfriend. My best friend and my girlfriend. My best friend and MY FUCKING GIRLFRIEND! That lying bitch is cheating on me! That sonuvabitch fucked my girl!*

Malcolm was losing it again.

"Man, I swear nothing happened."

Malcolm held the knife in a white-knuckled grip, trying to decide who to use it on, Reed, Natasha, or himself, and in what order.

"Reed, you'd better get the fuck out of here. Because I think I'm going to kill you."

His voice was calm and even. He almost didn't sound angry at all except for his words and the fact that he was holding six inches of deadly sharp steel.

"Look man, it ain't what you think …"

"GO!" He lashed out with the knife, slashing at Reed's throat.

Reed jerked away as the blade whispered through the air, nicked his throat, and drew blood. His eyes widened as a trickle of red dripped down and stained the collar of his T-shirt. Malcolm sneered as Reed quickly wiped away the blood, stared at the smear of red on his palm, then took off running across the lawn.

"Fuckin' coward!"

Malcolm stood in front of the house, a huge shadow raging beneath the full moon. He turned toward Natasha. She looked terrified.

"Baby, come inside. It's okay. I swear we were just talking." She was trying hard to sound normal, but she was afraid and Malcolm knew it, and that just made him angrier. She had tried to sneak off with Reed. She had run in fear from him. He wanted to show her exactly what there was to be afraid of.

Malcolm allowed himself to be led back into the house. Natasha sat down on the old mohair couch as he walked past her into the kitchen. He lifted up the stovetop on the oven and blew out the pilot lights, then he turned up the gas.

"Baby? W-what are you doing? Malcolm?"

"Remember when you said you wanted to die with me? Remember when you said you would die for me? I believed you then. I really believed you meant it. But now I'm not so sure."

"Baby, you know I'd die for you."

"Really?" He eyed Natasha suspiciously. "Then let's do it."

His voice held no warmth or emotion. Natasha searched his eyes and could find none of the love that usually burned there for her. Shadows slithered across his dark retinas as if someone had flipped a switch and turned off all the light inside of him.

Malcolm sat down at the kitchen table. The rotten egg stink of natural gas began to fill the room. Natasha's gaze darted around the kitchen in a panic. She looked back at Malcolm, and tears began to well up and cascade down her cheeks.

"Oh, Malcolm, I'm not ready to die!"

"Yeah? Well I am, and you said you would die with me, or have you changed your mind? Maybe Reed has changed your mind?"

"Malcolm!"

"Is it because he's the same color as you? Got tired of fucking a nigger? Started getting homesick for your own kind? Tell me, did you fuck him?"

"Malcolm!"

"Did you? Did you?"

"Pleaaase!"

"Just answer the fucking question! Did-you-fuck-him?"

"Malcolm the gas! We're going to suffocate!"

"Did you?"

"Yes, damn it! Yes, we did! I did! But so did your last girlfriend, Reneé. Last year when she was all buddy-buddy with Reed while you were at work. She was fucking him! You thought she was so damned perfect. I could never measure up to Reneé, right? Well she fucked him too, and it's your fault! You're mean, Malcolm. You're cold. You never let anyone close to you. You smothered Reneé by being so jealous and controlling, and then you tried to break me down. You made me feel like shit for not being Reneé. I'm not Reneé, Malcolm. I'm me. I just wanted you to love *me.* "

Malcolm's face twisted into a scowl.

"What the fuck did you say?"

"Reneé … she cheated on you too, Malcolm."

All the rage drained out of him. His entire body deflated as if his anger had been the only thing filling his skin. He wilted down into the recliner across from Natasha.

Reneé had been the first woman he'd ever loved. The only reason he hadn't checked out on life. She had shown him that life could be beautiful and not just the foul and murky sty filled with sewer rats, cockroaches, and dilapidated row homes that he experienced every day. That life could be more than broken beer bottles, crack vials, hypodermic needles, more than the hopeless drug addicts, the single welfare mothers, the teenaged dealers, the fights and shootouts that filled his nights and days. She had shown him that life could be more than poverty, madness, violence, and hunger, that there could be hope and joy. She had shown him that not everyone and everything in life was out to hurt him.

"She lied!"

Malcolm felt the most profound misery he'd ever known. It felt like he'd just lost everything. This world was no longer a place he wanted to live in. Reed, his best friend, had fucking betrayed him! The only man he'd let get close to him since his father. The only man he'd ever trusted. The only person he'd ever really thought came close to being his equal had betrayed him with the only two women he'd ever really loved! They were all lost to him now.

Malcolm's mind filled with fantasies of death, torture, and dismemberment. He wanted them all to suffer. He wanted them to feel the pain he felt. But what he felt was too vast. It seemed impossible. No matter what he did, they'd never hurt as much as he did now. He just wanted to be rid of it all.

He reached across the cracked and yellowing Formica kitchen table and pulled out a book of matches. He pulled one matchstick from the pack …

"Malcolm! Noooooo!"

… and lit it.

# PART ONE

## CONFLICT

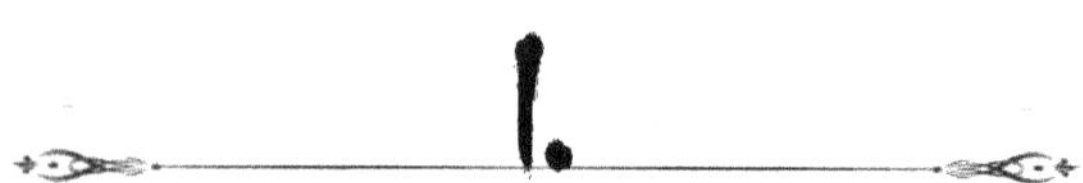

*Fifteen Years later ...*

Paul was silent as he sat in the car next to the tremendous Black man—the man he loved. He knew the violence Malcolm was capable of when he was in these moods, but his fear of Malcolm only fueled his passion for him. Malcolm was more than a man to Paul. He was like a primal, savage force of nature, a tidal wave or an earthquake imprisoned in human flesh.

Paul knew Malcolm didn't love him. He knew the big fearsome man only kept him around because Paul reminded him of Reed. Malcolm had even forced him to undergo cosmetic surgery to make him look exactly like his old high school friend. He knew that Malcolm wasn't really gay. To Malcolm, sex was just another way to humiliate and conquer Paul, to punish him for not being Reed.

Malcolm often beat him, whipped him, strangled him until Paul passed out, brutally raped and sodomized him while hurling threats and insults, cut, burned, and degraded him, and Paul just kept coming back for more. He was a glutton for pain and humiliation. For him, it was better than sex or love.

Paul had other lovers with whom he had

experimented with BDSM, but it had always lacked something. With Malcolm, he discovered what that something was—realism. He knew in his heart that Malcolm truly wanted to hurt him and that at any moment, he just might kill him. And that was the biggest turn-on of all, and after they killed Reed, he'd have Malcolm all to himself.

Paul sat quietly beside Malcolm, watching as his mood went from anger to depression. He had witnessed Malcolm's mood swings before and knew their sequence. Anger gave way to depression, which gave way to indifference, which turned to a wicked playfulness that preceded violence. A shudder of fear and an almost sexual excitement shivered up Paul's spine as Malcolm began to smile.

Malcolm was in a frenzy as he read through Reed's newest novel. He ripped each page out as he finished it, wishing it were Reed's living flesh. He was growling low in his stomach and grinding his teeth.

"That sonuvabitch!"

Malcolm grabbed the novel between his teeth and ripped it in half, tossing the remains of his kill in the backseat, where the pages fluttered to the floor like the feathers of a gull chopped down in mid-flight.

Malcolm started the engine and pulled away from the curb, startling a small flock of pigeons—"flying rats"—as he roared into the street, still growling, the bloodlust boiling in him like physical hunger. The air around him was thick, lush with his hatred. It weighted every movement with deadly purpose. Rage filled his shadow and gave it substance. Someone was about to catch a bad one … a very, very bad one.

The block-long, battleship gray '72 Impala purred like a lion with a belly full of antelope as it rounded the corner. For Malcolm, the menacing rumble was soothing. The power of the huge V-8 engine was comforting. It made him feel invincible. The sawed-off Mossberg pistol-grip pump shotgun that hung in its handmade holster under his sports jacket, his massive, heavily muscled, hormone-enhanced physique, and his irresistible homicidal rage completed the feeling of invincibility. He was a monster. And he blamed Reed for it.

Fifteen years ago, it had seemed impossible to him that Reed could've ever betrayed him. Even when he knew the truth, it had seemed unreal to him.

Didn't Reed know how much he loved him? Didn't Reed know what he would do to him? What he was capable of?

He would know after tonight. He would know and regret.

Reed took away the only two women that Malcolm had ever loved, taken them from right under his nose while they laughed, joked, and dreamt together every day, confided in each other, trusted each other. Reed had single-handedly made it impossible for Malcolm to ever love or trust anyone ever again, impossible for him to feel anything but his own pain, his own hate, his own sorrow, his own emptiness. Now he would have to bring the pain to the best friend he'd ever had. He owed that to him, and he always paid what he owed with interest.

The Impala cruised into the little cul-de-sac just as night smothered the day. He parked a few houses down from Reed's home and waited.

Malcolm had been watching the house for weeks. He'd seen Reed's family playing in the yard, peered into the bedroom window as Reed made love to his wife in the middle of the night. He wanted to murder them both at that exact moment, as Reed was pounding into her, poised on the edge of orgasm. He wanted to smash through the window and chop them to pieces, a double homicide O.J. style, but he restrained himself. He wanted the anticipation to build. He wanted Reed's pain to be exquisite.

Malcolm Davis slid silently from the behemoth

urban tank with a full-toothed grin chillingly contorting his face. In his mind, he was already in the house, already awash with blood. His body uncurled and rose to its full 6'5'' height. He was an impressive and intimidating figure in his loose-fitting Hugo Boss suit riding smoothly over his massive chest and shoulders. His onyx skin blended with the black suit, the black silk Armani shirt, and the night as the shadows began to knit together and he became just one more penumbra in the increasing darkness. He looked like the angel of death in that music video from Bone Thugs-N-Harmony:

*Meet me at the crossroads*
*Crossroad, crossroooads, crossroooads.*
*Meet me at the crossroads.*


"Hurry up, white boy," Malcolm growled, and the slender "white boy" with the long, brown, feathered hair and baggy pleated pants slid from the passenger side of the Impala, eager as a puppy to obey his master.

Reed's house was small and vulnerable looking. It was brand new. A production built tract home. A crackerjack box. It was a single story with three bedrooms, two baths, one dog, one couple, two kids, and one murderous sociopath grinning on the lawn. A fifteen-pound sledgehammer and a pair of wire cutters, and you could have leveled the house to its foundations.

The yard was professionally landscaped and perfectly manicured with neat little shrubs of sage and rosemary lined up by the front window and a midget evergreen tree in the front yard. A three-foot-tall wrought iron fence surrounded the entire property. It looked just like every other house on the block. Middle America.

Malcolm stepped over the gate without bothering to open it and strode across the lawn, leaving footprints in the soft, freshly watered sod. His shoes made wet, squishy sounds as they pressed into the earth. The sound made Reed's old, overweight Rottweiler go wild.

*The dog dies too*, Malcolm thought, almost giddy, a predacious smile tearing across his face like the grin of a piranha. And Malcolm had fangs. His canines were capped with platinum and tapered to sharp points. A diamond was embedded in each one. He looked like some kind of hip-hop vampire.

"Knock on the door, white boy," Malcolm growled again.

His longhaired accomplice slipped ahead of him and up the steps onto Reed's porch. Malcolm followed close behind, pulling the Mossberg from his coat and jacking a round into the chamber.

Paul paused for a moment at Reed's front door, breathing heavily from an overdose of adrenaline. He was dying to finally meet the subject of Malcolm's obsession, the author of the madness and misery that had engulfed them both. His whole arm shook as he reached out to ring the doorbell. He wanted to kill so badly his dick was hard.

# IV.

Reed was having a hard day. The sci-fi novel he was working on was three months past due, and he was no closer to finishing it now than he was three months ago. This was the twentieth time he had rewritten the last chapter, and it still didn't work. The characters had long ago gone stale for him. His writing seemed stiff and wooden. This was no longer a labor of love; it was just labor, pure and simple. His heart wasn't in it anymore. He was just imitating himself. Reed was nearly paralyzed by the fear that he had become the one thing he had always detested—a hack. He had already spent the ten-thousand-dollar advance, and the bills were starting to roll in again, but he couldn't let the manuscript go until it at least approached the level of talent he knew himself to be capable of. If he just turned it in as is, he would truly be a hack. Reed's perfectionism was going to drive his family to the poor house.

In the kitchen, his wife was creating one of her experimental gourmet vegetarian dishes from a recipe book she bought at one of those over-priced cooking stores, the kind that sold dried peppers, pickled mushrooms, and spices he'd never heard of. Whatever she was cooking, it smelled delicious. His growling stomach was one more distraction he didn't need. The kids were still another. They were getting on his fucking nerves. Slamming his hands down on the desk so hard the keyboard flipped over, he turned toward the living room and did what all fathers do when urgent, effective communication with their children becomes necessary. He clenched his fists and yelled.

"That's it! That is it! If you two can't play that damned thing together without arguing, I'm gonna turn it off and give it to the Goodwill! If you can't appreciate it, maybe they can find some kids that will."

"But, Daddy, Mark keeps playing that stupid hedgehog game over and over, and he won't let me play *Gears of War*!" Jennie's sweet, innocent voice came sailing out of the living room.

Reed's seven-year-old daughter, Jennie, looked every bit like her mother. She had her mother's long blonde hair, fiery emerald eyes, and long legs. Too bad she had her father's disposition. The face of an angel with the mouth and temper of a drunken sailor.

"That *Sonic the Hedgehog* is a faggot game!" she taunted, scowling at her little brother with disdain as if she'd caught him wearing his mother's panties.

"Hey, hey, young lady! You watch your goddamned mouth! Now both of you turn that crap off and get ready for dinner. I've got to finish working, goddamn it!"

"But, Daddy, I've almost got the high scoooore!" Mark whined in a high-pitched squeal that made his father cringe.

Mark looked exactly like Reed did at that age, the same crooked, pointy nose and Dick Van Dyke chin, except Reed's pants never hung off his ass like his son's over-sized black denims and Mark had a better haircut. Reed's hair had hung down his back until he was a junior in college, while Mark wore a short, neat crew cut. That was the first thing Linda changed about him. They had been flirting with each other in literature class for weeks before Reed had gotten up the nerve to ask her out. She had given him her phone number, and before their first date, they had nearly fallen in love over the phone. They were getting intimate for the first time when she told him, "Look, I think you're great, but I can't go out with a guy who looks like a damned hippie. If we're going to date, you've got to cut that hair!"

He did, and in exchange, she had agreed to another date, then another and then another, and then she agreed to marry him, and then she gave him two beautiful children. But sometimes, like when Mark did that annoying whining thing, Reed wondered if he should have kept the long hair.

"Stop whining and turn it off like I said!"

"Fuck! Man, this is bullshit," Mark whined.

Reed snapped.

"Damn it, that's enough! Both of you get in here now!"

"Damn it, Mark. See what the fuck you did? You got Daddy mad, you little punk!"

"Fuck you!"

"Fuck you too, faggot!"

"I said get in here *NOW* and close your mouths!"

Jennie and Mark walked slowly into the bedroom, where Reed had been banging away at his Mac, trying to wrestle out an opus. Now he stood in the middle of the room, glaring down at his two little brats with his hands on his hips. Jennie crossed her arms over her chest and huffed defiantly, rolling her eyes and stamping her foot the way she'd seen the Black girls at school do. Mark imitated his big sister, crossing his arms and huffing his own annoyance. Reed fought the urge to slap the shit out of both of them. He took a deep breath and mustered up the calmest, most diplomatic voice he could manage. He still sounded pissed.

"Now, both of you listen. It is absolutely *NOT* okay

to curse in this house. You are children! You do not use that type of foul language around your parents! Now I am trying to finish this novel so that maybe we can get some bills paid and perhaps have some money to live off. But if you think your stupid little video game is more important than food, clothing, and shelter, then go ahead and keep this shit up."

"Oh, but it's okay for *YOU* to curse," Jennie grumbled under her breath.

"What did you say, little girl!"

"The doorbell is ringing."

She turned and ran for the door, cutting short her father's lecture. Mark looked sympathetically at his father, shrugged his shoulders, and chased after his sister. Reed threw up his hands and shook his head in exasperation.

Jennie flung open the front door, and her jaw dropped as her mind slammed on the brakes. She couldn't make any sense of what she was seeing. Mark came running up alongside her, and his eyes grew large with surprise as he found himself staring at his father's face on another man. His eyes drifted to the darkness behind the daddy-clone. Something out there in the night was grinning at him with long, silver fangs. Fear raked its icy talons across his spine even as the darkness reached for him. He tried to grab his sister and pull her from the doorway, but it was too late. The darkness swept into the room and scooped him and his sister off the floor in arms that felt like what it must be like to be hugged by a granite statue.

"Reed!" the darkness yelled as it hurled the two terrified children into the living room. Their small, helpless bodies slammed headlong into the far wall, knocking the wind from their lungs. Dazed and frightened, they huddled together, crying for their father. The longhaired guy who looked like their daddy charged into the kitchen and attacked their mother, smacking her to the floor and dragging her across the linoleum by her hair. A huge curved knife with a spiked knuckle guard was pressed against her throat, and as she thrashed to free herself, it cut into her skin, drawing blood. That's when Reed charged in looking like he was ready to kill.

"Daddy!" the kids yelled, confident he would be able to save them. They were confident until the huge Black vampire turned to greet Reed and their father's face drained of all color. He looked small and helpless next to the tremendous Black man with the shotgun.

"What the fuck is—"

Reed's protest died in his throat and his eyes widened with recognition as he came face-to-face with all his guilt and fear.

"Malcolm?"

"Reed. I'm so glad you remember me after all these years. I never forgot you. I almost didn't recognize you with the haircut but I never forgot …"

Malcolm leered at Reed, his face mere inches away as if he were about to embrace him, that malevolent grin spreading even wider, splitting his face like a jack-o-lantern.

"Not for a second."

"What the hell do you want, Mal—" Reed again found his words choked off in midstream. This time it was due to Malcolm thrusting his thumb into Reed's Adam's apple. He fell to his knees, gagging and coughing, his eyes wide and teary.

"Do you know what I was doing while you were going to college and getting married and writing your cheap little books? Well, I'm going to show you." Malcolm's eyes flashed with an almost unbearable hatred. His eyes burned into Reed's as if he were trying to immolate him where he stood.

"See, your death had to be perfect because I can only kill you once, Reed. What a pity that is. I wish I could keep killing you over and over again. There are so many ways I could make you suffer. I have dreamt about it so many times. But I can only do it once. I have to choose one death for you. One perfect death. It has to make up for the pain you caused me all these years. So I've been practicing."

Reed swallowed hard. He looked from his son to his daughter and then back to Malcolm.

"W-what do you mean, practicing?"

Malcolm smiled again.

"I cruised the little back-alley bars on Pine Street, picking up pretty little long-haired white boys, taking them home and cutting them up … practicing." He spoke calmly and evenly, as if he were giving a lecture, but that searing hatred and madness still burned in his eyes, and his smile kept curling up on one side, making it look more like a snarl.

Reed looked over at the man who was threatening his wife and noticed for the first time that the man looked exactly like him. He wondered why Malcolm hadn't killed him. If what Malcolm said was true and he was the slasher who had been killing homosexual men plucked from the seedy little gay bars on Pine Street, then surely that's where he had found this guy. So why hadn't he killed him too? The Malcolm Davis he remembered certainly didn't need this anemic looking queer to pull off something like this, but then again, he had no idea what it was they were trying to pull off. At least that's what he told himself. But the terrible thing, the horrible, god-awful thing was that he knew … and he knew he couldn't stop it from happening.

"That kept me amused for a while. Their fear was like yours now, lush and pungent. It was a delicacy. Their deaths were pure ecstasy. But soon, it wasn't enough. I started doing couples and then … entire families. Then …"

He stared off into space, lost for a second in some distant memory.

"Nothing helped … it … It was never enough. I needed you. I needed to taste your fear, to drink your pain like hard liquor. I was in agony, hating the world, trying to understand how the people I loved, the people I trusted, could have done this to me. I could have had a lovely family like this." He gestured broadly at Reed's terrified wife and kids.

"I could have had an over-priced pre-fab house. I could have written novels better than the shit you write!" Reed flinched, wounded by that remark despite himself. "But you took all that away from me, Reed!"

Despite his cartoonishly fiendish dress, the silver fangs, and melodramatic little soliloquy that Reed was almost certain the man had rehearsed, the emotions appeared genuine, and that in itself was disturbing. Malcolm almost looked sad, on the verge of tears, as he glowered at Reed. His eyes were full of questions, full of pain. He almost looked vulnerable in a one-missing-plate-on-the-armored-belly-of-a-dragon  sort of way. Then the darkness and the madness and the flames came back into his eyes, and his face turned to carbonized steel. He bared his fangs in what passed for a smile. He was through talking. It was time to bring the pain.

Too late, Reed allowed himself to fully comprehend what Malcolm was planning.

"I've killed you in my mind more times than I can count, yet still you remain. So what is a brotha to do but cut off the problem at its source?" When Malcolm smiled this time, it resembled the slavering grimace worn by the alien in that movie before it tried to thrust its secondary mandibles through Sigourney Weaver's skull. Reed could vividly remember that moment in the movie theater when everyone shuddered in horror, imagining what it must be like to face such a relentless murdering creature. Then, he had been confident that he would never find out. Now he was.

"No ... no ... no. You can't! Malcolm, we were just kids! I made a mistake! I'm sorry! What do you want from me?!" Reed croaked, still clutching his throat and gasping for air.

The smile left Malcolm's face completely, and his eyes pinned Reed down like the barrel of the Mossberg he was leveling at the children.

"I want you to watch your family die."

The shotgun ripped the night in half and blew little Mark's chest open. Jennie's screams filled the silence before the thunder of the shotgun left the air. She recoiled in horror from the bleeding corpse that seconds ago had been her brother. Linda reached out for her dead son but was again smacked to the ground by her husband's doppelganger.

Reed seized the shotgun and tried to wrench it free from the maniac who had murdered his only son. A look of amusement crossed Malcolm's face as he looked down at Reed.

"Now, now, don't make me kill you so early in the game."

Malcolm let go of the shotgun with his right hand, just long enough to crush Reed's nose with an elbow that once more deposited Reed's ass onto the carpet. Barely conscious, Reed still tried to hold on to the Mossberg and delay for a second the carnage he knew was about to take place. Malcolm jerked it free from his weakening grasp and kicked him savagely in the chin with his mud encrusted Karl Kani boot.

"Don't go to sleep, Reed. The show's not over."

Malcolm reached under the coffee table and seized little Jennie by her ankle. She kicked and fought as she was dragged out of her hiding place.

"Take the shotgun, white boy!"

Reed's look-a-like dragged Linda across the room, the knife still cutting into her skin as she struggled, giving her a wet ruby necklace that hung down between her pale breasts in gory contrast. Malcolm handed the Mossberg over to Paul and took the knife. When he stood, he had Jennie in one hand, dangling by her ankle, and the wicked looking knife, her mother's blood dripping off the blade, in the other.

"Are you watching, Reed? Are you watching?"

The blade went straight through Jennie, cracking through her ribcage and out through her back. Pulling it out nearly ripped her in half. Blood erupted from the wound, sending a bright red arterial spray across the room. Malcolm's eyes gleamed with a kind of ecstasy, an almost religious fervor, as he drove the knife in again and again, hacking her tiny body to pieces. Her screams were deafening but mercifully short, settling into a gurgle and rattling wheeze bubbling up from her ruptured lungs.

Reed made one more effort to save his daughter. He staggered to his feet and charged at Malcolm, who smiled and promptly deposited the heel of his designer boot into Reed's solar plexus, forcing all the wind from his lungs and sending him crashing over the stained glass coffee table. Malcolm stepped over him, still carrying the little mutilated corpse of Reed's daughter, dripping blood all over the new carpet.

Linda was screaming. Reed was coughing up blood. Jennie was dead. Malcolm … was enjoying himself … and just getting started.

"Reed! Reed!" Linda screamed as her husband writhed on the floor.

"Oh, I'd almost forgotten about you, dear." Malcolm discarded the empty Jennie carcass on top of her battered father and stalked across the room to where Paul still held on to Reed's beautiful Barbie doll wife. Linda began struggling and crying, screaming out for help.

"Don't tire yourself out, sweetheart. This might take a while, and you're gonna need all your strength. I'm gonna fuck you to death!"

"Pleeeeeeeeease," Reed whispered hoarsely, vainly, from beneath his daughter's corpse. Her heart was still pumping blood out of a dozen wounds. The grief, the horror, overwhelmed him and his mind shut down, staring as the man with his face handed his wife over to Malcolm but really seeing only a wall of gray with eerily familiar shadows doing a bizarre and disturbing pantomime. Then everything went black.

Reed struggled desperately to free his mind from the dense miasma that had descended over it, struggled to stay in the present, but his mind kept retreating into the safety of the past, of playing in the sandbox, climbing the monkey bars, singing old pop tunes. It was a peaceful place, a safe place, a place where Linda wasn't screaming.

"Linda? Where is Linda?"

Reed's mind shook free of the cloud, and his eyes rolled around the room in a panic. In between Linda's screams and sobs, he could hear animalistic growls and grunts. When his eyes locked on the source of the pandemonium, his heart dropped and his stomach lurched. Malcolm was raping his wife and staring right at him. He wasn't just raping her. He was mutilating her, ripping into her with those bizarre silver fangs. Reed struggled to rise, but something pushed him back down, and he felt cold steel press against the back of his skull along with the unmistakable sound of a shotgun round being chambered.

"Don't move! You have no idea how much I'd love to kill you." It was the man with his face.

On the other side of the room, the savagery was escalating. Linda's screams were horrible as Malcolm tore chunks out of her breasts with his teeth, tearing off and spitting out each nipple. He was snarling and growling, still thrusting himself deep inside her, when he ripped her throat out with his teeth and began to chew. He was cannibalizing her—eating her alive. He brought the knife up—

"Noooooooooo!" Reed weakly screamed.

—and slashed open her chest, sawing through her sternum. He reached in and cracked her ribs open like an oyster shell, grabbed her heart in his fangs, and savaged it free from her chest. Reed was in shock. This was the most horrible thing he had ever seen, and he knew why it was happening. He knew that he had brought this horror down on his family. This was all his fault.

The Black vampire was grinning at him again. Blood was dripping from his fangs, down his chin, neck, chest. He was still chewing on Linda's heart, then, horribly, he swallowed.

"Are you still my best friend, Reed? Are you still going to look after Reneé for me? You going to be my brother-in-law?"

Malcolm was undoubtedly a monster, and Reed was certain that he had created him.

Dr. Frankenstein, I presume?

Detective Titus Baltimore refused to let the old timers see him gag. He knew that his partner was watching him, waiting to see if the tacky, red-black blood that formed a huge stain on the salt and pepper Berber carpet, the meaty copper smell, the children, the woman would be too much for him and he would have to pray to the porcelain god. True, he had never seen a murder this horrible up close. Not one this … grotesque … this savage and barbaric. The unsub who had done this bore scarcely any resemblance at all to the rest of humanity. But Titus choked back the scalding bile that was rising in his throat and focused his eyes to clear away the spots, forcing himself to check the little girl's mercilessly butchered corpse for fibers, hairs, any clue to the man who had done this.

CSU already had the entire room covered in silver latent print dust, and the forensic photographer was flashing pictures so fast it created a surreal strobe-light effect that gave the crime scene the look of a carnival horror show. But these weren't wax dummies. The grotesque wounds were not made with latex and stage blood. He had to turn away as the forensic boys wrenched the knife from Mrs. Cozen's body with a wet sticky *riiiiip* that made his skin crawl and the bile rise up in his throat again.

The CSU boys kept glowering at him as they vacuumed for hair and fiber and picked buckshot out of the drywall with tweezers, carefully placing them in plastic zip-lock bags. Titus knew they had a pretty good Crime Scene Unit, but he still wanted to check the scene himself in the hope that he might catch something the lab boys missed. He knew they hated anyone else working the scene but them. They always bitched about contaminating evidence, but this was his case, and he probably knew as much about forensics as they did. Besides, there was more than enough evidence to go around. The place was littered with it.

At 25, Detective Baltimore was the youngest homicide detective in the Philadelphia Police Department. He was a prodigy who graduated from high school at thirteen, received a PhD in Forensic Psychology from Princeton at eighteen, and made detective by the age of 21 after only two years on the street. After this case was over, the FBI would no doubt recruit him to investigate serial murderers full-time. It was what he always wanted. He just knew everyone resented him. They called him a kiss-ass, a brown-noser, said he hadn't paid his dues, that he had risen to the top off a high-powered education paid for by his rich daddy and by knowing the right people and saying the right things. They were right … and he didn't give a fuck. Why should he walk a beat rousting teenaged hookers and drug dealers when he didn't have to? He closed just as many cases as they did without their years on the street getting shot at and beaten up by crazed junkies, and he would close this one too.

Titus couldn't believe his luck. He was about to solve one of the worst serial killer cases in Philadelphia history. If what he was hearing was correct and all three cases were linked, the man who had savagely beaten, raped, murdered, and mutilated the Cozen family was responsible for more than two dozen murders dating back fifteen years. The frenzied over-kill, the stabbing, the cannibalism, the sexual assault, it was the same signature he had seen over and over again. "The Pine St. Slasher," who had murdered fifteen gay men between the summers of '90 and '95. The sadistic butcher they called "The Chaperone," who had raped and vivisected young women and their boyfriends between '95 and '99. And now the killer who beat, stabbed, and partially cannibalized six entire families, who the press had dubbed "The Family Man."

*Could they all be the same man?*

If this new information was correct, they were all the work of one psychopath. The same monster who shot little Mark Cozen with a shotgun at point blank range. The same sick fucker who hacked little Jennie Cozen to pieces while her mother and father watched, then raped and vivisected Linda Cozen and ate her alive.

The crime scene was scattered with enough physical evidence for a dozen convictions. Footprints, teeth impressions, semen, pubic hair, even bloody fingerprints on a murder weapon left sticking out from what was left of Mrs. Cozen's chest. And he had a witness, a survivor, who could not only give a description of the murderer but the killer's name as well ... Malcolm Davis. This case was solved, and "Tight Ass" Titus Baltimore was certain that he was about to be a hero.

"How can you be sure it was him? I mean, you hadn't seen him in fifteen years before tonight?"

"We were best friends in high school. I remember him."

"Well, you'll excuse me for saying this," Detective Baltimore surveyed the carnage that surrounded him, "but this doesn't look too friendly."

"We had a falling out. Years ago. Back in high school." Reed was in shock. The EMS technicians were trying to explain to him why they couldn't tape his shattered ribs while they bandaged his busted nose in place and pumped him full of painkillers. Detective Baltimore was trying to pump him for details.

"So he kills your family but leaves you alive? Did he say anything to you? Besides confessing to having killed all those people?"

"He told me that I'm the only one he'd let catch him. He told me not to get the cops involved because they couldn't stop him. That it was just between him and me."

"Well, like it or not, we're involved, and we're going to catch this bastard. I promise you. There will be justice for your family."

Detective Baltimore was the worst kind of asshole, the kind that knew he was a little shit but didn't care. He could see that Reed didn't trust him. That was going to be an obstacle. If he couldn't get Reed to trust him, getting information from him would be difficult.

Titus was used to distrust. He dealt with it every day on the job. There was too much swagger about him. His clothes looked too expensive, and he was too young and cocky. To most people, he looked like a con man, a politician, or a stand-up comedian rather than a cop. He was a pretty boy, and it was obvious that Reed hated pretty boys, especially pretty boys with authority. But Titus didn't care. He didn't care that Reed's entire life had been ruthlessly undone. He was only interested in making a name for himself in the department by solving the crime of the century. Reed knew it, and Detective Baltimore knew he knew it and didn't give two shits.

"Okay, do you mind if we go over the whole sequence of events step-by-step so I can get it clear in my head?"

"Yes, I do mind! My family is dead! Fuck your report. Just go catch that bastard!" Reed nearly passed out from the exertion of screaming. Titus leaned forward to catch him, but Reed shrugged him off, then winced and swooned again.

"Jesus! My fucking ribs." His eyes looked dazed and unfocused. He blinked several times and shook his head as he doubled over and held his ribs with both arms.

Titus was certain the man was about to either lose consciousness or lose his dinner. He had to lean on one of the EMTs to keep from falling off the gurney into a pool of his wife's blood. Titus sighed and tapped his foot, not sure if the man was really in that much pain or just putting on an act so he wouldn't have to talk anymore.

"Sorry, Detective. We need to get this man to a hospital. He may have a concussion, and his blood pressure is dropping. There may be some internal bleeding."

"Yeah, yeah, okay. I guess this can wait until tomorrow. We've got enough to go on so far, anyway."

The EMTs laid Reed back onto the gurney and wheeled him outside. Reporters were already crowding the sidewalk, swarming like flies over carrion. Titus followed the EMTs out to get his moment in the media spotlight. When Titus walked out, the first person he saw was Lieutenant Woo, the official head of the Family Man Task Force.

Woo was a figurehead. His job was mostly to handle the media and give them clever sound bites that painted the PPD in the best possible light. He hadn't stepped one foot onto the crime scene, but he was out there talking as if he personally had the whole case wrapped up. He made repeated references to *his* team and *his* taskforce. The press looked bored and annoyed. Apparently, they didn't buy his act either. Baltimore had been running the investigation long before the task force was established, and in spite of the so-called task force, it was still his show and everyone knew it.

"Detective Baltimore! Detective Baltimore! What

happened here? Are they all dead? Is it the Family Man again? Do you have any suspects?"

"You can get rid of that Family Man tag. I've got a better name for you ... Malcolm Davis. He has been positively identified, and we will have him in custody before the sun rises. I promise you that. Now if you'd excuse me. I have an investigation to conduct."

He turned and strode back into the house, ignoring all the questions and secretly patting himself on the back for how well he'd handled the ghouls. Always leave them hungry for more. And there would be more. There was still the arrest, the trial, and Titus would make certain that neither Lieutenant Woo nor some hot shot DA would steal his glory. He would make sure the press knew what an airtight case he'd handed the District Attorney's office, a case that a monkey could win.

Yeah, he would put it just like that, "a case that a monkey could win." That should make sure that credit went where it was due. He laughed to himself. They had given him this case because no one had been able to solve it so far, and they figured the hotshot PhD would do no better. They were all standing around waiting for him to fall on his face. He showed the fuckers.

The eight-man task force that was assigned to the "Family Man" murders, led by Lieutenant David Woo, who everyone called Big Bird because he was Chinese and nearly 6'8", had not done a damn thing. Officially, Titus and his partner, Detective Bryant, were part of the task force. Unofficially, they were the task force. The others were just leg-men, gophers, and backup in case they needed it. They were good for running down leads, cataloguing phone tips, and doing follow up research, but when it came to the crime scene investigations and interviewing suspects and witnesses, Titus wanted the other detectives as far away as possible. Lieutenant Woo wasn't a problem either. He only showed up to do TV interviews and get daily progress reports on how the investigation was going. He was still out there with the press, trying to put in the groundwork for a run at the Police Commissioner's office. Titus understood the man's ambition. He had ambitions of his own.

After nearly a year of work on these killings, the case had solved itself and two other serial-killer cases still on the books. Malcolm Davis. As Titus thought about the cases, he began to see the pattern. It was a downward spiral, a degenerative cycle. The increasing number of victims, from single men to couples to entire families, was a sign of control loss. It was like a drug addict progressing from smoking weed to snorting speed to smoking crack. The killer had developed a tolerance and needed more and more violence to satisfy his addiction. That explained the multiple victims and the increasing savagery of the attacks, progressing from stabbing to cutting to dissection to biting and, finally, to cannibalism. The killer was out of control and making mistakes.

In all the other murders, he had been careful to leave no physical evidence. He wore gloves to hide fingerprints, wore a condom to avoid leaving his DNA traces in his semen. He cut up the bite wounds to make it impossible for the police to cast the indentations to match against dental records—a remote possibility, but one that proved "our boy" was careful. They even suspected he vacuumed the crime scene to remove hair and fibers. But now he had left more evidence then they knew what to do with, had attacked someone who knew him and could identify him, and then left that victim alive. It was too good to be true.

# VII.

Detective James Bryant didn't believe the Cozen family's murder was connected to The Family Man. At 45 years old, he had seen a lot of horrible murders, but The Family Man was by far the worst. This bastard was careful, cunning, evil. He didn't buy that degeneration, self-destruction, downward spiral bullshit. This wasn't a guy who wanted to be caught. If he did, he would have been leaving clues all along—notes, taunting phone calls, any evidence at all. But the monster had never left them anything. It was the total lack of physical evidence that had marked his crimes as unique. It was what had first gotten Detective Bryant to thinking all the homicides were linked. That and the fact that the male victims in each case—The Pine St. Slasher, The Chaperone, and now The Family Man—all bore a remarkable similarity to each other. Of course, no one listened to him. He didn't have his partner's fancy PhD and high-powered IQ. All he had were his 27 years on the force and his instincts.

Right now, his instincts were telling him that there was definitely something wrong with this latest twist in the case. Killers like these didn't self-destruct all at once. There would have been signs that he was starting to slip, that he was getting sloppy. The murders would have started coming closer together, they would have gotten more and more random, and there would have been little mistakes here and there. But the murders had stayed two or three months apart, and they had stayed absolutely perfect. They had certainly grown more savage, but even that was predictable. Still, there was an element of control, a calculated, premeditated design to the crimes. This one just didn't add up.

He watched the crime scene guys going over the scene with tweezers, zip-lock bags, Dust Busters, brushes, and silver latent print powder. The forensic photographer was taking his grisly photos from every conceivable angle. Tight Ass was staring at Linda Cozen's half-eaten heart, peering into her vandalized chest cavity, trying to impress everyone with how calm and detached he could be. Detective Bryant only smiled and shook his head. He could see how pale the man had gotten and how his hand shook when he scribbled in his little pad. The cold sweat was another dead giveaway. How to deal with the smell of a corpse disposing of its waste products was something they didn't teach you in Criminal Psychology 101. Detective Bryant walked outside. For once, he was convinced that the answers were not to be found in the crime scene evidence. The answers were lying in a hospital bed at University Medical.

The forensic boys were busy doing their thing, so Bryant decided to leave them to it and wait for the report. The Medical Examiner had just arrived, looking appropriately somber. Tight Ass was still poking around the corpses, looking for God knew what. All this would be fine for convicting the killer once he was caught, but it wasn't going to help catch him, and that was all James was interested in. The fingerprints would help confirm the witness's identification, but James was pretty sure they had a good suspect. Malcolm Davis.

"Hey, Baltimore!"

"Yeah, you got something?" Detective Baltimore was beaming with enthusiasm.

"Uh, no. I'm done here. I'm gonna head back to the station and run these prints."

Titus glared at him like he couldn't believe what he was hearing. He gestured around the victim's living room at all the evidence to be collected and then shook his head.

"Yeah, whatever," he said.

"Tight Ass," Bryant hissed under his breath as he turned to leave.

Detective Bryant slid behind the wheel of the almost new white 2009 Dodge Intrepid the Department had given him and cruised away from the crime scene, headed for University Hospital. Tight Ass had promised the press he would have a suspect in custody by sunrise. Bryant wasn't so sure. Fools rush in. Detective James Bryant wanted to know a little more about the Family Man, The Chaperone, The Pine St. Slasher, the butcher who had hacked through the Cozen family like a lawnmower, Malcolm Davis.

# VIII.

Bryant had been with the force a long time. He'd already buried two partners and survived one brutal divorce. Rosalyn Ali had been his partner for fifteen years when she'd fallen to a stroke during the search for a serial child murderer ten years ago. The stroke left her partially paralyzed on her right side, relegating her to a desk for two years before another stroke relegated her to the grave. Rosalyn, Rosie, who was a double minority as a Puerto Rican/ Filipino female with the added handicap of being young and sexy, had fought her way up from the streets with him, even making detective before he did. She'd had to kick a lot of ass to prove that she was not the useless piece of fluff most policewomen were considered back then. Everything she did, every case she volunteered them for, every arrest she made seemed to be aimed at getting that gold shield, and she'd gotten it—years after other non-minorities in the department had already gotten theirs, but she'd done it. Even now, thinking back, he was proud of her.

The glass ceiling, which, from where they stood, was not transparent but opaque, hadn't bothered either of them at the time. They both knew the realities of racial politics in Philadelphia, particularly in the police departments, where minorities generally only came in handcuffs. They were both just happy to not be teamed up with one of the many corrupt and racist dinosaurs that polluted the PPD back in the 90s. Neither one of them wanted to have to deal with being forced to decide whether to turn in a fellow officer who'd gone buck-wild on some innocent or even guilty Black kid or to keep quiet and thereby become an accomplice. And they definitely didn't want to deal with a partner who took bribes or shook down dealers and prostitutes. Neither one of them wanted to feel like a sellout. It had been important to them that they feel like a benefit to their respective communities rather than yet another hardship. Back then, when the department was overwhelmingly white and male, they had been extremely grateful for one another.

When James finally made Detective, Rosie fought to have him partnered with her again. As James struggled to pass the detective's exam, she'd been partnered for nearly a year with Greg Jonieack, a lazy, moronic Polish Neanderthal who Mother Teresa would've made dumb Polack jokes about, and who was bringing her closing rate for murder cases way down by spending most of his time flirting with prostitutes. Every murder case seemed to take them to Broad and South, where they'd spend hours questioning prostitutes and Jonieack would inevitably take one into an alley for "questioning" while she waited in the car. If they hadn't gotten her a new partner, the department would've had a scandal on their hands because she was nearly to the point of turning him in.

As detectives working cases together, Bryant and Ali's closing rate had been incredible. They'd gotten all the shit cases that nobody wanted, and they'd somehow managed to solve most of them. In their first year together, they'd closed every case handed to them and had received the grudging respect of the other homicide detectives. Then, when their solve rate started to slip and cases started to go into the files unsolved, they'd caught other detectives looking into some of the cases they'd solved the year before to see if they'd faked or planted evidence. No one found anything, and even though Detectives Bryant and Ali didn't solve every case, their solve rate remained higher than most of the other detectives, which continued to lead to envy and suspicion. That envy and suspicion had even spilled over into James's marriage.

It was hard for a woman to accept that her man spent most of his day with another woman. Twelve-to-fourteen-hour days were common, and when James came home tired and sexually unmotivated, Lois's suspicion had grown. In truth, Bryant and Ali did have a brief affair, but they'd ended it when it started to interfere with work and they realized that, despite the depths of their friendship, they were not in love and what they were doing was just fucking and not worth ruining a career over. Lois didn't start suspecting them of having an affair until years after it had ended. It enraged him that when he was doing bad, she was blissfully unaware but now that he was innocent, every day was an inquisition.

The divorce was far from peaceful. She'd wanted the house, the car, and five hundred dollars a month in alimony. She'd gotten the car and the alimony. Now, he could barely afford to keep the house with all the money he was sending to her each month. Rosie felt bad that she'd caused the breakup of his marriage, but James knew that it wasn't her Lois had been jealous of. It was the job. And he'd chosen the job over her. She was a bitch anyway. He'd loved that car. He'd loved Rosie.

James remembers the day she died. Her brain had turned to mush from lack of oxygen, and there was no recognition in her eyes as she stared at him from the hospital bed. He'd left the hospital knowing that he'd just seen her for the last time.

Before Rosie, his first partner, back when he was a fresh-faced rookie, was a gung-ho ex-marine named Cliff Douglas who missed all the action in Vietnam and seemed to regret riding a desk through the war and never seeing front line combat. He made up for it with near suicidal recklessness on the street. For him, the streets were his second chance at seeing combat. Where many of the old-timers avoided any calls where there were shots fired or armed suspects of any kind, Cliff would go well out of his way to join a gunfight. Cliff regularly charged into dangerous situations with guns blazing. He had more courage than common sense and seemed to James to have a death wish. There were always jokes about "Crazy Cliff," but James didn't think they were funny. Having a borderline psychotic on the force made for amusing bar stories but not when you were his partner, not when his madness could lead to you catching bullets.

James was the only one on the force at that time who regularly wore a vest, and it already had dents in the breastplate from what would have been fatal impacts. He was constantly teased about it by the macho assholes who sat in pizza and donut shops half the day leering at and making lewd comments about every girl who passed by, only leaving long enough to gang up on some doped-up juvenile delinquent. They thought it was cowardly to wear a vest, but those idiots weren't partnered up with "Crazy Cliff." James quickly grew tired of the whine of bullets whizzing past his head. He pulled his service revolver more in those first few years partnered with that nutcase than he had in all the rest of his 25 years on the force. Bryant's GI-Joe partner finally got his wish during one of the many riots on South Street. He'd finally gotten his Purple Heart, chopped in half by friendly fire and left paralyzed from the neck down. Years later, after thousands of hours of physical therapy, he'd regained enough movement in his right arm to point a gun at his temple and blow his brains out.

Now he had Tight Ass. From the moment he heard about the youngest detective on the force, Bryant had hated him. James had been on the force for thirteen years before he finally made detective, and here this young punk got his detective's shield fresh out of college without spending a day on the streets. Regardless of his PhD and genius level IQ, James felt all cops needed to do their time, pay their dues. What they learned in the streets they could never learn sitting in a classroom reading case studies.

Detective Bryant aimed the Intrepid towards Broad and Olney with his mind still lost in the past and hiding from the present. It was easier to direct his anger at long dead partners, an ex-wife he hadn't seen in years, and a partner who was not here to defend himself than at the monster he was tracking. The man who had committed these crimes scared James worse than the shootouts he'd had as a rookie, worse than "Crazy Cliff" ever had. This man was completely outside his frame of reference. He'd looked all kinds of murderers and rapists right in the eyes without fear, but he had understood them. No matter how sick or depraved they were, he'd been able to relate to them. He knew what motivated them. The Family Man, he could not relate to, could not understand.

Detective Bryant knew that if he had any chance of catching Malcolm Davis, he had to find a way to comprehend his madness, and that meant finding out all he could about the killer. He needed to go where Malcolm lived, to breathe the air he breathed, smell the scents he smelled, see what he saw. He needed to talk to Reed Cozen and drag Malcolm Davis out of him.

James knew this case would take a toll on him. He wasn't sure he could afford to pay it anymore. He felt old, tired. Something this dark and ugly might destroy him. In some ways, it felt as though it already had.

He and Titus had been working the case for two

years, and it had already worn him down. Some of the things he'd seen still kept him up at night—especially the kids. The children made this whole thing so much more terrible. There was a reason why James didn't work vice. Seeing abused and exploited children every day was something he hadn't wanted to deal with. Now, he dealt with their corpses, and The Family Man left him knee deep in them.

It was more than simply catching the man. A part of him *needed* to understand him, if only to convince himself that he could never be like him.

James had been to enough Sex Addicts Anonymous sessions to know that he also had a problem. He'd talked to enough murderers, rapists, and child molesters to know that his problem was a little too similar to theirs. He was a sexual predator just as they were, only he used smooth talk instead of coercion and violence to trap his prey. What he did was not a crime. The women he'd seduced and told that he loved to get between their legs had come to him willingly. Still, he'd left them just as emotionally scarred as if he'd raped them, and the passion he felt when he was with them was a little too close to the passion he saw in Linda Cozen's mutilated corpse. He needed to know that he would never, could never, become *that*. He needed to know what made Malcolm tick.

Detective Bryant pulled up outside of University Medical Center, squealing his tires as he pulled into a handicapped-parking zone. An overweight nurse with the 2010 version of a bouffant hairdo started toward his car, looking unnecessarily irate. James backed the Intrepid out of the handicapped zone before Henrietta Hippo could initiate an argument. He had to cruise the lot for another ten minutes before he found another parking spot. He sat in the car for another five minutes, taking deep breaths and trying to clear all of his own problems out of his head so he could appropriately commiserate with the victim. When he finally stepped from the car, a nervous tremor went through him and he gritted his teeth against it, sucking the fear down deep in his guts where stomach acids would dissolve it. As he walked through the doors of the emergency room, he could feel his stomach acids at work.

47

# IX.

Reed sat and thought. His family was dead, murdered by a man he hadn't seen or thought of in over a decade but who had obviously been thinking of him. The police would catch him. They had all the information they needed. Something about that troubled him. He knew that Malcolm wasn't a stupid man. Why had Malcolm left him alive knowing that he would identify him and lead the police right to him? He knew Malcolm was crazy, but Malcom had always been crazy—smart, cunning, deadly, crazy. It didn't even surprise him to hear that Malcolm was The Family Man. The only thing unusual was that Reed was still breathing. Malcolm had to be planning something else. He remembered how Malcolm used to always quote from that movie *Shaka Zulu.*

*"Never leave an enemy behind or he will rise again to fly at your throat!"*

Well, Malcolm had left him behind, but Reed was in no condition to fly at anyone's throat. He hated Malcolm, wanted him dead, but he feared him too much to go after him himself, and his own feelings of guilt kept getting in the way of his anger. He knew that Malcolm was no doubt crazy before Reed took his girlfriends from him, but was he this crazy? Would he have killed all those people if it weren't for what Reed had done to him? Would he have murdered Linda, Jennie, and little Mark? Had Reed pushed over the first domino that knocked over dozens of lives and came back around to crush the lives of his family?

Reed began to daydream about his wife. He dreamt about Jennie's birth. He had been scared to death when all of a sudden, in the middle of the delivery, his wife had stopped dilating and had to be rushed into surgery for an emergency Caesarian section. He held her hand and they sang children's songs while waiting for the anesthesia to take effect. He would never forget the sound of his first child's cries. The smile on her face, on his wife's face, on his own face. He had a family now … then. Now he had no family. He was alone again. Reed began to weep quietly into the pillow.

A soft, respectful knock preceded Detective James Bryant's entrance into Reed's hospital room. Reed was almost thankful for the distraction. The silence was full of ghosts and demons.

"I'm Detective Bryant from the Philadelphia Police Department Homicide Division. May I speak to you a moment? I know it's been a long evening, but the sooner we get some facts from you, the sooner we can catch this guy."

"Come on in. I can't sleep anyway." Reed pulled himself upright, wincing in pain.

"Thank you." Detective James Bryant sat down in a chair by Reed's bed, looked thoughtfully at Reed's battered face, and got right to the point.

"Who is Malcolm Davis, and how do you know him?"

"Detective Bryant—"

"James. Just call me James."

Reed considered the old detective. In his crumpled old Botany 500 suit, he looked like a stockier Black version of Colombo. The chewed up, unlit cigar that hung from his mouth completed the effect. He looked kind, harmless, like someone's father or grandfather. But if you looked closely, you could see the thick sinuous arms and chest bulging through the suit, you could see the hard, determined look in his eyes.

Detective Bryant—James—was more than he appeared.

"Okay, James. Where should I begin? You want to know who Malcolm is? He's my very own Frankenstein monster. I made him, and now the chickens have come home to roost, so to speak."

"I wouldn't think a novelist would be so quick to mix metaphors."

Reed laughed, then winced in pain, curling into a ball and holding his sides.

"Please. Don't make me laugh or I literally will split my sides."

"Okay, so what do you mean you created him? What is it between the two of you?"

Reed continued to hold his sides. He rocked back and forth and stared at the television set, which had never been turned on. The pain in his ribs had subsided. The pain in his mind raged.

"Malcolm was my best friend in high school, and I betrayed him. I slept with his first girlfriend. The first woman he'd ever loved, maybe the first human being he'd ever loved besides maybe his mother."

"And what did Malcolm do? Did he know?"

"Malcolm suspected it, but he wasn't sure. He wanted to believe me. He trusted me. I think, maybe, he loved me."

"Loved you?"

"Not in a sexual way." The memory of Malcolm attacking him in the men's room of a train station long ago crept its way past his defenses. "I don't think. I … I think he just thought of me as an intellectual equal. His only peer in a world of morons. Without me, he would have been alone."

"Is that how you thought? That you were alone in a world of morons?"

"I never had Malcolm's ego. I never shared his contempt for everybody and everything. He found that charming. He thought I was naive and weak. He treated me like a pet."

"And so you fucked his girlfriend to prove to him that you were as much a man as he was?"

"To prove it to myself. I was jealous of Malcolm. He was the meanest bastard you ever met, and the girls loved him. They loved him! They always go for the assholes. I was too nice. I was the kind of guy girls dated because they knew I'd never have the nerve to ask them for sex. I was their best friend. They called me their little brother and talked to me on the phone about how much they wanted to fuck guys like Malcolm, but of course, Malcolm was obsessed with Reneé."

"Malcolm's first girlfriend?"

"He thought she was perfect, flawless, goodness and innocence personified. He had her on a pedestal so high she was dizzy. It was like he thought that if an angel like her could love him, then maybe he wasn't completely evil. But she was no angel. I proved that. His suspicions eventually led to their break up. Then, after he and Reneé broke up, he started dating this girl named Natasha."

"Did Malcolm love her?"

"He thought he did. All he ever did was torture her by telling her how she would never measure up to Reneé. See, he still thought Reneé was some type of angel."

"And what happened to Natasha?"

"I slept with her too. That's when Malcolm found out. He caught me over at Natasha's house, in her bedroom. I thought he was going to kill me right then. I was trying to talk my way out of it and he was trying to believe me. He still wanted to believe that I hadn't done it. I was amazed when he let me walk out of there alive. When I left, he went into Natasha's kitchen, blew out the pilot lights on her stove, and turned up the gas. He brought her down there in the kitchen with him and sat while the kitchen filled up with gas. He had a pack of matches on the table. She lasted maybe five minutes before she told him everything. She even told him about Reneé and I. Malcolm lit the match. There was a small explosion, but only the stove was destroyed. She had cracked too quickly, and there wasn't enough gas to level the house and kill them both like Malcolm wanted. They only suffered a few minor burns and bruises. The kitchen got burnt up pretty bad, but the firemen put out the blaze before it took the rest of the house. Malcolm walked back home during all the commotion of the fire trucks, police cars, and nosy neighbors. When the police came to arrest him for arson, he took a knife and slit his own throat, cut right through his trachea and his esophagus, and tried to saw through his cervical vertebrae. He was trying to decapitate himself."

"Jesus Christ."

"They rushed him to the emergency room, and the doctors stitched him up. The doctor who operated on him said she'd seen hundreds of suicides but she had never seen anyone try to cut their own throat, let alone remove their own head. They had him on suicide watch for twenty-four hours a day. A few weeks later, he left the hospital, and I never saw him again until tonight," Reed said. But that wasn't exactly true. He'd seen Malcolm following him one day after school, soon after he'd left the hospital.

He'd caught Malcolm's familiar shadow trailing him onto the bus, glimpsed it briefly between the dozens of passengers packed in like human cattle. The image was so brief he could almost convince himself that he hadn't seen it. But he had. Reed left the bus and tried to lose himself in the press of downtown shoppers, shoplifters, and pickpockets on Chestnut Street. Repeatedly, he glanced behind to see if Malcolm was following him, but the hundreds of bargain hunters formed an impenetrable curtain. A flash of dark clothing, black skin, a massive shape slipping between the human traffic pumped panicked adrenaline into Reed's step. He crossed Market Street at a near sprint, headed toward the train station inside the huge Gallery Mall.

As Reed walked nervously into the Gallery and down to the station, he thought he'd caught a momentary glimmer of two furious eyes burning from a face the color of liquid night. A chill raked his spine. Reed never saw more than a second or two of his pursuer, but he'd known he was there.

Electric tendrils of fear had snaked beneath his skin, making him shiver and bounce nervously from foot to foot. He looked around in a near panic, wondering what direction the attack would come from. Then he'd seen Natasha. She was smiling and heading towards him, and Malcolm was still somewhere close by. Even if he couldn't see him, Reed knew Malcolm was coming for him, and he knew that if Natasha so much as hugged him within sight of Malcolm, he would die right there on that platform. Malcolm would tear him apart where he stood. He had to get away from her.

Reed looked around for an exit and finally retreated to a men's room deeper within the mall. He'd been in there for less than a minute when Malcolm walked in. Reed's whole body shook convulsively when he saw him. Malcolm, his very own boogie-man come to drag him to hell … in pieces. It wasn't just the thought of dying. It was the way he would die. Reed's eyes traveled from the feral scowl on Malcolm's face, the flaming hatred roiling in his eyes, to the wicked looking switchblade in his right hand. Reed had seen the slasher movies. Most of them he'd watched with Malcolm. Reed knew what a determined man could do with a knife. He knew what Malcolm could do with one.

Reed remembered Malcolm moving toward him. He remembered feeling the big man's rage traveling before him like onrushing storm clouds. The temperature seemed to rise in proportion to Malcolm's anger. The bathroom grew thick and humid as if Malcolm's fury were heating the very air, boiling off his skin like steam. Sweat rolled from Reed's forehead into his eyes, making them sting.

A tidal wave of emotions crashed down on his mind; guilt and fear gripped him like a physical entity, impregnating his whole body with an oppressive dread. He could feel its weight pressing down on him, rooting his Nikes to the piss-stained tile floor. The realization of his own eminent death froze his tongue to the roof of his mouth and drained the phosphagens from his muscles. His eyes locked on Malcolm's, and his emotions grew deeper and more confused. A profound sadness, sympathy for his friend's pain, confused his self-preservation instincts, fear morphing with his guilt and remorse, and he found himself moving toward Malcolm, opening his arms to embrace him, waiting to feel the cold sting of the blade penetrating his skin, muscle, and organs, ripping him open. But he never felt the knife.

What happened next remained locked in the place where past pain hides from the conscious mind, a profound chasm half filled with chimerical nightmares, nebulous impressions, abstract sensations. A vague recollection of not being able to breathe, feeling Malcolm's powerful arms crushing down over his throat. Mixed feelings of pleasure and pain, of vulnerability, of surrender, of sheer horror, and something that he could not accept, could not believe. Even now, his mind retreated from it. What he'd felt had been sexual excitement simultaneous with the certainty of death.

But these memories were all obscure, wisps and shadows, shreds of memory coming to him as if from a dream. He'd awakened crumpled on the floor in a bathroom stall, not quite certain why he was alive.

Malcolm had not killed him.

That had been the last time he'd seen Malcolm until last night, and now, as he had then, he had no idea why Malcolm let him live.

Detective Bryant got up from his chair and turned to leave. He felt woozy, needed air. This case just seemed to get more and more horrible.

"Reneé and that other girl, Natasha, do they still live in Philly?"

"Probably. Nobody ever leaves Philly. It's like a black hole, but I don't have their addresses or anything."

"Where did they live back then?"

"Reneé lived in Frankford. Natasha lived in Germantown, a few blocks from Malcolm. Her mom was one of those liberal hippie types." Reed offered that last bit of information as a way of explaining why a white woman would live with her young daughter in a Black ghetto. Detective Bryant tried his best not to be offended and failed.

"I'll have Dispatch locate them for me. What were their last names?"

"Reneé's last name was Volaré."

"Volaré? Like the song?"

"Yeah, like the song. Natasha's name was something Indian sounding. I can't remember it."

"Take my card and call me if you remember it. If Malcolm went after you, he might go after them. I'm placing you under protective custody. There'll be an officer posted outside your door."

"You think he'll come after me again?"

Detective Bryant thought about everything he'd heard tonight and considered lying, but instead, he gave it to him straight.

"I think that a man who slit his own throat and tried to blow himself up isn't gonna stop until he feels he's avenged whatever wrong you've done to him or until we stop him."

*Never leave an enemy behind or he will rise again to fly*

*at your throat!*

A shiver slithered up Reed's back and scampered across his neck and shoulders. He stared at the detective, his eyes widening in fear. He swallowed hard and tried to speak, but he had nothing to say. What could he say? He wanted the detective to say something, to say that he would stop Malcolm, that he would keep him from ever hurting anyone again.

Detective Bryant, feeling guilty, like maybe he had been a little too harsh, offered Reed a few comforting words.

"Look, I don't know if it helps any, but I think Malcolm was deeply disturbed long before you came along."

"Yeah, but would he have become what he's become? Would he be a killer if it weren't for me?"

Detective Bryant didn't know, and he hated to think that there might be any justification for the horrible things that had been done to this man's family, but he also believed that friends didn't steal each other's girlfriends. Bros before hoes. That's what he'd always preached and practiced. This man had violated that male code and destroyed a man in the process. He had paid with the lives of his family.

"I don't know."

Bryant left without another word.

Reneé Volaré lived with her husband and three boys in Fishtown, the white trash district. Detective Bryant found the entire neighborhood depressing, pitiful, and just plain bizarre. Having grown up in a Black ghetto watching White people on TV who seemed to have everything except problems, seeing that White people lived like rats in this type of filth made no sense to him. White folks in America had a four-hundred-year head start on Black people, yet somehow, this entire neighborhood had not just fallen behind but seemed to have failed to even get out of the blocks. The houses were not only old and dilapidated but they seemed to be falling apart, covered in trash and garbage. The hollow-eyed people who ambled through the filth strewn streets looked like holocaust victims, depressed, angry, malnourished, defeated. G-town's citizens looked optimistic in comparison.

Every teenager Bryant passed was either drunk or high. Every couple he passed was fighting, some of them physically. Every elderly person he passed looked to be on the verge of tears. And here he was, about to bring more bad news into this neighborhood that already seemed to know too much. He could imagine the conversation to come.

"Mrs. Volaré, there's a very good possibility that a homicidal psychopath that you used to date is on his way to murder you and your family."

He hated it.

There were two patrol vehicles behind him, escorting him to Ms. Volaré's house just in case Malcolm happened to be there. Detective Bryant pulled up in front of the withered two-story shack and let out a deep, heavy sigh. The house looked like shit. He doubted if it had been painted for decades. What little paint still clung to the building's crumbling brick facade was cracked and peeling. One of the second-floor windows was shattered and had been covered in plastic rather than repaired. The veneer on the front door was warped, splintered, and water-stained. The concrete steps that led up to the door had huge chunks missing, and most of the corners were broken off. There was an old sheet that had once been white hung over the living room window in lieu of drapes. As he stepped out of his vehicle and up the crumbling steps, he saw what was perhaps the only thing that could make this whole miserable trip worse. There was dried blood on the sheet. Lots of blood.

Bryant pulled out his weapon and called for the officers to follow him as he kicked in the door. The old weather-beaten door split down the center and caved in on itself. Bryant stepped through it into the Volaré's living room. He waved the two officers in, and they fanned out into the house like commandos. They were apprehensive, scared. None of them wanted to be the first one to confront The Family Man or the gruesome aftermath of one of his rampages. They had their weapons drawn, and their eyes were darting everywhere at once. Bryant mentally prepared himself for another scene like the one at the Cozen's house.

The living room was in shambles, but the house was so dirty and choked with clutter that it was difficult to tell if the overall chaos was due to a struggle or merely bad housekeeping. The remains of a spaghetti dinner were strewn all over the floor amid broken dishes, empty beer cans, newspapers, old sports and fashion magazines, a spilled ashtray, broken toys, and baby bottles half-filled with spoiled milk. A child's highchair lay in one corner on top of a plastic tricycle, and there was a long orange and yellow food stain down the wall where the chair had apparently been thrown, splattering a plate of baby food.

The other officers were going through the house, checking it room by room with their guns still drawn. It was empty. All the rooms were in the same state of disarray. Much of the mess could've been attributed to slovenly tenants, but the only thing that could not be explained away was the bloodstained sheet that hung from the window. Blood had saturated the bottom half of the cloth, with splatters as high as six feet. Curiously, a large area on the carpet was completely clear. It looked as if it had actually been scrubbed and vacuumed.

Detective Bryant stared at the huge clean spot, remembering how The Family Man always cleaned up his crime scenes to destroy evidence. This one, too, had been cleaned but sloppily. Bryant got on the radio and called for the Crime Scene Unit. There was no doubt in his mind that Malcolm Davis had been there.

But where were the bodies? Why had he taken the bodies away? Was this some change in the pattern, or was there some special reason why he didn't want these particular bodies found? Was he trying to conceal this crime for some reason? Had there even been a crime here?

It made no sense.

Detectives Tony Vargas and Mike Willis, who were also assigned to the taskforce, showed up at the same time as the Crime Scene Unit. Vargas, who seemed to change styles and fashions like a chameleon, was wearing a black suit with gray pinstripes that was tapered at the waist and had big, wide collars like a zoot suit. On his feet, he wore black and white Stacy Adams with tassels. His hair was slicked back, and his moustache had been shaved to a thin line tracing his upper lip. He looked like a gangster from the roaring twenties. Willis, with his big feet, big ears, pointy-head, glasses, long neck, and oversized Adam's apple, looked like Gomer Pyle. Bryant was so overwhelmed by the case that he couldn't even think of anything sarcastic to say. Still, he couldn't resist shaking his head like an amused parent watching two slightly dimwitted though well-meaning children.

"Okay, so what the fuck've we got here?" Vargas drawled with a Newport 100 dangling from his lip, dropping ashes onto the carpet.

"I'm not sure. See all that blood on the sheet? That's not from no nose bleed." Bryant casually removed the cigarette from Tony's mouth and tossed it out the door. He didn't feel he needed to explain to him that a good defense attorney could convince a jury that those few cigarette ashes had contaminated the entire crime scene, calling into question the validity of anything they found there. If it was the detectives themselves who brought in the cigarette ashes, who's to say how much more of the evidence was in fact left by them? It was an old argument that had fucked every detective at one time or another.

"No shit!" Willis said, looking at the gory sheet hanging by a tack to each corner of the window. "And look at this. It looks like somebody's been doin' some cleaning, and it sure as shit wasn't the slobs who live in this dump."

Willis had a remarkable knack for looking like a complete moron while in fact possessing one of the finest investigative minds in the department.

"Let's wait and see what the CSU boys come up with," Bryant said

Two guys from Crime Scene, one Filipino and one

Black, showed up twenty minutes later. They took pictures, dusted for fingerprints, and bagged and tagged anything that looked like it could possibly be evidence. The last thing they did was spray everything with Luminal. The whole room seemed to turn green. There was blood everywhere—on the walls, the floor, the ceiling. A massacre had taken place here.

But where were the bodies?

"That much blood, I'd say we were definitely looking at a murder scene," the effeminate looking Filipino offered, though his observation was hardly needed. The way the blood was splattered floor to ceiling suggested an arterial spray that could only have come from mortal wounds.

"Could one body have produced this much blood?" Vargas asked.

"Not even if you drained every last drop of blood out of it," the technician replied. "See the way the blood sprayed all the way across the room here and almost hit the ceiling?"

He pointed to where the glowing trail of Luminal began at the larger puddle in the middle of the room, trailed across the floor, and climbed the far wall.

"That had to have been a powerful blow and most likely one of the first. But after a while, there wouldn't have been enough blood left in the body to spray like that. It would have just kind of dripped, but there is blood sprayed in every direction. That indicates to me that we are looking at multiple victims. Multiple casualties."

"The Family Man," Vargas said aloud to himself

"Yeah, but where is the family? Where are the bodies?" the CSU tech asked.

It was a rhetorical question. Nobody in the room had a clue what happened to that family and probably never would unless they caught Malcolm and he led them to the bodies.

Detective Bryant was exhausted when he finally

left Fishtown. The last thing he wanted to do was head to the station and toil over paperwork. He needed to lose himself for a while. He needed a place where the drinks, the thrills, and the women were cheap and plentiful. The Star Bar fit two of the criteria, and two out of three ain't ever bad. He cruised down Market Street slowly to make sure none of the vice cops he knew were hanging around. Even though every red-blooded American boy occasionally visited the local titty bar, he didn't want his fellow officers to see him out creepin'. He didn't want it getting around the department that he was some kind of degenerate.

The bright red, white, and blue neon that surrounded the huge marquee, featuring names like Misty Towers and Tawny Peaks, illuminated his car as he drove by the gaudy little strip club. Detective Bryant turned the corner onto Tenth Street and guided his Intrepid into the alley behind the club. Bryant briefly wondered if it was against policy to use an official vehicle to cruise for pussy, but then he dismissed the thought. After all, he was just going to look at the pussy. It wasn't like he was buying a taste. If confronted, he could always say he was looking for leads or an informant.

The back door was locked, so Bryant walked all the way around to the front of the building, an inconvenience that almost made him call the whole adventure off. He was still paranoid about being spotted by another cop, especially those gossipy hens in Vice. They'd once chased a cop out of town by letting it be known around the department that he'd been spotted cruising Pine Street where the transvestite hookers plied their trade. No one had actually witnessed him propositioning any of them, but the suspicion alone was enough for his fellow peace officers to make his life hell. They put dildos on his car seat along with AIDS awareness pamphlets and gay magazines. Finally, the poor guy had enough and transferred to some New Jersey PD. Apparently that wasn't far enough because his first day on the new job, someone taped a huge glossy picture of a penis clipped from a porno mag on the back of his squad car. The dishonored officer didn't even know it until some sweet old lady nearly had a heart attack and called in to report him for obscenity. He was let go soon afterward. Detective Bryant didn't need that kind of drama in his life.

No one that he recognized from the force was around, so he scurried inside. His guilty expression and body language screamed "perp." It annoyed him that the wrangler who stood out front, tempting sex starved perverts like himself with promises of the world's most exotic erotic dancers, knew him by name. It annoyed him to think about how much money he'd wasted in these types of places since the divorce. It annoyed him that the scandalous hoes that worked there charging twenty dollars a lap dance knew he was an easy mark.

The moment he walked in, his eyes zeroed in on an average looking young blonde with a remarkably above average ass. In fact, it was the most perfect ass he could ever recall seeing. A Prince song was playing as she dry humped the air. The Purple One wailed out "Irresistible Bitch" to an infectious driving bass beat, and the blonde bent over and did that little booty shake thing, then went into the butterfly. James loved T&A, but he was particularly partial to A. He found himself irresistibly sprung. Detective Bryant went straight to the ATM machine by the coat check, withdrew two hundred dollars, and immediately asked the cocktail waitress for a hundred one-dollar bills. He plopped down in a chair by the stage, still transfixed by the bounce and wiggle of that most perfect ass.

It annoyed him how easy it was to access and be parted from your money in these places. He hadn't had one sip of alcohol and he was already stuffing fifty one-dollar bills in the dancer's G-string. It was starting to look like a grass skirt. But she was smiling and bouncing that ass in his face, and for once, The Family

Man murder case was the furthest thing from his mind.

The more he looked at her, the more pedestrian her appearance became to him. She would never be called beautiful, but there was an aura of raw animalistic sexuality around her … or maybe it was just the ass. The song ended, and she stepped down from the stage. She suddenly looked shy and self-conscious. She was new at this. Bryant waved her over.

"Hi, you … uh … you want a dance?"

He wondered if the shy, innocent thing was just an act. If it was, it was working.

"Certainly."

She slid onto his lap and straddled his growing erection. A hip-hop song featuring a rap artist named DMX came on, and she began to gyrate her hips to the beat.

"What's your name, gorgeous?"

"Candy … um … CC. My friends call me CC."

"How long have you been working here?"

"I just started on Monday. Whoa, you've got some serious muscle under there." She ran her hands over his arms and chest, nodding and smiling her approval.

"I used to box. I still hit the gym every now and then." Actually, he spent about two hours every morning lifting weights, skipping rope, and pounding the heavy bag.

"What do you do now?"

Now it was his turn to hesitate. "I … uh … I'm a Homicide Detective."

He waited for the awkward pause in the conversation, the sudden chill in her mood. Being a policeman to most people was like being a wife beater or a child abuser. It brought to mind images of cops in riot gear siccing attack dogs and firehoses on peaceful demonstrators or, more recently, of racist assholes clubbing Black motorists half to death. Being a homicide detective was like being a mortician or, worse, a grave robber. To the average citizen, he was some kind of sadistic necrophile. But CC seemed different.

"That's cool! You ever kill anyone?"

"I haven't pulled my gun in almost twenty years."

"Oh yeah, and what about twenty years ago?"

"I shot a guy once. He had his wife and kid held hostage in this rat-infested little shack on Columbia Avenue. He'd already stabbed his mother-in-law to death. It was like a hundred degrees outside, and you could smell the blood beginning to rot. All of a sudden, he tries to sneak out the back door. All the other cops were parked out front with their guns pointed at the front door, and he comes creepin' out the back. It was just me and this other rookie in the backyard, and he comes out holding that knife with that old lady's blood still dripping from the blade."

"Did he attack you?"

"No. He didn't get a chance. I was so freaked out scared I shot him as soon as he stepped into the yard."

This time she did pause. She looked deep into the eyes, nodded, and smiled. Then she did something that completely shocked him. She reached down between his legs and started to stroke him.

"I like you."

"I like you too. You are the sexiest woman I've ever seen in this place," he lied.

"You're a pretty handsome man yourself."

The song ended, the next song began, and she was still working his lap. He pulled her closer to him and hugged her, nuzzling his face in her neck and then rubbing his cheek over her bare nipples. He then kissed her lightly on the cheek. CC seemed shaken up by it. She stopped dancing and stared at him curiously. The detective reached out and stroked her cheek with his fingertips. CC caught his hand. She rubbed the back of his hand softly against her cheek as she continued to stare at him. Then she kissed his hand and lowered it between her breasts, holding it against her heart.

"You are beautiful," Bryant told her, and this time

he meant it. She was gentle, tender, innocent, and vulnerable. He wondered what would drive such a woman to play whore for a living.

"You are so different. The other guys who come in here just paw and grope at me. But you … you cuddle and caress. You're almost loving." She was still looking at him like she was waiting for an explanation.

Bryant shrugged. He wanted this woman, not just sexually, though that was definitely the largest part of what he was feeling, but he wanted to hold her in his arms, fall asleep with her head on his chest. He wanted to wake up and see her smiling up at him and then make love to her all over again.

"You want to spend a little time with me?" He spoke from his heart and immediately regretted it. He had pushed too hard, too fast. He was afraid he would frighten her away.

"Well … see, I'm married but …"

"But?"

"But I think you're sweet."

"What time do you get off?" He couldn't help himself. He wanted her, had to have her.

Detective Bryant didn't normally mess with married women, but he figured that any man who would let his wife work in a place like that wasn't worthy of his respect or consideration.

"I don't get off until two."

"I'll be back for you."

The detective stood up and handed her $40 for the two dances. He kissed her forehead and walked out feeling superhuman. He didn't care if someone from the force saw him walking out of The Star Bar. He was thinking about CC … and The Family Man. Malcolm Davis had somehow leapt back into his head the instant he left the bar. By the time he got back to the Intrepid, he was no longer thinking about CC at all.

The 12th Precinct was only about a mile away, and he figured that it would still be buzzing with the excitement of the latest murder. They were very close to closing the most horrible murder case in Philadelphia. When he entered the station, he was surprised and relieved to find that Tight Ass was still out at the crime scene. First thing, Bryant checked the files to see if Malcolm had a criminal record. It took longer than he expected, but the search came up negative. Just as he suspected, the man had been careful. Knowing it was probably a waste of time, he went to work scanning the prints lifted from the murder weapon into the AFIS computer, searching for a match.

The system they used for tracking fingerprints was still fairly new, and less than one fourth of the fingerprints they had on file had been entered into the computer. He wished he had access to the FBI's Automated Fingerprint Identification System, which contained not only the fingerprints of every person ever arrested in the United States but also everyone who had ever served in the military. As tedious as it was to search through Philadelphia's fingerprint records, he quickly realized that searching the files of every felon in the US would be one hell of a chore, high-tech computer system or not. The AFIS could suggest possible fingerprint matches, but the human eye, his human eye, had to make the final call. The computer narrowed it down by weeding out the fingerprints that didn't match at all, but he still had to check each of the computer's suggestions, and that sometimes took hours.

The detective bit the tip off another White Owl cigar and stuck it in his mouth without lighting it. He quit smoking years ago, but he still enjoyed the taste of tobacco and he still had that damn oral fixation. His coffee was bitter and tepid. His shoulders ached. He could barely keep his eyes open, and his mind kept wandering back to the Star Club. He considered calling the guys at the Bureau and asking them to run the print through the VICAP computer, but he knew how stingy they could be with their technology when they weren't actually in on a case. Thanks to his stubborn ass, glory hog of a partner, the FBI was not a part of this one, not even as consultants.

He knew they were monitoring the case. The captain recruited them to help with a profile after the second killing, but that was the limit of their involvement. Since the killer apparently hadn't crossed state lines, it was still a PPD case, it was still his case. He might call the feds in on this one just to get some feedback from the big heads at their Behavioral Science Department. Maybe he could get them to work up another profile of The Family Man to see if he could really be responsible for all those other murders, see if he could really be Malcolm Davis. After a few hours of sifting through fingerprints, he gave up and called it a night. When he left the station, there was no question where he was headed. He made a beeline for The Star Bar, a beeline for CC.

She was just counting out her tips when he walked in. She had already changed out of her dance costume and was wearing a gray sweat suit with Reebok tennis shoes and no socks. All her makeup had been washed off, and her blonde hair hung limply to her shoulders. CC looked like she had just left an aerobics class. She was sexy as hell, even sexier than she'd been when dancing. When she saw him, CC beamed and then blushed.

"I've been waiting for you. I thought you weren't going to show. I … I was almost wishing you didn't."

"Why?"

"Because I knew that if you did, I wouldn't be able to say no to you." She blushed again and stared at her shoes.

"Let's go." He draped an arm around her, hugging her close, and started to walk toward the door.

"Uh … I'll meet you out back. I can't let the manager see me leave with a customer. It's against the rules. I could get fired. You know, some of the girls have been caught turning tricks, so they had to make it a rule or else the place could get shut down."

"Oh, yeah, that makes sense. I'm in the white Dodge."

"I'll be out in about five minutes. I don't want it to look too obvious." She had that shy embarrassed look again.

Bryant smiled and walked out. He was in his car, gnawing on another White Owl cigar, when she came out, looking nervous, excited, and still embarrassed. Bryant stuck the cigar in the ashtray and popped half-a-dozen wintergreen Tic Tacs into his mouth, chewing them up before CC reached the car. When CC slid into the passenger seat, he pulled her close and kissed her. He wasn't sure if the Tic Tacs had covered the taste of the cigar, but she didn't seem to mind.

He took his time that night. He made love with his heart, his soul, his lips, tongue, hands, his entire body. He wanted her to be thinking of him when she went home to her husband. He knew he would be thinking of her.

# XI.

Malcolm knew Paul was angry, but he held his tongue. The sidekick's anger hadn't yet made him stupid enough to be disobedient, which was good. Malcolm didn't want him to have die before the fun was over. But he could see that something was bugging him.

"Why didn't you let me kill Reed? You promised! Now the cops'll be all over us. We're going to get caught and sentenced to death. We had that bastard on his knees, crying and begging, and you spared him. Why?"

"None of your fucking business, white boy. You think I owe your ass an explanation?"

"When are we going back for Reed?" Paul asked.

Malcolm was deep in thought. He wasn't about to answer Paul's question, and if the white boy opened his mouth again, he would hurt him. Malcolm was thinking about Reed. He was reliving Reed's terror, his pain. It had been perfect, and he wanted more.

Didn't Paul understand that if he killed Reed, he wouldn't be able to hurt him again, that he wouldn't be able to enjoy the sweet ecstasy of vengeance?

Reed's pain would be over and so would Malcolm's whole reason for living. The hate that drove him would have no target, no focus. Reed had to live so that Malcolm could keep hurting him. The game was just beginning. Malcolm had made the first move. Now it was Reed's turn. Malcolm couldn't end the game, only Reed could.

*Never leave an enemy behind …*

*Don't worry, Reed, I haven't left you. I'll be coming back.*

Malcolm was smiling again. The memory of having Reed cornered in the bathroom fifteen years ago slipped into his mind, what he'd done, what he hadn't done, how that experience had affected him. He found himself getting aroused and angry at the same time. That would have been the perfect time to kill Reed. But he hadn't. He couldn't. He'd found himself homicidally impotent, but another, stronger impulse rose up in its place.

Detective Bryant was surprised to find CC still beside him in the morning. She woke him up by kissing her way down his body and then taking his morning erection down her throat. By the time he was fully awake, he was already approaching orgasm. She took that down her throat as well. He promptly reciprocated, then they both stepped into the shower to wash the evening from their pleasantly fatigued bodies and greet the day.

"I'm surprised you're still here. What about your husband?"

"I normally don't get off work until four anyway. I'll just tell him I stopped at my sister's house. He leaves to play golf at six in the morning on Saturdays, so he probably didn't even miss me."

"I'm glad you stayed. Do you want breakfast?"

"Sure." She lathered her body, and as Bryant watched, he found himself growing another painful erection. His penis had been overworked, and it ached as it swelled larger than he ever remembered it being before last night. It looked like a club. He stepped from the shower and dried himself off before he was tempted to do something that might rupture a blood vessel and leave his tender organ swollen for the next two weeks.

He slipped into his Calvin Klein boxers and stepped back into the bedroom. CC was humming softly as she shampooed her hair. Bryant slid down on the carpet to begin the first of three hundred abdominal crunches. As he sweated through his first set of one hundred, he listened to her offbeat version of "What's Love Got To Do With It?" turn into Lauren Hill's "Doo Wop." He smiled to himself as he ran last night over in his head. CC was the most giving, most unselfish, unselfconscious, uninhibited, sensitive lover he'd ever had. Sex with her was flawless. Nothing to add and nothing to take away. He felt like he was in love, but he knew he had a sucker's heart and was smart enough not to let it lead him.

Detective James Bryant had been with well over two hundred women in his 45 years on this earth, and he had probably fallen in love with 150 of them. Still, 90% of them he'd dumped within two weeks. All he had to do was imagine a woman raising his kids, and that usually sobered him right up. He didn't have any kids yet, but when he did, he didn't want it to be with some silly ho whose only notable asset was that she swallowed and didn't mind occasionally taking a load in the face. The mother of his children would have to be special, someone strong who could raise the kids without him if he should ever be killed on the job. He knew it was a morbid thought, but it was a realistic one.

After he finished his crunches and around 100 pushups, Bryant went into the kitchen to make breakfast. CC was done with her shower and was searching the bed for her bra and panties. He had to catch his breath as he watched her bend over to check under the bed.

"Man, that ass is incredible," he marveled under his breath.

She heard him and smiled. "So, what's for breakfast, Detective?"

"Please, just call me James."

"You know what's funny?"

"What?"

"I just realized I'd never asked you your name. I feel like such a slut." She found her underwear and slipped them on along with her sweat pants. She kind of looked like a Madonna wannabe in her black lacy bra, like Roseanna Arquette in *Desperately Seeking Susan.*

"No. You feel like heaven," Bryant said as he chopped up the onions and bell peppers for an omelet.

CC smiled and blushed.

"So, what are you making?"

"It's my own recipe. A cream cheese omelet. You chop up some onions, garlic, bell pepper, and tomatoes. Mix it with a few eggs, some basil and oregano. Then you cook it up, and just before you fold the omelet in half, you place about two tablespoons of cream cheese and some grated Monterey Jack cheese in the center."

"Mmmmm, sounds delicious. I guess after last night, I can't really call anything decadent, but it seems like a lot of effort and a lot of calories."

"Trust me, it's worth it. In a world like this, where everything is all fucked up, even something as trivial as making the perfect omelet can take on an almost Zen-like quality. That and the fact that the weekends are the only days that I eat fatty foods."

By the time Bryant and CC finished breakfast, it was already past eight o'clock. James drove her home, figuring that if her husband was at home pissed-off because she'd been out all night, he could flash his badge and make up a story about her being attacked or something. They took Lincoln Drive, doing 45 miles an hour through those ridiculously tight turns with the signs that announced a 25-mph speed limit and doing 70 on the straights as they left Mt. Airy, speeding down to South Philly. Bryant found it chillingly ominous that CC's home was right in the middle of one of Malcolm's favorite hunting grounds.

They pulled up to one of those little 200-plus-year-old, post-Revolutionary War row homes that the tourists think are so adorable and quaint but the residents hate because of the poor insulation, rusted plumbing, and walls so thin that neighbors could hear each other fart. There were gray-haired Italian grandmothers pushing their grandchildren around in strollers, dogs locked behind fences yapping at shadows, and normal nosy spinsters sitting on their front stoops, keeping their eyes on everyone's business because they had none of their own However, just as she'd predicted, CC's husband was already gone. They sat in the car for a few minutes before she went in.

"I had a great time, CC. You are an incredible woman."

"You sure you don't think I'm a slut? I don't usually cheat on my husband."

"I believe you," he lied. "And no, I don't think you're a slut. I think you are something truly special, and I hope that man of yours appreciates what he's got."

"He doesn't," she stated flatly. She kissed him deeply, then slid from the car.

"I hope you come to see me again. James."

"I don't think I could stop myself if I wanted to," the detective replied, meaning it a little more than he was comfortable with.

Bryant made it to the office at nine and was surprised to find his normally punctual partner had not yet arrived. He sat down at his desk and allowed his mind to go back into the case.

*Where are you, Malcolm? What are you up to? What is it you really want?*

*"Never leave an enemy behind or it will rise again to fly at your throat!"*

Something told Bryant that Malcolm Davis was not done yet. There would be more murders. Unless they could catch him, there would be a lot more.

# XIII.

Titus barely slept all night. His mind was wrapped around the case like a boa constrictor, but he couldn't digest it, couldn't make sense of it. A man the entire city had been hunting for years had stepped out of the night, slaughtered a family, practically autographed the crime scene, and vanished back into the night. They should have had him in custody an hour after they received the 911 call, but somehow, he had eluded them.

Detective Baltimore had been all over the Cozens' house, inspecting every bit of evidence as fast as the crime scene techs gathered it. He'd followed the medical examiner's van to the city morgue and sat through the preliminary autopsy. Afterwards, he went back to the precinct and pulled out all the files on the three murder investigations, covering 27 separate homicides. Malcolm Davis had been a busy boy. So far, they had been unable to turn up an address on the suspect, but they had his mother, grandmother, sister, and all three of his aunts under surveillance. At five o'clock a.m., Detective Baltimore finally crawled into bed, confident that when he awoke, it would be to a phone call telling him they had located their suspect.

When Baltimore's head rose from the pillow, it was nearly ten o'clock in the morning. He was late for work and no suspects were in custody. His lazy dinosaur of a partner hadn't even bothered to wake him. Of course, they hadn't picked each other up for work since they first partnered up two years ago. They rarely even rode together in the same car. Titus knew the captain hated it when he drove his own car on duty, but so far, he hadn't said anything. The only way Titus could work with James was separately. Not as partners but as two individual investigators working simultaneously on the same case.

Titus didn't understand Detective James Bryant. He couldn't relate to his lackadaisical attitude, his lack of enthusiasm for the job. He would bet anything that Bryant got a good sleep. The fact that there was a madman running around hacking up women and children probably didn't stop him from getting his eight hours in. If he just wanted to collect a paycheck every week, there were easier jobs than a homicide detective. No one waded through blood and guts everyday unless they were truly committed to the cause, and Titus was committed. Titus was a crusader. James Bryant didn't make sense.

"Baby, are you up? I made you some bacon and eggs and your favorite French toast!"

"Okay, I'm up, Mom!"

The smell of fresh bacon drifted up to Titus, pulling him from the bed and into the shower. It was time to begin the day. He needed to get over to the hospital to talk to Reed. If they couldn't locate Malcolm, maybe they could find his accomplice. Titus showered, shaved, and slipped into a gray Brooks Brothers suit and a pair of black Stacy Adams. He considered his new Armani silk tie and felt foolish as he turned it down in favor of a blue polyester tie from Jeans West, but he wasn't up to dealing with the whispers of "spoiled rich kid" from his fellow officers.

With his all-American good looks, Titus looked more like a model in a men's apparel magazine like *GQ* or *M*. Well, except for the tie and the fact that he was a good three inches shy of six feet and was showing the beginnings of a spare tire around his mid-section. His face was quite handsome, however, almost pretty. He had high cheekbones with thin lips and dimpled cheeks, ice blue eyes, and dark brown hair that he slicked back the way the Italian gangsters did in the movies. He would never be pegged as a homicide detective. Although on those special occasions when he wore his black Armani Tux, he did look a little like James Bond.

Titus walked downstairs and smiled. Mrs. Janet Baltimore sat at the kitchen table sectioning a grapefruit half with a paring knife. She was wearing the red flannel pajamas he'd bought her for Christmas along with the blue and white terry cloth bathrobe and slippers that he'd given her for her birthday. Her long silver hair was cinched into a tight bun, and her glasses hung off the tip of her nose as she carefully prepared his meal. She had looked exactly the same for the past twenty years. Titus couldn't remember her ever being young. The gray hair, the wrinkles, the fifty or sixty extra pounds, the extra chin, the loose flesh that hung from her triceps, the varicose veins that crisscrossed her legs, all seemed to have been there since his first birthday. Looking at pictures of the young, vibrant, sexy woman she had once been was like looking at a stranger. To him, she had always been the same woman she was today—a hard-working, church-going, house-cleaning, home-cooking mom.

Detective Titus Baltimore was a mama's boy. He had always been and probably always would be. His dad had never been around. Fitzgerald Baltimore was always too busy with his art gallery and borderline-legal import /export business that dealt mostly in ancient artifacts plundered from various sacred burial grounds around the globe and smuggled into the US from the same private airstrips the cartels used to fly out Columbia's most popular export.

Baltimore's dad was two-thousand-dollar suits that hung in the closet, the smell of expensive Cuban cigars that lingered in the air, the ninety-thousand-dollar Mercedes sports car in the driveway, a ten thousand dollar a month expense account supplementing the paycheck that cared for his son and his wife when Fitzgerald was away on one of his seemingly endless business trips. Baltimore's dad had never been there to tuck him in at night. That had always been Mom. His dad had never been there to show him how to throw a football or shoot lay-ups. Instead, he'd learned to play piano and ballroom dance. He'd had girlfriends, had even gotten engaged and moved out on his own. But those relationships had always failed, and when they had, Mama had happily been there for her little boy. Baltimore was a real mama's boy, and he was proud of it.

After finishing his breakfast, Baltimore kissed his mom goodbye and headed for the station. Feeling a little gutsier, he decided to take Dad's Mercedes instead of the '65 Ford Mustang he normally drove.

"Fuck those jealous assholes!" Baltimore yelled as he gunned the engine and pealed out of the driveway. He wasn't going to feel guilty just because he was rich and they weren't. He'd lost years of quality time with his father to the pursuit of money, so he felt he owed it to himself, and perhaps to old Fitzgerald as well, to enjoy some of the luxuries his father had abandoned him to obtain.

As he drove, Baltimore went over the case again in his mind. How could a six-foot five-inch, two-hundred-thirty-pound Black vampire in a designer suit disappear? He decided to skip the station and head straight for the hospital. He needed to talk to Reed and find out more about Malcolm's sidekick.

# XIV.

Veins and cords bulged through his skin. His back and bicep muscles ached from the super-set of seated row and military style pull-ups with a 25-pound plate dangling from a chain around his waist. Malcolm walked over to the water fountain, wiping the sweat from his brow and smiling appreciatively at the well muscled but still pleasantly voluptuous ass attached to the gym's sales manager. She was also some kind of fitness model or something. She seemed to live at the gym. Her breasts were perfect—implants, but natural looking. She obviously had large breasts in the first place and probably lost them when her body fat dropped below 10%. She had just filled the void with silicone. She was short but tough looking, and her eyes were jet black like her waist length hair.

*Italian? Sicilian maybe? Possibly Spanish.*

She was obviously down with the brothers, whatever her ethnicity. She always stared at Malcolm when she thought he wasn't looking and was constantly trying to make small talk. Malcolm liked her. That's why he hadn't fucked her yet. Let her enjoy life for a while longer.

Malcolm bent over the water fountain to get a drink

and saw her staring at his ass out of the corner of his eye.

*I guess what's good for the goose ...,* he thought. She sighed longingly, and he knew she had meant for him to hear it. *She keeps this shit up and I will haul off and fuck her!*

Malcolm went back to the free weight area and began to load up the bar on the preacher curl bench. He knew he shouldn't be out in public with all those cops after him, but he had lost the capacity to process fear anymore. He couldn't envision anyone possibly stopping him. He knew that would be his downfall eventually, but for right now, it was his strength.

Half the gym's muscle-bound troglodytes were staring at Malcolm and snickering derisively as he slid two 45-pound plates on each end of the 25-pound bar for a total of 205 pounds. Malcolm snickered back. He knew they thought he was crazy, trying to curl so much weight. He knew they were waiting to see him tear a bicep muscle just trying to lift it from the rack. But what they didn't know was that he *was* insane, stark raving mad, and he could easily toss this weight up for at least eight reps, thanks to a stack of Deca, Clembuterol, and the latest legal growth hormones that had swelled his biceps from eighteen and a half inches to a Herculean twenty-one inches in just the past two months. The thick, tentacled roots that were Malcolm's fingers wrapped around the curl bar and easily hoisted it into the air. His arms strained and burned with lactic acid, but the weight curled steadily upward, reaching its apex just below Malcolm's collarbone and then slowly lowering back down to mid-thigh twelve times. The snickering had turned to gasps of astonishment.

*Showed those fools!*

Malcolm slammed the bar back down on the rack and stretched his massive arms, smiling at his reflection in the mirror. He may not have been able to bench-press five hundred pounds like some of the juiced-up Italians that seemed to spend all day everyday doing the same three exercises—squats, bench presses, and shoulder presses—but he knew he had the strongest arms in The Atlas Gym.

The Atlas Gym was hardcore, for serious weightlifters only. There was no sauna or Jacuzzi, no pool, no aerobics room, only a handful of cardio equipment, and no juice bar. What The Atlas had was weight, massive weight. Each bench could hold up to a thousand pounds, and there was at least that much weight in iron plates stacked on weight trees beside each one. Even the dumbbells went all the way up to 150 pounds each. No one but hardcore bodybuilders and power-lifters, mostly professionals, worked out there.

Malcolm glanced around the room at the grossly over-muscled clientele groaning and straining beneath impossible stacks of weight and thought that if he got his arms around any one of their necks, they would never get away until their lifeless husks slumped to the floor.

Malcolm looked at himself in the mirror again, pleased with the way all eight sections of his rectus abdominus were as clearly defined as his obliques and serratus muscles, forming an armor-plated waistline that was only 31 inches around. He liked the way his lats fanned out under his arms but not so much that he couldn't lower his arms to his sides like some of those other muscle-bound freaks. Malcolm smiled as he flexed his bulging pecs, admiring their crisscrossed striations and how the pectoralis major was clearly separated from the pectoralis minor. He liked his rounded delts and the way his traps rose like a cobra's hood when he rolled his shoulders forward but not so much that they made his neck disappear. With the exception of his disproportionately large arms, he had the body of a supremely well-conditioned prizefighter, similar to Evander Holyfield or Lennox Lewis with Lee

Haney's arms. Unlike the bodybuilders who spent just as much time in the tanning booths and hair salons as they did in the weight room, Malcolm's muscles weren't just for show. They were more than cosmetic. They had crushed, bludgeoned, beaten, and stabbed the life from 27 innocent people that the police knew of and another 17 they had no clue about. His body was a perfect killing machine.

*You're a fucking monster!* he thought as he stared at himself in the mirror, and that predacious smile split open his face once more.

Malcolm had just finished his last set of curls when the twelve TV sets positioned above the treadmills and lifecycles began to broadcast the morning news. As Malcolm expected, it featured a headline story about the murder of the Cozen family, with a surprisingly accurate description of him along with a police artist's sketch that was also remarkably accurate. He was flattered that Reed remembered him so well. He regretted that he would not be able to workout at The Atlas anymore, but he did not regret neatly slicing the throat of the blond-haired, blue-eyed, pumped-up Aryan with the squeaky voice who shouted, "That's him!" as Malcolm attempted to exit the premises peacefully and quietly. He did regret not being able to stay and watch him drown in his own blood.

Titus Baltimore had one more question for Reed.

"Describe Malcolm's accomplice for me."

"I already did. He looks exactly like me … or rather like I looked fifteen years ago. He even has my old heavy metal/ hippie haircut. You could take one of my old yearbook pictures and put it out there. That's how much he looks like me."

The answer was unbelievable. Detective Baltimore didn't know whether it was Mr. Cozen's shock over losing his wife and kids confusing things in his head or if the man was just flat-out lying. Mr. Cozen seemed eager to help catch the killer, but then why make up such an absurd story? He seemed perfectly lucid, but what he was saying went way beyond creepy to become something else altogether, something perverse.

"His accomplice looked just like you? Identical? Like some kind of twin?"

"Yes," Reed replied with conviction, looking Tight Ass right in his smug little eyes.

"First a giant Black vampire and now your evil twin? What is this—a creature double feature?"

"Fuck you, Detective! Those are the bastards that murdered my family! I ain't making this up!"

Detective Baltimore stared at Mr. Reed Cozen for a long moment before he spoke again. He wasn't sure about this story. Something about it just didn't click for him. In fact, a lot of things about it made no sense to him.

*Why would a man wait fifteen years, then suddenly reappear and savagely murder a man's entire family because he'd messed around with a high school sweetheart?*

Even as violent as kids were today, he'd never heard of a teenaged romantic rivalry resulting in mutilation murders. Maybe a drive-by or ambush shooting, but never after over a decade had passed.

Titus had only been thirteen when he graduated from high school, a child prodigy with the highest SAT scores in his little private academy, and he could remember very little about the girls he dated at the academy, or even later at Princeton, for that matter. There had been too damned many of them. He couldn't imagine still being strung out on one of them after all these years. Certainly not enough to kill.

*And why would he leave Mr. Cozen alive as a witness if he were really the target of Malcolm's vengeance? Why would Malcolm Davis confess to Mr. Cozen about a series of homicides he had so far gotten away with and then not kill him?* It made no sense! And why did Reed seem to be acting so guilty, so defensive, as if he was hiding something?

As far as Titus was concerned, Mr. Cozen had just topped the suspect list.

"Please forgive me, Mr. Cozen, but I am just terribly confused by all this."

Reed's eyes searched Baltimore's face in helpless frustration. It was obvious that he wanted to strangle the detective and probably would have tried if he wasn't injured and Baltimore wasn't armed.

"What the hell is so confusing? I told you who did it. You just go get him. Lock him up! Shoot him! Anything! Just do your fucking job and leave me the fuck alone!

While you're in here fucking with me, that sonuvabitch is probably out there killing another family!"

"I assure you, Mr. Cozen, we have half the Philadelphia Police Department kicking in doors all over town, searching for Mr. Davis right now. We'll have him in custody soon. In the meantime, you get some rest. I understand you might be released later today or tomorrow. I may need you to come down to the station and answer a few more questions."

"What fucking questions? There's no more I can tell you."

"Well, that may be true, but you still haven't given us an official statement, and you might think of something else between today and tomorrow that might help us."

"I've already given you everything but the man's address and phone number!"

Titus straightened his cheap tie and flashed a cheap smile as he exited Reed's hospital room.

"Sleep on it. Maybe you'll remember something, something you may not even think was important but that might help us. Goodbye, Mr. Cozen."

"Yeah, fuck you very much."

Baltimore shut the door quietly behind him and nodded to the uniformed officer stationed outside Reed's door.

"I can't wait to interrogate that prick. Sonuvabitch is lying through his fucking teeth. He's involved somehow. I just can't figure out how. But I know he knows something. It's time to look a little into Mr. Cozen's background, see what kind of skeletons he's got in his closet."

Detective Baltimore decided to re-question Reed's neighbors. This time, he wasn't going to be asking about suspicious looking strangers lurking around the Cozen house or strange vehicles parked on the street. He wanted to know about the Cozens themselves. He would go through address books and scraps of paper at the crime scene, call up friends, family, coworkers, find out if they had a babysitter and question her as well. He would question the family physician, see if he had any suspicion that there was abuse taking place either against the kids or the wife, any suspicious bruises or injuries on any of them. He wanted to find out if the Cozens were seeing a therapist or a marriage counselor. Baltimore would track down and question anyone who might have any knowledge about what went on in that household. He wanted to know just how loving a relationship Reed Cozen had with his wife and kids.

Baltimore suddenly had an idea. He had just exited the hospital when he paused and started fishing through his wallet for a business card. Last year, he had worked a case where a ten-year-old girl was kidnapped, raped, brutally beaten, and murdered by an intruder who dragged the child out of her bedroom window in the middle of the night and took her across the street to the park, where her body was later found.

The family was on TV every night for weeks pleading for anyone with information about the crime to come forward. They offered a reward that would have bankrupted them. They looked so genuinely grief-stricken that the public never considered the possibility the parents might be suspects themselves, and the police only conducted a half-hearted interrogation of them. The crime scene evidence—the jimmied bedroom window and the screwdriver that had obviously been used to pry open the window, then used to repeatedly stab the child—seemed to all fit the pattern of a stranger abduction murder.

After one of the couple's tearful pleas for the killer to turn himself in or for anyone with information on the killer's identity to come forward, someone did. A caseworker from the Department of Human Services called the station and told the detective that the child had come to her office just two weeks before the murder to report her father and mother's brutal physical and sexual abuse. It turned the whole case around, and the police eventually got a full confession out of the couple, and the court put them each away for life without the possibility of parole.

Detective Baltimore sifted through the forty or more business cards he had stuffed into his wallet, which was at one time handsome sealskin but was now just a worn-out mess. Finally, he located the office number of Ms. Judy Hamilton, pulled out his iPhone, and called her up. She answered on the first ring.

"Hello, Department of Human Services, this is Caseworker Hamilton. May I help you?"

"Hello, Ms. Hamilton. This is Detective Baltimore with the Philadelphia Police Department Homicide Division."

"Oh, yes, I remember you from that terrible case of the little Simpson girl, Etta Simpson, the little girl that was killed by her parents. That was such a tragic case. I felt bad because we just didn't act quickly enough to save her. The day I went and talked to the parents, the little girl suddenly changed her mind and said she made the whole thing up or else we would have taken her out of there right then and there. We planned to come back and do a follow up investigation, but by then, it was too late. They murdered that poor child." Her voice was choked with emotion as she spoke.

Detective Baltimore was impressed with how much Ms. Hamilton seemed to care for these children. He wondered how such a woman could handle the type of horrors she no doubt witnessed every day—crimes and abuses perpetrated against innocent women and children, families torn apart from within—and still stay so compassionate, so caring. Most of the DHS workers he'd met were as hardened and cynical as cops. They treated the kids who came through the system like they all brought their misfortunes upon themselves, and of course, there were many that had— teenaged mothers, adolescent prostitutes, drunks, drug addicts, and juvenile delinquents kicked out by families who just couldn't take them anymore. The job tended to harden the heart to sob stories, but this woman's heart still had quite a bit of giving left in it. Baltimore, looking into his own heart, wondered how long either of them could last.

"I have to ask a favor of you, Ms. Hamilton. Have you seen the news? Have you heard anything about the family they believed was murdered by that guy they're calling The Family Man?"

"Yes, I've seen it. Are you involved with that case, Detective?"

"Yes, ma'am. I'm in charge of the investigation. That's the reason I'm calling. I have reason to believe that the same killer may not have committed this last murder, or at least, he may not have been working alone. I'm beginning to think the father may have had something to do with it. In fact he may *be* The Family Man or his accomplice. I need you to see if there's a file on him. Maybe his wife or his kid tried to reach you."

"What was the name?"

"Cozen. The father's name is Reed. The mother's name was Linda, and there was Jennie and Mark."

"Can you hold on while I check the computer? It should just take a second."

"Sure. I really appreciate this."

Detective Baltimore walked across the hospital parking lot with his iPhone wedged between ear and shoulder as he fished for his car keys. He slipped behind the wheel of his Mercedes and began to head back to Reed's quiet little neighborhood to check out the neighborhood elementary school. Maybe there was a teacher or a counselor, maybe even a school nurse in whom one of the children had confided.

"Uh … Detective? Are you still there?"

"Yes, Ms. Hamilton. Did you find anything?"

"Well, it seems like the daughter, Jennie, came to us about six months ago. The Vice Principal, a woman named Anna Lamb, at her school brought her in. She believed the little girl's father had molested the child. Little Jennie didn't seem to think anything was out of ordinary. When she was questioned by one of our staff assigned to her case, a Rita Franklin, Mrs. Franklin noted that she had gotten the impression that her father was perhaps a little overly affectionate, perhaps even inappropriately so, but nothing serious, nothing criminal. Mrs. Franklin said it seemed to her like a father who just really loved his little girl. She assured the vice principal that she would talk to Mr. Cozen and then warned her to be more careful with those kinds of accusations around children.

"Children have very active imaginations. Things can get all twisted in a child's impressionable young mind, and they can start to believe that they were victims of sexual molestation when it was actually something entirely innocent. The woman wasn't completely convinced, so Mrs. Franklin agreed to go with her to Mr. Cozen's house to drop off the child, and she talked to him there. She noted in her records that Mr. Cozen seemed rather confused and more than a little embarrassed by the whole thing, but that he was cooperative and assured Mrs. Franklin to her satisfaction that nothing illicit or untoward had taken place between him and his daughter. The child was returned, and no follow-up was ever done."

Titus scribbled down all the information in his notepad, steering the Mercedes with his knees and with an occasional quick turn of his left hand before returning to scribble something else.

"Would it be possible to interview Mrs. Franklin?"

"Um … unfortunately, she is no longer with us."

"Would you happen to know where she's employed now?"

"Detective … Rita Franklin died two months ago. She was very old, almost seventy, and she just went in her sleep. She was at work all day the day before she died. She could never stand the thought of retirement.

Such a sweet old lady."

"I'm sorry to hear that. Listen, thank you very much for the help, Mrs. Hamilton."

"That's Ms. Hamilton, Detective, and you can call me Judy."

"Well … uh … thanks, Judy. You have been a tremendous help."

Now there was an accusation of sexual misconduct between Reed and his daughter. What if Reed really was molesting his daughter? If the mother found out and threatened to leave him and take the kids or call the police, that would be a hell of a convincing motive for murder. It would definitely convince a jury. Juries don't have much tolerance for crimes against kids. Baltimore wondered what had made the vice principal so certain the little girl had been molested. He turned off Frankford Avenue onto Tarsdale. He was only a mile or two away from Frankford Elementary. He would ask her himself.

Frankford Elementary was one of the older schools in Philadelphia. It was right next to Frankford's low-income housing project, which was right next to an upper-middle class white neighborhood. The 50-year-old three-story red brick building covered in creeping ivy was a racial battleground. It was filled with over-privileged white kids and under-privileged Black and Latino kids.

The poor kids saw, in the clothes the white kids wore and the expensive cars that dropped them off in the morning, exactly what they would probably never have. The city planner who zoned the housing projects and the school for that area seemed to have been some kind of racist out to turn every white kid in that neighborhood into Philadelphia's version of Hitler Youth. Their whole perception of the Black and Latino community was of down-trodden, angry, rebellious black and brown faces that stared out at the white kids from their hellish projects and extorted lunch money, sneakers, jackets, jewelry, and anything else of value the white kids were stupid enough to bring into this war-zone. Every one of those white kids would grow up to hate and fear Blacks and Latinos, except the ones who idolized and emulated them, the so-called whiggers who would eventually join the same gangs and wind up on the same nowhere path the projects condemned the minority kids to.

Reed actually lived a little further east in the homogeneous, all white, northeast section of Philadelphia. Why he sent his kids to a school way down here in this combat zone instead of a nice, safe school in his own neighborhood, Baltimore could only guess. This was the first school that Reed and Malcolm attended together. It seemed that Reed was a little sentimental after all. If he remembered the school so fondly that he would risk his kids' lives and their social objectivity to send them there, Baltimore found it hard to believe that he hadn't thought of Malcolm in over a decade as he had claimed. Every time he dropped his kids off at school, he most certainly thought about him. Baltimore would bet his badge on it. But did Reed shudder when he thought of Malcolm, or did he smile fondly? That was the question, and Baltimore felt like he was getting closer and closer to finding the answer. He could almost see the far-off, wistful look in Reed's eye and the nostalgic grin on his face.

Detective Baltimore was instantly transported back to his own childhood as he walked into the bustling elementary school. His grade school had been just like this one, filled with students' artwork and awards, stupid motivational slogans about getting along with others, and anti-drug messages painted on the peach-colored walls. This school, however, seemed to contain four times as many kids as had attended his little academy. It seemed like there were more kids crowding the hallway between him and the principal's office than there had been in his entire school. Baltimore was fighting against the current on a seemingly endless tide of pre-adolescents making their way toward the schoolyard. He was stepped on, kicked, elbowed, and cursed as he struggled through the crowd. He felt like he should have worn full riot gear.

Finally, Baltimore made it to the principal's office without having to draw his gun. He was a little bumped and bruised, but he had survived the recess rush. A young blonde-haired woman, who looked as if she hadn't graduated from elementary school too long ago herself, sat behind the reception desk, appraising him with a bright Colgate smile as he walked into the office. She had big blue eyes and was dressed in the same oversized, baggy clothes as the kids.

"Excuse me, I'm here to speak to Vice Principal Lamb," Baltimore said, showing her his badge, at which point her smile faltered and her eyes hardened a little. *I guess I'm not so attractive anymore*, Detective Baltimore thought. Hating cops was in style these days.

"Do you have an appointment with her, Officer?"

"That's Detective Baltimore, and I'm sorry, no, I don't. I'm investigating the murder of the Cozen family, and I understand the children attended school here."

"Oh, yes. That was so tragic. I'll let her know you are here."

She sprang from her chair behind the desk and barged, without knocking, into an office only a few feet away. As she stuck her head inside to talk to the vice principal, her butt swayed from side to side as she shifted from one foot to the other. Baltimore wondered how he was able to tell that she had a nice ass when she wore jeans two sizes too large. But he could tell. He wondered if that show was for his benefit. The girl couldn't have been older than twenty, twenty-one at the maximum. True, he was only twenty-five himself, but the job along with his above average intelligence made him feel much older. Too old for this one, although she was tempting. She was more Bryant's type, he thought, and wondered where his partner might be right now, if he was even working the case or if he was off at some sandwich shop somewhere scarfing down a cheese steak hoagie. Everyone said he was a good detective, and maybe he was at one time, but in the two years that Baltimore had been paired up with the guy, he'd seen very little evidence of any commitment to the job. All the guy seemed to want to do was eat and chase pussy. There could be a body laying cut up on the floor, and while Baltimore was gathering evidence, Bryant would come out with some story about a girl he fucked two years ago who had tits just like the corpse.

When the fluffy little blonde returned, she had two people with her. A short, balding, over-weight Black gentleman stepped forward and seized the detective's hand in his stubby little fingers. He pumped Baltimore's arm enthusiastically and introduced himself as the principal. Beside him, in a tan skirt suit with a white silk T-shirt, stood a striking older woman with blonde hair streaked with gray, high cheekbones, full lips, and steel gray eyes like a timber wolf. She stepped forward and introduced herself as the vice principal. When she shook his hand, her breasts wobbled pleasingly beneath her shirt. It was obvious that she was voluptuously endowed, despite the great pains she took to hide it.

*A prude, perhaps?* Detective Baltimore thought. Maybe the whole child molestation thing was just the over-active imagination of a spinster who feared her own sexuality and was suspicious of any type of intimacy between men and women. He hoped not. If he could tie Cozen into a motive like this, he was certain he could use it to squeeze a confession out of him. Shit, he wouldn't need a confession to get a conviction. If he could prove that Reed Cozen molested his own daughter, he wouldn't need a shred of evidence to convict him for the murders. The jury's revulsion would guarantee that bastard a lethal injection. The only thing that bothered him was that the coroner had found no evidence of rape or sexual assault on either of the two kids, only on the mother. But rape didn't always mean penetration. Detective Baltimore knew there were any of a number of things a pervert could do to a young kid that wouldn't bruise or tear the vaginal walls or the rectum. The detective's stomach lurched at the thought of it.

He was led into the vice principal's office, where he took a seat on a leather couch across from a huge pine desk that had been stained a dark brown to resemble oak.

"What can we do for you, Detective? Of course, we heard about the murders, and we've all been racking our brains trying to remember if we saw anyone suspicious hanging around after school, looking like they were, you know, stalking the children. But, so far, no one can remember seeing anything out of the ordinary."

Detective Baltimore turned his attention to Ms. Lamb.

"I understand that you once took Jennie Cozen to the Department of Human Services to see an abuse counselor. May I ask why?"

"Well, Detective, she was called to my office repeatedly for cursing and extremely inappropriate sexual language and behavior."

"Behavior?"

"Yes. Grabbing little boys' penises, grabbing girls between their legs and on their backsides, making comments about her own sexual prowess. In short, we believed that this type of premature and somewhat oversexed behavior was consistent with what we have seen in children who have been sexually abused."

"And on the basis of this, you took her to see an abuse counselor?"

"Not only that. One day she was called to my office for pulling up her dress and showing her breasts to the boys in her class. When I called her into my office, she said that they had just developed and she was proud of them and wanted to show them off. It was simply the last straw, and I had to suspend her. When her father came down to pick her up … the way she kissed him …"

"You mean he used his tongue?"

The vice principal blushed.

"No … uh … not exactly. It was the way she draped her arm around his neck and he slipped his arms around her waist and they kissed right on the lips. You kind of got the impression that if they weren't in public, he *would* have French kissed her, and when they talked to each other, it was more like husband and wife than father and daughter. I mean, she spoke to him like he was another one of her little playmates. No respect at all. It was just unnatural. Even when they left, she wasn't just holding his hand, she was hugging it to herself the way newlyweds do. I know it sounds like I'm overreacting, but it just all started to add up. Even Tom here noticed it. As soon as they left, we just looked at each other, and we knew something about that wasn't proper. You would've had to see it. It was almost lewd."

"Thank you for your time, Miss Lamb. You have been most helpful."

The principal finally spoke up after sitting there quietly and letting Anna Lamb have her say.

"She's right, you know. I was here and I saw it. She's not just making this up. If you had been here and had seen the way they acted around each other, it was like watching that movie *Lolita*. You just knew that this wasn't how fathers and daughters acted toward each other. I have two daughters. One of them is just a little older than Jennie, and I have never touched her the way Mr. Cozen touched his daughter … not with that level of intimacy and familiarity. If you had a daughter, you would understand. When they hit puberty, you notice and your attitude changes. When they start to develop breasts and want to dress sexy and you notice that they are almost women, it makes a father a little uncomfortable. There's a stiffness in your posture when you hug them that wasn't there before because you notice that she has breasts now and you almost try not to rub up against them when you embrace, as if even that would be perverted. It's a subtle thing, but it happens. You become uncomfortable with the idea of your little baby girl becoming a sexual creature. Mr. Cozen did not seem uncomfortable. He was a little too damned comfortable."

"Detective, you don't think this has anything to do with why they were murdered, do you? I mean, I thought you already had a suspect?" Anna Lamb asked. She looked horrified.

"We have a suspect, not a conviction. Thank you very much for your time. Here's my card. If you think of anything else, please call me."

Detective Titus Baltimore left Frankford Elementary beginning to believe that perhaps something was going on with Reed and his daughter. The thought made him sick … and angry. At least now he had something to do rather than sit around twiddling his thumbs while he waited for Malcolm Davis to get picked up. He slipped behind the wheel of the Mercedes and headed back to the Cozen house.

As he drove, he thought about the first case he'd worked involving allegations of sexual molestation. A guy named Mitchell Allen murdered his babysitter and her boyfriend because he claimed he caught them sexually assaulting his son. He bludgeoned them both to death with a two-and-a-half-pound welding hammer, broke nearly every bone in their bodies. They had been, quite literally, beaten to a bloody, misshapen pulp. He was arrested and tried for second-degree murder. Titus gave his testimony about the forensic evidence linking Allen to the crimes, but since Mr. Allen was admitting that he did in fact kill the couple, Titus's testimony had been brief.

A medical examiner testified that they'd found no physical evidence of sexual assault on Mitchell Allen's little boy. All they had was Allen's word on what he saw and the word of his young son, and Allen had refused to allow his son to testify. He didn't want the kid put through any further trauma. Baltimore had stayed to hear the outcome of the case. Finally, on the third day of the trial, Mitchell Allen himself was called to the stand. The assistant DA asked him if he felt any guilt or remorse for the death of the couple.

Mr. Allen replied, "You know, I've been thinking about that ever since the night it all happened."

"And ...?" The prosecutor probed.

"Well, I guess I can't really answer that until I know how this all winds up affecting my son, Johnny. I mean, years from now, when he's an adult, I might find out that I caused him more harm than good by killing those two. Then again, I might have just saved him years of emotional trauma. Right now, I just don't know."

"Mr. Allen, I think you may have misunderstood my question."

"No, I understood you perfectly."

"What about your victims, Mr. Allen? Do you feel anything for them? What about their families and their loss?"

"The only victim in this was my son! Those two pedophiles, their families, The City of Philadelphia, The State of Pennsylvania, they weren't the ones being raped! I hope those two burn in hell for what they did! And as for their families, I read somewhere that behavior like this is passed down. The abused becomes the abuser. The victim becomes the victimizer. So, if those two sons-of-bitches molested my kid because they were molested by their parents when they were young, then my only consolation in all this would be to know that their parents were suffering. That every day, they feel the pain that they caused my child."

That wasn't what the jury wanted to hear.

Mitchell Allen was found guilty of second-degree murder and sentenced to fifteen years behind bars. As far as Baltimore knew, the man was still there, still unremorseful, still unrepentant, and the detective still agreed with every word the man said. Now more than ever, Detective Baltimore wanted to nail Mr. Cozen's ass to the wall. If he had molested his daughter, Jennie, and then had gotten his friend Malcolm to murder his own family to keep anyone from finding out about it, Detective Baltimore was determined to make the man pay.

Detective Bryant was back at his desk, staring at the computer screen as it tossed up possible matches from the over three million prints on file. Many of the prints were from convicts already dead, currently incarcerated, or drifters who had moved on years ago, but there were some that looked pretty good. But the computer, as good as it was, didn't replace the naked eye, and again and again, he dismissed the computer's suggestions. The AFIS had already gone through over a hundred thousand prints last night and nearly double that this morning. Finally, it tossed up a print for a guy who was arrested on Pine Street for soliciting for prostitution and again for public indecency (apparently got caught giving a blow-job in an alley). James shook his head in disbelief as the computer downloaded the suspect's picture.

"No! Oh my God. This is crazy!"

It wasn't Malcolm Davis, but it might be the next best thing: his accomplice, a longhaired gay prostitute named Paul Cooper. There was even a recent address. James sprang from his chair and rushed into the captain's office to give him the good news.

"Captain Kelly! I think we've got that sonuvabitch!

The computer found a match for one of the prints lifted from the murder weapon. It matches the fingerprint of a male prostitute we picked up a few times for solicitation, and get this, he looks just like Mr. Cozen! I mean they could be twins! Is that some creepy shit or what? But it's definitely a different guy. I already checked Mr. Cozen's prints against those on the murder weapon, and nothing. This is a different guy walking around with his face!"

The captain was silent. His elbows rested on the desk. His clasped hands supported his square, dimpled chin. He was staring at James as if he hadn't heard a word he'd said. James was about to repeat himself, but he paused, giving the captain time to respond.

Captain Roy Kelly was a huge man in his early forties. He was nearly six four with shoulders like a fullback and arms like Lou Ferrigno. He was often in the gym lifting weights in the morning when Bryant got there. Kelly was a stern and serious man who almost never yelled. He didn't have to. Kelly's demeanor did his speaking for him, and it was clear he would rather not talk unless it was absolutely necessary. He was economical with his words; his deep, gravelly voice and unwavering dead man's gaze carried weight. When he spoke, it was like the rumbling of an earthquake and could always be heard even across a noisy room.

"Detective, where is your partner?"

"I don't know. I haven't seen him since last night."

"And why don't you know? You guys are supposed to be working together."

"Captain, Tight Ass just has his own way of doing things. The guy just … I just can't work with—"

The captain raised his left hand to silence him, and Bryant's mouth snapped shut obediently. He hated the way the captain could do that to him. The man was definitely a born leader, even if he was a reluctant one, but what did that say about Bryant? He hated to think of himself as a born follower, reluctant or otherwise.

"James, before you go to arrest this suspect, the first thing you are going to do is pick up Detective Baltimore. He's at the crime scene trying to dig up leads. I want you two sharing leads and working together. Right now, you're both pursuing two entirely different lines of investigation, and I want to see you come together on this and solve this fucking case. I will have patrolmen standing by. As soon as you rendezvous with Titus, call for back up, and I will have them meet you at the scene. One more thing. I know you and Baltimore are on long leashes. That's my fault. You and I were in the academy together, and I know you should have been promoted long ago if it wasn't for your anti-authority kick. So maybe I feel like I owe you. But I want you and Baltimore to start reporting in to Lieutenant Woo. He's the head of the task force, and he should know everything you two are up to."

"If he brought his ass out to the crime scenes every once in a while, he'd know what was going on."

The captain lowered his eyes from where they had been burrowing into Bryant's and went back to some crime scene photos he had been examining before the detective walked in. Lieutenant Woo rushed into the captain's office as if he'd heard his name called. He began talking excitedly to the captain. Bryant considered himself dismissed and left to find his partner. He couldn't even remember Baltimore's cell number. He hadn't used it in months. Maybe Baltimore had his radio turned on for once. James started to try him on the police band and then decided to try later. He needed a few more minutes alone to think.

The squad room was bustling with nervous energy. This case had everyone uptight. It was the type of case that could either put a detective on the fast track to a promotion or put a black mark on his permanent record that would guarantee a stalled career. Half the department was trying to get in on the case, and the other half was trying their best to avoid it.

Officer Webb, a young Black kid who, despite his crisp blue uniform and Kiwi-black, spit-shined shoes, looked more like a gangsta rapper than a cop, rushed up to Bryant waving a yellowing 8x10. It almost made Bryant nervous to see the guy with a gun, which in turn made him feel guilty. He offered the guy a weak, insincere smile and then looked at the picture. It was Malcolm Davis's graduation photo, sans cap and gown.

"Here's the picture we got from Mrs. Davis, Malcolm Davis's mom."

The picture showed Malcolm in the same type of somber attire that Mr. Cozen described him in the night of the murders—black suit, black shirt, black tie. His head wasn't shaved then, but it was cut very short. His eyes were preternaturally focused and intense, boring into the camera, seeming to come right out of the photo. The photograph looked alive, like those portraits with the eyes that followed its viewers wherever they went. He was leaning forward as if he was about to spring off the stool.

Officer Webb was looking over Bryant's shoulder at the photo. He let out a long hissing breath and shook his head in disbelief.

"Does that look like a teenager to you? Intense sonuvabitch, isn't he? Those eyes! The original thousand-yard stare—I've got homies on death row with eyes like that ... assassin's eyes."

Bryant tried not to wonder what a cop was doing with "homies on death row." He looked at Malcolm's eyes, the smirk that was almost a snarl, the flared nostrils, and the slightly furrowed brow. The kid looked savage, feral, like something dragged from the wilderness that had gotten off its chain. Bryant thought it was the face people would give to a murderer when they imagined one without ever actually seeing one, all the features melodramatically menacing.

"I thought serial killers were supposed to look normal ... you know ... ordinary ... like the guy next door? This guy looks like a comic book super villain, like he should be chasing James Bond through Venice in a speed boat," Webb joked.

"Yeah, he is an unsettling, disturbing looking muthafucka, ain't he? Take this photo, make copies, and get it out to the press. It's old, but we can still use it. He ain't really changed very much."

"James!" The captain was slipping his sports coat on and rushing toward him. Lieutenant Woo was right behind him. Bryant looked at the Lieutenant and thought he must be getting old because every officer he saw looked young to him except for the captain. The detective was younger than Captain Kelly, but the years of witnessing one grisly example of man's inhumanity after another had prematurely aged him. He was only in his forties but looked like he was in his mid-fifties.

"Forget about picking up Titus. You're coming with me."

"What's going on, Captain?"

"Malcolm just killed again. He slashed a bodybuilder at a gym downtown."

"Jesus Christ."

Captain Kelly turned to Lieutenant Woo and told him to call Detective Baltimore and have him meet them at The Atlas Gym. James watched as the tall, lanky Chinese detective hurried off to do the captain's bidding. Once again, he would be a no-show at the crime scene. The only photo opportunities this time would be for someone to lay the blame on for this latest fuck up, a front-page crucifixion. No way Woo was going to make the scene for that. If his luck held out, Bryant probably wouldn't see the lieutenant again until the case was solved and there was glory to be usurped. That's the way he preferred it, anyway. He would much rather have reported directly to the captain than to one of his bootlicking underlings.

"Make sure Titus comes right away. Tell him to drop whatever bullshit he's up to."

"Great, that's just what we need," Bryant lamented.

The captain grinned sardonically. It was the only type of grin the man seemed capable of.

"Teamwork, remember, James?"

"Oh, yeah. Teamwork. Right."

When Captain Kelly and Detective Bryant arrived at The Atlas Gym, they found the worst possible crime scene imaginable. Over a dozen different people, from customers, friends, and co-workers, to EMTs and cops, had touched the body and were now milling about, contaminating the crime scene. Someone had the sense to put yellow police tape around the scene, but the tape had been torn down and trampled. It was complete pandemonium.

The captain was incensed. Detective Bryant was doing his best to limit his reaction to merely incensed. He felt like punching someone's teeth out.

"Who the fuck is supposed to be controlling this crime scene?" the captain growled

"Who the fuck is in charge here?!" Bryant yelled

The uniformed officers on the scene all stared at each other and then back at the captain. Finally, a tall Italian officer with sergeant stripes and a thin moustache that looked like it had been plucked rather than shaved stepped forward. Both the Captain and Bryant rolled their eyes and shook their heads. The guy looked like he should be on the cover of some fashion magazine from the 1920s or at a gay pride parade.

"Uh … I'm the ranking officer here, sir."

"Great. Get all of these people out of the fucking crime scene so maybe we can gather whatever evidence hasn't already been contaminated or destroyed. Get the witnesses outside! Get statements from them and then get them the fuck out of here! The man is dead, right? So why the fuck do we still have EMTs here? Get them the fuck out of here and call the ME! Until the forensic guys get here, I want everybody but Detective Bryant and me the fuck out of here! Oh, and when Detective

Baltimore shows up, send him in here too."

The Sergeant walked off, looking like he'd just been smacked. His face was red, and he was cursing under his breath.

"You can't blame the guy, really. All they're used to doing down here is catching shoplifters and harassing kids for skipping school to play video games," the detective said

"Yeah, that and taking bribes from the Mafia, flirting with the tourists, and eating pizza all damn day," the captain growled back.

The sergeant and the rest of the officers began herding the huge crowd outside, happy to have something to do that kept them out of the captain's direct line of sight.

"Who was the first officer on the scene?"

A young redheaded kid who looked barely out of his teens stepped forward.

"Uh … I was, sir."

"What's your name?"

"Officer Wyatt. John Wyatt."

"Wyatt, next time you arrive at a 187, the first thing you do is secure the goddamn scene! If I ever see some shit like this again, I'm going to snatch that badge right off your chest and stab you with it. Look at this shit! Now almost anything we find, a defense attorney will shove right up our asses if we try to bring it into a courtroom. Did you interview any of the witnesses?"

"Uh … yes, sir. The sales lady was standing right by the guy when the suspect sliced him. She said the TV had just showed a picture of Malcolm Davis and the guy pointed at the suspect and yelled out 'That's him!' Then Malcolm opened up the guy's throat with some kind of little knife he whipped out of a gym bag he was carrying. After that, the suspect just walked out the door, got into his car, and drove away. Obviously, no one else tried to stop him."

"Tell me the sales lady is still here," Detective

Bryant said.

"Oh yeah, she's the one with the incredible body standing over there in the red spandex."

"I want you to make sure you get a complete statement from her," the captain said

Captain Kelly and Detective Bryant knelt to look at the body. There were bloody towels everywhere from where the gym staff had attempted to stop the bleeding. Blood formed a huge puddle on the floor. People never realized how much blood was in the human body until they saw it pooled around a corpse. Kelly and Bryant studied the victim's lacerated throat, helplessly outraged.

"What the hell kind of monster would do something like this for no reason? He almost took the guy's head off," Captain Kelly said.

"The guy recognized him. That's all the reason he needed. It almost looks like the suicide attempt Mr. Cozen described to me."

"What suicide attempt?" The captain asked.

"Mr. Cozen said Malcolm tried to commit suicide after he found out what had been going on with Cozen and his girl. Crazy fuck nearly decapitated himself."

"I've never heard of anyone trying to commit suicide by cutting their own throat. Jesus. That's a guy who really wants to die."

"Yeah, that was my thought too. It'll be a lot of fun trying to bring this guy in," Detective Bryant said.

"Yeah, it looks like he's saying catch me if you can. This guy just said the wrong thing, and he's a corpse. Big sonuvabitch too, but it doesn't look like he had a chance to put up much of a fight. No signs of a struggle at all."

"I wonder if Malcolm knew the guy like with Reed, or if its every bit as random and spontaneous as it looks."

"Good question, Detective. I want you to go over there with Officer Wyatt and find out whatever you can from that witness. No, on second thought, leave that to Titus whenever he gets here. You grab some units and get over to Mr. Cooper's house and make some arrests. I want someone in custody by the time the news media gets wind of this."

Detective Bryant was getting a kick out of seeing the captain so animated. Captain Kelly had spoken more in the last ten minutes than Bryant could remember him speaking in the last ten years.

The next two hours were a nightmare. Detective Bryant made it to Paul Cooper's house and found him bound and mutilated almost beyond recognition, hanging from some metal contraption in the middle of the living room. His body bore hundreds of welts, cuts, burns, and bruises. He must have been tortured for hours before he was finally killed. His face was a swollen purple fright mask. His eyes were swollen shut, and there were cuts above and below each one from where someone's knuckles had repeatedly smashed into them. His nose was completely crushed and smeared sideways across his face. All the teeth had been smashed out of his mouth, and his lips were split in several places. Blood and saliva ran down his chest. His tongue was missing. Bones and muscle tissue showed through all over his body where someone had worked him over with a knife, flaying his skin off in long strips. His penis had been completely skinned, peeled like a banana. Parts of his buttocks, his pecs, and his cheek had been bitten away. His chest looked like someone had tried to chew right through him to get at his heart. It was missing as well.

Bryant knew without waiting for the coroner that most of this had been done while the victim was still alive. The Family Man never had much taste for necrophilia. He liked live prey. The most disturbing sight was the abundance of old yellowing bruises, half and fully healed scars and cuts. This man had been being tortured for a long time. Where did this type of depravity come from? He thought of Reed stealing Malcolm's high school sweetheart, but that just didn't explain … *THIS!*

All over the house, they found S&M and bondage paraphernalia. Metal and leather restraints, including the medieval looking iron shackles that Cooper's body hung from, whips, scalpels, branding irons, long steel needles, iron dildos, and all kinds of horrible "toys" were everywhere. The place looked like an Inquisition era torture chamber, something from The Marquis de Sade's darkest imaginings.

There was no sign of Malcolm anywhere. The forensic boys were going over everything, bagging, tagging, and dusting for prints. James knew it was pointless. This guy wasn't the type to stand trial. When and if he was finally caught, he would hold court in the street and go out blasting. A guy who tried to cut his own head off wasn't the "Come out with your hands up" type. He was the shoot-to-kill type. Right now, he was the armed and dangerous and still on the loose type. And they were running out of leads. Malcolm could be anywhere now.

# XVII.

No one had been to the Cozens' house since the night of the murders. The front door was still covered in yellow tape. Titus swiped the tape aside and opened the front door. The carpets had not been cleaned, and the smell of fetid blood wafted up his nostrils, causing his stomach to lurch involuntarily. Blood spattered the living room walls, the couch, the shattered coffee table, the television, and the Wii video game console. Even the stereo and CD tower were sprayed with splashes of dark red. The eggshell-white curtains looked like the linen from an operating room table. In his mind's eye, Titus could still see the position of each victim. He could almost see the death scene as it unfolded.

He imagined little Mark taking a blast from a shotgun in the chest at pointblank range, sending half his vital organs flying against the wall in back of him; Jennie Cozen stabbed a dozen times, then tossed aside; and Linda Cozen raped, stabbed, cannibalized. Alive. Alive as that monster thrust himself inside her. Alive as he chewed off her breasts. Alive as he drove his knife through her chest.

*But which monster was it? Malcolm Davis or Reed himself?*

Detective Baltimore turned away and began to walk into the Cozens' bedroom. The desktop computer was still turned on, and the novel Reed had been working on was still on the screen. *He must turn off his screen saver when he works.* Papers were littered everywhere, and Titus sat down at Reed's desk to sift through them. They were mostly bills, three letters from Reed's publisher in escalating degrees of urgency, begging him to finish his novel, a post card from Linda's mother on a gambling trip in Vegas, and notes for Reed's novel written on three by five cards, receipts, brown paper bags, and notebook paper of varying sizes. Every other scrap of paper that looked vaguely important had already been bagged and tagged and was sitting in an evidence locker.

Titus decided to browse through the computer again. He'd spent half the previous night printing out everything on the computer that looked relevant. He knew his way around Reed's database pretty well now. Within minutes, he located Reed's address book containing the phone numbers of Linda's mother in Delaware, their babysitter, physician, pediatrician, and their marriage counselor.

*So, things weren't perfect in paradise*, Titus thought.

He called the marriage counselor, a Dr. Elliot Berkowitz, and got his secretary, who was rather hesitant to put the man on the phone. She insisted that he was with a patient and could not be disturbed. Titus had to settle for leaving a message with his cell number. Next, he called Linda's mother, hoping that someone had managed to inform her of her daughter's passing before she'd seen it on television. It had slipped his mind, and he prayed that Detective Bryant had at least taken care of that one little detail. Maybe the hospital or Reed himself had thought to call.

"H-Hello?" The woman who answered sounded as if she had been crying

"Uh, this is Detective Titus Baltimore of the

Philadelphia Police Department. Is this Mrs. Reeser? Linda Cozen's mother?"

"Y-yes."

"I'm investigating your daughter's murder, and I was hoping you could answer a few questions for me."

"Y-y-yeah, sure. I-I just found out today. Reed called me and told me this morning, and then it was all over the news. All day, that's all I keep hearing about. I finally turned off the TV and the radio and unplugged the phone. I just plugged it back in. Those damn reporters keep calling me."

"I know this must be terrible for you, but I must ask you some questions. It will only take a second. Do you know anyone who would want to hurt your daughter?"

"What-what do you mean? I thought … Reed told me that it was that Malcolm Davis guy. That Black guy Reed use to be friends with."

"I know, but we just have to check out all possibilities. Now, do you know anyone who might want to harm your daughter?"

"No. Everyone loved Linda."

"How was your daughter's marriage? Any problems there? Between her and Mr. Cozen?"

"No more than any other couple. She wanted him to spend more time with the kids, help out more around the house. They had money problems. He wouldn't work a real job. Put all his time into writing those books. Sometimes they did well. Sometimes they didn't. They lived from royalty check to royalty check. It was often feast or famine. He didn't write the kind of books that stayed on the shelves long. There would be the initial excitement from his small body of fans, and then interest would peter out and the royalty checks would get smaller and smaller, and then they would stop coming entirely. Then it was time to write another book. That's hard on a woman, trying to stick to a budget when she doesn't even know what their income is gonna be from month to month."

"Is that why they were seeing a marriage counselor?"

"Well, not exactly. I mean she never said it directly, but I kind of got the impression that they were having some sexual problems."

"Is that what your daughter told you?"

"No, of course that's not the type of thing a daughter discusses with her mother, so it's more of a hunch. Just kind of reading into what she wasn't saying."

"I see. Is that it? No other problems?"

"No. They were a pretty happy couple, mostly. They just had the normal problems most young couples have these days."

"Okay, thank you, Mrs. Reeser. I'll be in touch if we come up with anything."

Titus hadn't learned much from his conversation with Mrs. Reeser, but that bit about sexual problems might be something. He needed to talk to their therapist. Maybe it had something to do with the allegations of child molesting. Talking to doctors could be touchy, though. That doctor/patient privilege thing was a pain in the ass. Even with a warrant, they often refused to cooperate, and Titus didn't have a warrant or the probable cause to get one. All he had was his suspicions and those of Jennie's teachers. His cell phone rang, and Detective Baltimore answered to the sound of Captain Kelly's low, rumbling, impatient voice.

"Detective, where the hell are you? Didn't Woo tell you we wanted you over here with us?"

"Yeah, but I figured you guys could handle that yourselves. I'm over at the Cozens' house, checking the scene for more clues."

"Well, Malcolm just left us another clue. A bodybuilder just got his throat slashed about two hours ago in broad daylight in front of a dozen witnesses, and guess who did it? I need you down here now. It's at The Atlas Gym on Walnut Street."

"Shit! All right, I'm on my way."

Titus was disappointed that he had to leave before

he could follow up with the marriage counselor or the Cozens' physician or their babysitter or pediatrician. He felt certain that one of them would confirm the story about Reed and his daughter, and he was not looking forward to facing the media without a suspect in custody. He locked up the house and jumped back into the Mercedes, instantly regretting having brought it instead of the Mustang. When the other cops saw him behind the wheel of this ninety-thousand-dollar rich boy's toy, he knew they would instantly distrust him, and the ones who already distrusted him would hate him. The reporters would be all over him. He could almost see the full color picture of him cruising up to the crime scene in his Mercedes under the headline: "Rich Boy Cop Fails to Catch Killer" or "Another Killed, Playboy Cop On Cruise Control." Titus groaned and reached into his glove compartment for the Advil. He washed it down with tepid, day-old Evian and chewed on a Rolaids. He hit the Roosevelt Expressway at 60 miles an hour, heading toward Center City and more headache.

Detective Baltimore's stomach was twisting in knots. His head started to pound before the Advil could kick in. His day had taken a very bad turn. Malcolm had left another body, in broad daylight, in front of a dozen witnesses, with half the city's police force on a full-scale manhunt for him. Worse yet, Baltimore promised the city of Philadelphia, on live television, that he would have him in custody by today. They were going to chew him up and spit him out. Baltimore let out another loud moan, popped another Advil, and hit the accelerator.

*Fools rush in ...,* he thought and chewed another Rolaids.

When Baltimore arrived at The Atlas Gym, he almost believed he had a chance of slipping in before the reporters noticed him. The Mercedes slid smoothly down the normally serene one-way street, narrowly inching past the news vans parked haphazardly along the street, half-on and half-off the sidewalk, with their gaudy satellite dishes protruding from the roofs. Baltimore felt like giving them all parking tickets. For a moment, he looked away from the pandemonium in front of The Atlas and studied the architecture of the surrounding buildings. Two-hundred-year-old colonials that had been restored to near original or better than original condition lined the street in peaceful harmony. Many of them had been turned into stores, and one of them was even a theater. This was Detective Baltimore's favorite part of town, next to Chestnut Hill of course, and perhaps Northern Liberties. Today, however, he was not at all happy to be there.

Titus was only a few storefronts away from the crime scene, looking for a place to park. The reporters hadn't spotted him yet. He knew what he looked like driving up in a vehicle that no police detective should be able to afford, and he had to struggle to keep his guilt from showing in his expression. The reporters had lain siege around a thoroughly harassed-looking Captain Kelly, assaulting him with microphones and TV cameras like a pack of hyenas ringing in prey. Almost no one seemed to notice the Mercedes slide into the no parking zone across the street. Titus started to feel a little better, but then as soon as he got out of the car, the hyenas came to feed.

"Detective! Detective Baltimore! You said you would have the killer in custody by now. Have you apprehended a suspect?"

"No. I—"

"Detective, do you have any leads on the whereabouts of Malcolm Davis?"

"No, but—"

"How could he walk right into a public establishment in Center City, murder someone in broad daylight, and get away when the police are supposed to be conducting a manhunt for him?"

"I can't answer that right now, but I assure you we

are doing everything in our power—"

"Can you guarantee the citizens of this city that one of them won't be his next victim?"

"As I said, the Philadelphia Police Department is doing everything we can to bring this killer to justice and fulfill our duty to the citizens of this town to keep them safe. This man will be caught."

"And if he isn't? Are you going to patrol the whole town in that Mercedes to make sure he doesn't murder another family?"

The hairs on Baltimore's neck raised, and his eyes shot daggers at the young reporter who had so brazenly attacked him, some punk from one of the local weeklies. A nobody. But now Titus was in front of TV cameras, in front of his shiny new Mercedes sport convertible with that searing question still hanging in the air like the caustic stench of an overcooked meal. Detective Baltimore gritted his teeth and leaned forward into the reporter's face, glaring at him with murder in his eyes.

"No comment," he hissed.

The young news hound recoiled and shrank back into the crowd. Detective Baltimore shoved his way through the hyenas to get to Captain Kelly's side. They began their chant of "No comment" in unison, a mantra to ward off the ghouls that came to feast on the remains of the dead, as the detectives made their way back into the gym. They slid under the police tape and past the five officers who had their hands full holding back the crowd of eager spectators. The ME was already on the scene making his preliminary examination of the body, knees splashing around in the victim's blood as he knelt over the body.

"Who is this guy? Do we have an ID on him yet?"

"Yes. He had a wallet in his sweat pants. His name's Michael Lipshutz. He owns a liquor store around the corner. A lot of these guys knew him. I've stopped through that store once or twice myself on the way home from a long day of the dead."

"What can you tell us right now?"

Doctor Medoff was a fastidious old gentleman who had been with the city morgue since computers were the size of Ford trucks, but he had changed well with the times and was quite good at what he did. He was always petitioning the city fathers for more money to upgrade the city's woefully outdated forensic equipment. Sometimes, he even managed to squeeze a nickel or two out of the budget.

"Well, it's exactly what it looks like. The victim's carotid artery was severed in one stroke that severed the jugular and sliced clean through his trachea and esophagus as well. My guess is he stabbed the knife in like this." Dr. Medoff made a hooking gesture towards the captain's throat. "Then grabbed the hilt of the blade with both hands and tore it across his throat. That would explain why the wound is so deep. He would have had to be tremendously powerful to slash clean through his neck in one stroke using only one hand. Hmmm?"

"What is it, Doctor?"

"You know, when I was in the Marines, this is how they taught us to cut a throat. Stab the knife in deep and then pull it across with both hands. Most people would just slash the knife across the throat. They wouldn't stab it in first. This guy may have had some military training."

"Not by our records."

"There are all kinds of ways to get military training off the record."

"You mean a merc school? You mean this guy might be some kind of trained mercenary? An assassin or terrorist or something? Fuckin' great!"

"Whoa! Whoa! I was just throwing that out as a possibility. These aren't exactly political targets he's going after. He could've picked it up in a book or one of those survivalist magazines. Hell, they have whole websites on the internet about physical interrogation techniques, tips on assassination, anti-personnel techniques. He could have learned this trick almost anywhere. But to do it so quickly and confidently, so automatically, means he's been practicing."

"That much I'm pretty sure of myself. I think this guy has been killing for a long time. We may never know what his real body count is"

"Well, he certainly knows what he's doing. There's no way anyone without medical training and equipment could have stopped the bleeding in time. He must have bled completely out before the paramedics even arrived. He died of asphyxiation. Drowned in his own blood."

"Did we find the murder weapon? He usually leaves it behind, sticking out of his victim's body."

"No, no murder weapon."

"The scene wasn't secure when we arrived. There were people walking all through here. I can't say one of them didn't walk off with it," Captain Kelly grumbled, looking like he was getting angry all over again.

"Great."

"Detective? Can I speak to you for a moment?"

"Yes, sir."

Captain Kelly and Detective Baltimore stepped around into the free-weight room, into the hamstring and quadriceps area, and leaned up against the squat rack.

"Have you made any progress?"

"Well, Captain, I haven't gotten any leads on Malcolm's whereabouts, but I think I might be close to some evidence that just might link Reed Cozen to the murders."

"That's just great, Baltimore. But right now, Reed isn't the one on a murderous rampage! Malcolm Davis is our primary suspect. So far, he's butchered Mrs. Cozen and her two kids, beat the shit out of Mr. Cozen, murdered this guy in broad daylight, and mutilated his accomplice, plus who knows how many other murders he's committed? Did you hear that James tried to track down one of Malcolm's ex-girlfriends? He went to her house, and there was no trace of her or her family, but CSU found blood everywhere. We're pretty sure they're dead. This Malcolm guy is out of fucking control. Fuck, Reed! You get me this Malcolm Davis guy!"

"But Captain, I—"

"Shut the fuck up. We need results! And we need 'em fast! Now I've already talked to Bryant, and now I'm gonna say it to you too. You two are partners. You WILL work together. I don't want to see you cruising around in your Mercedes while James is out doing god-knows-what. I don't give a fuck if you don't like each other. You put your heads together, and you solve this thing. Did you know that we just found Malcolm's accomplice? Yeah, Bryant said he could be Reed's twin. He found him trussed up in some kind of S&M contraption cut to ribbons. Finish up here and then you drive over there and take over."

"What's the location?"

"See? If you were in your damned patrol unit with your partner instead of that Mercedes, you'd have heard it on the radio. It's over on Eighth and South, by that little gift store."

Baltimore left, wondering if Captain Kelly would have been as adamant about him riding with Bryant in the patrol car if he had pulled up in the old Mustang instead of his dad's new Mercedes. Perhaps he was being too cynical. Maybe Captain Kelly only wanted to see him and Bryant acting like partners instead of two teenagers competing for the same spot on the football team. Maybe he was just tired of getting his ass chewed by the Police Chief, the DA, the Mayor, and whoever else had their canines dug into his backside these days. Baltimore was smart enough to know that whatever pressure he was feeling to solve these murders was nothing compared to the pressure the captain was under.

He made his way back to his car, reciting his mantra at the ghouls. It wasn't working, and they surged forward, engulfing him in their insensitive and insipid questions. Baltimore pushed his way through and drove off in a hail of flashbulbs. Now they had the pictures of him actually in the Mercedes. He'd probably be getting a call from IAD in the morning.

If The Atlas Gym scene was a circus, the scene at the Paul Cooper homicide was appropriately, if not excessively, funereal. There were more than a few officers still on the scene, two of whom were outside throwing up in the bushes. Another was regurgitating in the kitchen sink while James berated him about contaminating possible evidence. Still more were standing around, gawking at the swinging carcass gruesomely suspended from the ceiling like some kind of carrion stuffed scarecrow. The coroners had not arrived yet, but the crime scene techs were already busy reducing Paul's entire existence to a few dozen zip-lock bags with serial numbers on them. The only two cops who did not appear to be in shock were filling a box with S&M paraphernalia and carting it and a huge box of violent pornography out to the squad car. More evidence. None of which was going to lead them any closer to Malcolm.

"Hey, Baltimore." Bryant started to stride quickly toward him. For the first time, Baltimore noticed how powerfully Detective Bryant was built. He looked into Bryant's angry, bloodshot eyes and took an involuntary step back.

"Look, Titus, let's step outside. We need to talk."

Bryant rushed past him and out the door, not waiting to see if Detective Baltimore was following or not. Baltimore followed, wondering if the big blow up that had been building between the two of them all year was about to happen. He knew Detective Bryant had once been a pretty good boxer, while he'd never been in a fight in his entire life. Baltimore's only consolation was that Bryant would be suspended if he beat him too badly, and at least then they would no longer have to be partners. He felt like a punk when his legs began to shake and wobble slightly as he stepped out the door. He berated himself for not taking karate when his dad had suggested it. He'd be a black belt by now if he hadn't wanted those damn piano lessons.

"Uh, what's wrong, James?" He wanted to sound strong, but his voice came out hoarse and squeaky.

"Relax, Tight Ass. I'm not going to hit you."

Detective Baltimore's whole face turned red. Bryant knew Baltimore would think that he was calling him out for a fight. He had made him think that on purpose, and now he was laughing at him. Baltimore went from relief, to embarrassment, to anger.

"Okay, James! What the fuck did you call me out here like this for?"

"We need to get together on this case, and we can't do it by ignoring and working against each other. The captain is right. Malcolm is out of control, and we aren't going to catch him like this."

Baltimore calmed down. He hated the fact that Bryant had done the right thing, the mature thing, before he had, but Bryant was right, and Baltimore couldn't help but to be impressed that the man actually seemed to care. He was beginning to think the old bastard didn't give a damn about whether the case got solved or not and was relieved to discover he'd been wrong.

"Okay, so how should we start?"

"First, I gotta say you're completely wrong about Mr. Cozen. I know you think he had something to do with his family's murder, but you're wrong. The only complicity he might have had in this was in pissing Malcolm off."

"You have no idea what I've found out about that scumbag. Do you know he might have been molesting his daughter? Did you know that?"

Detective Bryant was shocked.

"Can you prove that?"

"Not yet, but if he was and the wife found out about it, that's a strong motive for killing them. And he could have found out how to copycat The Family Man by talking with Malcolm, finding out all the juicy details we've been keeping out of the papers so that he could duplicate the crime well enough to fool even us. Malcolm may have even helped. Because one thing's for sure, Malcolm is definitely The Family Man, and the fact that he's best friends with Mr. Cozen certainly makes things look suspicious."

"Well, Reed was telling the truth about there being a guy who looked just like him working with Malcolm. We found this guy's prints all over the crime scene."

"That doesn't prove anything. The guy could have been coerced into it. Especially considering how he ended up. And we've got a morgue full of guys who look like Reed, courtesy of his buddy, Malcolm."

"Okay, then we obviously can't proceed until we eliminate Mr. Cozen as a suspect. But first I want to head over to Malcolm's mother's house and get a little more background info on our suspect. Perhaps she might be able to tell us something that'll give us a clue to where he might be hiding. We've had her house under twenty-four-hour surveillance, but Malcolm may have found a way to sneak in past the stakeout. He might be sitting in there with his mother right now eating biscuits and drinking tea. "

Just as they were talking, the black ME's van pulled up and Dr. Medoff popped out, looking harried and flustered.

"Two for one, aye boys?"

In a rare moment of serendipity, both detectives had the exact same thought at the exact same moment.

*I've been seeing entirely too much of that guy lately.*

# XVIIII.

Malcolm was running out of options, and he knew it. The cops were all over Paul's apartment. Malcolm knew that was inevitable. Even if they hadn't tracked him down, the body would have started to decompose soon and the smell would have brought them. Now, Malcolm had nowhere to stay, and cruising around all day and night in the Impala was dangerous. If a cop stopped him for so much as failing to use his turn signal, it could be all over, and Reed would be off the hook. Besides that, he was tired, and tired people made mistakes. He had to stay alert to finish this.

Reed had betrayed him again. This time to the police. Of course, Malcolm knew he would, but he had warned him that it was between the two of them. That anyone else who got involved would wind up just like his family. He would make Reed understand the depth of his conviction. But first, he had to rest.

Malcolm drove deep into North Philadelphia, headed toward the Raymond Rosen housing projects where police feared to tread. He passed rows and rows of burned out, ill-kept, and plain old run-down homes. The worse the neighborhood got, it seemed the more people were out in the street. By the time the Impala rolled cautiously past the Raymond Rosen projects, it looked like he was in the middle of some kind of street fair. Teenaged prostitutes were everywhere, trying to raise money for the next hit of crack or heroin. Drug dealers of the same age strolled up and down the street, brazenly selling their product to their somnolent consumers. Young kids were all over the place with basketballs, making jump shots in milk crates nailed to telephone poles and playing handball against heavily graffitied brick walls. Malcolm went almost unnoticed as he cruised to a stop in an empty lot that was the community trash dump. He lay back in the Impala's long bench seat and rested his head on the passenger door's armrest. He began to dream about Reed before his eyes had even fully closed.

In Malcolm's mind, Reed was the cause of his madness, the one who stole the twinkle of hope and wonder from his eyes. Not the stepfather who filled his head with horror stories about the Vietnam War, who made his pre-adolescent years basic training for an imaginary invasion he was convinced was just around the corner. The man who woke him up at five o'clock in the morning to run military drills in which he shot live rounds at his stepson and punched and kicked him mercilessly to toughen him up. In his mind, he had been a good kid before Reed, a shy, sensitive kid who read horror and sci-fi novels and daydreamed most of the day. Not the kid who, at age ten, tortured a cat in his stepdad's basement, imagining that he was a Vietnamese soldier interrogating captured GIs. Not the kid who, at age twelve, would expose himself to the old ladies at the nursing home around the corner from the house where he grew up and who, at age thirteen, burned it to the ground, masturbating as he watched the flames engulf it, imagining the old ladies burning alive inside.

He didn't remember setting fire to a homeless man at the train station on Tulpehocken Street, dousing him with lighter fluid as he lay passed out drunk on a bench and tossing the match just to see what it would look like when his skin melted off his bones, watching as the man writhed and cried out in agony to see how long he would scream before he died. He didn't even remember stalking a female jogger in Wissahickon Park, dragging the frightened woman into the woods and raping her at knifepoint, telling her, "You should be honored. You're my first," as she struggled. He only remembered the poor, awkward, oversized Black kid that everyone picked on in junior high before he got smart and started to fight back, before he learned to walk, talk, and dress like the superior human being he always believed himself to be. Malcolm was one sick puppy long before Reed, but that was not the way he saw it.

Malcolm saw Reed as the villain in his tragedy. Reed had ruined him, shattered the safe illusion of karmic balance and order the rest of the world enjoyed. Reed had shown him that life was a cruel and capricious bitch.

So how could he not flirt with death?

Now, Reed was the famous novelist and he was … a monster. Malcolm used to dream of being a novelist just like Reed. It seemed ridiculous to him now, like he must have been someone else entirely, the dreams of another man in another time. But once, Malcolm had wanted to be an author, a poet, a philosopher. Back then, Malcolm believed he had a lot to say to the world that it needed to hear. Now, it had no choice but to hear him. He was telling his story in blood, a story that was nearing its climax, Reed's denouement.

For as long as he could remember, Malcolm had thought of life as something that had been done to him, inflicted upon him against his will, something to be endured like the torture his stepdad had told him about and inflicted upon him. Life was what people did before they died. His stepdad had taught him that. He had taught him about survival. And that was all living was about. Survival and domination. Reneé and then Natasha had been the only things in his life to ever contradict that philosophy. Then their actions had quickly reinforced it. Life was cruel, capricious, and pointless, and no one got out of it alive. The best anyone could hope for was to take their abusers out with them.

Malcolm thought about his mother, the only person who had never let him down and never betrayed him. He knew the cops would be putting her through hell. Especially that white GQ sonuvabitch who was on the news talking about how the cops would have Malcolm in custody by the end of the night. Malcolm knew that guy was probably the one knocking on his mother's door with a search warrant, tearing her house apart. In all of this, that was the only thing Malcolm regretted or felt any guilt about, putting his mother through the hassle of dealing with the gang in blue.

"Don't worry, Mom, I'll make sure that bastard pays for any pain he causes you."

The activity in the streets became more hectic as two rival drug dealers began arguing in the street in front of Raymond Rosen. They both reached for their guns, spitting out a vituperative stream of truncated English and brutal profanity. Malcolm fell asleep to the sound of gunfire, police and ambulance sirens, and screams. He was home.

"All right, what leads do we have so far?"

Detective Baltimore tried to sound gung-ho. They had just finished talking to the ME and watching the crime scene techs catalogue every possible scrap of evidence. The body was on its way downtown, and they were on their way to Malcolm's mother's house. They made a quick stop to drop off Baltimore's Mercedes at the station. Baltimore was thinking what sweet revenge it would've been to drive the Mercedes into G-town and then explain to his dad how crack addicts had stolen it.

"Honestly, I ain't got shit. We know who the motherfucker is. We know where every damn member of his family lives. We have pictures of him all over the place and enough sightings to fill an entire filing cabinet. The whole city's been chasing down leads all day, and not one of them has turned into anything."

"Well, even though it looks like Reed was telling the truth about his look-alike, I still think there's more going on that he ain't telling us. I think if we squeezed him, we might even find out where Malcolm is hiding."

Detective Bryant looked at Baltimore with hard, serious eyes, recognizing in him the beginnings of a potentially hazardous obsession, hazardous to their case.

"Look, Titus. That might be possible, but I doubt it. I think this is all about Malcolm. Period. Mr. Cozen just probably feels guilty for fuckin' Malcolm over when they were kids. He told me he thinks that his betrayal might be what pushed Malcolm over the edge. He feels like maybe he brought all this down on himself and his family. Forget about him. Tell me about Malcolm. I want to know what insights your PhD in psychology has given you on this type of psychotic."

"Malcolm's not a psychotic. He's a sociopath, an anti-social personality type. See, the rest of us have developed altruistic emotions that help us get along in society together, emotions like sympathy, empathy, compassion. Malcolm doesn't have these. He's extremely paranoid, a 'The world is out to get me' type, but he isn't crazy. There are no voices in his head telling him to kill. He knows the difference between right and wrong, but he justifies doing wrong, rationalizes his acts. That's all Reed Cozen is for him. A justification to do all the evil shit he's probably been dreaming about doing long before he ever met Reed. He probably feels about as much connection with the human race as a wolf feels with sheep."

Bryant nodded his head slowly, digesting everything Baltimore said.

"Whatever happened to that profile we got from the FBI on the Family Man?"

"I still have it, but I think we can pretty much discount it. They said he would be a White male between twenty-five and thirty-five, and Malcolm is Black. They said he would drive a van or a pick-up truck with a shell on it. Malcolm drives an Impala. They said he would be a reclusive, anti-social nerd with homosexual tendencies who has trouble meeting women and may even fear them. Malcolm definitely does not fear women, regardless of his tendencies, and he may be anti-social, but he is not reclusive. They said he would probably live out in the suburbs, and Malcolm definitely does not—"

"Okay, okay, so they were wrong, but that profile was done before we knew all the cases were connected. If they knew about The Pine Street killings and the Chaperone killings, maybe that might change the profile."

"I'm certain it would. The Pine Street slashings would indicate a very confident person, out-going, who can easily get people to trust him because the victims were lured away from public places without anyone noticing anything suspicious and then murdered in their homes. The repeated stabbing would indicate sexual frustration and rage, perhaps even a hatred of homosexuals, an attempt to deny those tendencies within himself. The fact that the men were all young and healthy would lead us to assume we were dealing with someone very strong and very confident in his strength. See, the men were not ambushed and rendered unconscious, as one would expect.

"Most serial killers are cowards at heart. They don't want victims who can fight back. They want the killings clean and easy. But these victims were not knocked out, not drugged, not tied up. They were struggling the whole time, but not one of them survived. This man was supremely confident and extremely sadistic. He wanted them to see it coming, to feel his power. The fact that they all look alike we know is because they were meant to symbolize Reed. He was killing Reed over and over again. The fact that they were all gay men may tell us something about his feelings toward Reed. He probably has conflicting feelings about Reed, kind of a love-hate thing. Most likely, there's some sexual ambiguity there as well."

"That's good. Keep going. What about the Chaperone killings? What does that tell us about him?"

"The Chaperone killings add a new element: the women. This is when the violence first escalates to include partial dismemberment and rape. He is feeling confident now with his prowess as a killer, but he's also frustrated. The fantasy isn't living up to the reality. He needs more. So he goes after couples. Probably still overcompensating for possible gay tendencies. He rapes to feel potent. To feel like a man. But he gets no real sexual gratification out of the intercourse itself. It's their fear, their pain, their humiliation that gets him off. He uses his penis as another weapon. Another way of inflicting pain.

"For him, it is interchangeable with his knife. He is a true sadist. He needs to feel in control of his victims. I'm sure he makes the men watch. That's another way of demonstrating his power and their powerlessness. It's all about control. He wants God-like power over his victims' lives. The removal of their hearts is a way to relive the experience. It is a souvenir, a memento of the experience. He uses it to masturbate, to sustain him between victims. Plus, with all the symbolism in our culture involving the heart, by taking the women's hearts, he could be trying to steal back the love Reed stole from him. "

"And now, The Family Man."

"This is more difficult. We see the same pattern re-emerge. The same male figures again, the overkill stabbing, the rape, the souvenir taking, the same themes of dominance and control. Even the cannibalism is a predictable escalation in the pattern. It must be the greatest high imaginable to literally consume his victims, the ultimate statement of dominance and control. This escalation in violence is consistent with the idea I first put out about him being on a degenerative cycle."

"I'm still not sold on that idea."

"Well, look at it. He's escalated the violence, the number of victims. He's killing more frequently. Even his choice of victims suggests he's out of control. He's not killing strangers anymore. He's killing people he knows, people close to him, Reed Cozen's family, Reneé Volaré's family, Paul Cooper. Then he lashes out and murders a guy in broad daylight, in front of dozens of witnesses. He's in self-destruct mode. He's making mistakes. He's got half the cops in the city after him now. This is not the same careful, meticulous killer who did the first homicides. Now, he's completely lost the plot."

James nodded.

"Yeah, but up until this most recent spree, he was still careful. He may have escalated the number of victims and the violence, but it still seemed controlled. It still seemed to be following some kind of pattern. Even in the middle of that frenzy of violence, he still took the time to clean up the crime scene, even to the point of vacuuming up all the hair and fiber, and using condoms during the rape. I don't see an out-of-control guy stopping to put on a condom. The Cozen murders were the first time he left any kind of evidence at all. That was the first time he seemed to lose control. I mean, all of a sudden, we have a messy crime scene full of physical evidence. Before that, nothing. I mean, even the way he killed the kids seems wrong somehow. It seems out of character, like there must've been some reason for it that we're just not getting."

"You're right. The kids don't fit. It looks like they were killed almost as an afterthought. The way they are killed is almost merciful compared to what he did to the parents. He discarded the bodies face down, sometimes even covered them up. This usually indicates guilt or remorse. He even brought along a gun and shot several of the children to further distance himself from their deaths. None of the sadism is displayed toward the kids. They are simply executed as a matter of course."

"So, why does he kill them at all if he doesn't get off on it? I mean, all that bullshit about Reed aside, these freaks kill because it gets them off. But if the children don't do it for him, why not just stick to couples? Why does he go after the families?"

"It's as if he finds it a distasteful but necessary chore. Like he has some purpose or cause that includes the kids somehow. Reed may not have made him this way, but that betrayal was definitely the stressor that sent him off on his murder spree. He's probably been fantasizing about these killings for years but just needed a push, something to get him started. Reed did that. Now he's acting out his fantasies, and Reed is the star. My God! It can't be! What if …? No."

"What is it?"

"I'm not sure. I just have this hunch. I think I may know why he goes after families. It all goes back to the fantasy and Reed. It's almost too sick. I don't know. I'm probably wrong."

"Tell me. What are you thinking?"

"Look, can you do me a favor and interview Malcolm's mother? I need to talk to Reed again."

"I'm going with you. I think we need to do this together. Besides, I have some questions of my own. Let's talk to his mother since we're damn near there anyway, and then we'll both head over to Reed's house. He got out of the hospital today, so he should be home resting."

The two detectives drove silently through the bizarre clash of classes that was Germantown. Within eight blocks, they'd passed through what looked like the suburbs, into a war-zone, then into a lush affluent landscape of Colonial Mansions and manicured lawns, and back into the urban asylum. They brought the white unmarked police cruiser to rest in front of a narrow three-story red brick row home adjoined on each side by its twin. About half a dozen young kids between the ages of nine and twelve were chasing each other up and down the street, hurling what appeared to be wet newspapers with deadly accuracy at one another's heads. The loud *Thwap!* of wet paper hitting flesh echoed loudly off the domino-like houses as one papier-mâché projectile after another found its mark.

Detective Baltimore leapt from the car and was about to pound on Mrs. Davis's door like the entire SWAT team had come calling. Bryant grabbed his arm and eased him back.

"Take it easy. See that car over there? Detectives Vargas and Jones have been staking this place out for days, and I can assure you, Malcolm ain't in there. And if he shows up, they've both got our backs. What we don't want to do is charge in there like the goddamned Gestapo and put this woman on the defensive. You sit back and take notes and try to figure out how what she tells us fits into the profile. I'll ask the questions. If you have a question, just whisper it to me and I'll ask."

"Why the hell do you get to ask all the questions?"

Bryant gave Baltimore a long look of irritation like the ones kids give to their little brothers or sisters when they say something embarrassingly stupid—the look little Jennie Cozen had often given her brother Mark.

"You've got the PhD, bright boy. You figure it out."

Detective Bryant shook his head in exasperation and knocked on the door. A surprisingly young-looking Black woman opened the door and greeted the two detectives with a sullen and baleful glare. She wore a tattered red terry cloth robe that was missing buttons and did little to hide the sensuous swell of her cinnamon brown breasts or the long, smooth, subtly muscular legs that seemed to grow out of the bottom of the robe and go on forever or the high round curve of her buttocks. Her face bore the hard lines of a hard life, and her wild, wooly hair was lightly speckled with gray. Still, she was far from the senescent old matron they were expecting. Bryant sized her up within seconds and decided without hesitation that she was beautiful and that if they'd met under different circumstances, he would have already propositioned her. Baltimore thought she was probably a very stunning woman years ago, but in his eyes, age and a hard life had weathered away her beauty even if her body had survived the storm remarkably well. Though he, too, acknowledged that if given the chance, he would probably still do her.

"What?"

"I'm Detective James Bryant and this is Detective Titus Baltimore of the Philadelphia Police Department Homicide Division."

"And?" Mrs. Davis rolled her eyes and tapped her foot impatiently, then focused an accusatory glare at Detective Baltimore. He tried to return the look but failed miserably and felt it. She smirked scornfully at his failure.

"You know why we're here. Just answer a few questions for us and we'll be gone."

"I have no idea where my son is."

"I'm sure you do not. I want to ask you questions about his childhood."

"If you know he ain't here, why are those cops parked over there all day and night? Why are there more cops following me every time I leave the house?!"

"It's for your own protection."

"I'm his mama! Malcolm would never hurt me!"

"Ma'am, I know this might be hard for you to accept, but Malcolm is out of control and is seriously in need of help. I don't think you or I really know what he might do in this state. I'm sure you believe you know your son. No parent wants to admit that they don't really know everything about their own children. But did you know that Malcolm would murder that man's family or that guy in the gym or any of the other people he's suspected of harming?"

Mrs. Davis's strong, defiant face began to crack, first with the trembling of her bottom lip, then with the tears that began to slowly weep from the corners of her eyes and slide along her pronounced cheekbones.

"Honestly, Detective, I'm sorry to admit it, but I'm not surprised by any of this."

"May we come in?" Detective Bryant placed a hand

gently on Mrs. Davis's shoulder and guided her back into the house.

The living room was small, paneled with fake wood that was starting to peel away from the sheet rock, and sparsely furnished with an old green leather lounge chair and ottoman, an eggshell white sectional sofa, darkened in spots by sweat and dirt, and a natural pine coffee table. The centerpiece of the room was an ancient Magnavox color TV set with the knobs missing. A pair of pliers sat atop the set, presumably to change the channels. The rug was a bizarre burnt orange that was gnarled, matted, and nearly bald, like the fur of a dog with a serious case of mange. The first thing Detective Bryant noticed was the lack of dust.

For such an old house with old rundown furniture, it was impossibly clean. Even the old Magnavox was free of dust and seemed to shine as if it had just been waxed. Titus instinctively looked at the old woman's hands and noticed that they looked raw and pinkish. From scrubbing, he assumed. Obsessive-compulsive behavior. He wondered if this behavior began before or after she found out her son was a murderer.

"Tell us, Mrs. Davis, why aren't you surprised by Malcolm's … uh … outburst?"

"You can call me Wynona. No one calls me Mrs. Davis except my supervisors at work, and I hate those arrogant little peckerwoods." She didn't even acknowledge the "peckerwood" that sat uncomfortably on the other end of the sofa. Bryant couldn't help the little smile that crept onto his face. He wondered if Baltimore still wanted to be the one to ask the questions.

"Okay, Wynona, tell us about Malcolm."

Wynona took a long, deep breath and rubbed the back of one dry hand across her forehead. When she spoke, her voice was strong and steady, and all the tears had left her eyes. She was once again the strong, poverty-hardened woman that greeted them at the door.

"Malcolm's had a hard life. Jerome, his stepdad, used to beat him and put him through these military exercises."

"Military exercises?"

"Yeah, he wanted him to be tough in case there was another war. See, Jerome was a Vietnam vet."

Detective Baltimore instantly thought of Dr. Medoff's comment about the man who'd killed the bodybuilder having some military training. He whispered to Detective Bryant to ask Wynona about it.

"What went on during these exercises?"

"Mostly just calisthenics. Lots of push-ups and jumping jacks, but sometimes he would teach him hand-to-hand combat stuff, teach him how to throw knives and even to shoot guns. Sometimes Jerome would get a little carried away and beat Malcolm up pretty bad. He said it would make him tough. They would stick fight full contact, and Malcolm would come in the house bleeding with lumps and bruises all over him, and Jerome wouldn't even let me take him to the hospital. Once, he even stabbed him."

"Stabbed him?"

"He didn't mean to. They were doing some kind of knife fighting drills, and it got carried away. Malcolm got stabbed in the shoulder. Had to have thirteen stitches, but Jerome had him back out there the next day. Tore open all the stitches, and Malcolm had to go right back to the hospital."

Titus and James looked at each other at the mention of knife fighting. The pieces were all coming together. Some people might be born bad, but most are made.

"How did Malcolm feel about his stepdad? Did he resent him?"

"Oh no, Malcolm loved Jerome. They were inseparable. Until ..."

"Until?"

"Well, we never told Malcolm that Jerome wasn't his real dad, and when Malcolm was about eleven, he found out. It devastated him. All of a sudden, he just seemed to withdraw. He would sit at the dinner table and stare at Jerome. Some of the most hateful stares you ever saw. They still wrestled and stuff in the backyard, but it didn't look very friendly anymore. Malcolm was getting bigger, and Jerome was getting older. Sometimes Jerome would come in the house as beat up and bloody as Malcolm. I tried to tell myself it was just normal male competitiveness, but those looks Malcolm would give him. Then Malcolm started trying to kill Jerome."

Both detectives lurched forward at the same time and stared at Wynona, trying to make sure they'd really heard what they thought they had.

"Malcolm tried to kill your husband?"

"Oh, he ain't my husband no more. He ran off one night, couldn't take it. He was scared of Malcolm. He made Malcolm into some kinda psycho with all that Vietnam shit, and then he ran off and left me to deal with it. One night, Malcolm crept in the room with one of those sawed-off broomsticks they used to fight with and tried to beat Jerome to death. Jerome had to knock Malcolm out to get him to stop. The next night, Malcolm came at him with a knife. Cut him up pretty bad before Jerome managed to get the knife away from him. Jerome was about to turn the knife on Malcolm, but I threw myself between them to break it up. That's when Jerome turned around and walked out the door. He never came back."

"And that's why you think Malcolm's guilty?"

"Not just because of that. Because of the fire."

"Malcolm tried to burn down your house?"

"Not this house, the old folks home over on Johnson Street. The one that *used* to be over on Johnson Street. I can't prove it, but I just know it. The day before it happened, two staff members from the old folks home called the police on Malcolm, accusing him of sneaking onto their property and peeping in at the old ladies when they were dressing. They said he exposed himself to one them. When the cops picked him up and I had to go down to the station to get him, I was so embarrassed. I was absolutely furious! When we got home, I took off my belt and tried to beat him half to death.

"See, I was a single mother now, dealing with the responsibilities of both mother and father, and that meant being the disciplinarian. It was ridiculous, really. I mean after all the stuff Jerome did to him. What the hell was my scrawny little ass going to do? But Malcolm seemed to take that beating really hard. He cried like I never remember seeing him cry. I couldn't take it. I stopped and hugged him to me and promised him that we would get him help. He kept saying he was sorry over and over. I told him that I loved him and everything would be all right.

"The next day, the old folk's home was burned to the ground. The Fire Marshall said it was arson. Someone had thrown a Molotov cocktail through one of the windows. Five people died, including two of the women that Malcolm was accused of harassing. The cops questioned Malcolm. He denied everything, and the whole thing just kind of went away. But I knew what he'd done, just like I know what he's doing now."

Detective Bryant asked Mrs. Davis more about Malcolm's childhood and learned that he had wet the bed until age 12, a humiliation for which he was badly beaten by his stepdad. He had been caught mutilating cats in the basement. Malcolm said he was interrogating them. He was beaten for that too. In school, his freakish size and poor hygiene made him a target for the other kids to pick on until he, in his mother's words, "turned mean." Right after he chased off Jerome, he put a stop to the teasing by breaking the school bully's leg. Malcolm became the new school bully.

The two detectives thanked Mrs. Davis for her time and left quietly. They were no closer to finding Malcolm, but they were a lot closer to understanding him. They sat silently, absorbed in their own little worlds, processing all that they'd heard as they drove out to the Northeast to question Reed.

"Arson, bed-wetting, torturing animals—this guy has all the typical warning signs of the classic serial killer," Detective Baltimore muttered, talking more to himself than to his partner.

"You know, I still can't believe that this is a Black guy doing all these murders. I would've never imagined the Family Man was Black. Even the FBI profile said we'd be looking for a middle-class white guy."

"Yeah, the fact that he targets white families is what threw them off. Serial killers usually stay within their own race. But Malcolm has demonstrated a lot of atypical behavior. The killing of both men and women is unusual. Though that could be attributed to bisexuality. The killing of both adults and young children is highly unusual."

"But aren't most serial killers white? I never heard of a Black serial killer before. I know it sounds prejudiced, but I always associate Black people with crimes of profit or crimes of passion. Drug dealers shooting each other over turf. Some kid shooting another kid for stepping on his sneakers or dissin' his momma or lookin' too hard at his girl. No offense, but when I think of sick shit like this, I think of white folks. I mean, a Black guy might rape a woman and then kill her, but I thought only a white guy would kill a woman and *then* rape her. And then chop her up into little pieces, eat parts of her, stick the rest of her in the freezer, and talk to it. I thought you sick bastards had the monopoly on that kind of crazy."

"That's some pretty racist shit, James. Wayne Williams, the Atlanta child murderer, was Black."

"Yeah, if you believe he did it. Look, I know that it's fucked up to think like that, but I'm a victim of that Black liberal mentality that says that minorities who commit crimes do so because they are underprivileged, undereducated, oppressed, and deprived. Evil, I mean pure evil, for me always wore a white face. Charles Manson, Ted Bundy, Jeffrey Dahmer, Adolph Hitler. I mean, even knowing that Malcolm was Black, I still half expected Mrs. Davis to come to the door and be this old white lady with a bible in one hand, a cat o' nine tails in the other, and a big confederate flag on the wall over the mantel, married to some leering pedophile with a history of child and spousal abuse, maybe a few sex offenses thrown in as well. That would've made sense to me. "

"The same factors that turn Caucasians into these types of monsters can do the same to Black people. There are fewer Black serial killers in America because there are fewer Black people in America. Actually, Black people are only twenty percent of the population but make up nearly thirty percent of all serial killers in America. So, a higher percentage of Blacks become serial killers than whites even though there are less of them.

"Malcolm was a very abused, very fucked-up kid who grew up to become a very fucked-up man. His mother didn't mention it, but I suspect that he was probably sexually abused as a child as well. White people don't hold the monopoly on child molestation."

Bryant nodded. "I've never heard of a Black serial killer on the level of John Wayne Gacy or Ted Bundy, though. Not someone killing thirty or forty people, carving them up, and eating them. I've never heard of that. The most famous, most prolific serial killers have all been white. I just can't see a Black guy acting like this. I know it's fucked up for me to hold that stereotype. In fact, I'm admitting it's a personal prejudice, one I definitely need to work on, but it is at least an understandable if not justified one."

Baltimore's jaw dropped open. He shook his head and blinked several times.

"What? Are you telling me you think there is

actually a such thing as justifiable bigotry? Really, James?"

"No, that's not what I'm saying. All I'm saying is that if you're on the job long enough, you start to notice certain patterns in crimes. You start to put a certain look and, yeah, a certain color to certain crimes. You can't help it. It's just human nature. You bust a meth lab, you're pretty sure the perp will be white. A crack house, Black or Latino. Someone shoots a guy outside a night club, you think Black guy. Someone dices up a family, tell me you don't picture a white guy? Tell me that isn't half the reason you're so convinced Reed Cozen had something to do with the murders? If Malcolm was white, would you be so convinced he must've had an accomplice? Shit, prejudice is just an occupational hazard. At least I'm man enough to cop to it."

"Yeah, maybe you're right. Maybe my feeling about Reed is really based on race and not the fact that he just smells so fucking guilty I could choke on the stench. But let me tell you, Malcolm is probably the worst serial killer I've ever heard of. He's the most sadistic sonuvabitch I've ever seen, white or Black."

"Well, you know how the saying goes, Black folks have to be twice as good to be just as good. Maybe Malcolm's just making a statement for equal opportunity." Bryant snickered.

Detective Baltimore knew Bryant was just trying to fuck with his head and get him pissed off. So he decided to ignore his little remark.

"Malcolm is the archetypal sexual sociopath, no different from Bundy or Dahmer except he's bigger and blacker, and I'm gonna be the one who puts his big black ass on death row. And if Mr. Cozen is guilty too, he'll be getting his hotshot ten minutes after Malcolm."

They drove along in a rigid silence for another ten minutes before Detective Bryant spoke again.

"Okay, so explain those damn silver fangs to me. What the fuck is up with that?"

Detective Baltimore grinned mischievously.

"Oh, that. I just thought it was a Black thang."

Bryant turned halfway around in his seat to face Baltimore and attempted his hardest interrogation room stare, the "crazy nigger" stare that was known to turn hardened career criminals into whining stool pigeons. But the ill-timed intervention of his sense of humor instead caused him to chuckle and shake his head.

"You know, you really don't know me well enough to joke like that." He tried the look again, and again, he started to chuckle.

"Yeah, but I'm getting to know you. Slowly but surely."

"Okay, smart ass, so what about the fangs?"

"Well, first off, I seriously doubt the fangs are made of silver. That's just not Malcolm's style. It doesn't seem to fit in with the designer suits. My guess is platinum. Malcolm likes money. If he wears any kind of jewelry, it would be diamonds and platinum."

"Okay, but why fangs? Why not a nice necklace or a ring if he wants to show off? I mean gold fronts went out years ago, except in the south, and I never heard of any brothas with fangs and definitely not platinum ones."

"Like I said before, all these murders are about Malcolm acting out a fantasy. The fangs are probably part of the fantasy. With his proclivity for cannibalism, it would be easy to imagine that he's acting out some kind of werewolf fantasy. Perhaps he sees himself as a vampire."

"He certainly dresses like one, in those morbid black suits. Dresses like a damn mortician."

"But I suspect that the fangs have more to do with how he sees us than how he sees himself."

"Yeah? And how does he see us?"

"As prey. He's the Big Bad Wolf and everyone else—"

"Is just a bunch of little pigs."

"Sheep for the slaughter. That's what I think the fangs symbolize. He's the ultimate predator, the top of the food chain, and the rest of humanity are his cattle."

They were nearing the end of one of the longest workdays either detective could remember when they pulled up in front of Reed's house. The police tape had been removed from the front door, and they could see Reed through the window, vacuuming the rug.

*How the hell do you vacuum up blood?* went through Baltimore's mind, but he kept the thought to himself, imagining a wet/dry vac filled with coagulated blood. *Maybe he shampooed it first,* he thought as he slipped from the car and started walking up the driveway toward the house.

Reed looked out the window, and he and the detective locked eyes. Reed threw down the vacuum cleaner and strode toward the door in a huff, swinging it wide before the detectives even reached it.

"Tell me you're here to tell me that Malcolm's been captured and not to ask me another bunch of stupid questions!"

Detective Bryant spoke up first.

"Relax, Mr. Cozen. We just have a few questions. It will only take a moment. It's good to see you've recovered so quickly."

"I still feel like I'm being jabbed in the ribs with an ice pick every time I sneeze, cough, or laugh. Of course, I haven't been doing much of the latter lately."

"May we come in? I promise we'll only be a moment."

Reed scowled, let out a long hissing breath, then turned and headed back inside the house, leaving the door open wide for the detectives to follow. His complexion was still pale and sallow, and he walked as if he was in constant fear of falling.

Detective Bryant bit the tip off a cigar and stuck it in his mouth without lighting it. Chewing cigars was, in Baltimore's opinion, one of Bryant's more disgusting habits, but he had to admit that actually smoking them would've been much worse. They followed Reed into the house that, for them, was still a murder scene, a particularly gruesome and nasty one at that. They knew that this was still Reed's home, but the idea of someone living there again seemed kind of sick, like someone taking up residence in a morgue. Baltimore noted that the vacuum he'd seen Reed running was in fact a shampooer, but that he had merely succeeded in making reddish brown suds where the huge bloodstains covered the carpet.

*He might as well write the Berber off as a loss,* Baltimore thought. It was unsalvageable. The coffee table was gone, and the walls had been scrubbed, spackled, and repainted, but no matter what he did to the house, it was still a murder scene.

"We found Malcolm's accomplice," Detective Baltimore offered.

"Did he tell you where Malcolm is? Did you catch him?"

"The man was dead."

"He was more than dead. He was destroyed, ripped apart," Detective Bryant added.

"Christ. Well, at least now you know I was telling the truth. You know that night, when it was all happening, I wondered why Malcolm hadn't killed that guy. It seemed out of character for him to have an accomplice. I think he brought the guy for my benefit … to make sure I knew that the killings were all about me. I knew that guy was a dead man. The way Malcolm kept calling him 'white boy.'"

"White boy? Why did that make you think he would kill him?"

"Malcolm never called anyone by their real names, not even Reneé and Natasha. He would call them white girl, white boy, bitch, ho, fool, nigga. That is, when he found it absolutely necessary to address someone.

Most often, he ignored people altogether. I was the only one he called by name. I asked him about it one time, and he said he was depersonalizing them. He said he'd read somewhere that in hostage situations, police always try to get the suspects to understand that their victims were real people with real lives and not just objects, so they would repeat the hostages' names over and over again and try to get the suspects to refer to them by name. He said this was supposed to make it harder for the suspects to murder their victims because it's easier to murder some anonymous white girl than it is to kill Mrs. Margaret Jones, mother of three, of 252 Greenblade Drive. So he made it a point to never call anyone by name in case he had to kill them one day."

Reed smirked and shook his head as memories from his high school years began to come back to him.

"He called me white boy for the first two weeks I knew him. He would walk by my table at lunch and smack me in the back of the head. Sometimes, he would knock over my milk or steal my dessert. Once, he just took my entire lunch. I stood up to say something, I don't know, 'Give me my lunch back, please, sir' or something like that, and he punched me in the gut so hard it knocked all the wind out of me and I nearly passed out. I fell underneath the table, and he sat down right beside where I'd fallen and ate my lunch. A few days later, he sat down and talked with me. He even bought me lunch that day. After we'd been friends for about a year, I asked him why he picked on me like that when we first met. You know what he said? He said he did it because he wanted me to know what it would be like to be his enemy before he could trust me to be his friend."

"Guess he was wrong," Detective Bryant mumbled.

"You know, the way you talk about Malcolm, like he was some psychopath, makes me wonder why you were friends with him in the first place. I mean, if he was as terrible as you say he was, why'd you become his best friend?" Baltimore was going into his interrogation mode.

"Everyone was afraid of Malcolm. Even back then, you knew the guy was dangerous, but that was the attraction. There wasn't a person in school who didn't want to be his friend."

"Why?"

"Seriously? You don't get it? Did you ever watch those Godzilla movies when you were a kid?"

"Godzilla movies? Yeah, sure. Who didn't?"

"Not the original one, but the campy sequels and remakes where Godzilla would rise out of the water, destroy half of Tokyo, make friends with a young Japanese kid, then save the world from some space monster? If you had the chance to be that kid, the one who made friends with Godzilla, would you turn it down? Every kid who ever watched one of those films wished *he* was the one. Imagine what it would be like to walk around town with Godzilla! You could do whatever you wanted. I mean, who's gonna say 'no' to you with Godzilla standing over your left shoulder? Well, that's what it was like being friends with Malcolm. It was like palling around with Godzilla."

"So, if it was so great, why did you fuck it up?"

"Because after a while, it's not good enough to just be Godzilla's friend … you want to be Godzilla."

Baltimore looked at Bryant, and they both turned back to look at Reed.

"Mr. Cozen, I have a very difficult question to ask you, and there's no delicate way to put it. Mr. Cozen, did you sexually molest your daughter?"

All the color drained from Reed's face, then returned in a scalding rush of red.

"What the fuck kind of question is that? Hell no, I didn't have sex with my daughter!"

"We understand that there were some accusations."

"That old bitch from the school? She's out of her goddamned mind! She brought Human Services to my house, and they almost took my babies away, all because she thought I hugged and kissed my kids too much. Fuck no, I never touched my daughter!"

"Mr. Cozen, exactly what were you and your wife seeing a marriage counselor about?"

"None of your fucking business!"

"We can get a warrant for the counselor's records, but we would prefer you volunteered the information. If we have to subpoena the records, we will." Baltimore lied. He knew no judge would break doctor/patient privilege, but he was hoping Reed didn't know that.

"Fuck you. Get a damn warrant then and get out of my house!"

"It's a simple question. If you've got nothing to hide, just answer it. There's no need to make this—"

"GET THE FUCK OUT!" Reed was shaking with anger, and tears were now rolling down his cheeks.

Detective Bryant turned and walked out the door, dragging Baltimore along with him. The young detective wasn't done yet, though...he still wanted answers.

"What're you hiding? We know you're hiding something!"

"GET OUT!" Reed winced, grabbed his sides, and plopped down on the couch, still glaring murderously at the two cops as they sauntered out the door.

"Come on, Titus. You've said enough."

When they got outside, Bryant grabbed Baltimore by the lapels and nearly lifted him off the ground.

"What the fuck was all that? That was completely out of line!"

"Fuck that! That sonavubitch knows something! You don't think it's a little strange that he just moved back in to the same house where his family was murdered? He could have gone to a motel, stayed with friends or family, but he goes back there and starts spring cleaning. Would you ever go back in that house if it was you?" He stared back at Bryant, not backing down.

Bryant let him go and walked to the car.

"Well, if he does know something, we're never gonna get it out of him now. He'll probably lawyer up and have a restraining order on both our asses by the morning, if not a fucking lawsuit."

They climbed into the car, and James hit the accelerator, stomping it to the floor and roaring away from the curb, taking his frustration out on the Intrepid's transmission. Baltimore was already planning to approach Reed again. He had to know what Reed knew.

Detective Bryant found himself back at the Star Bar, wondering what the hell was wrong with him. He was so exhausted he could barely keep his eyes open on the short drive from the precinct. He hadn't eaten since breakfast, which was contributing to his fatigue. He had maybe six hours before he had to get up and hit the gym for the first time since the case began and try to save his physique before his muscles began to atrophy. After the gym, it was back to work again. Still, he intended on spending every spare second until then with CC, even if that meant paying for lap dances.

Bryant had an anxious moment as he entered the club, when he was afraid CC wasn't there. He wandered the club, fending off advances from writhing, topless, silicone Barbie dolls eager to grind their g-stringed asses into his groin for twenty dollars. When he finally spotted CC, she was doing just that with an overweight, middle-aged financial district shark in a blue Botany 500 suit that was at least two sizes too small and bursting at the seams. Even though the club had a hands-off policy, it was loosely enforced. The man was eagerly rubbing his hands across her generous ass, which was bouncing mere inches from his face. Bryant was surprised that he felt not an ounce of jealousy. In fact, he felt pity for the shark-man. As soon as he ran out of money, CC would be gone and he'd be abandoned to deal with his erection all by himself.

CC spotted Bryant and winked, then turned back to her businessman, whispered in his ear, at which point he produced two crisp one-hundred-dollar bills and stuffed them in her G-string. CC smiled, winked at Bryant again, and went back to bouncing her ass in greaseball's face. Once again, Bryant felt sorry for the guy. He knew that CC would keep him hypnotized by her superior posterior until every large bill in his wallet and most of the small ones had found their way into her G-string, then she would go find another lonely, fat, horny businessman and liberate his paycheck as well. Bryant knew because such had been his fate on far too many nights. But not this night. Tonight, all he wanted was to take CC home with him and pretend they were married for a few hours before he had to send her home to her real husband. He sat back, ordered a drink, and waited for CC to drain her mark dry.

As he watched her work her latest sucker—hips swaying in a seductive bump and grind, eyes half-lidded, lips slightly parted, slightly puckered, slightly quivering in a convincing parody of ecstasy—Bryant found it amusing that so many moral activists thought it was the women in these places who were used and exploited. All he ever saw were the visually stimulated sex-drives of countless men being exploited to the economic advantage of the women and the people who employed them.

Bryant shook his head and chuckled to himself as yet another hundred-dollar bill slipped from the man's wallet into CC's underwear. He couldn't help wonder just how much these women made a night. He'd heard stories of women who made a thousand, up to two thousand a night. He thought those figures were just exaggerations and rumors started by the owners of these clubs to lure more girls into the profession. Now he wasn't sure those numbers were so farfetched.

Detective James Bryant was so engrossed in the parade of glistening, perfumed flesh that he didn't notice the shadow sitting motionlessly in a corner, a shadow darker than the other shadows, more substantial. A shadow that tensed and flexed, anxious but cautious, watching and waiting, smiling a savage silver smile.

# XXI.

Malcolm watched the old Black detective scan the crowd of jiggling naked bodies with a lust that seemed strangely similar to his own predatory hunger. He watched as, time and time again, the detective's eyes fixed on the blonde with the voluptuous ass and his hunger doubled and redoubled.

Malcolm smiled. It was the same choice he would have made were he in search of that particular type of game. Not because of her ass but because she looked like a victim, like prey. He noticed that the stripper was looking back at the detective, a less than inconspicuous smile playing across her lips. There was a connection. That was something he could use. The techno-rap song thundering through the small club ended, and the blonde slipped from the lap of the overweight suit she'd been grinding. She stashed his money in her G-string and walked off with a practiced wiggle that looked too deliberate, too unnatural, and too rehearsed to be sexy as she made her way over to the detective. The oblivious stripper passed Malcolm as he sipped club soda, grinned, and licked his lips, imagining what her heart would taste like.

Detective Bryant was so focused on CC that his eyes passed over the grinning shadow eyeing him from the corner without registering a thing. He was off-duty, and his alarms were all shut down for the night. The only thing Bryant was aware of was his own need, his own lust, and what he needed, what he lusted for, was CC. She flowed across the room toward him like something smooth and creamy that someone poured out of a jar. Something poured across chocolate. Bryant was pleased to see the same hunger in her eyes that he knew was in his own. She took his hand, then dropped it and wrapped her arms around him instead.

"I'm glad you came to see me."

"I'm glad I came too. You didn't have any problems with your old man about the other night, did you?"

"He doesn't care if I'm home or not as long as I keep money in the bank account so he can afford to sit on his ass and do nothing all day."

"Yeah, that's about the type of man I'd figured him to be."

CC's face turned sad for a moment. She seemed to grow weary and depressed all at once. Bryant instantly regretted his comment.

"He was a good man once, ambitious, motivated ... I spoiled him. I made things too easy for him. Why be a man when no one expects you to be? When you have a wife who lets you lay around drinking and smoking pot like some rebellious teenager, who lets you take her for granted, take advantage of her? I'd be the same way if I were in his shoes. You know, I started stripping to help pay his way through law school. He got his BA in Legal Studies, enrolled in Law School at University of Penn, and dropped out after the first semester. He keeps talking about going back, but why should he when he has a fool like me to keep paying all his bills for him?"

"You didn't make him that way, CC. Just because this asshole took your kindness for weakness doesn't mean it was weakness and not kindness. Some people would appreciate your sacrifices, not take advantage of them."

"Unfortunately, I didn't marry one of those type of people."

Bryant was trying his best to sound loving and supportive, but everything he said just seemed to make her more depressed. Her arms were still wrapped around his waist, her body still pressed against him, and he couldn't help feeling guilty for the erection that was poking through his pants into her stomach. Not very sensitive of him. His hands kept straying down her backside and lightly rubbing her buttocks, cupping first one cheek, then the other and softly squeezing. Detective James Bryant wasn't the "Alan Alda-shoulder-to-cry-on-best friend" type. He was the "face-first-into-the-pillow, banging-against-the-headboard, smack-your-ass, who's-your-daddy?" type.

Try as he might to stay focused on CC's problems, he was already wishing he could change the subject to something a little more likely to lead to them doing more in the bedroom tonight than cuddling and talking. Not that he was against cuddling or talking. He just preferred to do that after messing up the sheets a little.

"Look, let's just forget about your husband and go have some fun. I'll make sure you have no reason to think of any other man for at least an hour or two."

CC smiled.

"That sounds good to me."

"I'll meet you outside."

"Fuck it. I'll walk out with you. You're a cop. What the fuck can they say? I'll just tell them I'm helping you with a case." CC giggled and took Bryant's arm as they walked out the door.

"And you are, believe me. You're just the type of help I need right now … the perfect medicine." Once they were outside the club, Bryant reached down and squeezed her butt again.

# XXIII.

Inside the Star Bar, the darkness in the back of the club stirred. Malcolm rose and moved with the shadows surrounding him. He watched the pair slip from the club arm-in-arm and was pretty sure he knew where they were going. This was his chance to find out where the detective lived. He'd been following the man all day, learning his habits, studying him. That other detective, Baltimore, was fairly uncomplicated, predictable, and would be easy to deal with. He knew what made the man tick.

Detective Baltimore was full of illusions. He believed in right and wrong, good and bad, in justice, and he was fighting hard to hold on to these illusions even though his own chosen profession was so perfectly designed to dispel them. He'd convinced himself that he and the rest of the police force, and possibly the church and the little old lady who lived down the street and baked pies and cookies for the neighborhood kids on Christmas and the nurse who bandaged his booboo when he was ten and fell off his skateboard and the little kids who rode the school bus that he passed every morning on the way to work, were the good guys. They were all part of his world, the world of all that was good and just. They were what balanced all the horror he witnessed on the streets. They were what he was fighting to protect, even though every day, he discovered the kids on the school bus carried guns to class and sold dope behind the jungle gym. His fellow police officers were robbing drug dealers, raping prostitutes, brutalizing suspects, manufacturing evidence, and taking bribes. The nurse was stealing morphine from her patients to feed her own habit. The old lady who baked the pies was luring kids into her home and sexually abusing them.

Baltimore was the type of cop who could see all the sickness and corruption inside of people and still hold on to his illusions because he needed them. Without them, he could not function. He needed to believe that there were monsters like Malcolm and that there were the innocent people the monsters preyed on and then there were the heroes.

Reality, the way Malcolm saw it, was that they were all monsters, everyone. They were all evil and corrupt, and they all deserved to die. That punk-ass detective was weak and stupid and would soon be dead.

Malcolm didn't believe that Detective Baltimore could pose him any real threat. He didn't believe any man could, but the detective's nuisance factor was rising. Right now, Malcolm was sure that Detective Baltimore was harassing Reed again. After Bryant dropped Baltimore at the station, Malcolm watched him head over to the expressway, and he could guess where the man was headed. Baltimore held no surprises for him. He would be easy prey.

Detective Bryant was the more difficult man to figure. He held no illusions, no grandiose ideas about morality or justice, and he possessed the same type of hunger that burned in Malcolm. It was in his eyes when he looked at the stripper. He could see the violent passion burning like funeral pyres in the detective's dark irises. Malcolm wondered what kept a man like that from becoming a man like him. But he was pretty sure he knew the answer. There was no Reed in Detective Bryant's life, no huge traumatic event to wrench away his most integral, most necessary illusions, to take away the very beliefs that told him every day that the next breath was worth taking, worth the effort of inhaling and exhaling. That life was worth the struggle to acquire the commodities of existence. Reed had made Malcolm the man he was, and Detective Bryant had no Reed. But he did have a Malcolm, and that was even better … or even worse.

Malcolm slid into a stolen Jeep Cherokee, fortunate that none of the blood from the man he'd car-jacked was still on the seat to ruin his new Armani suit. The leather had cleaned up well. He'd finally ditched the Impala. Now that both his and the car's descriptions were all over the airwaves, he wouldn't stand a chance driving around in that thing. It would draw cops faster than a 24-hour donut shop.

Malcolm watched the detective drive off. He cradled the Mossberg pistol grip pump shotgun that hung down in the extra-long right pocket of his Hugo Boss trench coat, started up the engine, put the Jeep in gear, and followed after Bryant. Malcolm tried following several car lengths behind but, after nearly losing him twice, narrowed the space between them until he was directly behind the detective's car. The detective was too caught up in the stripper to notice him anyway.

Malcolm brought the Jeep to a halt and parked it down the block from the detective's house. He watched the detective pull the Dodge into the driveway and practically sprint into the house with CC in tow. He imagined the two ripping off each other's clothes with a passion that resembled fury, never making it to the bedroom, their last strips of clothing hitting the kitchen floor as the couple followed them down. Their bodies crashing into each other in a violent maelstrom of flesh against sweating flesh. Then he imagined what he would do to her, and his thoughts filled with blood and screams.

Up and down the block, lights burned bright behind drawn curtains and blinds, but Malcolm knew the residents had long gone to sleep. They left the lights on so that potential burglars would think they were still awake. It was an old trick that no longer worked. Criminals no longer cared if people were awake or not. He guessed the detective's neighbors had never heard of home invasion robberies.

From bedroom windows, the flickering blue light and muffled canned laughter of TV sets played for sleeping viewers. Somewhere down the block, a stereo blared. Cats stalked through the bushes and shrubs in front of the neighboring houses, hunting rodents. An occasional car passed.

Children's bikes and toys were strewn at random on several of the small patches of grass and dirt that passed for lawns in Philadelphia, although, as lawns went, Mt. Airy did tend to be a bit more lush than other parts of Philly. Dogs yapped behind fences, sensing something fierce on the wind, a coming storm.

Malcolm crossed the street and walked over to the detective's house. He cursed to himself as his boots sank into damp earth with each step he took on his way to the back of the house. He'd just gotten the damned things shined, and now, with all the heat around him, he'd have to shine them himself this time. He couldn't risk getting caught over muddy boots. A rose bush had grown wild on the chain link fence that separated the detective's house from his neighbor's, and Malcolm grimaced in anger as the thorns snagged his new suit. He was getting sick of Armani anyway. The next suit would have to be another Hugo Boss. They just seemed to fit his build better. Malcolm knew it wouldn't take the cops long to figure out that he was still buying suits with Paul's credit cards, but he wasn't about to walk around in rags. He'd have to use them once more and then destroy them before the cops could use them to track him down.

Malcolm crept up to the back door, making hardly a sound despite his muddy boots. Raccoons, possums, alley cats, and stray dogs called to each other beneath the moonlight. The racket was nerve-wrenching in the otherwise still night. Malcolm froze for a second, cursing the damn animals silently before peering through the small window in the backdoor. There were no lights on in the house, but Malcolm could still make out the entwined forms of the detective and the stripper coupling furiously on the vinyl floor just as he'd imagined it, minus the pain and the blood.

Detective James Bryant was not as dangerous as Malcolm thought, not like him at all. They never were. They all had weaknesses, and Malcolm was witnessing Detective Bryant's. He could smash through that flimsy kitchen door and kill them both if he wanted. But he had other plans. He would deal with the other detective first, the white boy, Titus Baltimore. Once the white boy had been dealt with, this one would drown his sorrows in pussy and leave Malcolm free to deal with Reed without interference. Malcolm smiled and slipped back into the shadows just as Bryant looked up at the little window in the kitchen door and convinced himself that he hadn't seen a face there.

# XXIV.

Reed was barely coherent when he called his attorney, ranting about police harassment, a field in which business and entertainment lawyer Jacob Lanski was not at all experienced. Jacob Lanski had been Reed's lawyer since he sold his first novel and was excellent at negotiating contracts to get both him and his clients the most money possible. But Reed doubted the man had ever been in a courtroom or been before a judge standing next to a client in handcuffs, which sounded exactly like where Reed was heading. Guilty or innocent, when the Philadelphia Police Department decided they had a good suspect, that suspect quickly became a defendant. Evidence got misplaced, witness's testimonies changed, and innocent men went to jail. Reed was certain the man wanted no part of this and would try to find any excuse to avoid getting involved in what was about to become a very complicated drama, but leaving Reed hanging now could mean losing a very lucrative client. Like it or not, the man was stuck if he still wanted Reed as a client.

"Calm down, Reed. Calm down. Just tell me what's going on."

"These cops, they're treating me like I killed my

own family. They think Malcolm and I did it together or something. Every time I turn around, they're showing up on my doorstep. They've got me so pissed off I can't even grieve! Jacob, my family's dead! Doesn't anybody understand that? It's like my whole life just ended, and these bastards are treating me like I'm a damn criminal!"

"Give me the two officers' names and we'll get a restraining order right away."

"Detective Titus Baltimore and Detective Bryant … uh … James Bryant, I think. I'm not sure. He's the quiet one. It's the other one, Detective Baltimore. He's the real asshole. Oh fuck! You're not going to fucking believe this! I can't believe this sonuvabitch! He's back! That fucking detective … Baltimore … He's walking up my fucking driveway right now!"

"You've got to be kidding me. I'll take care of this. Let me make a few calls. Be cooperative. Don't give him any reason to distrust you. You've got nothing to hide. I'm on my way over there."

"I don't want to say shit to this guy. I think he's trying to frame me or something."

"Then don't. Just wait for me to get there."

# XXV.

Immediately after he was dropped off at the police station, Baltimore decided to double back for one more shot at Mr. Cozen. He knew he'd blown it earlier, and if he didn't get to him tonight, there'd no doubt be a restraining order against him by the morning. Before he drove back to Reed's house, he made one more call to the Cozens' marriage counselor, a psychiatrist named Doctor David Berkowitz.

Baltimore spent nearly half an hour negotiating his way through the doctor's tedious message system before he finally managed to speak to his equally tedious receptionist. His lips were nearly exhausted from kissing the secretary's ass by the time he spoke to Dr. Berkowitz.

The doctor's responses were predictably guarded. Over and over, the doctor reiterated his stance: even in capital crimes, doctor/patient privilege still applied. But Baltimore was persistent. In a last-ditch effort, Baltimore described the condition of Jennie Cozen's body.

"Her attacker stabbed the knife in so deep that it went straight through her. Her ribcage was bisected. She was cut from her collarbone down to her pelvic bone, stabbed half a dozen times with a bowie knife nearly as big as her. He nearly split her in half. And she was alive through all of it. Can you imagine what that must have felt like? How terrified that little girl must have been? How much agony she must have been in?"

The doctor's voice choked with emotion.

"Stop. That's enough."

"Then help me, doc. I need your help."

"Talk to the babysitter."

He hung up before Baltimore could ask another question or thank him. Baltimore already had the girl's name and address in his notebook. He decided not to bother with a phone call and drove to the girl's house instead. The house was just around the corner from where the Cozens lived, on an identical cul-de-sac, in a nearly identical home.

Every new home development was filled with cul-de-sacs. It made them all mazes that were impossible to navigate without a GPS. Even with his Garmin, Baltimore got lost twice before he found the babysitter's modest single-story home, tucked at the end of yet another dead-end street.

The girl's father opened the door, looking tired and weak in the way middle-class people who overworked themselves in pursuit of wealth tended to look—world weary from the hours of overtime, the endless days of plotting and scheming, the mad, back-stabbing, cut-throat, free-for-all scramble up the corporate ladder, all for the sake of the next promotion, the elusive six-figure salary, and the newer, bigger, custom-built house. Suburbanites worked harder to escape the middle-class than poor folks worked to escape the ghetto. The babysitter's father had the $50,000 BMW, the $22,000 Ford mini-van, $160,000 cracker box house, and a wife with a dependency on cosmetic surgery and Xanax.

Keeping up with the Joneses had become their religion. The guy probably made a $70,000 a year income and carried $100,000 in debt. Detective Baltimore stared nakedly at the man's painful-looking hair plugs and his wife's tight, shiny skin. Her face was a mask of fine, smooth scar tissue like the skin grafts on burn victims, almost plastic. Her breasts were ridiculously round, like scoops of ice cream, and spaced too far apart. He could probably fit his entire foot between her breasts and not touch either of them. They looked about as natural as wax fruit.

Detective Baltimore stifled his urge to slap both of them and shake them until they woke up. Instead, he introduced himself, flashed them his badge, and asked to see Crissy.

"Homicide? But … what?"

"She's not in any trouble. I just want to ask her some questions about Mr. Cozen."

"Oh, that sick bastard."

"John!" Mrs. Green looked suddenly embarrassed.

"That sonuvabitch molested our little girl!" John Green was turning red. Anger flashed in his eyes, and then all of a sudden, it snuffed out and he just looked tired.

"Is this true?"

"Well, yes and no." Mrs. Evelyn Green spoke up. Her voice was low and husky, and she dragged out her words as she spoke like a phone sex operator. She was in her 40s but looked nothing like a housewife and more like a madam for a high-class whorehouse. She was what was known as a MILF or a cougar. She was a little *too* coy and sexual, and the way she stared directly into Baltimore's eyes when she spoke and then looked away smiling was unnerving. She seemed to be flirting almost unconsciously, like a woman who hadn't been fucked in a while and needed it more than even she was willing to admit.

"What do you mean, yes and no?"

"I mean that Crissy is a little …" She paused and looked away, smiling demurely. When she turned back to Baltimore, she stared deep into his icy blue eyes as if challenging him. "She's a little fast. She wasn't a virgin before Mr. Cozen, and she kind of made it clear to us that she seduced him."

*I wonder where she got that from?* Baltimore wondered, trying hard not to stare at Mrs. Green's unnaturally large breasts, squeezed into a T-shirt obviously purchased for the way they accentuated the plastic surgeon's handiwork. Her large, dark nipples poked shamelessly through the fabric. She smiled when she noticed him staring at them, then seemed to wave them at him, shaking them so they jiggled ever so slightly. It could've been accidental, but he doubted it.

"That's why we didn't press charges. It's bad enough with the reputation she already has. But seducing a man twice her age? What school could we send her to once that got out?"

Mr. Green flopped down in his chair and dropped his head down into his hands.

"Little slut," he moaned.

Baltimore talked with the girl's mother and father for nearly 20 minutes before spending another torturous half-hour with an emotional sixeen-year-old girl who cursed Mr. Cozen out of one side of her mouth while declaring her love for him out of the other. Detective Baltimore was shaken and angry when he left the Greens' house; the little girl had tried to flirt with him too. Crissy interrupted him midway through his questioning to ask him if he was as good in bed as he looked. He had to restrain himself from slapping the shit out of her. He called the parents into the room to make sure she didn't try anything with him that could get him thrown into jail. Once Mr. and Mrs. Green were in the room, she'd gone into graphic descriptions of her "love affair" with Mr. Cozen, delighting in the shock and discomfort on her parents' faces. When Baltimore left the girl's home, he felt like puking. Crissy definitely had problems, but Reed had still taken advantage of her.

Baltimore pulled himself together, shaking off his anger and revulsion, reminding himself that this was probably his last shot at Reed. He had tried the full frontal assault, and that was unsuccessful, so now he figured maybe he could sweet talk the man. After all, his lips were already in practice from Doctor Berkowitz's receptionist. Why let his newly acquired ass-kissing skills go to waste?

"Go away, Detective. I have nothing to say to you. Now get off my property!"

Detective Baltimore stood on the porch, ringing the doorbell, but Reed refused to open the door. Baltimore resisted the urge to kick it in.

"Look, Mr. Cozen. I just wanted to apologize for upsetting you earlier. I was completely out of line, and I am sorry if I caused you any inconvenience."

"Okay, so you've apologized. Now go!"

"I know you're upset, but Malcolm is out there killing people, and we've got no clue to his whereabouts. Something you know just might lead us to him. You've got to help us, Mr. Cozen."

Baltimore was getting better and better at begging for help.

"Detective, I'm on the phone with my lawyer. If you don't get off my porch right now, I swear I'll have your badge!"

"Please, Mr. Cozen. What if Malcolm takes another family tonight and something you know could've stopped him? Could you live with that? Because I swear, restraining order or not, if that happens, I will never leave you alone. I don't care if you're involved or not, guilty or not. Once I tell a jury about those allegations of child molestation and I get the little girl up the street to talk about your little love affair, you'll be lucky to get life without parole."

"Please, Detective, just go away."

"Just answer a few more questions, and tomorrow, I'm out of your life for good ... well, at least until the trial."

"Ha! You think you're gonna get Malcolm to stand trial? If you don't kill him the second you see him, he'll definitely kill you."

Baltimore smirked.

"Listen, I think that you having sex with your babysitter is just plain sick, but since the parents don't want to press charges and it doesn't have any bearing on my investigation, I really don't care. But if it turns out that you know something that you're not telling me, I'll use this little incident to bury you."

Reed finally opened the door. Baltimore's smile widened.

"Okay, Detective, you win. What do you want me to tell you?"

Baltimore stepped through the door and withdrew a pen and pad.

"Well, first off, I want you to convince me that you had nothing to do with your family's murder."

"Jesus Christ, Detective! If I was working with Malcolm, would I be so eager for you to catch him?"

Baltimore nodded and raised an eyebrow.

"Well, actually you seem more eager for me to kill him than to catch him—"

"I just want you to stop him before he kills me, and the only way you're gonna stop him is to shoot on sight. If you think I'm lying and just trying to get Malcolm killed so he can't implicate me, then go ahead and try and take him alive. I'll make sure to come to your funeral."

"Is this supposed to be convincing me?"

"Look, Detective, sure I fucked up by sleeping with Crissy. I fucked up my marriage, my reputation. But my wife and I were putting it all back together. She was sticking by me. I talked it over with the girl's family. They weren't gonna press charges. Everything was gonna be all right. So why would I want my family dead? And why would Malcolm help me if I did? Even if you don't believe that I loved my family, you know enough about Malcolm to know that he hates me. Why would he do me any favors?"

Baltimore was visibly annoyed at Reed's logic. But he couldn't deny it either. He was starting to believe the man.

"Okay, then the next thing is ..."

Detective Baltimore leaned forward, looking deeply into Reed's eyes. He was still looking for the guilt he'd seen there before, but now all he saw was fear and profound sadness. The man was scared half to death.

"Where do you think I can find Malcolm?"

"I told you, I have no idea where he is. I hadn't seen him in fifteen years before he showed up on my doorstep. "

"But he's been watching you. He's been right there with you for the last fifteen years."

"What do you mean?"

"Mr. Cozen, when did you and your wife get married? Or rather, when did you first get serious? When did you two move in together?"

"I don't remember the exact date. It was back in 2000. In February, I think. We got married in June."

"The Chaperone killings began in July of 2000. And when was Jennie born?"

"Um ... January seventeenth, 2001."

"The same year the Family Man killings began. Your life is the pattern. When you were single, he stalked single guys. You get married, he switches to couples, and even more telling, the attacks become more sadistic. Most of the violence is now aimed at the woman, as if Malcolm was punishing them for being with their husbands and boyfriends. That's why we started calling the killer The Chaperone, because it seemed like he was punishing the couples for some moral indiscretion. But now it's obvious that the increased violence was due to jealousy. Malcolm wanted you all to himself. That's why we never made the connection between The Pine

St. Slasher and The Chaperone. The women didn't fit the pattern. A guy stalks gay men and then suddenly switches to couples and starts raping and mutilating the women? It didn't fit. But, if he was rehearsing you and your wife's murder, it fits."

"You know, it slipped my mind before now, but that's how he put it to me. He said that the other killings were practice runs."

Baltimore scribbled a note in his pad.

"See, that makes sense. You start a family and he starts killing families. That explains the children. We could never understand why he killed the kids, but that explains it. He was patterning his killing spree after you."

Reed went silent for a second, and his eyes glazed with a far-off look that Baltimore recognized as horror and resignation.

"So, then he definitely won't stop until I'm dead. My death completes the pattern."

Baltimore said nothing.

"Did you check his mom's house?"

"We've got round-the-clock surveillance on Mrs. Davis. And Malcolm definitely isn't there."

"If Rick is still around, he might go to his house."

"Who's Rick?"

"He's mini-Malcolm, another little psychopath who used to hang around with Malcolm because he got off on violence. I would have expected him to be Malcolm's accomplice in this. They grew up in the same neighborhood, just a few blocks from one another. Rick wasn't that bright, though, and he had severe anger management problems. He might be in prison already, or dead.

"He was extremely vicious and would fly into a rage without provocation, but he was just a little guy, a few inches shorter than I was. About five-foot-five inches, five-foot six-inches, only a hundred-twenty, a hundred and thirty pounds. He had wet dreams about being as big as Malcolm. The rest of us had nightmares about him getting that big. A stupid, out-of-control Malcolm who could flip out on anyone for any reason was about the worst thing I could've imagined."

"Well, now we've got a highly intelligent, extremely cunning, out-of-control Malcolm who could murder anyone for any reason."

"Oh, I've got a reason," Malcolm said as he stepped into the room behind Detective Baltimore, grabbing Baltimore by the hair and jerking his head back. Baltimore cried out in surprise and groped for his Glock. When he saw the glint of surgical steel in Malcolm's free hand, he knew he would never get to his weapon in time to save his life.

# XXVI.

Reed jumped as if someone had sent 1000 volts through the floor. He hadn't locked the door behind the detective and had left it half-open, anticipating the detective would be leaving soon. So neither of them heard Malcolm slip into the house. Death was once again standing in Reed's house, and Reed was once again at its mercy.

Reed shuffled backwards, yelping and screaming like a frightened infant, knocking over the rug shampooer, stumbling, and splashing down in the bloody foam and suds. Malcolm was smiling. He ran his tongue over his platinum tipped canines as he stabbed a long Japanese tanto knife into Detective Titus Baltimore's neck and ripped it across the man's throat with one hand, twisting his head in the opposite direction with the other. Detective Baltimore struggled to free his Glock nine-millimeter from its shoulder holster.

Malcolm smiled as the gun came out of its holster and the detective attempted to point it over his shoulder at Malcolm's head. The huge Black man appeared to be amused by the detective's valiant struggle for survival. Reed clamped his hands over his ears to muffle the whistling, wheezing gurgle coming from the detective's throat.

Despite Baltimore's obviously mortal wound, he still tried to aim the gun at Malcolm's head. Reed paused, hopeful that the detective would succeed and it would all be over. Malcolm would be out of his life forever.

The good guy couldn't die, could he?

In Reed's upright and moral world, the hero would somehow aim the gun over his shoulder into Malcolm's face and blow him away. Then Reed would get to the phone and call the paramedics, who would arrive just in time to save the detective's life. But Reed was learning more and more that his world had changed. Everything he'd known, all the laws and rules he'd come to believe in were gone for good. And this new world he now found himself trapped in was a dark and terrible place where no one escaped unscathed.

Malcolm laughed, a harsh, guttural, feral bark that made Reed cringe. Then he thrust the tip of a long, thin knife that looked like a miniature sword through Detective Baltimore's eye socket, sinking the blade into his skull up to the hilt. Reed watched the detective's gun hand fall limply to the ground, the Glock tumble down across the blood-stained Berber carpeting, and all hope fall with it.

Reed backed up across the room as far as he could and curled up in a corner, holding his knees and moaning, waiting for the killing blow, hoping Malcolm would have more mercy on him than he'd had on Linda and feeling like shit for it. But he didn't want to suffer like Linda had. Oh god, he didn't want to hurt like that.

"If you kept him out of it like I told you to, he'd still be alive. Who you gonna call now, Reed? How many more people you want to get killed? It's just you and me now, Reed. This is between you and me."

Reed was trembling and weeping.

"Please. Please don't. Don't hurt me."

Malcolm dropped Detective Baltimore's ruined corpse to the floor, studied it for a second with a look of satisfaction, turned, and walked out the door.

Reed was still curled into a fetal position, watching the blood gush from the detective's lacerated throat onto the carpet that was still stained with the blood of his wife and children. He stared at the hilt of the knife sticking out of Detective Baltimore's eye socket. The blade completely disappeared into the detective's skull. He stared into Baltimore's remaining eye. It was completely still, empty of any life. The detective was gone. His life had fled and left its bleeding shell in Reed's living room. It was only then that Reed became aware of his own inexplicable survival. He was still alive. For some bizarre reason, Malcolm had once again allowed him to live when he could have snuffed him out as easily as blowing out a candle.

"What the hell do you want from me?"

But Reed knew. He knew what Malcolm wanted the day he killed his family. He wanted Reed to come to him, willingly, to try to stop him. He wanted Reed to come at him with the same rage and hatred Malcolm had shown his family. He wanted Reed to come to him with a heart craving vengeance so he could carve that heart from his chest. Reed's head filled with memories of his lost family smiling, laughing, and then finally screaming in horror as Malcolm tore them apart. He remembered his childhood, his high school years with Malcolm. He saw again the day he met the huge Black kid, the day he first accepted Malcolm's friendship, the day he betrayed that friendship. He saw the blade ripping across the detective's throat. He saw it ripping across his own throat.

Reed felt the scream rising inside him, not in his throat but in his mind, a loud, agonized screech that rattled his teeth and twisted his thoughts. It was the sound of his family dying, and it stayed in his head and never reached his throat, becoming a chorus of screams. He could hear Jennie, Mark, Linda, and others, many others. It was the others that scared him the most. It sounded like hundreds. It grew louder and louder, wiping every thought from his mind, every thought but one … killing Malcolm. That was the one thought that seemed to quiet the screams. He seized it and followed it out of the madness. Reed knew he would stand almost no chance against Malcolm. Still, he picked up Detective Baltimore's Glock and stepped out of the house in search of his tormentor. He had only one clue to Malcolm's whereabouts, the same one he had given to the detective before Malcolm had taken him.

Rick's house.

# XXVII.

"Where the fuck were you! You were supposed to be watching the house! Where the fuck were you?"

Detective James Bryant attacked the two detectives, grabbing both of them by their throats and nearly driving them over the hood of the car. The entire eight-officer Family Man Task Force was there, and all of them rushed to pull Bryant off Detectives Trinidad and Nellis. Bryant fought them as they wrenched his hands from the detectives' throats and pulled him backward until he and the other officers all fell back against another squad car. Bryant pulled himself free and tried to go at the two detectives again, but the others grabbed him again. Trinidad was no punk, and he stepped up to Bryant as he raged in the arms of his fellow Task Force members and pointed his finger in Detective Bryant's face.

"Fuck you, James! Titus told us he had everything covered, and he was the primary on this case, not you. He told us we could go home. We'd already been watching the house for twelve hours straight with no sign of Malcolm. So we left. The next watch was coming on in two hours anyway. We figured the department was just trying to save some overtime. Baltimore made the call, not us. So fuck you. And don't you ever put your hands on me again, motherfucker."

Bryant glared at him, and Trinidad glared back.

"Besides, there was still one more surveillance team in place. Where the hell were they?"

All eyes turned to Detectives Wilson and Jones, who had been watching the Cozen house from a house directly across the street, taking pictures of everyone who came and went from that residence. They were unable to get a warrant to tap the phones or install listening devices, so they were virtually deaf, relying solely on visuals and long-range listening device. Wilson stepped up, unable to look Bryant in the eyes. He looked like a beaten fighter flinching at blows that hadn't even been thrown.

"All right, so what tha fuck happened?!"

"Well … uh … Mike went to pick up dinner, and I just turned around for a second to load the film. I … uh … had to go to the bathroom too. When I got back to the window and adjusted the camera, I saw Mr. Cozen coming out of the house with a gun in his hand. I hadn't heard any shots or anything, so I didn't think it was an emergency. I figured maybe Titus had already left. So I called Titus's cell to tell him the suspect was moving and that he was armed. After I didn't get an answer, I started looking up and down the street. That's when I saw that Baltimore's car was still parked up the block, and I knew something was wrong. I got down there as fast as I could, but by the time I got to the house, Mr. Cozen was gone and Titus was already dead."

"Reed couldn't have done this himself. Did you see Malcolm go in there?"

"No, but like I said, I was on the toilet for a few minutes, and he could've slipped in from the back of the house or something."

"Fuck! Fuck!" Bryant yelled at no one in particular. He shrugged off Lieutenant Woo, who was still restraining him, and stormed back into the house.

"We keep making mistakes and this motherfucker keeps getting lucky! I don't believe this shit!"

"But what if it wasn't Malcolm? What if Reed did it himself?"

Captain Kelly showed up, looking like he was ready to kill. Lieutenant Woo's eyes shifted from Captain Kelly to the patrol car as if seeking an escape route.

"Woo? What. Tha-fuck. Happened. Here?" He spoke calmly and deliberately, his deep voice rumbling like an engine revving up in some terrible machine.

The lieutenant was still looking around. He looked at each detective as if wondering why he had been singled out when he wasn't even at the scene, conveniently forgetting that he was supposed to be the head of the task force even though he had pretty much relegated that position to Baltimore and Bryant, whose case it was before the task force was ever established. Baltimore had been considered by most to be the primary on the case. The task force was more a public relations gimmick to make it look to the press as if the police were doing more about the case than they actually were. It looked better to say that they had an eight-man task force assigned to the case than two overworked detectives. But everyone here knew the truth. Still, Lieutenant Woo couldn't exactly point fingers at a dead man with his partner just yards away, ready to rip the head off anyone who looked at him sideways. Officially, this was Woo's case. So he was responsible.

"Uh … Detective Baltimore has been murdered."

"I fucking know that! How? How the fuck did this happen?"

"Well, um, Detective Baltimore went to interview the suspect without his partner. He dismissed his back-up and the surveillance team was … um … taking a break."

Captain Kelly looked at Wilson and Jones as if they were something he had scraped off his shoe.

"A break?" he grumbled.

"Well, see, um, Captain, I was in the bathroom and Mike had already left to get some cheese steak hoagies. I mean, we hadn't eaten in over six hours so ...."

The captain snarled with contempt and stepped up to the two detectives, staring them down until Wilson's mouth finally stopped moving.

"Wilson, if you say one more word, I'm going to unload an entire magazine in your ass, and the way you motherfuckers handle an investigation, I'm sure I'll get away with it. Now, where's James?"

"He was just here. He must be in there ... in the house." Lieutenant Woo pointed back toward the open door to Reed Cozen's house, which was now a crime scene for the second time in fewer than 72 hours.

"Has Crime Scene arrived yet?"

"Not yet, but they're on their way. The ME should be here soon too."

"Fine."

Bryant looked up when the captain walked in. He was sitting on the floor beside his fallen partner, and Captain Kelly squatted down next to him. Bryant and the captain stared at Baltimore's body in silence. The blade was still sticking out of Baltimore's eye-socket, and Bryant resisted the urge to pull it out himself. He didn't want to disturb the crime scene before it could at least be photographed and the Crime Scene Unit had gone over it for possible evidence, but he couldn't stand to see Baltimore like that.

"Where's his gun?"

"I think Mr. Cozen took it. We've got an APB out for him." Bryant was still staring at the body, his eyes unmoving. He seemed to be in shock.

"Wilson said he didn't hear any gunshots."

"I can't find any bullet holes either, and no shell casings. The CSU boys are bringing the metal detector, but I don't think they'll find anything. I don't think Titus had time to get off a shot. It looks like he was ambushed from behind."

"Do you think it was Reed?"

"Well, I'd like to think that Titus would have been able to take that little wimp, but who knows? My gut feeling is that it was Malcolm. But maybe it was both of them. Maybe Titus was right and they were working together. Wilson said he saw Reed walking out of the house with a gun. It might have been Baltimore's. And if he wasn't involved and it was Malcolm, why would he leave Reed alive again?"

"Why did he leave him alive the first time?"

"I don't know. It's all fucking crazy."

"I'm sorry, James. I know you two didn't always get along, but this must still be hard. I mean, losing a partner ... like this."

"I was just starting to like the little sonuvabitch too." Detective Bryant's eyes teared up for a moment. He shook his head, took a deep breath, and the tears were gone.

The CSU arrived and began their horribly efficient task of raking the crime scene for evidence. Bryant sat and stared while they went over Baltimore's corpse. He watched them dig under his fingernails. He watched them dust the knife sticking out of his eye socket for prints. He watched while they pulled little bits of fiber from his sports jacket with tweezers, then vacuumed the carpet from the door to where his body lay in case they missed anything. They vacuumed his jacket as well.

Dr. Medoff arrived, and Bryant was still kneeling at Baltimore's side. Captain Kelly intercepted the ME before he could tell Bryant to move out of the way and possibly wind up lying beside Baltimore in his own pool of blood. Dr. Medoff worked around Bryant ... and Bryant watched. After the ME was through making his preliminary report, his assistants lifted the body into a long, black, zippered bag and carried it out to the coroner's van. Bryant followed. The other officers stared in silence as their fallen comrade was carted off to the morgue.

Reporters were already on the scene. They buzzed about like flies. The smell of carrion was in the air, and they had come to glut themselves on Baltimore's remains. Bryant ignored them even when their buzzing rose to an annoying whine in his ears. He shrugged them off as he ducked under the yellow tape and crossed the street. He climbed into his patrol car and followed the coroner's van down to the city morgue.

# XVIII.

Captain Kelly was watching Detective Bryant's zombie-like stagger over to his squad car and was about to intercept him and suggest that he have one of the officers drive him home when Detective Nellis ran over to him in a panic.

"Captain Kelly! Sir, I can't get Vargas and Johnson on the radio. They're staked out at Mrs. Davis's house!" Nellis was holding his balding head in his hand, and his eyes were jittery and frightened.

"Now I can't get them on the radio. I can't think of a reason they'd  be out of their car."

"There ain't no toilet in that car is there?"

"No, sir."

"And you can't think of one reason why they'd be out of their car? Try them again before we call SWAT."

Nellis looked like he was about to cry as he raised the cell phone to his lips. The captain was playing it cool even though the hairs on the back of his neck were standing up. If he lost any more officers tonight, he'd probably be looking for a new job.

"Damn it, Angel! I thought something happened to you. Why aren't you guys answering your radios?"

Captain Kelly snatched the phone from Nellis and

barked into it at Detective Angel Vargas.

"Vargas, we just lost one of ours tonight. This shit has gotten serious. No more disappearing acts from anyone. I want everyone on their toes. Malcolm is now a cop killer. If you see him, do not try and apprehend him yourself. Call for backup and stand by. Maintain visual contact. Nobody try to be a hero on this. I don't want any more funerals."

Captain Roy Kelly spoke loud enough this time for all the other task force members to hear. Minutes later, the same message went out from police dispatch citywide. Every cop in town was now after Malcolm's scalp.

At the end of the block, slumped down in the front seat, peering out through the Jeep Cherokee's dark tinted windows, Malcolm watched. The coroner's van drove past his Jeep, followed by Detective Bryant's white Dodge. The headlights from the Intrepid momentarily illuminated the inside of the Jeep. Malcolm slipped down even lower in his seat. He saw the Detective's face—a cold, hard mask—absolutely expressionless.

Malcolm turned the key in the ignition, noting that the keys still had blood on them from their previous owner. The solemn procession of coroner and cop turned the corner. Malcolm followed. It felt more natural for him to hunt than to be hunted. As long as he was watching the police, he was comfortable they would never catch him. Soon, he would have to get rid of Detective Bryant too. The man was starting to get in the way.

Bryant always thought there was something humbling about a morgue. Being inside one brought him to an immediate awareness of his own mortality that was as real and palpable as if he were on his deathbed or facing execution. No one felt invincible or immortal in a morgue. As a cop, Bryant had gotten used to it. That is, until he watched the Medical Examiner wrench a seven-inch Japanese tanto knife from his partner's eye-socket and realized that the man who put it there was still out on the streets and it was up to Bryant to go after him. That's when Bryant began to wonder what it might feel like to have his throat slit. What went through people's minds when they were gargling their own blood and watching it spurt from their throat and two feet in the air?

Watching the ME's assistant saw open the top of the skull of a teenaged runaway who'd been brutally raped and beaten by a person or persons unknown while a guy from the University of Pennsylvania's Neurology lab waited impatiently for the kid's brain made him wonder if there really was a heaven or if it was all just an endless hell.

*And if hell is all there is? Are we already there? Are we*

*foolishly running from death when that is the only real peace we can hope for? If there is a heaven, how did the death of this kid fit into the divine plan?*

*Fuck. I'm trippin'. I need to pull it together,* Bryant thought.

The young boy had purple bruises all over his emaciated, tattooed body, along with older, yellowing ones. The streets had not been kind to him. Bryant looked around the postmortem room. He avoided a glance at Baltimore's corpse but found the other sights no more comforting. Next to the street kid, a tiny infant who'd stopped breathing in her sleep was being plundered for her liver and kidneys. Bryant wondered which lucky little kid or kids were going to get those and what the hell were they going to do with that other kid's brain? Then he noticed the university name tags on their lab coats and realized all the organs they were taking would likely be dissected by first year med students or used in research experiments. Bryant remembered that Baltimore was a registered organ donor just as the ME's assistant removed the boy's eyes and plopped them in a jar. Detective Bryant turned and left when they began sawing open Baltimore's chest. In his mind, he kept hearing that old saying: *"Today is a good day to die!"*

It wasn't. Not in Philly. Not ever. Here, death was always ugly, never peaceful, and never glorious. He wished he were one of those people who passed out at the sight of blood. At least then he wouldn't have to walk around with the image of Baltimore's corpse being sawed open, an image seared into his mind like the ghostly, electric-blue after-images when a camera flash flared.

Now it was time to go after Malcolm, and that thought made his Beretta, his badge, his handcuffs, the bulletproof vest, and the Remington pump shotgun in the trunk of his car feel like one of those $1.99 toy cop sets you got from the supermarket with the little plastic gun, plastic billy club, and little plastic handcuffs. He felt like a thirteen-year-old Masai warrior about to try to claim his manhood by hunting down a lion with nothing but a spear.

Bryant had faced down countless murderers in his career. He'd confronted gangbangers with rap sheets a mile long, gangsters and Mafia hitmen, husbands who'd murdered their wives, wives who'd murdered their husbands, parents who'd killed their children, cold-blooded killers who'd murdered for profit. But this was his first serial killer, and he found this one so different from the rest.

He could usually put himself inside a criminal's mind. He could think like they thought, understand their motives. He knew why a guy would kill someone during a robbery. He even knew why someone would kill someone during a rape. He knew why spouses killed each other. He'd never admit it to anyone, but he could even understand why someone would kill their own children. But Malcolm was a different breed. His were not crimes of passion or profit. His were crimes of perversion. They came from a place that Bryant's mind could not go, and that terrified him. Malcolm was motivated by pure rage and hatred. It seemed to be the only emotion he felt, an overwhelming hatred that had been festering inside him for decades. It had twisted into a murderous bloodlust that consumed more than two dozen lives, and the body count was still rising.

Bryant tried to tell himself that his fears were irrational. He was safe. He had the entire Philadelphia Police Force behind him ... But so had Baltimore. Bryant couldn't help wondering if he was next, if Malcolm was out there sharpening his blade for him. Instinctively, Bryant reached for his gun. Feeling its lethal weight normally made him feel confident, but today it felt small and cheap, like a plastic toy.

Detective Bryant took the drive from the morgue to the station, cursing and beeping his horn at the early morning traffic. A fat guy in a business suit riding one of those little scooters with the knobby tires pulled out in front of the Intrepid. Bryant tried to tell himself that his foot just slipped off the brake, causing him to tap the scooter's rear tire with his bumper, that it had nothing to do with the fact that the guy riding it looked like the man who'd been shoving hundreds into CC's G-string the night before. Bryant wasn't a jealous man. At least that's what he told himself when his foot once again slipped off the brake and he nearly drove the scooter off the road into the gutter. The man struggled to keep the bike from falling over. He turned and gave Detective Bryant his middle finger in the all-American "Fuck you" salute. Bryant gave him a cold, tight-lipped smile in return.

Bryant hadn't had time to shower. He could still smell CC's scent on him—cigarettes, alcohol, Obsession, and pussy. He wished he were still lying in bed beside her. The news of his partner's murder reached him just as he was falling asleep in CC's arms. He'd put her in a cab and headed directly to the scene without sleep. Now, he'd officially been up for twenty-four hours straight. It had been four days now since he'd been to the gym, and despite his fatigue, he figured an hour on the heavy bag would help him shake off the fog around his mind. At this point, an hour of sleep would only make him more exhausted.

Bryant drove to the police headquarters downtown, where they had the nicest gym facilities and the most corrupt cops in the city. When he worked there, he made it a point not to get too friendly with anyone he didn't know. He never discussed cases with any of the downtown boys or the South Philly boys. They were all in the Mafia's pockets, and he didn't want them leaking any information to the local wise guys about his cases, whether it involved them or not. Being on the task force made him multi-jurisdictional, which meant he worked all over the city. Bryant didn't necessarily like everyone he met. It was probably unfair to say all the downtown cops were corrupt, but it was probably safer to keep in mind that they just might be.

Detective Bryant entered the gym and was relieved to find it empty except for Captain Kelly, who was bench pressing half the weight in the gym. It seemed like the captain was always there. Roy Kelly was one of those mutant freaks who never did any cardio but seemed to have virtually no body fat. Unlike Bryant, who, despite countless hours skipping rope, shadow boxing, and hitting the heavy bag, had watched his gut grow nearly half an inch a year since he turned thirty. At forty-five, it had just reached the point where other people commented on it.

"Haven't seen you in here all week," Captain Kelly said. He was not the least bit out of breath, despite the three hundred and fifty pounds on his chest. He pumped out a dozen repetitions with little effort before resting the bar back on its rack.

"Yeah, it's been a rough week," Bryant said as he stepped into the locker room.

The smell of sweat was so strong that Bryant wanted to gag, but he thought it would've been unmanly. Guys were supposed to be used to the smell of jock sweat. He peeled himself out of the navy blue suit he'd worn on Monday, planned to take to the dry cleaners on Wednesday, but had instead run an iron over and thrown back on. It had shiny spots on the sleeves and pants legs from the steam iron. Bryant didn't care. He wasn't trying to win any fashion awards.

His thick, wooly hair had begun to grow into an Afro, and his goatee was growing into a full beard. As he looked in the mirror, even he had to admit he looked like shit. He decided to shave the beard before going out into the gym. Captain Kelly was probably trying to find the right time to comment on his grooming. Bryant decided to save the captain the trouble. He watched his ragged beard disappear down the sink as he ran the electric shaver across his cheeks.

As his moustache and beard fell away, a face emerged that was almost handsome. Bryant allowed himself a brief moment of vanity when he looked at his smooth chocolate skin, bow-shaped lips, high cheekbones, and dark, almond-shaped eyes. He tried to see what CC saw in him, and for a moment, he could see a man who was at least mildly attractive. He checked to make sure he was alone before he flexed his powerfully muscled chest and arms in the mirror. They were his finest assets. If he could only get rid of his gut, he might even manage to be sexy. He laughed at the idea of himself as a sex symbol. He knew what had always gotten him over with the women were his gentle manner and his sweet talk.

Unlike most men, Bryant had never been afraid to be corny. He would shower women with compliments and poetry, and they invariably fell before the onslaught. It was the same technique he used with witnesses and, occasionally, with suspects as well.

After he'd freed his face from its fur coat, he quickly shrugged his thick, stubby legs into a pair of satin Ringside boxing shorts and a Joe Boxer tank top. He walked back into the gym, wrapping his fists in long, yellow Mexican hand wraps with a pair of Reyes bag gloves tucked under his arm. Captain Kelly was still on the bench press, straining beneath what Bryant estimated to be 425 pounds. Bryant picked up a jump rope with one-pound weights in the handle and began skipping rope. He watched the clock while he twirled the heavy rope faster and faster.

Over and over, the image of Baltimore's corpse slithered its way into Bryant's thoughts. He tried to concentrate on the workout, but his anger kept getting in the way. He wondered where Reed Cozen had gone and what he planned to do with Baltimore's gun. If he had gone after Malcolm, they'd no doubt be finding another mutilated and cannibalized corpse soon. Then Malcolm would disappear and they'd have no way of finding him again. Not until he started to kill again in some other city, some other state, where they were less equipped to deal with evil of that magnitude.

For some reason, Bryant could never skip rope with shoes on. They threw off his rhythm. He often paid for this inability with scraped and bruised toes. The rope cracked against Bryant's toes whenever he missed a turn. He bit his bottom lip and cursed under his breath. He started jumping again, once again struck his toes, then threw the rope across the room into a corner. Captain Kelly looked up from the bench but said nothing.

Bryant slid the bag gloves on and began pounding the heavy bag with all the strength and speed he could muster. He imagined the 80-pound leather bag was Malcolm, and he pounded his fists into it with increasing ferocity, grunting with each shot. Rather than making him feel better, it was beginning to depress him. The bag wouldn't go down. It just bounced right back. To Bryant, it seemed like an omen.

Captain Kelly walked over to the curl bar to do some bicep curls. Bryant began beating the stuffing out of the heavy bag, grunting and cursing. His short, muscular arms were pumping faster and faster as jabs, hooks, and straight rights flew in rapid, vicious combination. Bryant bobbed and slipped punches from his imaginary opponent, then countered with vicious body shots and hooks. He looked insane. Bryant threw one more violent flurry. The bag nearly bounced off its chain. He stood still, breathing hard and staring at the bag as if he believed he could disintegrate it with his eyes.

"James? Are you okay?" the captain asked.

"No. Not at all. My partner is dead."

"I think maybe you should take a break for a while. Maybe use up some of those sick days and see Dr. West."

"I'm not crazy, Roy. I'm just pissed off. I think I have

a right to be angry. Our boys fucked up, and now my partner's dead. You should have let me kick every one of their asses. The whole damn task force is useless!"

"James, Malcolm killed Detective Baltimore. Not Trinidad, not Nellis, not Wilson, not Jones, not Lieutenant Woo. Malcolm is the one who needs his ass kicked."

Bryant fell silent for a long moment. He stared at his feet with his hands clenched into tight fists. He was sweating so heavily it was forming a puddle at his feet.

"Look, James, it's okay to be pissed off. It's okay to be a little scared. After what happened, I'd be kinda worried if you weren't both. But you cannot let that fuck up this investigation. I talked to Lieutenant Woo last night. He's going to be taking a more active role in the investigation, which means you're gonna have to start acting like part of the task force. If you want to remain a part of this investigation, you're gonna have to start checking in with Woo and getting your assignments from him. I can't have you going renegade on this one. I gotta cover my ass too. So just do this by the numbers."

"Yeah, right. Whatever."

The door to the gym opened, and Detective Vargas strolled in grinning.

"We finally got a muthafuckin' lead!"

"What have you got?"

"Paul Cooper, Malcolm's little butt buddy, the one you found filleted the other day? Well, he had credit cards, platinum ones, close to $20,000 in credit. We didn't find any cards when we searched the apartment. We checked all over and couldn't find any identification of any kind."

"How the hell does a street prostitute get $20,000 in credit?" Captain Kelly asked.

Bryant shook his head in amazement and chuckled, thinking about how he was turned down at Sears for $600 of credit to buy a refrigerator.

"Cooper was a long way from a street prostitute. Before he died, he was working for an escort company that specialized in creative fantasy experiences. The place was perfectly legal. They even filed taxes," Vargas said.

"Let me guess. Cooper's particular specialty involved bullwhips and cattle prods? Creative fantasy experience," Bryant laughed.

"Cooper was pulling down about five-thousand-dollars a night."

"Five Thousand! Dollars? Some rich homo pays this guy what … a thousand dollars a pop just so he can beat the shit out of him? Fuck is wrong with this world?"

"The dude who ran the place said it was all pretty mild, no real sadistic stuff, and there was absolutely no sex. All those scars and bruises must have come from Cooper's personal life."

"Like he's going to admit that he has guys coming to him, paying for violent sex," Bryant barked

"Okay, so what happened to the cards?" Captain Kelly interrupted.

"You think Malcolm took them?" Bryant asked, hopeful but skeptical.

"This morning we ran his Visa and American Express cards, and they've been used twice since Cooper's murder, and guess what the purchases were?" Vargas asked, drawing it out like a good joke, building the suspense, waiting to spring the punch line.

"What?" The captain asked.

"Someone spent close to five thousand dollars at Kran Bros. on Seventh and South. You know, that fancy menswear shop? I called down there, and they said a tall, bald Black guy came in and bought one black Armani suit two days ago, and then just this morning, he came in and bought a Hugo Boss suit, size fifty-two extra-long, and a pair of black lizard skin Stacy Adams, size fifteen."

"Mu-tha-fucker. I just can't believe the balls on

this sonuvabitch! He kills a cop one day and then goes shopping the next? We just can't be as stupid as this guy thinks we are!" Bryant threw his hands up in exasperation.

"You mean to tell me this bastard's picture is all over the news and nobody in the store recognized him?"

"I asked them that too. The two old Italian guys that work there, they own the place, they said they work all day and when they get home, they're too tired to watch TV. Said they knew there was some guy out there killing people, but they had no idea what he looked like."

"Yeah, and they were probably in too much of a hurry to sell one of their expensive-ass, over-priced suits to worry about little things like getting an ID with that credit card. Do you really buy that they didn't know Malcolm's description? A six-foot Black vampire? His description has been getting as much attention as the murders themselves!"

"Do you think he'll use the cards again?" Captain Kelly asked.

Bryant bit his lip hard, trying not to scream. He stalked back and forth like a panther in a cage. The captain was staring at him. Detective Vargas was staring at him too.

*Fuck 'em both*, Bryant thought.

"Uh … I don't know. I mean, he's a cocky enough, but he's not stupid either. I'm sure he knew he was taking a risk buying that suit. I can't see why he even did it. It would be crazy for him to try it again."

"Malcolm ain't crazy. He wants us to think he is. But he ain't crazy. He's just bad, just fuckin' evil." Spit flew from his lips as Bryant spoke. Suddenly self-conscious, he wiped his mouth with his sweaty hand wrap and fell silent again.

Captain Kelly turned away from Bryant and looked at Detective Vargas.

"What the hell are you wearing? What do you think—you're back in Vice?"

Vargas was wearing an oversized Ben Davis shirt, oversized FUBU jeans that hung low off his ass, revealing the tops of his red and white checkered boxer shorts, a pair of black and white Air Jordans, and black gangster loc sunglasses. With his hair slicked back, he looked like a Mexican gang-banger.

"Sorry, Captain. The Lieutenant thought it would be a good idea to go under cover and check out Malcolm's old neighborhood. See if any of his old homeboys know where he's hiding out."

"Yeah, but this is Philly, not LA in the nineties. Nobody dresses like that out here! You're Puerto Rican. Do any of your friends dress like that? You go into G-town lookin' like American Me and they'll have you made in a second. Go change your damn clothes, will you, and take James to get a damn haircut. I've been trying not to say anything, but you look like shit, James. Well, at least you shaved, but that haircut is way past regulation."

"Yeah, I'll take care of it."

"It's almost time for the morning briefing."

Bryant rolled his eyes.

"And you *will* be there, James. By the numbers. You hear me?"

"Yes, sir!"

"Fuck you, James. Just be there."

Captain Kelly walked into the locker room, and Bryant followed. Vargas was still standing there, looking at himself in the mirror. Bryant shook his head. The guy watched too many hip-hop videos. Out of the corner of his eye, Bryant caught Captain Kelly staring at him again, visibly troubled.

"Are you sure you're gonna be okay, James? I mean, you just lost your partner. It might not be a bad idea to take a few days off."

"And how many people will die while I'm home convalescing?"

"You are not the task force, James. You are part of

the task force. The investigation can and will go on if you need to take a rest."

"Yeah, I'll think about it."

"One more thing. We're still focusing on Malcolm here. We have an all-points bulletin out on Reed Cozen, but forensics found skin under Baltimore's fingernails, black skin. He must've scratched Malcolm during the attack. So that pretty much lets Cozen off the hook for the murder."

"He might still have been an accomplice. He and Malcolm could've set Baltimore up."

"Do you honestly think Cozen might be involved?"

"It doesn't matter what I think. Until we know for sure, we gotta consider him armed and dangerous."

"Yeah, but you know what it's like out there. What if he's innocent and he winds up getting gunned down by some overzealous cop? A murderer that we failed to catch kills his family and then we murder the guy. The press will crucify us."

"Captain, there is no way we're gonna come out of this looking good. We're already screwed, so fuck the public relations."

The captain held up a hand to silence him.

"We got the DNA tests back from the lab."

"You can't get DNA tests done in less than a week."

"No, *you* can't get DNA tests done in less than a week. I can hire another lab to do all our tests if those bastards don't rush a little when we need them. Anyway, the semen we found in Mrs. Cozen didn't match the DNA samples we took from Mr. Cozen. Now, I'm willing to go out on a limb and say Mr. Cozen might want to kill his wife, but it's hard to imagine that he'd let a guy fuck her in front of him and his kids. I say bring Malcolm in dead or alive, but handle Reed with kid gloves. The guy's innocent, James. We can't afford more bad press on this. We've already made enough embarrassing mistakes on this case to put all our pensions in jeopardy."

"Yeah, like getting Titus killed." Bryant balled his hands up into tight fists and stared at them.

"James, enough. I need you on this. All of you. If you can't put this behind you—"

"I'm not taking a vacation, Roy. Let's just do everything we can to catch this bastard. Once his ass is in jail, the press will forget all about how bad we fucked up the investigation. Until then, I'm the only one whose pension's in jeopardy. You'll be fine. You always are."

"We're in this together, Detective."

"Okay, Captain. Whatever you say."

"I keep thinking about the cop who returned that little Asian boy to Jeffrey Dahmer's apartment. *After* Dahmer was caught is when all that information came out and the shit hit the fan. The press crucified that guy. I wonder what mistakes they'll dig up from this investigation."

"Sorry, Roy. But you'll have to excuse me if I don't give a fuck. I just want to catch this asshole."

Bryant dropped his shorts and stalked off into the shower. He turned back around and looked at Captain Kelly in amazement.

"Were any of Titus's credit cards missing?"

"His what?"

"Credit cards! Did we check his wallet and make sure everything was still there?"

"No."

"Damn it! If that bastard buys a suit on Titus's credit, he'll never see the inside of a courtroom! I promise you that. I'll shoot him dead on sight!"

"You might have to wait in line."

# PART TWO

## MALCOLM AND REED

# XXXI.

It was the first time since the ordeal began that the tears came uncontrollably. Sobs racked his body as grief overwhelmed him. He felt empty, like some vital part of him had been unceremoniously excised and lost forever. His life was over. He had lived the last ten years for his wife and family, and they were dead, and so were the next ten years of the life he and Linda had planned out so meticulously.

The dream of Linda owning her own vegetarian restaurant—dead. The dream of finally writing an award-winning novel—dead. Buying Linda a larger stone for her engagement ring—dead. Putting Mark and Jennie in private school—dead. He and Linda joining a gym and working out together—dead. Vacationing in Thailand—dead. Growing old and retiring in Las Vegas—dead. All of his dreams died the night Linda, Jennie, and Mark were murdered, and he knew he would most likely be dead soon too. Still, he had to try, for his family. He had to try to stop Malcolm.

Reed cried so hard he had difficulty steering the 2008 Ford Taurus through the cracked and potholed streets of Germantown. He thought he saw Malcolm in every Black face he passed. This was Malcolm's neighborhood, and he was omnipresent, a dark shadow of menace that seemed to fill every nook and crevice with the threat of violence. Reed started questioning himself, doubting the sanity of going after Malcolm in his own neighborhood.

*If I have to confront this monster, shouldn't I at least do it on my own terms, in a place where I would have the advantage, where I might at least stand a chance?*

This was suicide. But perhaps it would give him the element of surprise. Reed laughed. The sound of his own laughter frightened him. It had been so long since he'd heard it. It sounded warped, insane. He was so scared, angry, emotionally exhausted, it felt like he was losing his mind.

It had been fifteen years since Reed last came to Germantown. He hadn't been avoiding the place. He just never had a reason to go there. He drove slowly up Germantown Avenue while memories of his first few trips into G-town came back to him in a thrilling rush of frightening, amusing, exhilarating emotions. Even knowing how it all ended, his emotions were conflicted as he recalled his past with Malcolm. Much of who he was, many of the things he liked most about himself, he owed to Malcolm. He was a shy little nerd who everyone overlooked until Malcolm took interest in him. Malcolm taught him to believe in himself and his abilities because Malcolm had believed in him. Malcolm showed him things about himself and the world he might never have seen.

Reed crept his vehicle past the rows of seedy bars. In front of these graffiti-covered, rundown establishments, teenaged drug dealers "slang rocks" and crack-whores peddled their diseased sex. He recalled when Malcolm smacked a young drug dealer outside the AMPM mini-market 17 years ago for offering him crack.

"Do I look like a fucking piper to you, fool? Huh? You think I use that shit? Don't you ever insult me like that again, muthafucka! Ever!"

He grabbed the young dealer by his leather jacket and cracked the back of his hand across the guy's mouth with a sound like a gunshot. The kid reached into his pocket and fumbled out a small, silver automatic pistol. Malcolm paid no attention to the gun. He slapped him again and again. He didn't even respect the guy enough to punch him. The drug dealer dropped the gun, and Malcolm slapped him again. The kid turned to run, and Malcolm kicked him, stomping down on his tailbone so hard the guy's knees hit the pavement. All the other dealers started laughing and cheering. Malcolm reached down, picked up the kid's gun, then turned to look at the other "slangers" with an expression of utter disgust. They all stopped laughing. Malcolm turned and threw the gun in the trash.

Reed was scared shitless, but Malcolm seemed oblivious to the fact that he had almost gotten shot. Reed was impressed. He wanted that kind of power.

The AMPM was still there, and there were still drug dealers all around it. Reed turned down Washington Lane and headed for Burbridge Street, where Rick lived. Reed remembered the day he met Rick. He and Malcolm were walking to the corner store. They passed dozens of people in the street, on the corners, sitting on porches, and no one spoke to him. No one said hi. Conversations seemed to halt when Malcolm walked by.

"Don't you know any of these people? Ain't some of them your friends?" Reed had asked

"Yeah, I know 'em, and no, they ain't my friends. These are the same muthafuckas that used to tease me when I was little. Made my life hell. Now that I've gotten big, they ain't got shit to say!" He raised his voice and glared at a bunch of girls on a porch across the street. There were two guys on the porch as well who were not all that small themselves. They appeared ready to stand up and say something, then seemed to think better of it.

"Muthafuckas all scared now. Fuck 'em!"

"Yeah, fuck you too!" a voice called out from the porch, sounding almost identical to Malcolm's, same inflections, same rumbling bass. Reed turned to see who the dead man was and was surprised when a short, skinny, light-skinned Black kid came off the porch, smiling. He was even more surprised when he saw Malcolm was smiling too.

"Aw, this is my dog right here. This little nigga's crazy!" Malcolm was grinning from ear to ear when he slapped hands with the skinny Black kid. If Malcolm thought the kid was crazy, then he must be ready for a padded room, a daily cocktail of lithium and Prozac, and a jacket with the sleeves in the back.

"Who's the white boy?" Rick had asked, staring at Reed greedily, like he was a toy that he wanted and he was just waiting for Malcolm to say he could have him. Reed was pretty sure Rick was the type who broke all his toys.

"He's cool. Reed, meet Rick."

Rick just smiled at him with the tip of his tongue sticking out between his teeth. He looked both goofy and dangerous, like a hyena. Reed didn't offer to shake his hand. He was afraid he'd draw back a nub.

"Damn, and I was gonna suggest we go over to Chestnut Hill and jack some of them rich-ass white boys. I guess that's out now." He scowled at Reed, looking both hurt and angry at him for spoiling his plans. He didn't look so goofy anymore.

"Well, let's at least go find some bitches."

"Nah, nigga. Me and Reed gotta work on some shit for school. I'll check you later."

Rick scowled at Reed, flaring his nostrils, curling up his lip, and rolling his eyes.

"Punk-ass white muthafucka," he hissed venomously. He spit through his teeth, then walked back up to the porch.

Malcolm continued walking down the street, oblivious to Rick's subtle tantrum. Empathy was not a part of Malcolm's makeup.

"That nigga right there, you never want to fuck with. He'll kill your ass just 'cause he can't think of nothin' else better to do. He just don't give a fuck. He ain't headed nowhere but to the pen. He's one of them dumb muthafuckas that'll still be standin' over the body kickin' it and spittin' on it when the cops pull up. If I ever kill a muthafucka, I'll get away with that shit 'cause my ass ain't never goin' to jail. Rick expects to go to jail. He can't see any way to avoid it. That's what makes that nigga dangerous. Jail don't scare him."

"Does it scare you?" As soon as Reed asked it, he knew he shouldn't have.

Malcolm stopped in mid-stride. His head turned so slowly it was almost mechanical. Thick veins and cords bulged in his neck as his head swiveled 90 degrees. Reed tensed for the blow he was certain would come. Then a bone deep dread settled on him like a weight as he realized that if Malcolm struck him, he wouldn't stop, not until someone stopped him or Reed stopped breathing. Malcolm was staring down at Reed like he was trying to hold back a storm. His face seemed ready to fly apart under the strain of keeping the murderous emotions contained. Then it slowly began to harden, to lose all animation; nothing on his face looked alive except his eyes, and they were burning through Reed like lasers. When he spoke, his neighborhood dialect was gone. His voice was a deep, harsh bark. His nostrils flared and his lips curled back. He sounded like he did at school, intelligent and deadly serious.

"It's a non-issue because I'll never see the inside of a jail cell. Never. If it ever comes down to it, I'll hold court in the street."

Reed nodded without comment. His eyes were as wide as the barrels of a shotgun. He couldn't break Malcolm's gaze, frozen like a deer in the oncoming lights of an eighteen-wheeler. He trembled from head to toe as it slowly dawned on him exactly where he was—in the middle of a Black ghetto, the only white face for miles, standing in front of a very large kid who was probably a psychopath, a very large psychopath. It was all he could do to hold on to his bowels. Malcolm was still staring down at him, and he was not smiling.

Reed felt like a man who had been read his last rites, strapped into the electric chair, and then suddenly released and taken back to his cell, still tasting his own death. Malcolm had issued no threat, verbal or physical. It had been a spiritual awareness that had come from Malcolm's murderous gaze, an awareness of just who and what the man was. That was the first time he'd realized that despite their friendship, Malcolm was fully capable of killing him. It had been too late. By then, he'd already started sleeping with Reneé.

That was seventeen years ago, and now Reed was back in the same place. He hadn't learned his lesson. And this time, Malcolm was not his friend.

The Ford Taurus wagon looked completely out of place, like a poodle in a wolf's den, as it rolled warily down Duval Street amongst the old Cadillacs, Lincolns, Fords, and Chevys that lined the block. He passed Ambrose Street and gripped the steering wheel tighter, clenching his teeth. He peered cautiously down the narrow dead-end street and spotted Malcolm's old house. Of course, Malcolm wasn't there, but what was undoubtedly an unmarked police car was.

A white Crown Victoria with a spotlight mounted beside one of its oversized rearview mirrors sat midway down the block with the silhouette of two bored and frustrated detectives in its windshield. It was parked just a few houses down from the weathered three-story row home where Malcolm had once vivisected a cat in front of him to see how long it would live with its guts hanging out. Reed remembered watching it crawl around the basement floor, howling in pain, dragging its entrails behind it. His stepfather had stormed down into the basement, enraged by the noise, and had beaten Malcolm severely, the way you would beat a grown man, using his fists instead of an open hand or a strap, then he threw Reed out of the house and locked Malcolm down there with the dying cat all day.

Reed brought the car to a halt, remembering how Malcolm's eyes lost their feral intensity when he heard his stepfather coming down the basement steps. He seemed lost and afraid, like the teenager he was. Reed felt sorry for him then. Now he was ready to kill him.

Reed stared hard at the two detectives in the unmarked cruiser. He could almost make out their faces. They appeared to be taking a long look at his car as he passed. He hit the gas and sped past before they could recognize him. He knew the cops were probably looking for him almost as vigorously as they were hunting Malcolm. For all they knew, he'd killed Detective Baltimore himself and he was running the streets with the dead cop's gun, irrational with grief. Reed chuckled nervously when he realized that was exactly what he was doing.

The very next street after Ambrose was Burbridge Street, where Rick lived. Burbridge was on a long hill paved with red cobblestones and lined with lush trees. Three-story houses with stone facades rose like monuments on either side of the street. Reed was amazed at how the neighborhood changed so drastically from block to block. Compared to Ambrose Street, Burbridge Street was middle-class splendor. But compared to the cozy little street that Mark and Jennie grew up on, the house where he and Linda consummated their marriage, it was a slum. Reed's bottom lip trembled, and his eyes welled up with tears, but he fought them back. He picked up the Beretta from the passenger seat and chambered a round as he slid the Taurus into an empty spot between a Mustang 5.0 and a Hyundai Excel in front of Rick's house. His eyes scanned the block. No sign of the Impala. No sign of Malcolm. He slid from the car, took a deep breath, and walked up the front steps, the Beretta held behind his back, safety off, hammer cocked, his forehead and hands sweating, trembling.

*You are about to die. You're going to join Linda and Jennie and little Mark. It'll all be over soon.*

Reed could hear the voice as plain as day. It froze him right in his tracks. The voice was coming from inside his head, and it wasn't his. It was Malcolm. Quickly, he looked around, pointing the Beretta at the bushes on either side of the steps, at the parked cars, up at the porch, the roof over the porch. Malcolm wasn't there. He was in his head. Only crazy people heard voices. Reed knew that, but he'd heard it.

*You are about to die!*

The voice frightened him because he knew it shouldn't be there, because it meant that he was going insane, but the words didn't frighten him. They were simply points of fact. He was going to kill Malcolm, so in all likelihood, he himself would die because Malcolm was the killer and he was not. He was prepared for this. He had been living on borrowed time ever since he fucked Reneé and Natasha. He owed the devil his due. But Malcolm would die too. He was sure of that as well. And he didn't need a voice in his head to tell him.

"Can I help you, sir?"

The voice startled Reed, but at least it wasn't coming from his head this time. There was a rotund, elderly Black woman standing on the porch with her thick meaty hands on her rather substantial hips. She wore huge Bermuda shorts that came just above her knees, which were half swallowed in fat. Her plump feet ballooned out of a pair of broken down sandals, and her titanic breasts swung like bulbous pendulums in an oversized T-shirt bearing the face of Mickey Mouse. She wore curlers in her hair covered by a hair net. It was Rick's mom.

"I'm looking for Rick. I'm a friend of his—"

"I know who you are, Reed. I remember when you

used to come 'round here with that devilish nigga, Malcolm. I didn't want Ricky hangin' out with either one of you. I saw the way you got off on slummin' with Malcolm, how you fed off that nigga's evil. I heard about how that evil came back at you. I heard about what happened to your family." Her eyes bore down on him, full of accusation and not a shred of pity. "Now, you comin' around here lookin' for Ricky. For what? So you can find Malcolm and get yourself killed too? You should've never come around here in the first place. Should've stayed up there with the rest of the white folks."

"Ma'am, please, is Rick here? I just need to talk to him and then I'll be gone." Reed was struck by the irony of his words. They sounded exactly like what Detective Baltimore had said to him.

"Rick ain't here. He moved out years ago, right after college, when he got married."

*College? Married?* That didn't sound like the Rick he had known.

"Where did he move?"

"You're a fool if you go after him. You know Malcolm will kill you."

Reed knew. The voice in his head was telling him the exact same thing.

*You're going to die, white boy!*

"Please, Mrs. Brown."

"South Philly. He moved to South Philly."

She gave him the address and watched him turn to walk back to his car. He had shoved the Baretta down the back of his jeans, and the butt of the pistol was sticking out from under his shirt.

"Rest in peace," the old woman said solemnly at Reed's back.

Reed cringed. Even with the gun, he knew he was a dead man if he managed to catch up with Malcolm. It was like a caterpillar hunting a praying mantis. Prey stalking predator.

The drive to South Philly was a blur. Reed was on autopilot, taking the hairpin turns on Lincoln drive at lethal velocity without thinking. His mind was on Malcolm and the very real threat he would pose when they met face to face. Reed was no killer, but he had to try. Malcolm was.

The Taurus wagon's steel belted radials squealed in anguish as they burned across asphalt, leaving long skid marks on the road. Reed stomped down hard on the brakes and fought to keep the wagon from slamming into the median.

*I've got to slow down,* Reed thought.

There was plenty of time for him to die. No need to rush things. He flew down Kelly Drive, past the art museum, and down the parkway. He had no choice but to slow down now. He was approaching Center City. There would be cops.

Cops out to stop him from getting to Malcolm.

Thoughts of Malcolm turned to thoughts of his dead family. He remembered how he'd yelled at Mark and Jennie for cursing. The last words he'd spoken to them had been words of anger. Over and over, he rehearsed alternative ways he could have handled the situation.

If only he'd known. He would have held them, told them he loved them, played *Crash Bandicoot* with Mark and whipped Jennie in *Duke Nukem*. He thought about all the times he hadn't told Linda he loved her because he was too tired and his novel wasn't going right and he just wanted to lay down and shut out the world. He even thought about the times when he had ejaculated too quickly even though he knew he could've held back and waited for Linda to orgasm. But he'd been tired and selfish, and now she was gone and making love to her, holding her, telling her he loved her, were the only things in the world he wanted to do ... besides pulling Malcolm's heart out of his chest and stuffing it down his throat.

He turned onto 11th  Street and fought to keep

the wagon below 35 miles an hour. When he passed Catherine Street, he could hardly look at the huge, four-story, red brick institution where he, Malcolm, Reneé, and Natasha began their fatal courtship. In his stomach, thousands of huge Monarch butterflies began their migration. His hands were shaking again. He was almost there.

The street on which Rick lived looked surprisingly affluent. As affluent as South Philadelphia got, anyway. Manicured lawns were creatively landscaped with trees and shrubs. Some even had stone fountains on the front lawn. The houses all looked as if they'd been recently painted, and they even had garages, an almost unheard of feature for a home in Philadelphia, least of all South Philly. Further down the block, the houses regressed back into the claustrophobic row homes that no matter how well maintained, still looked like the immigrant ghetto it had been when the Italians, Jews, and Irish first came over the bridges from New York and New Jersey after their initial landing at Ellis Island. It wasn't depressing like a Black or Latino Ghetto. In fact, it could almost be called quaint by one of the privileged class, but Reed couldn't help noticing how much these homes resembled the houses in Germantown and North Philadelphia but were just better maintained.

Reed checked the address he'd written down and pulled up in front of a house that was almost a carbon copy of Malcolm's house on Ambrose Street. He kept driving further down the block, thinking it might be safer and less conspicuous to approach on foot. He double-parked the wagon and left the motor running. He hoped that Rick's wife wasn't home because there was a new voice in his head; it sounded like little Jennie, and it was screaming for revenge. An eye for an eye. A life for a life. A wife for a wife.

*Kill him, Daddy. Kill the bad man.*

Reed cringed and fought back tears, squeezing his eyes shut and clenching his teeth as Jennie pleaded with him.

*He hurt us, Daddy. He hurt me and Mommy and Mark. He hurt us real bad. Kill him, Daddy. Kill him. Kill his friends. Kill them all. Make those motherfuckers pay! An eye for an eye, Daddy. An eye for an eye!*

Jennie still talked too much and cursed too much, but Reed was in no mood to scold her. Even in her fury, it was good to hear her voice. He could hear Linda as well, cool, calm, humanitarian, pacifist, vegetarian for ethical reasons, echoing Jennie's wrath and screaming for Malcolm's blood. Death seemed to have changed her political outlook.

*He has to die, Reed. You know what you have to do. He hurt us, Reed. Kill him! Kill that FUCKING NIGGER!*

The cacophony continued in Reed's head as he walked up the street toward Rick's house. A wild, nervous energy seemed to be vibrating through him. His face was a riot of tics and twitches. Restless ghosts raged and stormed through his fragmented mind. He tried to quiet the voices by pressing his hands over his ears and closing his eyes. He stood on the sidewalk for nearly a full minute with his hands cupped to the sides of his head. It felt like his brain was flying apart. He knew what he needed to do, the only way to quiet the ghosts. Find Malcolm. Kill Malcolm.

Reed knew he was going insane. He surprised himself with how easy the idea was to accept. His sanity had been severed cleanly. It hadn't shattered. It had simply snapped like the stem of a dandelion in a harsh wind. Now he had the voices. The voices of the vengeful dead. He didn't mind. As long as the voices were there, he wasn't alone. He had his family. But now he needed to focus, and it was hard with the voices nagging him. Reed reached into his waistband and closed his hand around the Beretta. Feeling its cold, deadly weight seemed to calm him. Suddenly, his head was clear again. Quiet. He was ready.

# XXXII.

Malcolm showed up unexpectedly at Rick's door. He needed a place to lay low. He knew that Rick was married, but that didn't matter. Bros before hoes. That was law.

"What up, my nigga?" Malcolm slipped easily back into the lingo of the streets. It was as familiar to him as breathing.

"Malcolm! What's up, dog? I ain't seen your black ass in years. Man, you all over the news. Them cops want your ass bad!"

"That's why I'm here. I need to stay with you for a while."

Rick's eyes slid sideways back toward the house, then swept the floor. He looked nervous.

"Is that gonna be a problem, nigga? You still my nigga, ain't you?"

"Yeah, Malcolm. You know I got your back. It's just that I got a woman, a wife, and this shit you involved in …"

Malcolm leaned closer until his face was inches from Rick's.

"Are you my dog, or are you your bitch's bitch?"

Rick had lost a little of his craziness. It showed in

his clean, white Hanes underwear and terrycloth house coat, his neatly groomed hair, and, most telling, the can of Bud Light clutched in his right hand instead of the 40 of malt liquor that had once been permanently attached to his palm. Along with his insanity, he'd lost the quality Malcolm had most admired in the man, his fearlessness. There was a time when Malcolm saw in Rick something to be feared, a little nigga who didn't give a fuck. Now, marriage, college, and comfortable living had softened him. He wasn't street no more. He was still ghetto, that you couldn't escape, but now he was soft pillows, cable TV, recliners, and house slippers. He was domesticated. Weak.

Malcolm sneered in disgust, the fangs making the expression twice as menacing. If the man didn't remember where he came from real quick, Malcolm would have to turn Rick's crisp, new white T-shirt all red.

"You know I'm your dog, Malcolm."

"Yeah. I know, Rick. I know." Malcolm slipped past him into the house, carrying a garment bag filled with expensive designer suits from Georgio Armani, Hugo Boss, and Gianni Versace.

"So, where is your woman?"

Malcolm laughed out loud when he saw Rick flinch and shudder in horror.

"Don't worry, nigga. I'm not gonna hurt her. I just want to meet her. I mean, since we are going to be roommates for a while."

Rick's shoulders slumped. His face hung with the defeated look of a whipped dog. If Malcolm still cared for the man, he would've killed him for that just to put him out of his misery.

"She's upstairs asleep. She works at night."

"All right, I'm gonna drop my shit here. Then you and me are gonna go on a little mission."

"What's up?"

Malcolm smiled carnivorously, baring his fangs in

a ghastly expression somewhere between pleasure and naked aggression.

"Did you know that Natasha lived around here somewhere?"

This time Rick did smile, that old goofy smile with the tip of his tongue sticking out from between his teeth like a hyena. His eyes began to gleam with a kind of lust. Perhaps he hadn't changed as much as Malcolm had first suspected. He still had his old taste for violence, especially when it carried a sexual component.

Rick shrugged into a thick, black, goose down jacket with *Southpole* emblazoned across the front in two-inch-high silver lettering. He wore baggy Southpole jeans and a Tommy Hilfiger skullcap. A pair of silver and black Nikes completed the look—urban thug. He draped a huge platinum chain that resembled some type of wild animal restraint around his neck. Malcolm glared at him.

"Why the fuck are you trying to look like a fucking drug dealer when we got heat on us already? If we get stopped by the cops, you know damn well I ain't goin' to jail."

"Man, if we run into a cop, they'll spot your spooky lookin' ass long before they spot this chain. So, fuck it. It ain't like your ass is incognito. You couldn't be low profile now if you tried."

Malcolm looked at himself in the living room mirror and considered maybe changing from the black suit into something a little more understated, but the fangs would give him away no matter what, and he wasn't about to try and pull his own teeth. At least, not now.

"Fuck it," he said, then tightened the belt on his trench coat and stepped out the door.

"Cops down here are a bunch of cowards anyway. Ain't no way a patrol cop is gonna try and stop two killers by theirself. If they ain't got SWAT behind them, they ain't shit," Rick said, digging in a desk drawer for his pistol and hurrying close behind Malcolm.

They left with the shotgun tucked deep in the pocket of Malcolm's trench coat along with a long straight razor. Rick had a 9mm Smith and Wesson that Malcolm guessed had never been fired. It had no doubt sat in its fancy case ever since it was purchased. Malcolm knew Rick wanted a gun just so he could say he had a gun, and the 9mm had been featured in so many rap videos that every wannabe thug who knew nothing about guns now owned one. Malcolm wasn't the type to carry a 9mm. The 9mm shot sleek, high-velocity bullets that left neat, clean, through-and-through wounds that were easy for surgeons to stitch. Malcolm liked blood. The grislier the wound, the better. He preferred his .40 caliber Sig-Sauer with its big, slow bullets that left exit wounds the size of children's fists. A 9mm was like a .40 on stun, and compared to the shotgun, it was a squirt gun.

Natasha's place was thirteen blocks from where Rick stayed. She lived alone, as far as Malcolm had been able to figure, though she had a boyfriend who spent several nights a week at her apartment. Malcolm was hoping he had chosen this night to sleep over. The detectives were right about one thing. Killing only one victim no longer satisfied him. He needed more.

The little apartment atop the hoagie shop on Federal Street where Natasha lived was surprisingly nice. It had new carpeting in a gray that was almost silver, with thick upgraded padding, new furniture in that artsy antique style from Z-gallery made of iron and steel. The counter tops were either cultured stone or tumbled marble. The cabinets, tables, chairs, and bookcases were oak, mahogany, or cherry wood. A black leather sofa and a laptop iMac computer completed the look of nuevo urban success. Malcolm couldn't help wonder what she did for a living.

"Where is this bitch?"

"She'll be home soon. She probably went out on a date with her little boyfriend."

Malcolm looked around her apartment. There were pictures of Natasha's mother, her older sister, and her current boyfriend. He picked up a photo album and began turning through the stiff, yellowing pages. He wouldn't admit it to himself, but he was secretly looking for a picture of himself, an old letter or a poem, some sign that he had actually meant something to her, had made some impact on her life.

There was nothing. He began tearing her high school pictures in half with his teeth, remembering what that smooth, supple flesh had felt like beneath his lips years ago, imagining what it would feel like between his teeth now.

Natasha had ripped his heart out fifteen years ago. He would rip hers out today. His eyes began to tear up. Malcolm roared and threw the photo album across the room. He smashed everything he could get his hands on, shattering the beautiful, expensive furniture with his fists, splintering the rich wood, and sending shards of marble and granite flying. His elbows cracked through table and counter tops with psychotic fury.

Rick watched without comment. He muttered a silent prayer that Natasha made it home soon, before Malcolm got so out of control he turned his fury on the closest living substitute, on Rick. He took hold of the 9mm tucked in his waistband and jacked a round into the chamber. Just in case.

# XXXIII.

Natasha tried to pretend that Edward's calm, soothing words were having some impact.

"Everything's going to be fine. The cops have it under control. You know I wouldn't let anything happen to you."

She had changed her name and moved out of Germantown after high school. Her phone number and address were unlisted. She had no contact with anyone she knew 15 years ago. Even the cops were unable to locate her. She had avoided contacting them out of fear that they might lead Malcolm to her. So far, she'd been safe. More than a decade had passed since she'd seen Malcolm, but she knew he was out there looking for her, and all her precautions, all of Edward's soothing words, all of the police efforts to catch Malcolm weren't going to stop what was coming. She knew it the day she slept with Reed. She'd told herself that Malcolm loved her enough to forgive her, but she'd known. When she told Edward what Malcolm did to Reneé, she could feel the knife sliding into her own gut, opening her up, spilling her intestines onto the floor. Edward didn't understand. The cops didn't understand. But she knew.

"He's probably just running from the police now.

He did kill a cop, after all. If they catch him, he's done. Natasha? Natasha, are you still listening?"

"Uh huh. Look, I've still got a lot of work to do here. I'll give you a call when I get home."

"You sure you don't want to stay at my house? At least until this whole thing is over?"

Natasha thought about it and quickly dismissed the idea. She knew Edward wanted to protect her, but he couldn't. If Malcolm found her at Edward's house, they were both dead. Alone, maybe she could reach him. He loved her once. Maybe that meant that he wouldn't murder her?

How could a man love someone and then kill her?

Those others, yes. Even Reneé she could understand. But she and Malcolm had been something special. Reneé was his lover, but she'd never been his friend. They'd never laughed together the way Natasha had made Malcolm laugh with her. She had been his friend. But then, so had Reed.

The fear started in her again. She'd been fighting it all day, but now it gripped her deep in her stomach, twisting. It clamped down on her spine and shook her. Natasha dropped the phone and grabbed hold of the desk, holding on as the world turned and flipped at odd angles. She squeezed her eyes shut and tried to resist the urge to crawl under the desk and curl into a fetal position. If she gave up now, she was dead for sure. Malcolm would eat her alive. She picked up the phone and let out a long breath to steady her nerves.

"Natasha? Natasha?"

"I'm here, and thanks for the offer, but I think I need to be alone tonight. I'm pretty worn out, and I sleep better in my own bed."

"Are you sure?"

"Yes. I'll see you tomorrow."

There was a long awkward pause as Edward struggled with the idea of saying, "I love you." Natasha felt his struggle and wasn't in the mood for it. She hung up the phone, helping him to solve his dilemma. She knew Edward loved her, but he didn't want to be the first one to say so. It was one of his insecurities. He didn't want to be the only one in the relationship who was "in love."

Natasha didn't want to be in love at all, not with anyone ever again. Love scared her. She'd loved Malcolm. Malcolm had loved her. And because of that love, she'd probably be murdered.

Natasha dropped her head to the desk and cried. She hated herself for it. They were tears of self-pity and fear. She felt weak and pathetic, but the crying helped. She could feel eyes on her as people walked past her office and looked in at her, watching her sob like a baby.

She'd always hated the fact that all the offices at Creative Computer Concepts were made of glass. She felt like a bug in a child's ant farm. Natasha loved her job. It wasn't what she thought she'd be doing when she was an art major at Creative and Performing Arts. By now, she figured she'd be showing her Picassoesque oil paintings at galleries all over Greenwich Village, Paris, and Italy. Now, she channeled all her artistic talents into putting a good 21st century face on automotive supply stores, furniture warehouses, restaurants, and discount stores. She spent the greater portion of her day in cyberspace. The good thing was that computer geeks were supposed to be eccentric, so she could come to work in Birkenstocks, paisley skirts, loose, blousy, midriff shirts that revealed her pierced belly button and sunflower tattoo, and she could read comic books at her desk and call it research. In other words, being a professional didn't mean she had to grow up.

There was a soft knock at her door, and Natasha knew it was one of her fellow geeks coming to be supportive, probably hoping that her moment of weakness would make her an easy lay for the right comforting shoulder. The last thing she wanted to do was hear trite words of support and encouragement from some leering quasi-virgin whose sexual vocabulary included computer jargon.

One of her co-workers, a disheveled computer-game junkie with an Adam's apple the size of a golf ball, opened the door without waiting be invited and stuck his head in.

"Are you okay?"

Natasha sighed heavily and slammed her hand down on the table.

"Go away. Yes, I'm sure. No, I don't want to talk about it."

She didn't even bother to look up to see his reaction.

She heard the soft footsteps tentatively creep away. She hated to admit it, but her own cruelty energized her and shook her out of her depression. She got up from her desk, picked up her Carhartt bomber jacket and Kenneth Cole black leather purse, and walked toward the elevator. The closer she came to the street, to abandoning the safety and mundanity of the office, the less confident she felt. By the time she reached the elevators, she felt like she was walking toward the gas chamber.

It was the same dull, hopeless dread she'd felt since she heard Malcolm's name on the news. When she heard that he was wanted in connection with Reed's slaughtered family and that Reneé and *her* family were missing, when she learned that Malcolm was the prime suspect in the brutal murders of half a dozen families over the years, Natasha felt every meal, every breath, was potentially her last. She felt every person she spoke with was goodbye. Her senses were aroused and fevered as if for the last time. She was a condemned woman, and she'd never felt more alive.

The elevator doors slowly shut, locking her in its tomb, and began to descend. Going home was the scariest part of her day as she waited to feel his powerful hands clamp around her throat.

Each evening at the end of her workday, when she

stepped through the door to her apartment and found it empty, the relief, the release of tension, was almost sexual, orgasmic. She would collapse onto her couch and stare out the window, wondering where Malcolm was and when he was coming for her, how much longer she had.

The elevator doors opened with a whoosh, and Natasha stepped into the lobby, walking briskly, her heels tip-tapping across the granite tile and through the glass revolving doors. Cold air hit her face. The chill afternoon air on her skin felt refreshing, invigorating, strangely soothing after eight and a half  hours in her little office inhaling stagnant air and staring at her computer screen. She walked quickly toward the subway, weaving between slower pedestrians as she lengthened her stride into the walking sprint that she'd used ever since she'd been in high school, walking home beside her 6'5" boyfriend.

She stood on the subway platform waiting for her train and staring at the other passengers, wondering how many of them were worried about being murdered when they got home.

The moment Malcolm heard Natasha's keys in the front door, a rush of adrenaline and endorphins dumped into his bloodstream. The excitement was luscious, sensual. He hadn't seen Natasha face to face since he'd left the hospital fifteen years ago with stitches and staples holding his throat together. He wanted her now more than he'd known possible.

The apartment was a tomb. Malcolm hadn't turned on a light. The sun set, and night crept in to slowly leech away all light. He sat in the living room, staring at the front door, watching the shadows slip along the floor toward him. He hadn't spoken to Rick, who was nervously pacing from one room to the next, in hours. The tenebrous shadows had occupied all of his attention as the night slowly absorbed him, sucking his black skin down into darkness, leaving only his feral silver smile glinting in the faint moonlight.

When the door opened, the widening triangle of light from the hall reached across the floor, slicing a wedge out of the darkness that left Malcolm's legs and feet revealed. Natasha was so busy with her oversized purse and shrugging out of her extra-large bomber jacket that she almost didn't notice. Then, just before she shut the door and turned on the light, she stopped, frozen. Her breathing became quick and audible. Malcolm leaned forward in his chair until the bottom half of his face entered the funnel of light so that only his mouth and chin were visible, leaving his eyes still enshrouded in night. He smiled ear to ear and ran his tongue over the tips of his platinum canines.

Natasha's silhouette shook and swayed, backlit by the hall light. She didn't speak. Her hand was on the light switch, but she hadn't turned it on. Her other hand was still on the front door knob, but she hadn't shut it or tried to run. She seemed confused about what to do. She was just frozen there. Her breath came faster and faster. Malcolm could see her chest heaving. It looked as if she might be having a heart attack. She took one long, ragged breath and exhaled long and slow. Her breathing then returned to normal. Malcolm was impressed.

"Hello, Natasha."

"Malcolm," Natasha finally said in a calm, measured tone, not a question or a welcome, just an acknowledgement.

"Close the door and leave the lights out."

"Yeah, I remember. You and your thing with the dark."

Her tone held the glimmer of sarcasm, but there was something else there, a hint of sexual innuendo, the same fatal flirtatiousness, the same fearless, careless mischievousness that had first attracted him. That same devil-may-care attitude had no doubt led them to this moment the way it had once led her to fuck Reed.

Natasha shut the door to enclose them in crypt-like darkness. Malcolm's eyes had adjusted to the darkness. He could see her clearly without the light. He felt his own pulse quicken as he realized that she looked exactly the same as she had 15 years ago. Not a wrinkle or a gray hair or a pound of extra weight. She still dressed the same. Her mannerisms were the same. Her hair was still cut short like a boy's in what was almost a crew cut. She still had that slight, slender frame with small breasts and large ass perched high on her back that almost seemed out of place on a body so skinny. It was disconcerting. She was a woman in a child's body.

Natasha had never been very tactful, and 15 years hadn't seemed to have added much finesse. Even faced with violent annihilation, she got right to the point.

"So, did you miss me, or did you come here to kill me too?"

Love died hard in Malcolm. But so did hate. He smiled but didn't reply. He rose from the overstuffed leather lounge chair and stretched, drawing out the moment, luxuriating in his own power.

He looked bigger than Natasha remembered. In high school, Malcolm had been tall and skinny. Now, he was huge. Even in his suit, she could see his powerfully built shoulders and chest, his biceps stretching his sleeves, ready to rip through the seams of his finely tailored jacket. His body seemed to have been engineered for violence. His eyes were boiling pits of dark flame. She could see her reflection in their hard, dark surface, boiling on his retinas like ink in a cast-iron skillet. As he approached her, Malcolm seemed to bring the darkness with him, swallowing up all the light in the room. He was like a black hole about to suck her down into the void.

"Yes, I missed you, and yes, I'm here to kill you."

Rick also stepped out of his shadows, and Natasha visibly recoiled from him. She obviously remembered him. She'd never trusted or liked him. Malcolm remembered the way Rick used to leer at her when he thought Malcolm wasn't looking, like a starving mongrel slavering hungrily beneath his master's table, waiting for his chance to eat. Rick was a sneaky little psychopath, and seeing him in her apartment, waving a big shiny gun at her, was freaking her out even more than did Malcolm's presence.

"Wait," Malcolm barked.

"What's he doing here?"

"Back up," Malcolm answered.

"You were afraid I'd be too much for you?" She was taunting him.

Malcolm responded with another gruesome smile.

"I don't want anyone interrupting us."

Malcolm wanted her so badly he could taste the smell of her skin. He wasn't ready to see her die. Killing her would be hard, not like doing Reneé had been easy.

She had disappointed and disgusted him. Fat, filthy, living in squalor with her dimwitted, overweight husband and her litter of dimwitted, overweight kids. She'd been the first woman he'd ever fallen in love with, and even more special to him, she'd been the first woman to fall in love with him, the first to look at him and not see a monster, the first to see something special, something good that could be loved, something he couldn't even see in himself.

Then she'd fucked Reed, turned her back on Malcolm, betrayed him. He was sickened by what she'd allowed herself to become. It had been a pleasure to end her existence, to make her suffer, scream, beg as he cut open her torso and fucked her insides, ejaculating within her ribcage and onto her still beating heart. He didn't know how she could've possibly imagined that life with that slovenly, lowbred, peckerwood she married would be better for her than the life Malcolm offered her. There was nothing that Malcolm would not have done for her. He would have conquered the world for her and laid it at her feet. Instead, she'd chosen to lay her pearls before swine. So he'd come to take both the pearls and the swine to slaughter. He'd turned her filthy white trash home into a butcher shop.

Malcolm remembered how Reneé looked when she opened the door and saw him. Her face twisted in terror, and Malcolm saw something else in her fear: guilt. And that had been enough. He ripped that family apart. He'd wanted to destroy every part of her, every part of the life she'd built without him. Even the kids had not escaped his wrath. That was the first family he'd taken, and afterwards, he'd been ashamed at what he'd done to the kids. So he hid the bodies. He wrapped them in trash bags and stuffed them in the Impala, the kids in the trunk, Reneé and her pig of a husband in the back seat.

The drive back to Germantown had been nerve-wracking. A casual inquiry from any traffic cop and he'd have been fucked. When he finally made it back to his neighborhood, he buried the bodies in the basement of an abandoned house on Duvall Street. He felt nothing as he shoveled dirt on top of her lifeless body. She was dead, her whole family was dead, and he still felt the emptiness, the sadness, the rage, but not guilt, not remorse.

When he packed the dirt down with his foot, he began to smile. He did feel something. Joy. This killing had been exhilarating, electric. He felt a euphoria wash over him as he replayed the moment he ripped the trench knife from Reneé's belly to her throat, feeling her hot steaming guts boiling out of the incision, the blood wash over his hands in a warm, red torrent. Malcolm savored the look on her face as she begged for her life, promised to love him again as she tried to tempt him with her disgusting fat body. He'd felt nothing but contempt for her. In his heart, he'd still thought of her as perfect all these years, and seeing her as she really was freed him from delusion. She was disgusting, inferior, not worth the years he'd spent suffering over his false memories. Malcolm wanted to reclaim those wasted years from Reneé one pound of flesh at a time.

He'd left their burial scene in a walking dream, not seeing the streets as he whizzed past at nearly 60 miles an hour, but instead, the mortal terror of his victims played out before his eyes as if he were watching them on a VCR. Finally, he'd had to pull off to the side of the road to release the roiling storm of sexual agitation building within him. After he satisfied himself, he went back to Reneé's house to clean up the evidence, worried that someone would make the connection between them. But that connection had been severed fifteen years ago. No one even noticed that they were gone. That killing thrilled him more than any other.

So, when he found out that Reed was having a child, The Chaperone had become The Family Man. Soon afterward, Malcolm tracked down Natasha. But he knew that if she disappeared too, the police would start to get suspicious, and the only connection between the two girls were Malcolm and Reed and Rick. But Rick would never tell; he was loyal. Reed would have pointed the cops right to his doorstep. That was all a moot point now. Everyone knew Malcolm was The Family Man, so now there really was no reason not to kill Natasha.

Rick wanted to kill her, and Malcolm knew Rick, the type who let his emotions better him, the type to do something impulsive. Malcolm wasn't so sure he wanted her dead just yet or so fast. But he knew he wanted to hurt her. He needed to hurt her like she'd hurt him.

"What do you mean, wait?!" Rick's face was screwed up in a scowl of anger and disgust.

"Don't mad dog me, nigga!" And though Rick turned away from Malcolm's fury, his expression hadn't changed.

"I thought we came here to kill this bitch."

"Oh, I want to do much more than kill her."

Malcolm reached out and gripped Natasha's jaw in his hand, digging his long, spidery fingers into her cheeks. He pulled her closer until her face was less than an inch from his. With his other hand, he reached around and grabbed her ass.

"Daddy's home," he growled.

With one hand, Malcolm grabbed hold of the front

of Natasha's shirt, nearly jerking her off her feet as he violently ripped it from her. Her small, perfectly round breasts bounced and bobbled when he ripped the shirt down off one shoulder and tossed it to the ground. Her other shirtsleeve remained on her shoulder, strings dangling where the stitches popped. She didn't bother to try to cover herself. She let her arms dangle limply at her sides, and the rest of her shirt slowly slid down her arm to the floor.

Malcolm licked his canines. His eyes roamed her creamy, silky white skin. As Malcolm's arousal increased, so did his aggression. He unsheathed his straight razor and grabbed Natasha's skirt, ripping that off as well.

"Don't move."

With the straight razor in his hand, Malcolm knelt down in front of her and sliced off her panties.

Once again, he reached out and grabbed her naked buttocks, gently caressing each cheek. He pulled her closer until her pubic hair was pressed against his lips. Lovingly, he kissed her vagina, slipping his tongue up inside her. She shook with fear and what might've been excitement. He released her, looked up into her eyes, and smiled, again dragging his tongue over the gleaming tips of his platinum canines.

# XXXV.

Natasha trembled as she remembered sex with Malcolm. His feral aggression had been exciting at first, intense, then it had started to turn violent. He once choked her unconscious during sex. He used to bite her so hard on the neck, shoulders, ass, and face that he drew blood. He had only been seventeen then.

Now, he was a man and, more than that, a killer. Then there was Rick, a sadistic bully who needed to humiliate others to feel good about himself. Watching Malcolm touch her as she stood there naked and vulnerable was obviously exciting Rick. He was grabbing and tugging at his crotch, bouncing around as he watched the two of them and grinning his wild, goofy hyena grin. Again, Natasha shuddered and began to wish she was already dead.-

"Grab her. We're going back to your place. I don't want us getting interrupted."

"Yeah, man, but my lady's there. We can't be doin' this shit in front of her!"

"Fuck her. Just grab this bitch and let's go."

All the madness drained out of Rick's eyes. He was seeing his meal ticket fluttering away on the breeze. He looked at Malcolm and amended that thought; it was blowing away in a hurricane.

"Malcolm, it ain't just that she's my wife. She takes care of me, man. I ain't got to work. I don't cook or clean. Nigga, I'm set for life! And you about to fuck it all up bringin' this bitch to my house!"

"Look, nigga. Someone is gonna get fucked tonight. Fucked, tortured, and put to sleep. And it don't have to be *this* bitch," Malcolm growled. "It's all up to you."

Malcolm stepped up to loom over Rick and turned his face downward to watch the smaller man cower. Rick cowered.

"All right, man. Shit!"

"Yeah, nigga. That's what I thought."

Rick tucked the 9mm back into his waistband and grabbed Natasha's wrists.

"I can't believe he's got me involved in this shit," Rick whispered to Natasha. He walked her toward the door when Malcolm stopped him.

"Fool, are you just gonna walk her naked ass outside like that? Give her your fuckin' jacket or something."

Reluctantly, Rick handed Natasha his jacket. She snatched it from him and quickly wrapped it around herself. It came nearly to her knees and only served to emphasize how naked she was beneath it.

# XXXVII.

They stepped out of the apartment, slowly closed the door, and began walking down the stairs to the street. Malcolm stopped Rick and Natasha on the stairs. He put both hands on Natasha's shoulders, squeezing firmly.

"You know me, Natasha," Malcolm purred in a voice so low and rumbling it sounded more like a tightly tuned high-performance engine than human speech.

His eyes seized hers and held them.

"Scream, try to signal anyone, try to get away, and you will die.

"I know what you're thinking. You're thinking that I'm going to kill you anyway, and you're probably right, but as long as you're alive, there's at least a chance. A chance someone might rescue you. A chance I might spare your life. But your chances can run out real quick if you fuck with me, Natasha."

Malcolm released her shoulders and walked down the stairs. Natasha knew he felt certain she wouldn't try anything. She also knew he was right. She wouldn't try to run. As long as there was a chance to live, she couldn't throw her life away.

Rick drove the Cherokee back to his house, complaining the whole way about what his wife would say when he walked through the door with this naked female hostage. Malcolm and Natasha sat in the back seat. Malcolm seemed to be drawing inward. He stared at the back of Rick's head and gnashed his teeth, growling low and deep in his throat.

Natasha had seen him like this many times during their relationship. It was never a good thing. She looked out the window, watching the streets go by in a blur, watching the people rushing to and fro on the sidewalk, oblivious to her peril. She wished she were out there with them. She smelled the crisp night air and imagined herself hurrying along the sidewalk on her way to her apartment but turning around at the last minute and heading to a bookstore or a coffee shop instead, spending the night sipping hot chai instead of being chauffeured to her own murder.

"Man, my fuckin' wife is gonna fuckin' kill me!"

Malcolm reached around the seat and grabbed Rick's windpipe, squeezing the Adam's apple in his powerful fingers. Rick thrashed about in a panic, trying to free himself from the crushing vise around his throat, wheezing hoarsely as he tried to suck in oxygen.

With his other arm, Malcolm removed the gun from Rick's waistband and held it to Rick's right temple. The Jeep swerved as its driver struggled for air, bounced up on the median and then back onto the road, narrowly avoiding a garbage truck heading down the street in the opposite direction.

"Shut the fuck up. Do you hear me? Shut the fuck up!"

He squeezed even harder, bringing tears to Rick's eyes and causing him to see spots as he choked and gasped for air. Malcolm released him and sat back, still glaring at the back of his head and with the gun still pointed at his back. Rick coughed and wheezed, struggling to get air back into his lungs and coughing even more as the air he inhaled seemed to burn his throat.

"And if you crash, I'm gonna kill you."

Rick was silent for the remainder of the ride. Natasha silently prayed for the first time in over a decade.

# XXXVIII.

They stepped out of the Jeep, Rick's eyes cast downward, avoiding Malcolm's.

Malcolm barely noticed. He looked up and down the block. The sidewalks were empty, and there were no nosy neighbors peeking out of widows as far as he could tell. The lights were on in the house. Rick's wife was awake.

Rick pulled his keys from his front pocket, and Malcolm noticed with amusement that the man's hands trembled as he used the key. The man was losing it and quickly becoming a liability. Malcolm would have to do something about that soon.

The living room was empty, but the lights were on, and the aroma of baked chicken and hot biscuits drifted from the kitchen along with the sounds of pots and plates lightly clanking together.

"Uh … honey? Uh … we've got guests."

Malcolm stepped into the house with Natasha in tow. He turned, locked the door, and pushed the naked woman down onto the couch as Rick's "better half" rushed from the kitchen. She ran to Rick, simultaneously wiping gravy from her hands with a dishrag and smoothing down her hair. It had started to frizz from too long in the steaming kitchen and was sitting up on her head like she'd been struck by lightning. She turned her back on Malcolm as she gave Rick his welcome home kiss.

Out of habit, Malcolm looked down at her ass, and her ass was magnificent. Perched high on her back, bouncing and jiggling as she moved. Even in the baggy sweatpants she wore, he could make out the perfectly rounded outline of each buttock. Malcolm's first thought was that he couldn't remember ever seeing an ass more perfect, then he corrected himself. He could remember. He could remember exactly where he'd seen it.

When CC turned around, Malcolm was smiling … and licking his fangs.

It didn't take CC long to figure out who Malcolm was either.

"Oh my God, Rick! That's the guy! That's the guy all the cops are after! The one who's been killing those families!"

Malcolm stepped closer to her, still grinning. She recoiled, taking several steps backward and wincing as if anticipating a blow. Rick made a move to shield her, and Malcolm gently, almost casually, pushed him aside without even looking.

"The cops? Looking for me? Imagine that. Oh, that reminds me. How is Detective Bryant?"

The guilt that colored her face with a scarlet red confessed everything. Malcolm turned to Rick and waited for him to put two and two together. Rick looked from Malcolm's rather amused if still sinister countenance to his wife's guilt-ridden face, and his jaw dropped open.

"Fuck is he talkin' about, CC? Who da fuck is Detective Bryant?"

"That's the nigga she's fuckin' behind your bitch-ass back. The same muthafucka that's tryin' to hunt me down."

With that, Rick slapped CC so hard that she spun 180 degrees and fell to the floor. He straddled her hips, punching her repeatedly. She screamed and struggled, trying to buck him off and raising her arms to shield her face. His fists struck her in the chest, shoulders, and stomach. Malcolm noticed how, even in his rage, he avoided hitting her in the face with a control that indicated he'd done this before. When Rick clamped his hands around CC's throat and began to squeeze, Malcolm reached over and pulled him off of her.

"Don't kill her. I think I can use her to get at that detective. The nigga's in love with this bitch."

Rick's chest was heaving, and his eyes were wild with rage and starting to well up with tears.

"Man, get your shit together and tie this bitch up! You got any duct tape?"

Rick went to get the duct tape. As he walked down the hallway, he punched a wall and cursed loudly. From the sound of his voice, it was obvious that he was crying. Malcolm laughed, a horrible sound somewhere between a witch's cackle and a dog's bark. He bent down to help CC to her feet. She offered no resistance as he tossed her across the room like a rag doll. Natasha pulled CC up onto the couch with her. The two women hugged each other and stared over at Malcolm. Malcolm stared back at them with a massive erection in his pants. Natasha shuddered and turned away. CC continued to stare. She appeared to be in shock.

Rick returned with the tape and immediately began binding CC's hands and feet. Tears ran down his cheeks, and he muttered curses under his breath. He slapped her twice more before he finished taping up her feet, split her lip and caused it to bleed. Malcolm grabbed Natasha and dragged her upstairs, leaving the unhappy couple to settle their differences in private.

"We're gonna use your guestroom for a while. Don't kill that bitch. I'm serious. When you're done, come on up and we'll have some fun."

Malcolm pulled Rick's jacket off of Natasha's shoulders and ran his hands over her naked body. "I'll save you some."

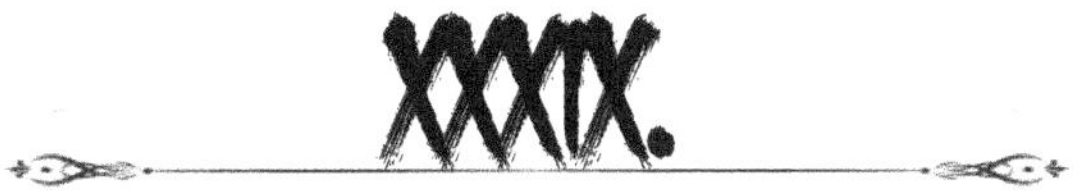

Natasha closed her eyes and tried to shut out the pain while still pretending to enjoy herself. Maybe if he thought she liked it, maybe if he thought she still wanted him, thought she still loved him, he wouldn't torture her too badly. Maybe he might even let her live, or at least kill her quickly. Maybe he wouldn't let Rick have his turn.

She tried not to show her fear, her disgust, her anger. She tried to ignore the penis slamming in and out of her, feeling as if it was pushing up into her guts. When the teeth clamped down on her shoulder and the fangs punctured her flesh, she tried not to scream. But she did.

*Oh, God, it hurt so bad!*

When he turned her over and she felt his penis ripping into her anus, she couldn't help herself. She screamed and cried and begged and cursed. Malcolm only laughed and pounded into her harder. His laughter sounded like something rumbling up from hell. She could feel his penis swelling inside her as he approached an orgasm; she felt his hand clamp around her throat and begin to squeeze. She couldn't breathe. Everything went gray, and then it all went black. She was grateful for the escape, the peace of oblivion.

When she awoke, Rick was on top of her, inside of her. His tongue was lolling out of his mouth, and his eyes were wild. He was muttering something about CC fucking some other guy. She could feel him thrusting inside her, but it was a dull, distant pain, more like the memory of a pain. Out of the corner of her eye, she could see a huge shadow, pregnant with menace, so dark it stood out against the backdrop of night. She closed her eyes and tried hard to slip back into oblivion, but the pain kept her wide awake. She opened her eyes again and looked back at the huge shadow that filled the corner of the room. It was moving toward her, its fangs reflecting the moonlight.

Malcolm bound Natasha's arms and legs to the bedposts and left her. He wasn't finished with her. He wanted her to suffer for a long time, and he wanted to derive as much pleasure as possible from her suffering.

She had tried to convince him she was still in love with him, hoping to be spared. Malcolm didn't care whether she loved him or not. Even if he still loved her (and he wasn't sure he didn't), he'd still have to hurt her. He had made a promise to himself long ago that he would repay every injury ten-fold. He owed her pain, lots of pain.

When her hands and feet were firmly secured, he kissed her once on the forehead, turned, and left. He walked downstairs with Rick walking closely behind.

In the living room, CC sat on the couch, immobile. There were a just few more bruises on her than when Malcolm left Rick alone with her. Tears trickled from her eyes, down her bruised cheek as Malcolm moved toward her.

"Congratulations, whore. You get to live."

He grabbed CC by her hair and yanked her up from the couch.

"We're going to see your boyfriend."

Rick made a sound like he was choking and punched the wall again. Malcolm laughed and led them both out the door and over to the Jeep.

Several police vehicles cruised by as they made their way through Center City, Philadelphia. Malcolm was calm. He knew that slouched down in the back seat behind the dark tinted windows, he was almost invisible, and Rick was far too scared to start speeding or do anything stupid that might attract police attention and get Malcolm angry and himself dead. CC was catatonic.

Malcolm had seen this before. CC had checked out. Her mind couldn't handle the stress and had simply shut down. Even if he were inclined to let her live, he knew her mind would never reassemble itself. No amount of psychotherapy could put the pieces back together. CC was gone.

# XLI.

City Hall loomed above them, covered in gargoyles, angels, thousands of pigeons that seethed as if the building itself were alive and breathing, and, of course, the monolithic statue of Benjamin Franklin watching over the city like a silent golem. Beneath the famous statue, a single vehicle rolled down Broad Street, past the clothing stores, record shops, and hotels where young urban professionals sipped martinis in posh restaurants. Violin music floated like a funeral procession of one.

CC watched a couple laughing in the window of an expensive seafood restaurant. The woman threw her napkin at her companion, who caught it and laughed even louder. CC's eyes clouded with tears. The last man who'd made her laugh like that was about to be murdered, and she was about to be murdered. She was certain of it.

Rick might think he was Malcolm's accomplice, but CC saw the way Malcolm looked at him. She heard the way he spoke to Rick. There was no respect there, no warmth. There was a distance between them that Malcolm carefully maintained, and he was widening it by the second. There was only one reason for that.

CC had no illusions about what was going to happen to her once they reached their destination. Hers would not be a quick, painless death. She, like everyone else in Philly, knew all about Malcolm and what he did to his victims. She'd seen the TV reports, read the newspapers, imagined the horror his victims must have felt, the pain, the helpless woe. She knew how he tortured his victims, ripped them apart with those gruesome silver fangs while they were still alive and conscious.

One news reporter had commented that he apparently "had no taste for carrion." The horrifying accounts of his rampages had replayed every evening in her nightmares. The news stories had disturbed her so much that she'd stopped watching television altogether.

Now, she was about to become one of those gruesome stories. The thought paralyzed her. The tale of her death would doubtlessly keep some folks awake at night. Her stomach rolled in revulsion as she imagined those silver fangs shredding her breasts.

They passed the steps of the Art Museum, made famous by Rocky Balboa's triumphant run, and CC remembered sitting with a handsome law student beneath one of the many ancient statues standing guard over the Art Museum's ornate courtyard. It was the 4th of July, nine years ago, and they were there to see the fireworks display. Now, that handsome law student would be an accomplice in her murder.

CC turned her thoughts away from what was about to happen. She could see no way to avoid it, so there was no sense dwelling on it. She wanted her last moments before the end to be as happy and peaceful as possible. She sought refuge in her memories, deep within her own mind. She transported herself away from Rick and Malcolm and back to her wedding day, the happiest day of her life, when she'd been hopeful, confident of a future filled with love and joy. When that memory faded, she thought of Detective James Bryant, how he'd held her, kissed her, made love to her. She held on to his memory like a talisman against the evil that surrounded her, and held on to the slim hope he would save her.

245

# XLII.

The house was empty when Reed smashed through the front door, brandishing the Beretta in a shooter's stance. He called out for Malcolm but heard no reply. He rushed from room to room with the 9mm held out in front of him. He dashed up the stairs into the master bedroom and found it empty. Reed was screaming Malcolm's name at the top of his lungs, or rather, he thought he was. When he realized that he hadn't uttered a word, that it was the voices in his head screaming for blood, he was already past caring.

He turned around and headed to the little guestroom. He stopped abruptly, just outside the room. There was someone in there. He'd heard a noise, a muffled cough. Malcolm was in there, waiting to ambush him. Reed aimed the Beretta at the door and fired half of the fifteen-round magazine through it. He waited a second and listened. This time he heard nothing. He kicked open the door and looked around for Malcolm's bleeding corpse. What he found was a naked woman bound to a bed with duct tape, her eyes wide in terror. He recognized her immediately. It was Natasha. She looked exactly as he remembered her, her slight, delicate body that appeared only recently matured frozen between childhood and womanhood like some kind of sensuous changeling.

Her eyes, even while terrified, still had that glint of mischief and sexual energy. She'd always been wild. It wouldn't have surprised him one bit to discover that her current predicament was consensual. There were two bullet holes in the headboard. One was less than two inches from her head. Reed scanned her body for bullet wounds. He could've killed her, shooting through the door like that. But she seemed to be unhurt. At least unhurt by him.

Reed was amazed at how seemingly unchanged she was. She looked only slightly older than when he'd last seen her, 15 years ago. Her body was still that of a teenager. Her pubic hairs had been shaved cleanly, making her look even younger. Reed wondered if Malcolm had shaved her or if she just kept it that way herself.

A trickle of blood dripped down from her shoulder where Malcolm's fangs had bitten into her skin. Again, Reed checked to make sure he hadn't shot her. There were no bullet wounds that Reed could see. It looked like two of the bullets had hit the ceiling and three others had buried themselves in the floor. His nervous breathing had caused his gun hand to bounce up and down, sending the bullets high and low. If someone had been standing right in front of the door, only one or two of the eight bullets he fired would've hit. Reed was not confident that two bullets would've been enough to stop Malcolm.

Reed looked back at Natasha, bound and helpless. God she was beautiful! A look of impatience came into Natasha's eyes, and she began struggling against her bonds. Still Reed stood in the doorway, staring at her exposed breasts. Even lying on her back, they didn't sag much. Her hard, pointy nipples pointed skyward.

Malcolm had bound her legs, one to each post, so that she was spread-eagle on the bed. Reed grazed her smooth legs with his eyes, and a hunger started to rise in him. He knew he was staring at her naked body for too long and that his pants were ill equipped to hide his growing excitement, but something about seeing her bound and gagged, helpless, was turning him on.

He snapped free of the spell and stepped forward to free her, feeling ashamed for that unbidden response.

All fear had left Natasha, and she was staring at Reed with a look of impatience and annoyance. She knew what he'd been thinking. Reed flushed with embarrassment. He knew how inappropriate those thoughts were with her terrorized and raped by a madman. Reed made sure that he removed the tape from her mouth last and gently.

As soon as she was free, Natasha jumped up and pulled her pants back on. She threw on an oversized sweatshirt that hung to her knees, and Reed looked at her quizzically.

"These aren't my clothes. They ripped off all my clothes back at my apartment. These are Rick's."

Reed wanted to ask her what they'd done to her, but it was obvious from her attitude that she wasn't interested in reliving her recent torture. She was putting on the same tough front she'd maintained in high school. Back then, he'd believed that she really was that tough. Now, he knew better. Nobody was that tough.

"Where's Malcolm?"

"I don't know. He probably went after you. He's obsessed with you. He told me he was gonna pull your heart out and feed it to me."

Natasha looked away from Reed as she finished the rest.

"I was laying here, trying to work up the nerve … uh … to get myself ready to … I uh … I was thinking that if he did try to feed me your heart and I ate it, he'd …"

"Yeah, maybe he would. Or maybe he'd cut you up anyway."

Reed tried to catch her gaze, but she refused to meet his eyes. Instead, she busied herself trying to stuff balled up tube socks into the toe of Rick's sneakers so they'd fit her feet.

"We'd better hurry up. Who knows when they'll be back."

"You go. I'm staying. I've got to end this."

Now, Natasha did look at him. Her face filled with shock and then concern. She opened her mouth to speak, to try talking him out of staying, out of confronting Malcolm, then her expression changed to solemn acceptance, and she turned away and gathered up Rick's ski jacket. She shrugged it on and zipped it up, turned to leave.

"You came here to die then."

"Maybe," Reed said.

Natasha was halfway out the door when she stopped and looked back at Reed.

"That's why you came here, huh? For Malcolm? Yeah, how could you know I'd be here? You always seemed to be in the right place at the right time, but it was all just a coincidence, wasn't it? You were never the type to make things happen. Things happened and you just got caught up in them. When we made love back then, I was just looking for a way to make Malcolm notice me and there you were. Right place. Right time. Now you're caught up in this, another situation you can't control. You can't win here, Reed. Just get out. You don't have to do this."

"It's too late now," Reed whispered.

"You spent all of high school following Malcolm around. You don't have to follow him anymore. Malcolm brought you here. He *wants* you here. And if you stay, you'll die."

"Or he will."

Natasha looked down at the 9mm clutched in Reed's hand and shook her head with what looked like pity. She slipped out the door, walking quickly down the stairs. Reed heard the front door slam and her footsteps down the street, running. He knew she'd go to the police, and he knew that they would interfere. They'd want to arrest Malcolm, put him on trial, and execute him legally, humanely, but that could never happen. Reed had to see this out himself. It had to end.

# XLIII.

Detective Bryant was not doing much to hide his boredom. In fact, he was doing everything he could to let it be known. "Big Bird" Woo was briefing the taskforce on the newest developments in The Family Man case.

Among others, Detective Bryant felt his time would be better spent out on the streets, looking for Malcolm. He'd heard everything the lieutenant was saying before. After all, most of it came straight from his notes.

"We know that Malcolm has some type of vendetta against Reed Cozen stemming from their high school friendship. This friendship ended when Mr. Cozen had an affair with both of Malcolm's first two girlfriends. For some reason, Malcolm has never gotten over this betrayal and has come back to ruin Reed Cozen's life. This is the most likely scenario. How all of that ties into The Family Man murders, we are not entirely certain, and perhaps only Malcolm himself can explain that to us. We do know that all the victims in each case bear an uncanny resemblance to Reed, including Paul Cooper, Malcolm's former roommate, accomplice, and most recent victim.

"Another scenario we have to consider is that Reed

and Malcolm are somehow working together. That Reed Cozen contacted Malcolm to kill his family. I think we've pretty much discounted this theory; however, we still have to keep it in mind as a possibility, especially considering the fact that Reed is currently missing and armed with Detective Baltimore's gun. We are going to search the Germantown area thoroughly in the hopes that Reed is heading there to find Malcolm. We are also going to stake out Reneé Volaré's house on the possibility that either Reed or Malcolm may show up there."

Detective Trinidad raised his hand, and Lieutenant Woo acknowledged him with a nod.

"What about the other woman ... ummm ... Natasha? Has anyone located her yet?"

"No. Still no luck there. We are researching her social security number in case she changed her name, but she has probably left town. Maybe with the help of the FBI, we can cut through some of the red tape at the IRS and get copies of her tax forms. That should at least tell us where she works."

"The FBI?" all the detectives seemed to speak in unison.

"Yes, the FBI. As soon as a police officer was murdered, this became a federal matter. So now the Feebs are in. They are not going to take over the entire investigation. They are going to work with us to bring this whole thing to a speedy resolution."

"Yeah, bullshit," Detective Bryant barked.

"Excuse me, Detective?"

There was obvious annoyance in Lieutenant Woo's voice.

"I said bullshit. The Feds don't assist. They commandeer! They'll have total access to all of *our* files, and we won't have access to any of *theirs*! They won't tell us shit about what they find. We'll wind up being their fucking errand boys, doin' all the work while they take the credit. *We* lost a detective, not *them*. This should be our case. They'll muscle their way in and squeeze us out like they always do."

"I promise you, that will not happen."

"Yeah, right," Bryant grumbled, and this time Woo ignored him.

Captain Kelly stood up and, in a voice that for anyone else would've been a whisper but from him sounded like the roar of a full grown male lion, addressed Detective Bryant directly.

"You're worried that they'll take over the investigation? Well, your new job is gonna be to make sure that doesn't happen. Meet your new partner, Agent David Malcovich of the Federal Bureau of Investigation."

Detective Bryant stood as the man who'd been seated beside the podium, next to the captain and Lieutenant Woo, rose and took the center of the room.

"What tha fuck are you talking about, *partner*?" Bryant asked.

Agent Malcovich was another tall, slender, nondescript white boy whose beady eyes, weak chin, skinny neck with comically large Adam's apple, and crooked front tooth would forever keep him from being called handsome. He was average. He was the type of average that people pass every day in the halls at work. The guy people pass on the street, in the aisles at the grocery store, and think that they might know him or that they've seen him before only to realize that he just reminds them of every other average looking guy they see every day.

"This was the lieutenant's suggestion, and I support it," Captain Kelly said.

"This is the best way for us to share information on this case. Agent Malcovich is going to be partnered with you for the duration of the investigation," Lieutenant Woo added.

"Nah, Fuck that!"

"Detective!"

For the first time since Bryant had known him, Lieutenant Woo's eyes blazed with genuine fury. It was one thing to talk about him behind his back or to disrespect him in private, but to show such blatant disrespect in front of the whole taskforce and the FBI was going too far. Woo started down from the podium, moving at Detective Bryant as if he were about to tackle him. Reflexively, Bryant stepped back into a boxer's stance, with his fists clenched and his jaw set, waiting for the blows to fall. Captain Kelly stepped between the two men, instantly neutralizing them.

Detective Bryant dropped his hands and hung his head. He knew he was out of control, but he couldn't pull it together. He still wanted to hit someone. He just didn't know who.

Malcolm was killing cops, and Bryant was now saddled with an FBI agent who, to him, was no better than a rookie. The FBI may handle the big jobs, but those were few and far between. They spent years on a single case. The average first year rookie metropolitan police officer got more from experience six months on the street than an FBI agent got in six years. As a matter of principle, Philadelphia PD looked at the Feebs as glorified desk jockeys fighting crime from a computer keyboard.

Lieutenant Woo had already regained his composure. He straightened his meticulously pressed jacket and turned to retake his place behind the podium. Captain Kelly was breathing heavily and glared at both of them as if he was disappointed they hadn't tried to take swings at each other. A uniformed officer stuck his head inside the door and looked around, instantly absorbing the tension and hostility still boiling in the air. His body language said retreat, but he seemed to steel himself, at least enough to stutter out his message.

"Um, uh, Captain?"

"What!?" The captain growled, and the young officer literally turned as if to run out of the room before he caught himself and turned around to continue. No one in the room would've made fun of him if he had bolted out of there. They all knew exactly how he felt.

"Um, uh, there's a lady downstairs who says she knows where Mr. Cozen is. She said that Malcolm kidnapped her and Mr. Cozen rescued her."

Led by Captain Kelly, Detective Bryant, Lieutenant Woo, and Agent Malcovich, an avalanche of detectives rose like one living thing and thundered through the door. This time, the officer did bolt from the doorway, just in time to save himself from being trampled.

Sitting in the "nice" interrogation room, the one with the coffee machine, the water cooler, and the comfortable chairs that was actually more of a detective's lounge, Natasha sipped a cup of pungent black coffee and tapped her foot like a drum machine as Captain Kelly and Detective Bryant funneled through the door, followed by Agent Malcovich of the FBI. Bryant recognized her immediately. They'd been trying to locate her all day.

The captain and the FBI agent stood in opposite corners of the room. Detective Bryant pulled up a chair directly across from her. He fixed his expression into the hard, expressionless mask he used when interrogating suspects, then when his eyes met hers, his face softened into a friendlier, more understanding expression, the one he used when consoling victims. He'd done it just this way a thousand times before.

Bryant looked into her eyes and could see that she'd been through hell. He knew enough about Malcolm now to guess some of what she'd suffered. How she'd managed to survive amazed him. That she was somehow coping with it, that she wasn't suffering from shock, that her mind hadn't completely shut down and left her catatonic was what impressed him.

"Natasha Little?"

"It's Natasha Green now."

"Married?"

"No. Just hiding from Malcolm."

"So, tell me about what happened to you?"

While Bryant listened intently, taking notes and interrupting occasionally to ask for detail, she told him how she'd come home to find Malcolm and Rick in her apartment. How they'd dragged her to Rick's house and raped her. She told how they'd left her tied to the bed and how Reed had found her and set her free, about how he was going after Malcolm. Bryant passed a look to the captain. She was holding something back. He could see her choosing her words carefully, deciding what to tell and what to withhold.

"Why did Malcolm leave?" the FBI agent asked from his corner of the room.

"I don't know. What do you mean, 'Why?'"

"I mean, why are you still alive? Why didn't he stay and finish you off?"

Bryant studied her face as she looked at the agent, then she dropped her eyes to her lap, where she was twisting and wrenching her hands.

"What? What is it?" An unexpected sense of dread washed over him, as if deep down, he could sense what was coming.

"He's got CC," she whispered

Detective Bryant leaped from his chair and grabbed Natasha by her shoulders. The chair fell over and struck the hard tiled floor with a loud *clack* that filled the small room.

"What did you say?"

"CC is Rick's wife. Malcolm's got her, and he's coming after you. He's probably on his way to your house right now."

Detective Bryant backed away from Natasha, reaching for his chair as his legs went numb and threatened to give out. Not finding it, he continued to back away, shaking his head and seeing a montage of Malcolm's ripped and ravaged victims. They all had CC's face except for a few; those bore his. He tripped over the toppled chair and plopped down on the floor in the lotus position. He sat there, staring at Natasha, trying to deny what he'd just heard.

Captain Kelly waved off Agent Malcovich moving forward to help.

"Agent Malcovich, would you take Ms. Little … uh … Green out and get a statement from her, please?"

Kelly knelt down and put a hand on Bryant's shoulder.

"You wanna tell me about it?"

"Do I have a choice?" Bryant was still staring at the seat vacated by Natasha.

"No, not at all. You can certainly put the idea of going after Malcolm by yourself out of your head. And if I were you, knowing that I know how emotionally involved you are, I would be working hard to convince me to keep your black ass on this case. The suspect has killed your partner and has now kidnapped a woman I can only assume is your girlfriend. By all rights, I should sit you at a desk until this case is over."

"But you need me. None of those other clowns out there has a prayer of catching Malcolm."

"Malcolm is self-destructing. He'll catch himself."

"And how many more people will he kill when he explodes? How many cops?"

"Okay, then tell me about this girl."

"I met her in a strip club."

"Jesus, James! What is it with you?"

"Do you want to hear this or not?"

"Go ahead."

"We started dating a week ago. Things were getting pretty serious pretty fast. I think … I think I love her."

"Did you know she was married?"

"Yes."

"You fuckin' asshole." Captain Kelly wiped his palm down his face as if wiping away a sheen of imaginary sweat. He paced the floor, casting looks of disgust and disappointment at Bryant.

"Did you know she was married to Malcolm's fucking best friend?"

"No! Of course not."

"Well shit, James. I don't see how I can keep you on this case."

"What?"

That woke Bryant up. He leapt to his feet with a look of anguish and desperation stenciled across his features. His arms were flung out in supplication, as if he were preparing to drop to his knees and beg. His eyes were wild in his head, darting around in amazement as his mouth worked soundlessly, trying to find the words to convince the captain, to make him see, make him understand. Finally, he let his arms droop limply at his sides. Closing his eyes, he took a long, deep breath. His whole body shuddered with emotion, stiffened, hardened, and settled, like molten ore cooling into iron. When he reopened his eyes, iron filled them as well.

"Captain, I don't see how you can keep me off of it."

"If you get killed, don't expect a police funeral."

"What tha fuck does that mean?"

"It means that you are officially off this case, and if you go near Malcolm, you are officially fired."

Detective Bryant didn't bother to argue. The captain knew he would do what he had to. He had no choice in the matter. His destiny was scripted by his nature. It was not in his nature to sit on the bench when the game was in its final quarter.

Bryant turned his back on Captain Kelly and stormed out into the station house, where Agent Malcovich was seated at his desk with Natasha. He stepped behind his desk, glaring at Natasha intently and started to take his seat. With obvious embarrassment, Malcovich scrambled out of the detective's chair before Bryant sat right on top of him.

"Are you sure they're going to my house?"

"He'll go there. And if you're not there, he'll wait

for you. If you are there … he'll kill you." Natasha felt it was only fair to warn him.

"What about Reed?" Bryant continued to question her, ignoring her fatal prediction.

"He'll still be at Rick's house, waiting for Malcolm to come back."

Detective Bryant turned to Lieutenant Woo, who was still standing by his desk looking like a lap dog who suddenly discovered it could bite, trying to decide if it should.

"Big Bird! Why don't you make yourself useful and send a couple cars over to pick up Reed."

The Lieutenant started across the room toward Detective Bryant. He had had enough. The lap dog had decided to bite.

Bryant smiled as the tall, lanky Chinese cop strode toward him and the other police officers cleared a path for him. He raised his balled fists and curled his body into a tight defensive stance.

"Bring it, Big Bird." He growled.

"Stop it! Lieutenant! Detective! Back off!"

It was the first time anyone could remember actually hearing the captain yell.

"Woo, go ahead and get somebody over to pick up Reed Cozen. Bryant, get the fuck out of my precinct or your ass is on suspension!"

"For what?!"

Captain Kelly snarled in reply. Bryant left.

Agent Malcovich chased after him. He caught him on the stairs.

"Detective Bryant! Detective Bryant!"

"What?" It sounded more like a threat than a question.

"I'm supposed to ride with you."

"I'm off the case."

"You're what?"

"Captain took me off the case. You're gonna have to find another driver."

"What about Malcolm? He's going to your house. He's coming after you. What are you gonna do?"

The detective smirked. Then he grinned. Then his eyes went flat and lifeless, hard like the smooth surface of a river rock. The grin died from his face like a heart monitor flat lining. It was like witnessing a death.

"I'm going home."

# XLIV.

Reed didn't know what to do when he heard the first sirens shred the night air. He couldn't remember how long he'd been sitting on Rick's couch, listening to the voices of his dead wife and dead children raking his brain, no longer a comfort but a mind-rending cacophony, watching headlights from passing cars travel past the living room window. In between reality lapses, where he found himself arguing back at the voices, telling them to be patient, that their deaths would be avenged, he toyed with the gun in his lap. He was no longer certain that Malcolm's death would stop the voices, and despite the turmoil they caused in his head, he wasn't sure he wanted to lose them. He would be very alone without them.

Reed had never been this close to his family when they were alive. He had never heard them so clearly. The characters in his novels had been more real to him. They had received most of his attention, attention stolen away from his family. Now his family had his full attention, and if their voices were suddenly gone, his loss would be complete. Perhaps killing himself now and joining them was the better answer, he thought.

The voices screamed out in protest.

*Come to us, Daddy! But kill the bad man first. Make him pay, Daddy! Make him pay, and then you can come to us!*

But Reed wanted to join his family now. He missed them more every second, and as lost as he knew he'd feel without their voices in his head, it killed him to hear their pain, to hear their rage. He wanted to hear them laugh again, and he knew that couldn't happen until Malcolm was dead.

The sirens were closer now, and there were a lot of them. There was no longer any doubt that they were coming to Rick's house. Reed abandoned his post on the couch and slipped out the back door, into the miniscule yard with its ill-kept lawn and bald patches like a human scalp during the latter stages of chemotherapy. His body felt weak and numb as he scrambled over the weather-torn wooden fence that ringed in the yard. He staggered and swayed down the alley, away from the wail of the sirens. The need for sleep was pressing on him, but the voices would not let him.

*Not yet, Daddy. Not yet.*

The alleys became a maze, and Reed had no idea where he was when he finally emerged onto the street after twenty minutes of climbing fences and wandering alleys. He looked up and spotted Willard Rouse's two phallic monoliths and began heading in their direction, toward Broad Street and the subway.

Reed had neglected to ask Natasha where the detective lived. He knew Malcolm was going there, but he didn't know where "there" was. Malcolm was out there killing, and Reed didn't know how to get to him. He sat on the subway, traveling toward Germantown, with no idea how he would locate Bryant's home. His eyes closed, and he had nearly fallen asleep when he heard a staticky radio voice mention Malcolm's name.

His eyes snapped open, and he saw that there were two police officers standing above the subway bench where he had been slumped, nearly asleep. They didn't seem to be paying him any attention. They were eyeing a group of Black teenagers at the end of the subway car who didn't seem to be doing anything particularly illegal. Their radios continued to squawk, and through the police jargon, Reed could make out enough to know that half the cops in the city where converging on an address in Mount Airy.

Malcolm. It had to be where Malcolm was headed. Reed almost blew it and shot the two cops on the train. The police officers had suddenly shifted their attention to him as he rose from his seat to exit the subway, and Reed's hand gripped the Beretta, clicking the safety off and aiming it toward them beneath his jacket. But their attention returned to the group of teenagers, and Reed simply slipped past them and out the door, his nerves vibrating beneath his skin. Nervous perspiration rained down his forehead, but the cops hadn't noticed.

Reed got off the subway at Broad and Erie and caught the H bus to Mount Airy. The bus driver eyed Reed suspiciously as he boarded, but Reed didn't care. He would not be an obstacle. The transfer was so soaked with sweat when he handed it to the driver that the man almost handed it back.

The rocking and swaying of the bus as it navigated the minefield of potholes began to lull him to sleep. He was so tired.

*Reed? You have to find him, sweetheart. You have to kill him. He hurt me, Reed. He ... he ... raped me ... and ...*

Reed snapped awake with the sound of his wife's voice still whispering in his ear like a lullaby.

*You can do it, Reed. You have the gun. You can put two bullets in that Black bastard's head, and then I'll be yours again.*

"Yeah, I can do it."

Reed fell back to sleep, nuzzled safe in the memory of his wife's warm embrace, her arms wrapped protectively around him and her voice curling into his eardrum like cigarette smoke. The bus hit a pothole, and his head banged against the bus window. He continued to snore.

Reed woke up just as the bus pulled up two stops past where he'd intended to get off. He dashed from the bus with his head spinning from waking up too quickly and standing up too fast. He paused on the sidewalk and stared into the darkness while he brought the vertigo under control. Police cruisers whizzed past him, lights flashing, sirens silent. He slowed his pace and followed.

Reed focused on what he had to do. Kill Malcolm. Kill Malcolm's friend. Kill the man he'd betrayed. Add insult to injury. Rip open those old wounds and rub salty vinegar into them.

Jennie's voice protested.

*What the fuck are you saying, Dad? He murdered us. He tortured Mom! He raped her! He killed your family! He's not your friend! He's not even human! He's a monster! A vicious monster! KILL HIM, DADDY!*

Another voice in his head countered. This one sounded exactly like Malcolm.

*You started it, Reed. You brought this shit down. I return every injury, every injustice ten-fold. You knew this. You knew this, but you hurt me anyway. You fucked Reneé! You fucked Natasha! You killed your family, Reed! You brought this on them! You, Reed! You!*

Reed screamed. He pressed his hands to his head and screamed his throat raw. Lights went on, and shocked, curious faces pressed to windowpanes as he passed houses, shrieking his anguished wail. Tears rolled freely down his face. Again, he wondered if perhaps he should simply turn the gun on himself, but he missed his family, and Reed knew they wouldn't take him back if he tried to join them in that way.

# XLV.

Malcolm's every muscle was tense, poised for violence, when he pulled up in front of the detective's house. Rick was getting on his nerves, even silent in the front seat. His pathetic domesticity sapped Rick of all the qualities that had allowed him to rank among Malcolm's friends. Malcolm could no longer count on Rick, and this realization increased his feeling of isolation. Rick was now a pale mockery of what he'd been.

Now, the only person alive who Malcolm still considered qualified to be his friend was Reed, and Reed betrayed him. That left Malcolm completely alone. He wanted to kill Rick for that, for not being worthy. He wanted to kill everyone, to torture CC nice and slowly while the detective watched. He wanted to see the look in the detective's eyes as he pulled his woman apart. Perhaps he would even let the detective live, let him live with that sight forever seared into his mind, forever a scar on his heart. Perhaps he would rip the detective apart too.

"Bring the bitch," Malcolm growled as he stepped from the Jeep.

Rick seized a fistful of CC's hair and dragged her

with him out of the Jeep.

The detective's door caved in beneath Malcolm's foot. Malcolm wondered why a man who dealt with crime every day wouldn't have a steel door with locks and an alarm system, but James Bryant had neither.

Like many people, Detective Bryant had faith in his gun. But guns didn't fire themselves. To shoot an intruder, he had to be home, and Detective Bryant wasn't.

Malcolm didn't mind waiting. Perhaps he could pass the time carving up Rick. Rick's comparative passivity had reached beyond the level of an irritation. It felt to Malcolm like betrayal. He considered for a moment that it might have been good that love had been stolen from him. Love made bitches of men.

He stared as Rick flopped to the couch, still wrestling with CC even though the woman had long ago ceased to struggle. It was then Malcolm saw the car pull up outside. A white Intrepid with oversized cop mirrors on the sides. Bryant's car.

"Stay here." He jacked a round into the shotgun and started to slip out a window at the side of the house. He would catch the detective by surprise.

Rick climbed from the couch with his fingers still entwined in CC's hair, lifting her up with him. He turned around to face the huge bay window, to see the show. He could see the detective now as he climbed from his car.

"Him? That's who you cheated on me with? That old fat bastard?" Rick shrieked hoarsely in her ear, trying to yell and whisper at the same time while he dragged her deeper into the house, away from the front door but still close enough to watch the detective die.

"James, run! It's a trap!" CC screamed and then braced for the slap she knew would come from her husband.

Detective Bryant ducked, drawing his weapon as he heard CC's voice call out from the darkness where his front door had been. He heard the sound of knuckles colliding with flesh and heard a soft whimper he also recognized as CC's. Malcolm would die for that.

Bryant moved to the left of the walkway, ducking down by the bushes, out of the sight line from the door, right next to where Malcolm crouched with the shotgun.

Bryant still could not see into the house. He had no idea where Malcolm or CC were. He couldn't start shooting in there and risk hitting her. His breath was coming faster as he tried to figure out his next move. The darkness over his right shoulder smiled silver like the moonlight. Then the whole street turned red and white as a dozen police cruisers converged on his home.

Malcolm had been about to press the shotgun to the detective's temple when he heard the squeal of tires as the first police cruiser pulled up to the house, followed by another and another and still more. Malcolm slid back into the night, slipped away down the side of the house into the maze of alleyways just as Reed had done across town hours earlier. Rick would have to fend for himself. A few seconds after the first police car slid into position, Malcolm was already gone.

Rick, however, was panicked. The detective wasn't dead, and the street was filled with black and whites, and he had no gun.

*Where is Malcolm?*

He had CC, but they had guns. Lots of guns. A dozen laser sights crawled blindly across the room, searching for him in the darkness. He watched twin beams of red light travel up his leg. He pulled his leg behind CC. He could use her as a shield. They wouldn't shoot and risk hitting her. Even with the lasers, they couldn't see in the dark.

When he saw the first officer turn his spotlight toward the house, his heart sank. He was fucked. Spotlights and all the red dots previously wandering the floor gathered on Rick's forehead quickly, voraciously, gobbled the darkness up. He had no time to give himself up. No voice bothered to call out for his surrender. He had no time to duck behind CC. No time to ask for forgiveness before the first shot propelled Rick's brain from his skull. Five more shots followed, and each removed a bit of his skull. CC fell to the floor as Rick's grasp slackened. When Rick finally fell beside her, his head was simply gone from the nose up. What was left of his brain flopped out of his shattered skull onto the carpet.

# XLVI.

Bryant rushed into the house when he saw CC's husband fall. He'd hoped that it was Malcolm who been taken down, but he knew as soon as he saw the corpse that it wasn't. Rick's skin was far too light. But at least they'd deprived Malcolm of an accomplice. He was running out of friends to help him, running out of places to hide.

And at least he'd saved CC. That now made three people who'd survived The Family Man. Perhaps Malcolm *was* slipping. Maybe they did have a chance of stopping him. Bryant still had no idea what Malcolm was really after, what all this killing was supposed to mean. This was the first real lead they'd gotten, and Malcolm still somehow got away.

Bryant spotted CC curled up next to Rick's corpse and gathered her into his arms.

"It's okay, baby. No one will hurt you now."

"Malcolm is here! He's here! He was on his way out there to kill you!"

Bryant looked around in a panic. Malcolm was still close. Maybe they hadn't missed him after all. Bryant turned to the other officers, who were staring at him and the far too familiar way that he held the witness.

"I want a net over this whole area, six blocks in every direction! Nothing gets out without a top to bottom search. Rip everything apart, but find this muthafucker! We just missed him! He's out there somewhere. That bastard was in my house!"

They all understood what that meant. He had gone after one of them. If "armed and dangerous" didn't say it loud enough, his assault on a fellow cop's home and loved one did. There would be no arrests that night. They would shoot to kill.

They all turned away and started back out the doorway as Detective Bryant kissed the victim/witness. Most of them didn't know that they'd just killed this woman's husband, but somehow, they knew what they were seeing was not right.

Bryant looked at his bullet-riddled living room and felt all his anger drain away. What remained was fear. He felt as if he was into something way over his head, about to be pulled completely under by a riptide where the sharks waited. The sharks with the silver fangs.

Agent Malcovich stepped into Bryant's house. It was then that the detective realized this was no longer his home. It was a crime scene. Malcolm had taken away his sanctuary. Captain Kelly walked through the door behind the FBI agent. When he saw Bryant standing with the half-naked, bruised CC in a desperate embrace, a stern look of disapproval and borderline disgust twisted his face. Bryant saw it and wanted to break the captain's jaw, but he wasn't sure he could take him, comfort CC to the best of his abilities, and keep his job. The EMTs came in, and the issue was settled. Bryant was reluctant to let CC go and certainly not until he knew where Malcolm was headed.

"I'm going with her."

"In a minute, James," Captain Kelly said, pulling Bryant and CC apart as the EMTs removed her from Bryant's protective grasp. "I need to talk to you first."

Bryant watched the EMTs begin their work on CC

and felt his life slipping completely out of control. Malcolm was killing him.

"James, why didn't you take some units with you to apprehend the suspect? If Malcovich hadn't notified me that you were going to try to take Malcolm in yourself, you could have gotten yourself and that girl killed. And I thought I told you to ride with Malcovich."

"That was when I was on the case. You took me off it, remember? All I was doing was going home. I have the right to do that."

"James, somehow, this lunatic has set his sights on you, so that means I have to keep you where I can see you. That means you're back on this case but *with* Agent Malcovich. Everything you do, I want him along with you. Your girlfriend is going under protective custody. I'll put her up at one of the hotels downtown and post someone at her door as soon as she gets out of the hospital. If you want to get a hotel too, the department will pick up the bill." The captain looked around the ruined living room and sighed. "You obviously can't stay here."

"Thanks, but I'll stay with CC tonight."

"Afraid not. You want to stay on this case? You can't be fucking the witness."

"You say 'witness' like you really think there will be a trial. You and I both know this muthafucka won't ever live to see the inside of a courtroom."

David Malcovich spoke up to change the subject. Murdering suspects was not something to discuss out loud, even in a room full of cops.

"Okay, so where do we look for him now?"

"Assuming we don't catch him tonight, all we have to do is find Cozen. Where Reed is, Malcolm will be."

"Unless, of course, he's switched targets," Malcovich said, staring emotionlessly at Bryant, obviously wondering how he might use him as bait.

"No, Reed is still his primary target. I'm just an obstacle he wants to remove."

Detective Willis strolled in, followed by Vargas, who was now dressed in a sharkskin suit with no tie and his hair slicked back like an Italian gangster.

"Bryant, where did you say you were when the shooting started?"

"I was crouched over there beside those bushes."

Willis and Vargas gave each other a look. Detective Willis's huge Adam's apple bobbed as his eyes slid sideways.

"Why? What?"

"We found two footprints on the other side of those bushes. One of them was size 15."

Detective Bryant began to sweat. He fought to control the tremor in his knees. He knew what the detectives were trying to say. He wanted to run out of there before they finished, to just jump in the back of the ambulance with CC and get away from all the madness.

"He was right next to you, man. If those units hadn't shown up ..."

Bryant didn't say a word. He turned and walked out of the room. He'd heard it, but he didn't have to react to it. Agent Malcovich followed as Bryant headed toward the ambulance.

CC looked terrible. Her already limp hair was thinning. Vivid purple bruises stood out on her face, and she seemed smaller, weaker, helpless. Her eyes were closed, but tears streamed from beneath her eyelids. Bryant wanted to comfort her, but he felt too responsible for her pain, for her husband's death, and for her own near death. He hadn't earned the right to comfort her.

Malcovich was hovering nearby at a respectable distance, watching as the EMTs helped CC onto the gurney and into the ambulance. Only after the ambulance sped off did he approach.

"Come on, Detective. We've got a killer to catch. I need to look at the crime scene photos. I need to see all the files on The Family Man," Agent Malcovich said as he climbed into the car beside Bryant.

"Then I'll drop you off at the station because I've looked at enough pictures. I just want to catch this bastard. Besides, everything that was relevant has already been sent to the Bureau. If you didn't do your homework, you'll have to catch up on your own time." Bryant didn't even look at Malcovich when he spoke. He pulled out of the parking lot, keeping his eyes on the road, gripping the steering wheel so hard the skin on his knuckles felt ready to rip, the muscles in his jaw fully flexed.

"There're enough files on The Family Man to fill two filing cabinets. I didn't pack that many suitcases. I need to review the files because there's something I haven't quite figured out."

"Yeah, and what's that?" Bryant smirked.

"The Family Man was so organized, so calculating, a stone cold sociopath, but ever since he's been identified as Malcolm Davis, he's been reckless, disorganized, psychotic."

Bryant shook his head.

"No. You still don't get it. Not ever since he was identified, ever since he went after Reed. The Cozen family was not the work of the thrill killer that murdered for sexual gratification like those other killings. He wasn't The Family Man when he went after them. He was just Malcolm Davis, and it was personal. It's been personal ever since. These aren't signature killings anymore. They're crimes of passion. Now it's all about revenge. What we have now is not a serial killer with a predictable pattern. It's a pissed off muthafucka who knows how to kill, enjoys killing, and who's out to kill Reed and anyone else who gets in the way … including us."

Agent Malcovich looked frightened for the first time. He looked exactly how Bryant felt.

# XLVII.

Reed was dreaming again. He was still walking, following in the direction of the sirens, but his mind had flown free of his exhausted body. Linda was cooking for him again. He could smell mushroom and zucchini casserole with too much garlic and cayenne pepper baking in the oven, filling the entire house with a heavy exotic musk. He was hungry, but he couldn't get Crissy out of his mind. They had a date, and he knew she was waiting for him. He told Linda he was going for a walk, and he walked around the corner to meet the babysitter in her daddy's car. Minutes later, Crissy's father caught his little girl lifting her head from Reed's lap with his cum dribbling off her chin.

Linda was crushed, but she stuck by him. He could see her tears rolling down her beautiful cheeks, see the pain and anger in her eyes wrestling with her determination to hold her family together. He'd felt like shit, helpless, useless, unworthy of her, the same way he felt the night she died.

Reed stopped walking. He stared up the block where several patrol vehicles were gathered, then he looked down the street. A hundred yards or so from where he was standing, something moved. He saw something slip across the street, illuminated for a second by the street light overhead … something large and black. A piece of the night had separated itself from the rest of the darkness and slid across the street to rejoin the night again. Reed recognized the way it moved. It was familiar, anthropomorphic. It was Malcolm.

Reed felt his feet moving before he consciously decided to run after the darkness. He saw a silhouette dashing across the dark. It slipped over a fence, moving fast. He followed. He pulled out the Beretta and pointed it into the solid wall of night, looking for the human shape he'd glimpsed there. Reed could hear the sound of heavy footprints thudding across dirt. He followed blindly, slowing down so he wouldn't overtake his prey in the dark.

He heard the sound of cloth flapping around brisk moving limbs, the sound of a lock popping open, the sound of a car door slamming. Malcolm had found wheels. Reed leapt another fence and found himself huffing, wheezing, out of breath, and standing next to a state liquor store back on Germantown Avenue.

There were six cars parked on the street at that hour: a red Chevy Nova with a white racing stripe, a green Hyundai Sonata, a candy-apple red Toyota Tercel, a white Ford F150 with a dent in the door, a ten-year old white BMW with dented fenders, and a black, drop-top Mercedes coupe. Reed aimed his gun at the coupe, but it was already pulling away from the curb. He couldn't see the passenger, but he knew. The Mercedes was just Malcolm's taste.

Reed had no idea how to steal a car. He hailed a cab. The cab driver slowed down and looked at Reed, appraising him. He looked wild, but he was white. White people never looked dangerous to people in G-town unless they were wearing uniforms or white hoods. Reed knew nothing about the cab driver. He didn't know the man was a recently legalized immigrant from Haiti; had a wife, three kids, a young sister, and a mother that he supported back home; was trying to raise the money to bring them to America with him. When Reed opened the car door, pointed the gun at the bridge of the driver's nose, and told him to get out, all he knew about the man was that he would never see another day if he didn't do exactly as Reed told him. The driver did not hesitate a moment and gave up the cab without resistance. No job was worth never seeing his family again.

The Mercedes cruised up Germantown Avenue at exactly five miles over the 25 mile per hour speed limit. Not too slow or too fast, nothing to raise suspicion. The top was up, the windows were tinted, and not even the driver's outline was visible. Reed followed the Mercedes down Germantown Avenue, through the Richard Allen projects, where angry kids threw empty bottles at the taxi but not at Malcolm's black Mercedes, as if they knew. He followed 11th street downtown into Center City. Reed had been following Malcolm for over half an hour when he recognized where they were going. He should have known.

# XLVIII.

Malcolm pulled up outside of the police station and parked the car. He was tired, but anger made him sharp. He knew Natasha had gotten away. How else had the cops known he was headed for the detective's house? They had gotten close this time. It enraged Malcolm to think of himself gunned down on the detective's front lawn with Reed and Natasha still alive, free to fuck each other all over again, to cum on his grave. Malcolm gnashed his teeth and punched his fist into the dash, sending little chips of high impact plastic flying back at his face. He didn't even blink as they struck his cheek. His eyes were glazed, staring deep into the night, trying to see through the walls of the police station. He wanted Natasha back. She belonged to him, not to the cops, not to Reed. She would always be his. She would die for him.

Malcolm knew he'd never get his time alone with Reed until he rid himself of the fleas that were tracking him, drawn to his heat. He knew that killing the cop had been a mistake, but now that he'd done it, there was no choice but to kill more. He'd kill them all if necessary, if that's what it took get them to back off. He'd drive a stake of fear through the police department's heart, reacquaint them with their own mortality, paralyze them. That would give him the time he needed to finally bring full closure to his relationship with Reed. And he still needed to reclaim Natasha, which meant going through her protectors, killing more cops.

Malcolm watched for over an hour, his focus never wavering, his anger ebbing and then crashing back upon him like waves upon a jagged shore, never noticing the taxi that idled down the block and across the street. Finally, two unmarked squad cars pulled up in front of the station house. A tall, awkwardly built white cop along with a foppish Puerto Rican hurried out of the station house flanking Natasha. She was wearing Rick's clothes and jacket. Malcolm felt a tug of desire as he watched her stroll defiantly down the station steps with no outward signs of nervousness despite the peril she must feel. His sex drive and homicidal instincts had long become indistinguishable, and the thought of drawing her blood heated his own. This would not be a cold, merciful execution. He had waited too long for that. Malcolm needed time with her, time to enjoy her again.

The three ducked into the back of an unmarked Ford LTD and headed up 11th Street, followed by the second car, which no doubt held additional security. Malcolm waited a few seconds to give them some distance. He swung the Mercedes into a tight U-turn and began to follow them, never noticing the taxi making a U-turn in his rearview mirror, nearly running down a pedestrian hurrying across the street to flag it down for a ride.

The procession of cars traveled up 11th Street and then turned right on Walnut Street at the Gay and Lesbian bookstore where a book signing was taking place. A small gay pride parade had formed outside its door, and the police slowed down to let several conservatively dressed businessmen, perversely attired Leathermen, and flamboyantly dressed drag queens saunter arm in arm across the street. Malcolm slowed to a complete stop and avoided coming too close to the police vehicles.

He smiled, recalling the day he'd picked up Paul at that same bookstore. He'd watched Paul flip through the pages of a leather and latex fetish magazine, then turn his attention to another book lower down on the rack, flipping through an illustrated adult comic book featuring X-rated renderings of Marquis De Sade's *Philosophy in the Bedroom* while his modest erection became apparent. He looked so much like Reed, Malcolm wanted to kill him on the spot.

When Paul spotted Malcolm staring at him with homicidal lust sizzling in his retinas, he recognized it instantly. He was drawn to it. He could see the want in Malcolm's eyes. Malcolm made sure that his intentions were clear in his expression, his need, his lust, his love as only the starving wolf can love the wounded deer, an obsessive adoration, a relentless hunger. Paul needed to be needed, to be consumed in the intensity of another human's passion. It had been destiny. Paul was born to be Malcolm's victim. They both knew it with the certainty of faith at the instant their eyes met. They lived together for months, with the promise of torture and death hanging between them like an unconsummated marriage. Even as Malcolm began slicing into him, he'd seen nothing but ecstasy on Paul's face. Pain, fear, yes, but greater than those had been an almost religious rapture. He had been the perfect sacrifice. After him, Malcolm knew it was finally time to kill Reed.

The parade moved on, and the cops continued down Walnut Street all the way to Front Street, where the car pulled into the parking lot of a huge apartment complex. The safe house. Malcolm parked his car across the street and smiled in the dark. His platinum fangs shined even through the tinted windows.

# PART THREE

## DENOUEMENT

# XLIX.

The second unmarked police car circled the block before driving off. It paused for a second in front of each car parked on the block in front of the safe house, and the officers inside recorded license plates. Malcolm held the shotgun between his legs and slid lower into the seat as the detectives pulled up alongside the black Mercedes. They wrote down the license plate and continued down the block. As soon as they ran the plate, Malcolm knew they'd be back. A car this expensive had surely been reported stolen almost immediately.

Malcolm watched as the cops continued down the block. After they turned the corner, Malcolm waited another ten minutes to be sure they weren't circling the block again before he left the Mercedes. The shotgun was still cocked as it hung down in the long pocket of his trench coat. Malcolm quickened his steps, crossing the street into the building. He walked over to the apartment's entrance and cursed aloud when he saw the doorman. The man had surely been alerted to call the cops if he spotted a six foot-five, 235-pound Black man with platinum fangs creeping around, and just killing the man would bring the cops too quickly. He might even be a planted cop bodyguard.

A young yuppie chick with flaming red hair piloted a black Chrysler 300 into the parking lot and drove around the back of the building. Malcolm followed her. If she wasn't parking in the lot, then there must be a garage, a garage with its own entrance to the building. Malcolm avoided the front of the building and the doorman's vigilant gaze, sticking to the shadows as he slid through the parking lot and ducked around the corner in time to see a gate starting to lower on an underground parking garage. Picking up his pace, he ducked under the gate before it closed completely.

Malcolm spotted the redhead stepping out of the Chrysler, slinging a black Prada bag over her shoulder. She wore a red leather jacket and a tight black miniskirt with black leggings. She looked like a high-priced call girl only a year or two of hard tricks away from walking the street. Malcolm followed her to the elevator door.

She pushed the button for the elevator, and Malcolm thought about following her up, but he knew he wouldn't be able to control the urge to kill her. She was attractive, and it had been awhile. Malcolm took the stairs.

Walter Essex was the security guard on duty that night. He'd been a real estate broker in better years and a thief in worse. He'd lost a wife to alcoholism and chronic drug abuse and two daughters to an abusive and irresponsible nature. The kids were both grown and gone now, in therapy and in denial of their father's existence. His wife, their mother, acquired some of his vices over the years, and last Thanksgiving, she ODed on heroin while in the kitchen. The turkey burnt and so did the house. The urn over the mantle at his daughter's house probably held more ashes from their old house than it did her mother's. The girl blamed him for that too.

Walter didn't expect much out of life. He had learned to pray for the best but prepare for the worst. Still, he was unprepared for the grinning black demon that roared out of the fire exit. It never occurred to him to reach for his gun. At least, not until he saw it in Malcolm's hands, pointed at his chin. He hadn't cleaned his gun in months, but it was loaded. He was sure of that, and the bullets, however old, were still fresh enough to kill him.

"Oh shit," he croaked. He was sure that this man would take his life. He didn't value it enough to beg for it.

"You can save yourself some pain if you tell me where those cops went with the girl," Malcolm whispered in a voice like wind whistling through a graveyard.

Walter didn't believe that this man would spare his life even if he did tell him what he wanted to know. There was something in those eyes—hardness, a coldness—that looked inhumane, the way a fisherman looked at the fish before he gutted and filleted it, but Walter told him anyway. It was worth a try.

"Top floor. Room 1016."

Walter hated cops. He didn't feel any regret imagining what the huge, ferocious-looking Black man would do to them. His only regret when he saw the blade come out from under Malcolm's jacket was never having apologized to his daughters. And finally, deep in his heart, he accepted that their mother's death truly was his fault.

"I'm sorry, Bethany," he whispered as Malcolm savagely bared knife and fangs.

When the knife slammed into his belly and began slicing upward, Walter tried not to scream. He tried to grab the man's wrists, and he tried to prevent the knife from rising, but the man was impossibly strong, and all Walter could do was try to slow him down a little. Blood rained from the ever-widening wound in his gut from beneath his naval to just below his saggy man-boobs. The man withdrew the knife and turned to walk away as ropes of bluish-purple intestines erupted from the enormous gash in Walter's belly.

The old security guard struggled to push his guts back inside his belly. The pain was overwhelming, sickening; his stomach roiled even as it flopped out of his body, and Walter vomited into the growing pool of bloody intestine at his feet, which in turn sent a new wave of pain through his bowels. He collapsed amid the blood and vomit, convulsing from pain and blood loss with the onset of terminal shock. He had forgotten the struggle to hold back his screams, and agonized cries now filled the entire lobby as Walter's killer disappeared into the stairwell.

Malcolm took his time walking up the stairs. The detectives wouldn't be as easy as the security guard had been. They would be cautious and on guard after the death of their peer. Malcolm had to be careful. He had to be smarter than they were. He knew that someone would be outside watching the hall. He had to take him out quietly. Malcolm still had the knife, now dripping wet with the security guard's blood. If one of the cops was outside in the hall, Malcolm would try to catch him by surprise with the knife and take him out silently before he could squeeze off a shot. Cops put too much faith in the ten-foot rule. Malcolm knew that he could close twenty feet and slice the detective open before he could even free his weapon from its holster. Acting was a lot quicker than reacting, and Malcolm would have surprise on his side. If both cops were inside the apartment, things might get a little more complicated.

Malcolm made it to the top floor and stared out the fire exit's thick glass window at the long, empty hall. There was no detective in the hallway, not even a bored, half-conscious uniform. No one to ambush, no one to force to open the door, to hold hostage and make the other cop give up his gun, to use as a human shield as he charged into the apartment blasting. Malcolm could see room 1016 halfway down the hall, only 100 feet away. It would be a pointless trip. Going through that door would be suicide. He looked around the stairwell and spotted a window that led to a rusting fire escape.

Malcolm slid through the window onto the rickety steel framework. The winds were 30 miles per hour, and Malcolm had to hang on as the entire structure rattled and shook. Malcolm climbed from the fire escape onto a thick ledge that wrapped around the building. The wind threatened to tear him from the ledge as he crept from window to window. He counted the distance from the fire escape to where he'd seen the apartment as he passed one dark window after another, slipping unnoticed past entangled or embattled lovers. He stopped just outside the apartment where Natasha was supposedly safe. The shade was pulled but the lights were on, and he could hear voices. He could also hear the unmistakable squawk of a police radio. This had to be the right place.

Malcolm slid the sawed-off Mossberg out of his coat pocket and aimed it at the window. He waited until he saw a large male silhouette fall across the shade before he pulled the trigger.

Natasha was lying on the couch, watching television and falling asleep, when the window imploded and Detective Willis went down in a spray of glass shards and blood. She heard the unmistakable sound of a shotgun chambering a round as Malcolm smashed through what remained of the window and stepped into the living room. Detective Vargas drew his guns and fired shots in the vicinity of the window, not aiming, just trying to buy time and distract Malcolm long enough to get to Natasha.

Malcolm smiled as bullets flew past him and punched chunks out of the drywall. Detective Vargas dove for the couch, reaching out for Natasha to shield her from the monster who'd just murdered Willis. If the detective could reach her and pin Malcolm down with gunfire long enough to get her to the door, she might have a shot at surviving this. But Malcolm was moving far too fast. In one leap, he moved from the window to the couch, firing the shotgun as he landed between the detective and Natasha. Vargas landed behind the sofa with a steaming hole in his chest. His silver sharkskin suit turned red as his life drained from severed arteries and perforated organs.

Natasha curled into a tight ball on the couch, waiting for the shotgun to turn on her. Malcolm put his dark cavernous eyes on her. She could see terrible things stirring deep within them.

He was breathing hard, like a prizefighter in the 12th round. Natasha could not believe the chance he'd taken to get her. She knew that he'd be even angrier because of the extreme risk. He'd almost lost his life getting to her. He could have died falling off the ledge or been gunned down stepping through the window, but he'd risked death for her. Another time and she might have been flattered, but now, all she could do was scream, explode from her fetal ball, and scramble to her feet to run away from him just like she'd run from him when he'd caught her fucking Reed.

Malcolm reached out and caught her arm as she tried to make it past him to the door. Natasha screamed again. Her one chance to escape, to survive, was gone. She continued to struggle but knew it was hopeless. Malcolm locked one iron-muscled limb around her neck and lifted her off the ground. She was choking, but she had enough air left in her lungs to continue screaming.

"Shut the fuck up," he growled, but there was no way she could.

She kept hoping that there were other cops around who would hear her screams and come save her. There had to be someone who could save her. She couldn't die. There was so much more she wanted to do with her life. Murder was what happened to other people, like those cops there on the floor. People like her didn't get murdered.

Malcolm opened the door and marched past the curious and frightened neighbors as they came out of their apartments. He still had her by the throat and he still had the Mossberg; his finger still hovered over the trigger. Natasha still screamed.

A long time ago, she'd loved this man. She'd told

him she'd die for him, that she'd wanted to die with him. Now all she wanted was to live, to go back to her perfect job, her perfect apartment, and her mediocre boyfriend. But Malcolm was going to take it all away. Malcolm was going to kill her. She knew that now, even if she still could not fully accept it. She had to keep fighting until the end.

"Help me! Someone help me! My god he's going to kill me! Help! Help!" Natasha screamed, but the other residents had come out to look, not to get involved. None of them wanted to become a victim. They watched as she was dragged to the fire exit by the tremendous Black man and down the stairs. They watched as she was thrown into the trunk of Malcolm's car. They were still watching, dialing 911 on their cell phones, while Malcolm sped away from the scene in the Mercedes, Natasha still screaming her horror under the listless stars.

Somehow, Reed had lost Malcolm in the downtown traffic. It surprised him when the entire procession had suddenly stalled before the parade of freaks at the gay bookstore, and Reed had continued up 11th Street, afraid to stop directly in back of Malcolm's vehicle and risk being spotted. Malcolm was apparently not as concerned about the cops spotting him. Reed didn't have enough room to turn onto Walnut Street anyway, with the three vehicles stopped on the corner.

Instead, he continued up 11th Street. His intention was to circle the block, but he'd forgotten that 10th Street was one-way in the opposite direction, and by the time he made his way all the way to 9th Street to come back around, they were gone. He turned down Walnut and drove all the way to 4th Street, then retraced his path when he couldn't find them again. When he saw squad cars race down Walnut Street with sirens and lights blazing, he knew he was too late. He followed anyway on the remote chance that they'd actually managed to capture or kill Malcolm.

Reed had to pull over to the curb to allow an ambulance to pass, heading toward Front Street, where the street was lit up like a discotheque by what looked like the entire police precinct and was most likely more. As he passed Second Street, the somber, angry faces of the police officers barricading the next block told him all he needed to know.

He pulled the taxi as close to the parking lot as possible before the cops told him to move on. A plainclothes Puerto Rican officer that Reed recognized from the night of his family's murder came storming from the apartment building with his face twisted into an angry scowl and tears streaming down his sallow, hollow cheeks. He punched one black-leather-gloved fist into the other and looked around for something else to hit.

Reed spun the taxi into a U-turn and drove off. Malcolm hadn't been captured here, and he'd gotten away with Natasha. Reed was once again left with no clue where to find Malcolm. His only consolation was that Malcolm wouldn't know where he was either.

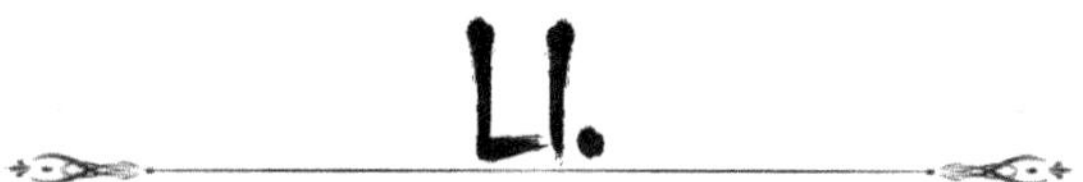

# LI.

Detective Bryant drove back to the station with fatigue, anxiety, frustration, and fear weighing down his limbs and coating his mind in a thick sludge that mired his thoughts and slowed the flow of ideas to a trickle. Malcolm had been inches away from him, hiding in the dark, preparing to ambush, preparing to kill him. He'd come to rescue CC and, instead, nearly became another victim of the man he was supposed to be saving her from. This case had turned as bad as any case possibly could. When Bryant thought about the pain CC had gone through, he felt his own pain, the pain of his failure, pour down over him like a flash flood. He almost allowed himself to weep before he caught himself. He bit his lower lip until it bled. The new little pain helped him hold back the tears.

Bryant wanted off this case. Fuck pride. Fuck revenge. He didn't even want to be the guy who found Malcolm anymore. He just wanted to wake up, turn on the news, and hear that some zealous cops had riddled Malcolm with bullets.

His near-death experience was causing a short circuit in his mental computer. Things were no longer adding up. This case made no sense to him and was making less sense every passing minute. He wanted no more part in this madness. Catching Malcolm was no longer nearly as important as not being caught by him and not letting him catch CC again.

Malcovich, conversely, had a hard-on for Malcolm now. A killer who callously, brazenly hunted cops threatened what little safety and authority the badge retained. Respect for the badge was often the best protection a cop had on the street, more than his gun, his vest, or all the backup available. There were far more criminals than cops. Respect for the badge kept them from storming the walls and overwhelming the city's meager police force. On the ride back to the station, Malcovich told Bryant about places in Sicily where cops were no safer walking the streets than an average citizen. He told him about places in Mexico where they were actively targeted.

"Last year, in Juarez, Mexico, on Christmas Eve, they found a police detective's head outside the police station wearing a Santa hat. Just his head. In his mouth, there was a list of ten other police detectives. It was a hit list. Half those cops are dead now, and a bunch of the rest immigrated to America to escape the drug cartels. At least it isn't that bad."

It was every cop's nightmare. When the uniform and the badge no longer held any fear and all they had to hold order was the gun and the billy club, their lives wouldn't be worth a vial of crack. Malcovich was right. It wasn't that bad in Philadelphia, not as bad as they had it in Juarez, but it felt like it was getting closer. There was a psychopath hunting and killing cops. It may not have been an entire criminal organization, but what was the difference? Dead was dead. He told Malcovich to shut the fuck up, and they drove the rest of the way without speaking another word. That was when Bryant decided he wanted off this case. Catching a madman wasn't worth his life. The other cops would understand, and if they didn't, if they thought he was a coward, then they could go fuck themselves. He was done.

Malcolm's arrogance in the face of the full might of the Philadelphia Police Department threatened to undermine the authority of the entire force. It threatened to reduce the badge to useless adornment. If for no other reason, Malcolm had to be made an example. Malcovich wanted to see him on death row. Bryant wanted to see him in a casket. Malcolm had long ago ceased to be a suspect. It was a war, he was the enemy, and it was kill or be killed.

Malcovich was eager to get back to the station. He wanted to look at the crime scene photos again, try to get a handle on Malcolm's psyche. Maybe something in the files would give a clue as to where Malcolm might be going, what he might be planning. His bubbly enthusiasm was annoying Bryant. He just wanted to see CC again. She was being treated at Washington Hospital and was safe for now.

Bryant parked in front of the station, and he and Malcovich started up the steps. They had just entered the building when they heard the call go out over the radio. The safe house had been compromised. Natasha had been kidnapped, and Willis and Vargas were dead, along with an unfortunate security guard who'd been disemboweled. Bryant punched both fists into the sides of his head and clenched his teeth as if biting down onto something desperately trying to get away.

"My God! We can't be as helpless as this guy thinks we are! This bastard is walking right through us!"

David Malcovich stared at his feet. When he looked up, Bryant could tell he was searching for some words of reassurance.

"Save it," Bryant said.

Bryant shook his head. Agent Malcovich still believed they would catch this guy, even with the scorecard lopsided in The Family Man's favor. He hoped the agent was right because right now, Malcolm was kicking their collective ass.

Half the station house poured out into their vehicles, heading toward the scene. Bryant ran to the Intrepid. Malcovich followed.

"Whoa, partner, you'd better find another ride."

"I need to see the scene while it's still fresh."

"I'm not going to the scene. I'm going to the hospital. I need to see CC."

If Malcolm had so quickly located and penetrated the safe house, then CC wasn't safe either.

"Two detectives were killed and a witness is missing. We need to get over there!"

"Wrong." Bryant pointed a finger directly at Agent Malcovich as if he were aiming a gun. "*You* need to get over there. I need to see CC."

Bryant slammed the car door and nearly took off Malcovich's toes as he sped away from the curb.

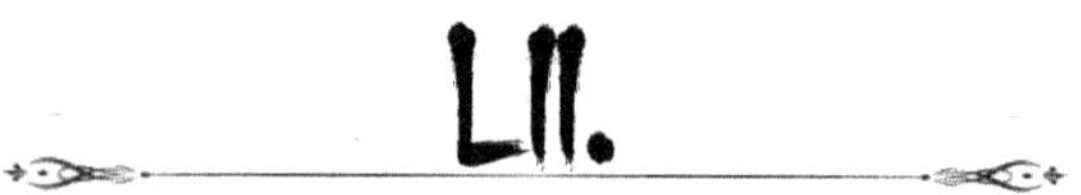

# LII.

During the brief drive to the murder scene, Special Agent Malcovich once again ran the case in his head. Malcolm had a very unique and disturbing signature. It was rare to encounter a serial killer whose need to control and dominate others led him to take on more than one victim at a time. It was too difficult, too risky. Controlling one victim was hard enough, but two or more increased the margin for error. Those serial killers who assaulted multiple victims at once generally only did so once or twice at the end of their degenerative cycle, when they no longer cared whether or not they were caught. There were, of course, a few exceptions.

David Berkowitz had gone after couples, and The Nightstalker, Richard Ramirez, had assaulted couples as they slept. But in both those cases, the males were killed quickly and were not part of the ritualistic rape/murder. A killer who hunted entire families again and again as a part of his signature was almost unprecedented. It indicated a megalomaniacal psychopath with an overwhelming need to control and dominate others. Malcolm was some bizarre hybrid of what the FBI termed the "anger-excitation killer" and the "anger-retaliatory killer." In other words, Malcolm was a very pissed off killer who was turned on by death and believed he had a legitimate reason to murder. A serial killer on a mission.

The use of surrogate victims to substitute for the true target led Malcovich to label Malcolm as an anger-retaliatory killer. That and the overkill stabbing and beating. The sexual sadism, the prolonged torture, the obvious planning and premeditation, the ritualistic mutilation and cannibalism were all the signatures of the "anger-excitation killer," who derives sexual gratification from rape, torture, homicide, and mutilation.

The way the parents were discarded face up and posed indicated a definite sexual motive to Malcolm's crimes. Conversely, the children were all found face down or with their faces covered, as if, having sated his anger upon them, the killer was overcome with guilt. There was no sexual assault on the children, despite what, in some cases, were a profusion of stab wounds that would indicate the killer was in a complete homicidal fury. He was, in his meticulous cleaning of the crime scenes and removal of physical evidence, extremely organized, even to the point of wearing condoms during rape.

Organized. Pre-meditated. Then, during his assault on Reed Cozen's family, no condom, no attempt to destroy evidence, witness left alive, and, ever since, no attempt to hide his identity, as if Malcolm didn't care whether he was captured or not. Either that or he didn't believe he could be stopped.

Malcovich thought about what Detective Bryant said about the first killings being signature killings and the rest being personal revenge killings. It made sense. If anything about this case could be said to make sense.

Agent Malcovich nervously checked the magazine in his Glock 9mm as he pulled up in the parking lot of the Society Hill Towers, where, upstairs on the top floor, the officers' bodies still lay where they'd fallen.

He watched the faces of the police officers who were busy handling the crowds of civilians and press. Their expressions ranged from anger to cool professionalism, but behind each pair of eyes, Malcovich could see the dark tint of fear. No one was safe anymore.

Malcovich clicked the Glock off safety as he climbed from the rented Plymouth Concorde and flashed his badge at the uniformed officer who rushed forward to guide him under the yellow police tape.

"This way, Special Agent …"

"Malcovich. Thanks."

The same officer guided him into the building, past the doorman, who was speaking excitedly to a female detective hurriedly trying to scribble down his account of the incident. He led him to the stairwell, where the body of the security guard was still crumpled on the floor of the lobby. Blood had pooled two inches deep around the body. The guard's mouth had fallen open, and his head was turned at an awkward angle so that his glazed, vapid eyes were looking backwards over his shoulder. The most gifted contortionist would not have been able to mimic the pose. The scene on the top floor was even worse.

As he entered the apartment, Malcovich examined the shattered window, the body lying amid glass fragments, the other body lying alongside the couch, and developed a pretty fair picture of how it had gone down. It was easy to imagine Malcolm coming through the window blasting away with the shotgun. Malcovich poked his head out the window and felt the powerful gusts that whipped around the building. He looked at the narrow ledge that led from the fire escape and thought how easily someone could be blown off. The man who'd risked a ten-story fall to come through that window and confront the two armed detectives had been recklessly, fanatically determined.

Malcovich began to scribble notes on his pad while trying not to think about how he'd been discussing the case with these very same detectives just hours before. It was hard to think of them as mere corpus delicti when he could still remember the sound of their voices. Once again, he found himself fearing for Detective Bryant's safety and his own. Malcolm was like no serial killer ever encountered. There was no telling what he was capable of.

Malcolm had changed cars again. He'd found another Impala parked in an empty lot with a For Sale sign on it. The ridiculously optimistic owner had tagged it with a $20,000 price tag. If Malcolm had had the money, he might have actually bought it because it was beautiful. A huge eight cylinder '95 Super Sport with smoke tinted windows, black leather interior, a burgundy paint job so black it looked as if it were bleeding oil and blood at the same time. The speedometer stopped at 160 miles per hour.

"Gangster!" Malcolm hissed as he ran his hands over the dash. It was a compliment.

He tapped his foot on the gas, revving the engine, marveling as the tachometer jumped from 0 to 80 every time he even touched the pedal. Malcolm popped the trunk on the Impala, walked to the Mercedes, and lifted Natasha from the trunk. When her feet hit the dirt, she wobbled on unsteady legs and nearly fell. She turned angry eyes on Malcolm. Her chest heaved with each breath drawn between her clenched teeth. He could see in her eyes that she wanted to fight. She'd no doubt been lying back there gathering her courage, formulating a plan. Malcolm had no fear. He had her, and there was nothing she could do to get away.

"You want to fight? I'm going to hurt you no matter what. Do you want the pain to start right now?"

He could see all the resolve drain out of her. Her bottom lip quivered with emotion, and her face cracked and sprang tears.

"No, no, no, no, no. Please. Please! Just let me go. Let me go!"

Malcolm wrapped one massive hand around Natasha's neck and dragged her to the Impala, tossing her headfirst into the trunk with so much force that she nearly flipped head over heels. Malcolm slammed the trunk lid down, almost catching her leg before she pulled it inside with her. He could hear her muffled screams as he walked around and slipped into the driver's seat. He smiled, imagining hearing those screams in a more intimate setting.

Malcolm pulled the Impala out of the lot, jamming his foot down on the accelerator and whipping the steering wheel, fishtailing the tremendous vehicle into a violent turn before speeding off down the block with the 400cc engine growling like a dinosaur.

This car, he would keep.

Malcolm had one more risk to take, one more message to send to the PPD before he could finish things between him and Reed. He headed back down 11th Street, piloting the Impala through the bitter night, cutting the tense evening air, heading back toward the police station for another confrontation. He knew the detective would be in a panic to get to CC. He'd have no idea how Malcolm had found the first safe house and would figure that CC was also in danger.

When Detective Bryant leapt into the Intrepid and raced off toward Washington Hospital, Malcolm was watching. In his rearview mirror, City Hall receded. The statue of Ben Franklin shrank to the size of a toy soldier. Ahead, the Spectrum arena grew to fill the windshield.

Reed was driving in circles, and the voices in his mind had multiplied. He could no longer recognize most of them. There was now a great chorus, an ethereal choir of rage, howling for retribution. They were the voices of all the people Malcolm had murdered, disembodied spirits because Malcolm had slashed their bodies to gore-streaked ribbons. Now they possessed Reed, haunting his thoughts. They had chosen him as their champion, their avenger, and he was failing. Not only was Malcolm getting away but he was killing more people, adding more souls to the maddening choir screaming through Reed's head.

*Kill him, Reed!*

*Kill that bastard, Daddy! Find him! Find him and kill him! He hurt us, Daddy!*

*He's hurting people, Reed! You have to stop him! Find him, Reed! Kill him, Reed!*

There were dozens of them crying out their rage, their pain, their hatred. The inside of his skull resounded with their shrill cries, echoing like a cathedral. The noise was deafening, drowning out the sounds of city traffic, drowning out every coherent thought that attempted to surface when Reed needed his mind clear. He had to figure out where to find Malcolm. He gripped the Beretta tight, using it to anchor him to reality, to fend off the ghosts, as he steered the taxi through the somber Philadelphia streets.

Steam rolled from the gutters, creating the atmosphere of a foggy London night from a Hammer Films horror flick. Reed could almost imagine Peter Cushing skulking through the dark alleyways. He caught the quick, furtive movements of sewer rats darting through the shadows and wondered what other beasts were lurking just beyond his sight. Reed's paranoia was escalating. Every shadow seemed to resemble Malcolm. His finger repeatedly jerked on the trigger as he caught movements from the corners of his eyes that his mind hastily misinterpreted as potential attacks.

He drove nervously down 11th Street, almost to the police station, then turned around and started back. His eyes scanned the street for any sight of the Mercedes or Detective Bryant's white Intrepid. He cut over to Broad Street and began driving aimlessly up and down, avoiding the pedestrians who tried to hail down the taxi for a ride. There was no sign of Malcolm. Reed was about to make another U-turn and head back up Broad Street, but he spotted a patrol car at the next intersection, so he continued straight ahead. Getting stopped for an illegal U-turn would end it all. It would take all night to extricate himself from the cop's tiresome questioning. Who knows where Malcolm would be by then?

Reed was trying hard to hold his mind together, but the longer Malcolm remained alive, the harder that task would become. Malcolm had to die soon. Reed wanted desperately to join his family, but first he had to wash his sins clean with Malcolm's blood, wash away the years of neglecting Linda and his family, wash away the betrayal, his guilt, the smell of Crissy's young pussy.

The tears were starting to flow again. Reed could hear weeping. But they weren't his tears. He recognized the heart-wrenching sobs. They belonged to his wife. They were the tears she shed the night she found out about him and Crissy, the same tears she shed the night she was murdered. Only Malcolm had ever hurt Linda as much as Reed, and he'd had to kill her to do it. Reed felt his heart crack open and spill out all its dreams. They boiled like a corrosive poison in his chest cavity. Everything he'd ever hoped for was now just more pain. He continued down the street, checking his rearview mirror for the patrol car. Linda's anguished tears echoed through the haunted night. He let his own tears join hers as he hunted down Broad Street, chasing demons.

Bryant was relieved to see the familiar sight of Detective Jones's old LTD parked in the Washington Hospital parking lot. Mathew Jones was a veteran of the force, a timeworn soldier who the District Attorney's office often called upon to guard Mafia witnesses before trial. He once protected a member of the Junior Black Mafia who'd turned state's evidence. While Jones was out in the hall, his partner had allowed the witness to make a phone call to his cousin to tell him where the police were hiding him. His cousin was also an enforcer in the JBM, and Jones had soon found himself in a shootout. When it was over, two ranking members of the JBM were dead and four others had been captured fleeing the scene in a bullet ridden Lexus LX. Every single one of them was wounded. Jones had taken a couple slugs too, but the witness had never been touched. His partner took one in his forehead, but miraculously, the bullet traveled around the back of his skull and exited without touching his brain. He was back to work in a month, but not with Jones. Jones never worked with a partner again, and he hadn't lost a witness yet.

Just as relief started to settle in, Bryant remembered again his own dire pronouncement to Reed just a few days ago:

*A man who slit his own throat and tried to blow himself up isn't gonna stop until he feels he's avenged whatever wrong you've done him or until we stop him.*

Detective Bryant was sick of trying to stop Malcolm. For one night, he just wanted to forget about the case for a while. He wanted to lose himself inside of CC, but he wasn't sure that would ever be possible. She was beyond traumatized; her husband had been decapitated, she'd been brutally raped and beaten beyond comprehension. She was in shock, physically, mentally, and emotionally, if not forever catatonic and withdrawn from her last slender link to reality. She could blame Bryant for everything. If he'd heeded

Malcolm's warning and backed off the case, her husband might still be alive; Baltimore might still be alive. If he had stayed out of her life, Malcolm might never have come in. But that was just Bryant's guilt talking. Being married to Rick had inescapably entwined her destiny with Malcolm's long before Bryant entered her life. Being a homicide detective just meant her destiny also entwined inexorably with his, even if it was his sexual addiction that brought him to her first.

Bryant mulled over the effects of destiny upon the outcome of this case; he couldn't help but wonder which was the bigger rationalization: his guilt or his attempts to answer to it.

The second floor, where CC had been moved from the ER and Trauma Center, was well lit with no visible way to approach unseen. Bryant scanned the parking lot quickly for anything that looked out of place. He was further encouraged when a patrol vehicle rolled into the parking lot and two serious looking police officers pulled up alongside his car and shined a light inside. Bryant held up his badge. The officers lowered the light but didn't turn it off.

"Sorry, Detective, but when I saw you parked over here casing the hospital ... well ... you know what happened to Vargas and Willis? I just wanted to make sure everything was safe?" the angry looking young cop offered, phrasing it like a question.

"Yeah, it's all safe."

They gave him one last suspicious look before driving hesitantly on. Bryant parked the car and headed inside to where Jones stood guard over CC. He climbed the steps to the second floor, still looking around nervously, in fear of being ambushed. Jones had scouted this location well. Detective Bryant had to walk past a large window to get to CC's room, giving whoever was inside the room a full view of who was coming as the overhead light cast his shadow on the drawn curtains.

When Bryant knocked on the door, he heard the frighteningly familiar sound of a shotgun chambering a round. He stepped back from the door and back over to the window.

"Matt? It's me, James … James Bryant. Don't shoot me, man. You don't want the paperwork."

The door slowly crept open, and Jones appeared, still aiming the shotgun at Detective Bryant's midsection. He looked at Bryant for a long moment, then looked beyond him over his shoulder, and then left and right. Bryant had an uncomfortable second or two when he thought Jones didn't recognize him or recognized him but was so determined to protect his witness that he would shoot him anyway. Finally, Jones lowered the shotgun and let the detective in.

"Sorry, I just had to be sure there wasn't anyone with you. Someone might've had a gun on you, forcing you to knock."

"Damn. You're hardcore, man."

"James!" CC called to Bryant from her bed, trying to open her arms to his embrace as if afraid someone would pull them apart.

"Are you okay, sweetheart?" He brushed her limp hair back from her eyes, revealing a gruesome black and blue hematoma swelling beneath her left eye. His heart crumpled like used newspaper at the sight of it.

"I'm okay, really. It doesn't hurt … much." She smiled crookedly through bruised, lacerated lips and Demerol as Detective Bryant felt that pang in his heart again.

He kissed her gently on her battered lips, hugged her close, and stroked her hair. Jones turned self-consciously toward the window. He gripped the shotgun and bounced nervously from foot to foot. Bryant and CC were embracing more urgently, so fervently engrossed in their ginger passion they'd forgotten that they were not alone. They needed each other's comfort to soothe the pain and stress they'd so recently endured. Finally, Jones could no longer take it.

"I'm going outside to watch the hallway. Holler if you need me and stay away from the window."

Jones left the shotgun by the door as he stepped outside, shaking his head in annoyance at how unprofessional it was to be outside guarding a door where inside a fellow cop was about to try fucking a witness in her hospital bed. He slammed the door behind him and never even saw the knife until it was sticking out of his throat.

Malcolm dragged Detective Jones's corpse next door, where the bodies of the two patrol officers were already piled on an empty bed, their blood saturating the mattress. Next door, Detective Bryant was slipping beneath the sheet covering CC. Malcolm could hear the sounds of their painful lovemaking. He sat down in a chair in a dark corner of the room. Artificial light from outside spilled through the curtains, casting a twilight glow on half the room. Malcolm sat just beyond its reach. He found even this mild light harsh and invasive and physically recoiled from it. The light fell across the faces of the dead policemen. Detective Jones's eye sockets filled with shadows. He seemed to be winking at Malcolm.

Next door, the bedframe began a rhythmic smack against the wall as Detective Bryant got his groove on with CC. It built to a thunderous climax, and for a second, Malcolm was afraid they would come right through the wall. Then everything went silent. Malcolm waited for several more minutes until he heard the bathroom door open and close and the sound of a running shower. He knew the patrol cops would be missed soon. Their radios continued to squawk and hiss with staticky voices that Malcolm could just barely discern.

Malcolm stood up and began to undress, shrugging out of his expensive clothes. He flexed and stroked himself slowly as he imagined killing CC. He waited a while longer, then slipped out of the room, carrying Detective Jones's keys and his own clothes tucked under his arm.

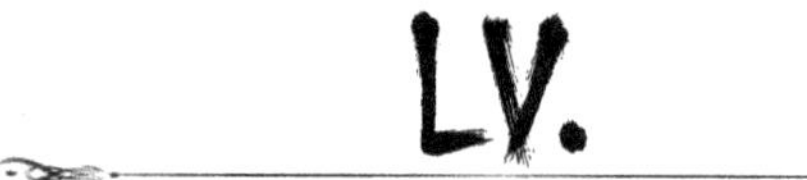



CC was just slipping down into a drug- and orgasm-induced sleep when she felt the cool breeze wash over her. Unconsciously, she pulled the covers up over her shoulders and slipped down deeper into an exhausted slumber that bordered on collapse. CC had been so nervous and agitated, wound up tight as a drum, wired by fear. Releasing that pressure had completely drained her. She had needed that orgasm, needed to let go, to release the tension and fear, needed to feel loved. Bryant was a giving and considerate lover. After being kidnapped by Malcolm and watching Rick die right beside her, she had needed to feel safe. Wrapped in Bryant's arms, she had felt like nothing in the world could hurt her. Their lovemaking had been furious, passionate, not hurried so much as urgent. Hungry. Their need had struck them so suddenly, so powerfully, that they were consumed by it. When she climaxed, it felt like dying, like letting go of the world and all its troubles.

She was past dreaming, in a dark peaceful oblivion, when the weight of a body pressed down upon her and kisses fell on her face and neck. CC could feel hot breath on the back of her neck and gentle nips and bites. She knew it was Bryant, but she was so tired that she couldn't awaken. She felt hot, wet lips kiss their way down her spine and two large hands knead her buttocks. There was a low, guttural purr as he slid a tongue across each cheek, then an animalistic growl that seemed to vibrate through the bed. Hard, sharp teeth bit into the soft flesh of her ass, and she awoke with a start and turned over.

"That hurt!" she mumbled sleepily.

A large, dark shape rose up from between her legs and came down over her. The shape was much too big to be Bryant. Fear vibrated through her flesh and locked her muscles. CC felt her legs being torn apart and a large phallus push up into her. She could hear the shower still running. She screamed, and powerful arms locked around her waist, yanking her from the bed and hoisting her into the air.

# LVI.

Bryant rushed out of the bathroom and felt the bile rise in his throat as he absorbed the sight of Malcolm standing in the center of the room with one arm gripping CC's naked ass, holding her off the ground with her legs wrapped around his waist. Malcolm was almost completely nude, with nothing but a long trench coat hanging from his shoulders. It took only a second for Detective Bryant to realize that Malcolm was inside of her, raping her. Bryant started toward him, meaning to tear him from CC, tear Malcolm's head from his shoulders, when he spotted the shotgun pointed directly at his chest.

"Detective Bryant. You have really been fucking up things between me and Reed."

Malcolm pumped his hips to punctuate his words, sliding himself in and out of CC with a wet, squishy sound that withered the detective's spirit and brought a drugged whimper of pain from CC.

"Tell me, what should I do about that, Detective Bryant? Should I kill you and this bitch?"

Bryant noted that Malcolm had referred to him by name, which gave him some hope that he wasn't intending on killing him, but just as quickly he noted that he was still referring to CC as simply "bitch," a thing with no name, completely depersonalized. He was still vigorously raping her as he stood pointing the gun at Bryant. He was pounding harder, more angrily. The sound of his hard, unyielding flesh slapping against CC's soft skin was sickeningly loud.

"Let her go, damn it! Let her the fuck go! I'll kill you, you sick motherfucker! I'll fucking kill you!"

There was an invisible wall between him and Malcolm that began at the tip of the shotgun's huge barrel. Bryant began pacing like a tiger on a leash, wanting to launch himself at Malcolm and beat him to a pulp, but the shotgun remained as an insurmountable obstacle. The detective's pistol sat across the room on the nightstand.

*He gets no real sexual gratification out of the intercourse itself. It's the fear, the pain, the humiliation that gets him off. He uses his penis as another weapon ... I'm sure he made the men watch. That's another way of demonstrating his power and their powerlessness.*

Bryant remembered Baltimore's words as he looked into Malcolm's eyes. Locked onto his, Malcolm's eyes calmly studied Bryant's, studied his expression, relished his pain, his powerlessness, while reveling in his own power.

Malcolm's mind seemed to be completely disconnected from his body. His attention remained unblinkingly focused on Bryant even as he slammed himself into CC with still increasing ferocity. She was crying now, sobbing in pain. Her body was limp as a rag doll. Bryant was desperate to kill Malcolm, but he knew that psychopath would not hesitate to pull the trigger, and at that range, with a shotgun, there was no way he could miss.

Bryant watched helplessly as Malcolm began to roar, his whole body shaking with what could only have been an orgasm. Bryant was repulsed at the thought of Malcolm's evil seed erupting into CC's womb. Malcolm bared his platinum fangs and bit down on CC's shoulder. Blood squirted into his mouth and ran down CC's shoulder. She squealed in pain and began to thrash as he tore into her. Malcolm's eyes remained pinned on Bryant. He let CC fall away like an empty sack, dumping her onto the floor. Malcolm's erection was now bobbing in the air, pointing directly at Bryant, enormous, dripping with sexual fluids and blood and showing no sign of diminishing. It looked violent, lethal. Malcolm was still smiling. He moved toward Bryant, bearing his erection in one hand like a weapon and the shotgun in the other hand like it was a phallus.

Bryant backed away from Malcolm, now more afraid of the swollen, angry penis than of the shotgun. He backed into the bathroom, and Malcolm continued to advance. He could see CC writhing across the floor, trying to get away. Malcolm forgot about her. All his attention was now focused on the detective, mind, body, and diseased spirit. Bryant felt fear grip him, shake him like never before as, for the first time, he could picture himself as Malcolm's victim.

The detective backed into the bathroom knowing he had nowhere else to go. He squared his shoulders and prepared to fight. It was better to be shot outright than submit to whatever Malcolm had planned. Bryant heard a shot ring out, and Malcolm staggered, his face twisted into a horrible rictus of rage and pain. He spun around, letting out a bloodcurdling roar.

Bryant didn't know what had happened. Had Malcolm been shot? There was blood on the bathroom floor, but it was not his. He saw Malcolm flying toward CC, who stood her ground, holding the detective's misplaced pistol. She fired another shot that brought another horrifying roar from Malcolm and caused him to drop the shotgun, but just as quickly, his other arm came up with a huge survival knife gripped in his fist.

In one blurred movement, he slammed the blade

into her stomach and knocked her nearly across the room. She struck the wall and fell in a heap with the blade still in her, a long gash yawned open to split her torso where Malcolm had ripped her from her belly all the way to her sternum. Malcolm charged past her, moving fast, as Detective Bryant charged out of the bathroom and scooped the Mossberg off the ground.

Bryant fired at Malcolm's back as he leapt out the closed window. All that buckshot couldn't have missed, but Malcolm fell to the pavement and came up running. Bryant leaned out the shattered window, again firing as Malcolm dashed through the hospital parking lot.

# LVII.

Malcolm climbed into the Impala and started the engine. He had fucked up badly and was now wounded. Patrol vehicles screeched into the lot, sirens flashing. Malcolm jammed his foot down on the accelerator, and the Impala flew. A dozen police vehicles were in pursuit as the Impala went careening up Broad Street. Malcolm had a bullet in his hip, a bullet somewhere in his chest, and smaller .12 gauge balls scattered into his back. It didn't feel like anything immediately vital had been hit. A rib felt shattered, but his heart and lungs seemed fine as Malcolm brought his pulse and respiration under control. Shock and blood loss were his only fear.

The Impala's speedometer showed 90 miles per hour. The police cars struggled to keep up. Malcolm wove in and out of traffic with recklessness beyond courage. He charged through slower moving traffic and late-night strollers, leaving the cops behind. They had to consider the safety of others. Malcolm made no such considerations and ran down two pedestrians as he turned the Impala up onto the sidewalk and then barreled through an intersection. The falling bodies created a barricade for the police, who could not so casually run them over as had Malcolm.

The Impala picked up speed, opening up the distance between Malcolm and his pursuers. He checked his watch. It was four o'clock in the morning. There were already early morning commuters out getting a head start on the rush hour traffic. At this hour, Malcolm knew the school would be unalarmed. The first of the janitorial staff would have already arrived and would be busy mopping floors and emptying trashcans. No one would look for Malcolm there. No one but Reed.

# LVIII.

Reed was cruising down Broad Street when he heard the thunder of the shotgun blast and saw the police cars descend on the hospital. He turned the taxi toward the commotion and barely avoided a head-on collision with the massive Impala as it came hurtling from the parking lot, a three-ton fiberglass and steel projectile. Reed slammed on his brakes so hard and so quickly his forehead struck the windshield, smeared it with his blood, dazed him for a moment. Shaking off the momentary wooziness, he could still hear sirens but could no longer see the police. He pulled the taxi into the lot and spotted Detective Bryant slumped out of a second story window. There were several other cops visible in the room, but they were keeping their distance from the detective, surrounding him but wary of him as well. The detective appeared to be muttering to himself. Reed wondered if Bryant could now hear the same voices that filled his head.

Detective Bryant had had more than enough. Malcolm had thoroughly beaten him. If someone else wanted to play the hero, that was fine with Bryant, but he was through. He felt it for the first time tonight.

He had finally felt what victims felt, that terror, that helplessness, knowing that death was coming and nothing could not stop it. He had been powerless. Malcolm had wanted him to feel it and he had. He was powerless as Malcolm raped CC, powerless as he punched the knife into her. He had been powerless as Malcolm came at him, looking as if he might rape him too. He had thought of Reed's hunt for Malcolm as prey chasing predator, but now he realized that he was prey as well, they were all prey for Malcolm, the entire police force, the entire city. Chasing him just meant bringing him more victims.

Bryant couldn't turn around to look at CC. He heard other officers telling him that she was still alive, that she would be okay, that the trauma team was on its way. But Bryant knew better. People didn't survive wounds like that. CC had trusted him to protect her, and he had failed, and now she was dying. Bryant wanted no more. He could not stop Malcolm and had lost all will to try.

# LIX.

When Reed approached him, Detective Bryant was still on his knees by the window and still cradling the shotgun. Reed simply walked through the ring of cops that were surrounding the detective.

He glanced into the other room and saw a stack of bodies on the bed, uniformed bodies. Some of the cops standing around the bodies were in tears. Others were enraged. The next room held several cops hunched over a bleeding woman, trying to bandage her wounds with towels. He looked back toward the detective who had his back turned to all of it. He was still staring off down Broad Street, in the direction that Malcolm had gone.

Reed knelt beside him and, with eyes that were wildly insane, asked, "Where did he go? Where's Malcolm?"

Reed could no longer distinguish his own voice from the choir of voices in his head. He wasn't completely certain he had actually spoken. His own voice may have just been another voice in his head. Then the detective answered.

"I can't stop him. No one can. We can't stop him."

"Don't quit now, Detective. He wants you to think he's invincible. He wants you to be afraid. But he's just human, just a man."

Detective Bryant shook his head and sighed heavily. He turned to look up at Reed, tears streamed down his face.

"I'm through. I quit."

"You can't quit! Malcolm won't stop. He'll just keep killing. We have to stop him!"

Detective Bryant rose from his knees and pushed his way past Reed and past his fellow police officers.

"I quit."

Reed ran past him, down the stairs, and outside into the parking lot. He could hear the cops ordering him to stop and to begin chasing him as he leapt into the taxi. Then he heard Detective Bryant's weak voice croak, "Let him go."

When Reed spun the taxi out onto Broad Street, no one followed.

The howling in his head was constant now. The voices no longer resembled human speech. They became the auditory embodiment of pain, the sound of death, the sound of rage. His head shook with their horrible racket. His bones vibrated with the sound of their agony and anger. His head felt as if it was breaking apart. The taxi swerved all over the road as he steered it toward …

What? Where? Reed was lost again.

*Where would Malcolm go? Think. Think. Think!*

He punched his temples with his fists, trying to quiet the din and jar his thoughts back into place.

*Where? Where? Where is Malcolm? Where would he go?*

It came to him like a flash of inspiration.

*Where it all began … back to the school … the High School of Creative and Performing Arts.*

# LX.

Natasha noticed right away that Malcolm was hurt. He wore no clothing except the trench coat. Blood from at least two major wounds streamed down his naked chest and down one leg. He limped as he dragged her out of the trunk and through the teacher's entrance. She knew he was taking her to the fourth floor. That's where they used to all hang out. There, she would die. She was certain of it. Despite his blood loss, it was obvious that Malcolm's virility was unaffected.

As they started up the stairs, she began thinking fast. She had only three more flights of stairs left to figure out a way out of this, and then it would be too late. Malcolm was hurt, but he was still dangerous and still too much of a physical match for her. If she could hurt him again, just enough to get free, she was sure she could outrun him. He no longer had the shotgun, although he still had Rick's 9mm. If she could hurt his arm, perhaps he wouldn't be able to aim, but she had no weapon. She wondered if Malcolm had another knife. When she'd dated him in high school, he'd had dozens of them, but she knew he'd left many of them at the scenes of his slaughters. Still, he might have more. Who knew how big his knife collection was by now and how much of it he carried with him?

There was only one place for Malcolm to conceal a knife—the trench coat. He'd left all his other clothes at the hospital. Natasha rubbed up against him as he dragged her up the steps and felt something heavy in his pocket. It had to be a knife. They reached the fourth floor, and Natasha made up her mind that it was now or never. She plunged her hand deep into the trench coat's blood-soaked pocket and cut her hand on the knife as she wrapped her hand around the blade and drew it out. She barely had time to switch her grip to the handle before he understood what she'd done.

She raised the blade, eager to thrust it through Malcolm's black heart, shrieking as she tried to stab him. Malcolm struck first, punching her in the chest with such force that she collapsed to her knees, gasping in pain, the air in her lungs burning. The knife clattered to the floor, and Malcolm casually picked it up. Natasha was determined not to die passively. She knew she was going to die, but if she was going to be his victim, she was determined she would be Malcolm's last.

"You can't kill me, Malcolm. You love me."

"That's exactly why you have to die."

Malcolm was standing directly above her now. He was still naked. His penis dangled semi-erect just inches from her face, close enough to bite.

"We were supposed to die together, remember? Give me the knife and I'll help you leave all this madness behind. We can be together in death like we couldn't be in life. I'll be all yours again. Just the two of us. I know you can't kill yourself, and I know you can kill me even without the knife. This is how it was supposed to end. This is how it was always supposed to end for us. Give me the knife and let's end this together."

"Don't flatter yourself, bitch. I ain't dyin' with you. I'm just going to rape you and kill you. You're dying alone tonight, you fucking whore."

He spit in her face. That was when Natasha

launched her final attack.

# LXI.

The sounds of a struggle echoed through the halls as Reed searched classroom after classroom on the fourth floor. He could hear screams, grunts, curses, and savage growls. He recognized both voices, Malcolm's and Natasha's. He was killing her, but she was fighting back. If she could only hold out until he got there. He still had the gun. He could —

Reed turned a corner, and there, in the middle of the hall, he saw the dark, familiar shape of Malcolm Davis crouched over a prone figure that could only be Natasha. Malcolm was tearing into her with his knife and his fangs as she kicked, scratched, and bit him. She had done some damage. Malcolm was bleeding and in obvious pain, but her struggles were subsiding, her strength waning. Reed watched Malcolm raise the knife and slam it down again and again. He could hear the sound of the knife slamming through her chest and puncturing the vinyl tiles beneath her. The blade dug into the subfloor, and Malcolm had to wrench it out each time in order to bring it down again. Finally, her struggles ceased, but the horror wasn't over. Malcolm bent down over her lifeless body to feed.

Reed could tell by his motions that he was also

fucking her. He'd been fucking her while she struggled for her life as he'd stabbed her repeatedly. He was fucking her as her life bled out on the dirty school floor. He was fucking her and eating her alive. Reed aimed the gun at them and fired. He wasn't worried about hitting Natasha. By now, he was sure that she wished she were dead if she wasn't. If Natasha was dead, perhaps she'd thank him when she joined the infernal choir in his head.

The bullet punctured a locker above Malcolm, and he looked up, pausing in his feeding frenzy. Reed ran toward him, firing the Beretta. Malcolm rolled off Natasha and fled down the hall. Reed continued to pursue him. He was determined not to lose him this time. He glanced at Natasha as he passed. She was torn apart but still breathing shallowly, gurgling out her last breath. Their eyes had locked, and her voice joined the chorus.

*Kill him, Reed! Get that bastard, Reed!*

Reed continued running.

## LXII.

Uncannily, the shadows swallowed Malcolm whole. Reed darted from room to room with the Beretta leading the way. Malcolm was still there, still somewhere. He was stalking Reed as Reed was hunting him.

Reed roamed the school, carefully checking every room that held specific memories for him and Malcolm. The Creative Writing Room where he and Malcolm worked side-by-side for four years. The English Room, Expository Writing, Journalism, the cafeteria. He found no sign of Malcolm. The sun was starting to rise, and Reed found a blood trail. Malcolm was hemorrhaging heavily. Reed followed the blood as best he could in the growing light.

The trail led to an art room with large crimson splatters on the door and shadows dancing across the walls as if a candle was burning within. Reed slid the door open and spotted the source of the flame. A Bunsen burner sat atop the teacher's desk, casting just enough illumination to reveal a decomposing skull with long blonde hair. Even in its advanced state of decomposition, even though it had been fifteen years since he'd last seen her, Reed had no trouble recognizing her.

*Who else would it be?*

Reneé Volaré. He backed out of the room, pointing the gun at the shrinking shadows. Any one of them could have been Malcolm, but none of them were. Still, he felt Malcolm's ominous, suffocating presence emanating from every dark corner of the room.

The sounds of the early morning janitorial staff making their way up the stairs came to him through the riot of voices in his rapidly fragmenting mind. They were all in danger. Reed fired the gun, aiming it down the stairwell. He waited a moment and listened. When he heard the sound of running feet, he knew that they had left the building. Fewer victims for Malcolm.

Reed continued to search for Malcolm. He passed Natasha's lifeless form several times as he hunted through the dark. The last time he passed her, Natasha's chest was cracked open and her heart was gone. So was her head.

Haunting echoes surrounded Reed. His family, Natasha, Reneé, Detective Baltimore, those other cops, the faceless victims that stretched back over a decade. He tried to isolate each voice, hoping they could help him, give him some clue of where to find Malcolm.

*He proposed in the gymnasium.*

The gymnasium was where Malcolm proposed to Reneé. He'd interrupted the entire gym class and produced the modest diamond ring. The gym teacher tried to interrupt his proposal, and there was a tense moment where Reed was sure that Malcolm would kill him. That was followed right away by another long tense moment as Reneé looked across the gym at Reed, begging for help. Malcolm appeared to be growing impatient and angry as Reneé stalled and continued to stare at Reed. Reed had been afraid that Malcolm would notice the way Reneé was looking at him and know that he'd been fucking her, but just as Malcolm seemed ready to snap, Reneé said, "Yes."

*Look in the gymnasium. Kill him, Reed. Kill him!*

Taking the steps two at a time, Reed hurtled down to the school's basement, to the gymnasium, where Malcolm was waiting for him. He opened the door to the gymnasium and was struck in the chest by something heavy that knocked him backward, bounced off, and rolled across the floor. He looked down and watched Natasha's severed head roll across the floor and disappear into the darkness. Malcolm stepped out of the shadows and kicked the head back across the room at Reed.

"You still want her, Reed?"

Malcolm's voice reverberated in the empty gym. His face was covered in blood. He smiled carnivorously. His platinum fangs were streaked with gore. His mouth was a horror. Reed didn't need to ask what had happened to Natasha's heart.

"You're a fucking animal!" Reed brought the Beretta up in what seemed like slow motion.

Malcolm charged.

Before Reed could get off a shot, Malcolm was on him, stabbing. Reed felt the blade sink into his chest and rip downward. Then it was in his gut, tearing its way upward. Finally, Reed managed to get off a shot. The bullet ripped through Malcolm's abdomen and exploded out of his back. Malcolm howled and spun away into the darkness. No way he could survive a wound like that without immediate medical attention.

When Malcolm charged from the shadows, Reed spotted his other wounds. He was bleeding profusely from his chest and hip. His penis looked like it was missing a chunk. He had a wound in his stomach. Malcolm was starting to look like one of his own victims.

Reed looked no better. His guts were on fire, and blood spurted from the wound in his chest. He slid down to the gym floor, still clutching the Beretta but losing sight of Malcolm. He looked around in a panic. Maybe Malcolm was dead? But the voices said no. They were just as loud as before. If anything, their agitation had increased.

*Kill him! Kill him! Kill him! Killhimkillimkillim!*

The chant began to swirl around his head, the words blurring together into a steady roar. The shadows shrank as the morning sun beat the night into submission. Reed took it as a good omen.

Then Malcolm attacked again. This time, Reed popped off two rounds before the blade sank into him. He felt the knife ripping a new wound open as Malcolm stabbed him again and again. He could feel Malcolm's fangs in his skin. Then Malcolm rolled off, onto the floor, wheezing and coughing blood. Reed was hacked up bad, dying, but Malcolm was dying also. Reed had no more fear. He had nothing.

The voices were gone as well. They were finally alone. Just Reed and Malcolm. Reed struggled to catch his breath. Waves of gray obscured his vision as he struggled to hold on to consciousness, to hold on to life. Malcolm lay beside him, dying. Listening to Malcolm's ragged breathing, Reed finally allowed himself to remember what had happened in that bathroom fifteen years ago.

# LXIII.

Malcolm walked in, wielding that black switchblade with the leopard on the side he'd had that night at Natasha's house. He knew about Reneé. He knew about Natasha. He had just spent weeks in a hospital, recovering from a self-inflicted throat wound. He was murderously angry. His rage rippled from him in shimmering microwaves of pure hostility. He started toward Reed, and there was nothing but hatred in his eyes.

Reed had watched Malcolm raise the knife. He felt the weight of his own guilt bend him, crush him. He lowered his head, bowed by the sudden force of his remorse. Malcolm had been the best friend he'd ever had. Malcolm had taught him more about life than his own parents, taught him more about himself than he would have ever learned alone, taught him his own potential, to believe in himself. Malcolm had loved him, and he'd repaid that love with betrayal. He had acted out against Malcolm like a spoiled child trying to get its parent's attention through some shocking act of disobedience. Now, he was about to be punished. Reed had known he was going to die, but still he'd wanted Malcolm's forgiveness.

Before Malcolm could bring the knife down, Reed stepped forward and wrapped his arms around him. He kissed Malcolm on the neck and whispered:

"I'm sorry. I'm so sorry."

Malcolm had paused then, unsure of himself. The knife hovered in the air, ready to strike, but it didn't descend. Malcolm looked down at Reed with questions in his eyes, uncertainty distorting his hatred. He stared into Reed's eyes and saw his remorse and his love. Then Reed rose up on his toes with tears streaming down his face and kissed Malcolm on the lips. Malcolm dropped the knife. He wrapped both hands around Reed's throat and began to squeeze the life from him.

Reed never struggled. Tears continued to roll down his face. He mouthed the words "I'm sorry" again, and Malcolm let him go. Reed staggered, choking and dizzy. Malcolm again lifted the knife, and Reed closed his eyes, again waiting calmly for death.

"I love you, Malcolm."

Reed had heard the words leave his mouth before he decided to speak. They came from a place in his heart to which his conscious mind was not privy. They had an immediate effect on Malcolm. The knife clattered to the ground. Reed opened his eyes and saw Malcolm's face warp, contorting as if he were in pain. He turned and walked out of the bathroom.

"Why didn't you kill me then, Malcolm? Why didn't you kill me fifteen years ago, back in that bathroom? Why all this? All this death, all those families, my family, those cops, why?"

"Because I loved you too."

It took a moment before Reed was certain the voice had not come from his head.

"I loved Reneé with all my heart. I never loved anyone like that besides my own mother. I loved Natasha too. But deep down, I expected them to betray me. But not you, Reed. I never thought you would. I thought you would always be with me. When you hugged me … I … I realized that losing you was what really hurt."

Malcolm began to cough, and blood bubbled up out of his mouth.

"Why did you kill all those families? All those people? Why didn't you just kill me?"

"Because I loved you! But I wanted to kill you so bad … so bad it was all I could think of. I hated you so much, knowing you were happy and that you had forgotten all about me that … that … I wanted to hurt you over and over again. So, I did. Every time I murdered one of those faggots, I was killing you … and … and killing that part of me that still wanted you, the part that still wanted to forgive you, that still wanted to be your friend."

"Did it work?"

Malcolm laughed, and more blood bubbled up out of his mouth. He coughed again, wincing in pain.

"Well, here we are."

"Yeah, but we're still alive. You could still forgive me. I could still forgive you."

"You still want to be my friend? After all this?"

Malcolm's face was a rictus of agony, but it was unclear whether physical or emotional. He pulled Rick's 9mm out of his coat pocket and slid it under Reed's chin.

"Sorry, Reed but I can't forgive. I can't forget."

He pulled the trigger. Reed's head exploded like a rotten jack-o'-lantern. The spaghetti-pulp of brains sprayed across the gymnasium floor.

Detective Bryant emptied his entire magazine into Malcolm.

Malcolm growled and gnashed his teeth savagely as each bullet tore through him. He'd finally killed Reed, even after being mortally wounded himself. But now this detective had come, and Malcolm wasn't sure he had enough life left to avenge his own death.

He held Rick's 9mm in his hand, trying to raise it by the sheer force of his murderous will, but a bullet shattered his arm. He felt as if every major organ had been pulverized. The short, fat, middle-aged detective loomed above him. Malcolm snarled with rage even as his life fled.

# 

Bryant came as soon as he heard news of the break-in hit the air. The janitorial staff reported that someone was shooting inside the High School for the Creative and Performing Arts. Bryant had been halfway home when he heard the call. It didn't take much to figure out that it was Malcolm and Reed, and he kicked himself in the ass for not thinking of it before. It was the school they'd attended together with Reneé and Natasha. It was where all this began.

Bryant had to go stop Malcolm despite his fear, guilt, shame, and fatigue. If he didn't face Malcolm, he'd have to quit the force because this fear would never go away. Unless he turned toward this fear, Bryant would forever be a victim.

A Latino woman in her 40s came running out of the building just as Bryant pulled up. She told him there was a headless woman lying in the hall on the fourth floor. Bryant drew his weapon and crossed the parking lot in a flat-out run. He was starting up the stairs when he heard the shots coming from the basement.

He turned and crept cautiously back down the stairs, toward the basement. The morning sun was blazing, but there were still shadows, still places for

Malcolm to hide. Bryant heard voices, a harsh pained laugh, coughing, more voices. He pushed open the gym door in time to see Malcolm blow Reed's head off.

Bryant opened fire, pumping bullets into Malcolm until all the darkness was gone.

The stark, white early morning sunlight crept across the room and illuminated the brutalized bodies. Reed was a mess. His guts were trailing out of an abdomen ripped open by the foot-long slashes crisscrossing his torso. His head looked like a science fair volcano with a steaming crater instead of the top of his skull. Malcolm was bleeding from bullet holes, bites, and slashes that had turned his surrounding tissue to tenderized meat. His chest no longer rose or fell; his last breath had long exited his ruptured lungs. The terrible dark flame in his eyes, his searing hatred, had winked out, and all animation had ceased. There was no need for an ambulance. Both were beyond any resuscitation.

As the sun crept higher, Bryant squinted against the glare, unable to tear his eyes from these two fallen foes/friends. He still clutched his pistol, and his finger still depressed the trigger. The morning light continued to tear large rifts in the few lingering remains of doomed night.

The horror that bled itself out on the gymnasium floor had no place in the light. In the morning sun, it all turned easily from horror to tragedy. Even Malcolm lost all menace and became an object of sympathy, even empathy. Bryant found himself wondering what this monster might have become if not for the years of abuse dealt out by his stepfather, if not for the betrayal of his best friend, if not for the hell he'd managed to drag them all into.

Bryant walked out of the high school building as it began filling up with his police brethren. They walked about so casually that it seemed none of them were even aware of the danger that had been living, breathing, and still killing just moments before.

Cynical teenaged artists, writers, and musicians were lined up in the chill November air, waiting for the all clear so that they could enter the school and resume their mild flirtation with education. Bryant was too beaten down to tell them that school was cancelled that day. He walked pensively through their gauntlet of stares, ranging from curious to disinterested to openly hostile.

One of the fashionably angst stricken kids—long haired, overweight, tragically pimpled, wearing pinstriped bell bottom pants and a New Age hippie version of a dashiki—commented on how happy he was to be missing first period class no matter who had to die to make it happen. Yet another pale, anemic, black lipsticked, black nail-polished, black eye-shadowed, trench coat Mafia type yelled out, "Scrape the muthafuckin' bodies up off the floor and let us get to class!"

Bryant looked to see if any of the teachers who were corralling the unruly gaggle of teens would reprimand the boy for his language. None of them even seemed to be paying attention. They had no doubt heard worse and had long learned to ignore it all.

None of the kids seemed the least bit awed by the fact that their high school was now a murder scene. Growing up in Philadelphia had accustomed them to tragedy. Every street they passed between home and school had at one time or another been cordoned off with yellow crime scene tape, with a chalk outline drawn on the asphalt. Bryant couldn't help but wonder how many of these kids had actually witnessed a murder, how many had watched blood being hosed off a sidewalk and down the gutter, how many would someday be murderers themselves. In fact, none seemed to be the least bit impressed by Malcolm's death. Bryant could see them distancing themselves from the horror already. The forced laughter masked a collective sigh of relief.

Last night, Malcolm was the most serious topic of discussion in Philadelphia, talked about in hushed tones, the reason mothers didn't let their kids stay out past dark and fathers slept with shotguns by the beds. Today, all the pain and death and fear of the last few days would become nothing more than bad jokes and interesting dining room conversation.

Except for the friends and families of Malcolm's victims. For them, the memories would hold their terrible power for years to come. Malcolm was a boogieman who had merely left the world of the living to be reborn in their memories and nightmares.

As exhausted as Bryant was, he was in no hurry to face a rejuvenated and revitalized Malcolm Davis in his dreams. He would much rather delay that inevitable battle and stay awake a few more hours. He knew he would have years yet to contend with Malcolm's ghost. Bryant shivered at that thought and pulled the collar up on his trench coat to shield his neck and face from the cold air, which, of course, had absolutely nothing to do with why he was shivering. He bumped into David Malcovich on his way across the school parking lot.

"I thought you said you were off this case."

"I figured if another cop had to die trying to stop this wacko, it might as well be someone worn out and expendable like me."

"So, tell me, Detective, did you give Malcolm a warning before you shot him? Did you identify yourself? Who shot first?" Malcovich asked.

"You don't know me well enough to ask that question," Bryant replied and slid behind the wheel of the Intrepid.

Agent Malcovich leaned his head through the car window.

"I thought you'd be interested to know that your girlfriend just got out of surgery and they think she's going to make it. She's in the ICU right now."

"Thanks, Malcovich," Bryant replied and whipped the Intrepid up onto the curb as he spun it into a U-turn and headed to the hospital. He wondered if the curiously emotionless FBI agent was planning to report him to IAD for violating Malcolm's civil rights. It sounded ridiculous, but he'd seen stranger things happen, and Malcovich was strange.

No one would ever know whether or not Bryant gave Malcolm a warning before he shot. Other detectives were writing his shooting report for him right now, and the report would say the shooting was justified. Only Bryant would ever know for sure. He shrugged his shoulders, deciding that he really didn't give a fuck what anyone thought about how he handled the shooting. The bastard deserved to die and was right where he belonged. End of story.

Bryant fought off his final image of Malcolm, bloodied and dying, blowing Reed's head apart with the 9mm. Everyone on the force would give Detective Bryant the credit for stopping Malcolm, but Bryant knew that Reed had really done the killing, Reed and CC and Natasha. The bullets from Bryant's gun were merely the smallest and the last contributions to Malcolm's death.

As he pulled into the hospital parking lot, the image of Malcolm growling savagely as bullets smashed into his chest played in Bryant's head. There had been a brief second when Malcolm had continued to glare at him, his eyes still savagely alive, vibrant with murderous hate, his hand still gripping the 9mm.

Bryant emptied his entire magazine into Malcolm, yet Malcolm still radiated an aura of invincible menace. In that moment, Bryant had been once again at Malcolm's mercy. Malcolm smiled a horrible, blood-drenched grimace as his entire body shuddered, and then he died, but Bryant knew that he would never be free of that moment. It would haunt him forever. Malcolm was immortal.

A dart of pain lanced Bryant's heart as he watched CC's battered body lying motionless in ICU. She looked even worse than she had when he'd last seen her. It was more than a miracle that she was still alive. A nurse checked one of the many IV drips in CC's arm. Bryant sat by her side as the elderly nurse checked CC's bandages. She acknowledged Bryant's presence without taking her eyes off her patient.

"Are you her husband?"

"No. Her husband helped do this to her. I'm the cop who killed the bastard."

The nurse, who, to Bryant, seemed ready for her own hospital bed, looked at Bryant with what could only be described as horror, then, when she saw the pain written in lines of stress and worry all over his face, her expression softened into pity. A shaky, wavering smile tried to take root on her face and failed. She turned on her heels and walked to the door. She paused before stepping out into the hall.

"Good job, Detective."

CC's eyes fluttered open and focused on Bryant with a tentative smile. She reached out for the detective's hand.

"Is Malcolm dead?"

"Yeah. You killed him, baby. No one will ever hurt you again."

She smiled and fell back to sleep, cradling Bryant's fingers in her taped and bandaged hand. Bryant closed his eyes and found Malcolm waiting for him just beyond consciousness. He snapped awake, breathing heavily and shaking with fear. Sweat soaked through his clothes, adding yet more stains to the already dirty and wrinkled suit. He touched his holster for reassurance, flipped a White Owl cigar between his lips, and began to chew it nervously as he sat watching CC the rest of the morning. He popped a No-Doze and asked a nurse for some coffee.

He didn't know when he would gather the courage to sleep

WRATH JAMES WHITE is a former World Class Heavyweight Kickboxer, a professional Kickboxing and Mixed Martial Arts trainer, distance runner, performance artist, and former street brawler, who is now known for creating some of the most disturbing works of fiction in print.

Wrath is the author of such extreme horror classics as THE RESURRECTIONIST (now a major motion picture titled "Come Back To Me") SUCCULENT PREY, and it's sequel PREY DRIVE, YACCUB'S CURSE, 400 DAYS OF OPPRESSION, SACRIFICE, VORACIOUS, TO THE DEATH, THE REAPER, SKINZZ, EVERYONE DIES FAMOUS IN A SMALL TOWN, THE BOOK OF A THOUSAND SINS, HIS PAIN, POPULATION ZERO, IF YOU DIED TOMORROW I WOULD EAT YOUR CORPSE, HARDCORE KELLI, and many others. He is the co-author of TERATOLOGIST co-written with the king of extreme horror, Edward Lee, SOMETHING TERRIBLE co-written with his son Sultan Z. White, ORGY OF SOULS co-written with Maurice Broaddus, HERO and THE KILLINGS both co-written with J.F. Gonzalez, POISONING EROS co-written with Monica J. O'Rourke, MASTER OF PAIN co-written with Kristopher Rufty, and BOY'S NIGHT co-written with Matt Shaw among others.

Wrath lives and works in Austin, TX.

# MORE FROM
# MADNESS HEART PRESS

Czech Extreme by Edward Lee
isbn: 978-1-955745-06-2

The Bighead by Edward Lee
isbn: 978-1-955745-22-2

The Television by Edward Lee
978-1-955745-28-4

Extinction Peak by Lucas Mangum
isbn: 979-8-689548-65-4

You Will Be Consumed by Nikolas Robinson
isbn: 978-1-7348937-7-9

Curse of the Ratman by Jay Wilburn
isbn: 978-1-955745-19-2

Trench Mouth by Christine Morgan
isbn: 978-1-7348937-9-3

Warlock Infernal by Christine Morgan
isbn: 978-1-955745-24-6

Addicted to the Dead by Shane McKenzie
isbn: 978-1-955745-15-4